A COURSE IN PHONETICS

Fourth Edition

COLLEGIVM·EXONIENSE
IN·ACADEMIA·OXON.

A COURSE IN PHONETICS

—■—

Fourth Edition

PETER LADEFOGED

University of California, Los Angeles

HARCOURT COLLEGE PUBLISHERS

Fort Worth Philadelphia San Diego New York Orlando Austin San Antonio
Toronto Montreal London Sydney Tokyo

PUBLISHER	Earl McPeek
ACQUISITIONS EDITOR	Bill Hoffman
MARKET STRATEGIST	John Meyers
PROJECT EDITOR	CJ Jasieniecki
ART DIRECTOR	Garry Harman
PRODUCTION MANAGER	Lois West

ISBN: 0-15-507319-2
Library of Congress Catalog Card Number: 00-101369

Address for Domestic Orders
Harcourt College Publishers, 6277 Sea Harbor Drive, Orlando, FL 32887-6777
800-782-4479

Address for International Orders
International Customer Service
Harcourt, Inc., 6277 Sea Harbor Drive, Orlando, FL 32887-6777
407-345-3800
(fax) 407-345-4060
(e-mail) hbintl@harcourt.com

Address for Editorial Correspondence
Harcourt College Publishers, 301 Commerce Street, Suite 3700, Fort Worth, TX 76102

Web Site Address
http://www.harcourtcollege.com

Printed in the United States of America

0 1 2 3 4 5 6 7 8 9   066   9 8 7 6 5 4 3 2 1

Harcourt College Publishers

This book is for:

Lise

Thegn

Katie

and for Simba, who faithfully attended
nearly all the LBFS meetings
at which it was written.

———————————■———————————

PREFACE

This is a *course* in phonetics, not a book about phonetics. It is intended to be useful to students of linguistics and to those who are concerned with studying the sounds of English, as well as to speech pathologists and communication scientists who want to know about the sounds of speech. It is divided into three parts, so that readers may pay attention to the particular parts that are appropriate for the objectives of their course. If you are not using this as a textbook for a course and want a shorter, general introduction, you should read another of my books, *Vowels and Consonants* (see Further Reading page 269).

The first part of this book focuses on introductory concepts and contains two chapters, one presenting an overview of articulatory phonetics and the technical terms required for describing speech and the other providing the basic notions of phonetic transcription and a set of symbols for transcribing English. Everyone should master the terminology and symbols in both these chapters before going further in the book.

The second part of the book focuses on English phonetics and contains three chapters that provide a solid foundation for the study of the sound pattern of English. Those who are not primarily concerned with the phonetics of English may prefer to skip much of the material in this part and go straight to the third part.

The third part examines general phonetics and deals with the phonetic structures of other languages, but it also includes a great deal of material on English. Chapters 6 and 7 are of most importance to students of foreign languages and of general linguistics; but these chapters should also be studied carefully by speech pathologists and others who are concerned with deviant forms of English.

Chapter 8 is important for all students of phonetics. It outlines some of the main concepts of acoustic phonetics and describes the acoustic structure of English sounds. This chapter is a prerequisite for the discussion of vowels in Chapter 9, which illustrates the vowels of different accents of English, as well as those of other languages. It is also useful to have some knowledge of acoustic phonetics before reading Chapter 10, which discusses the nature of the syllable and the use of stress, length, tone, and intonation.

The final chapter considers some general linguistic concepts and also reviews much of the earlier part of the book by considering the latest version of the International Phonetic Alphabet (IPA) and by presenting a set of linguistic phonetic features.

Toward the end of the book, the chapters have fewer exercises—largely because varied assignments seem most rewarding at the beginning of a course. Toward the end of a course, students should be able to concentrate on a single project. The kind of project that is most useful for students of general linguistics is to give a description of the major phonetic characteristics in some other language. Students of English might profitably try to describe an accent of English that is very different from their own. Each student might try to find a speaker of another language (or a speaker with a different accent) with whom to work. Then, using grammars, dictionaries, or whatever sources are available, the student could try to compile a list of words illustrating the major characteristics of that language. If possible, a tape recording of this list of words should be prepared and submitted along with written observations.

At the end of nearly every chapter there is also a set of performance exercises that involve making and hearing differences between sounds. Nobody can hope to get very far in the study of phonetics without developing this practical ability. Phoneticians should be able to produce the sounds they describe and to reproduce sounds described by others. Some people are naturally better at doing this than others, but students can improve their ability to a considerable extent by conscientiously working through exercises of the kind suggested here.

There are some small changes in the style of phonetic transcription used in this edition, which are aimed at bringing it more in line with the two major dictionaries that give an accurate record of American and British pronunciation, Daniel Jones's *English Pronouncing Dictionary*, 15th edition, edited by Peter Roach and James Hartman, (Cambridge: Cambridge University Press, 1997) and the *Longman Pronunciation Dictionary,* 2nd edition, (Harlow, U.K.: Pearson Education, 2000), by John Wells. Choosing a transcription for a book of this kind is still a no-win situation: you cannot please all the people all the time. This is especially true in the case of this book, which has a large international circulation and has to be designed so that it can be used by speakers of British and American English. However, it is obviously appropriate to use the style of the major reference books. I should also note that I (and, I am sure, the editors of the two dictionaries) are aware that there is no such thing as British English or General American English. There are numerous dialects in both countries. The remarks on transcriptions appropriate for different groups of readers should be taken only as general guidelines.

In addition to the comparatively small changes in transcription, there are a number of changes bringing the book more up-to-date with respect to current linguistic and phonetic theories. Many new findings have been added. The latest version of the IPA chart has been used. The acoustic phonetics chapter has been rewritten and new spectrograms and pitch analyses have been made using contemporary computer techniques. I have deleted the texts for transcription at the ends of the chapters, partly to keep the size of the book within reasonable limits and partly because instructors do not seem to agree on what they wish students to transcribe. This does not mean that I think that making phonetic transcriptions is not a necessary part of a training in phonetics. On the contrary, learning to make good observations of one's own speech is a skill that should be developed. But there are many different kinds of material that can be used for this purpose.

Many of the sounds discussed in this book are available on the Web through www.harcourtcollege.com/english/ladefoged. In addition to the sounds of the words in most of the tables, each pronounced by a native speaker, the symbols of the IPA charts are illustrated, and the exercises at the ends of the chapters are pronounced.

The sources for some of the less familiar data are acknowledged in a separate section at the end of the book, but I cannot properly acknowledge all of the material I have incorporated. From a personal point of view, my greatest debt is still to David Abercrombie of the University of Edinburgh, from whom I first learned what I took to be the commonly accepted dogma of phonetics; only later did I discover that many of the ideas were his own contributions to the field. But, as he was always eager to point out, many are part of the general tradition of phonetics in Britain that goes back through Daniel Jones to such great nineteenth-century phoneticians as Henry Sweet.

Numerous improvements suggested by students and fellow teachers have been incorporated in this edition. I would particularly like to thank my colleagues Bruce Hayes, Sun-Ah Jun, Patricia Keating, and Ian Maddieson. Other reviewers who have been especially helpful include Geoffrey Pullum, William Katz, and Jackson Gandour.

Takehiko Makino made numerous astute observations while translating the third edition into Japanese. I have also received useful comments from Peggy MacEachern, Paolo Matteucci, Peter Roach, Renetta Garrison Tull, John Wells, and Sandra Whiteside.

Harcourt College Publishers have provided excellent editorial assistance. I am particularly grateful to CJ Jasieniecki and Lynn McGarvin.

As always, without my wife this would have been an incomparably poorer book.

CONTENTS

ARTICULATORY PHONETICS

Phonetics is concerned with describing speech. There are many different reasons for wanting to describe speech, which means that there are many different kinds of phoneticians. Some are concerned with the sounds that occur in the languages of the world. Others are more concerned with helping people speak a particular form of English. Yet others are looking for ways to make computers talk more intelligibly, or to recognize whatever is said to them. For all these purposes phoneticians need to find out what people are doing when they are talking and how the sounds of speech can be described.

THE VOCAL ORGANS

We will begin by describing how speech sounds are made. In nearly all speech sounds, the basic source of power is the respiratory system pushing air out of the lungs. Try to talk while breathing in instead of out. You will find that you can do it, but it is much harder than talking when breathing out.

Air from the lungs goes up the windpipe (the trachea, to use the more technical term) and into the larynx, at which point it must pass between two small muscular folds called the vocal folds. If the vocal folds are apart, as they normally are when breathing out, the air from the lungs will have a relatively free passage into the pharynx and the mouth. But if the vocal folds are adjusted so that there is only a narrow passage between them, the airstream will cause them to vibrate. Sounds produced when the vocal folds are vibrating are said to be **voiced,** as opposed to those in which the vocal folds are apart, which are said to be **voiceless.**

In order to hear the difference between a voiced and a voiceless sound, try saying a long *v* sound, which we will symbolize as [vvvvv]. Now compare this with a long *f* sound [fffff], saying each of them alternately—[fffffvvvvvfffff-vvvvv]. Both of these sounds are formed in the same way in the mouth. The difference between them is that [v] is voiced but [f] is voiceless. You can feel the vocal fold vibrations in [v] if you put your fingertips against your larynx. You can also hear the buzzing of the vibrations in [v] more easily if you stop up your ears while contrasting [fffffvvvvv].

The difference between voiced and voiceless sounds is often important in distinguishing sounds. In each of the pairs of words "fat, vat; thigh, thy; Sue, zoo" the first consonant in the first word of each pair is voiceless, whereas in the second word, it is voiced. To check this for yourself, say just the consonant at the beginning of each of these words and try to feel and hear the voicing as suggested above. Try to find other pairs of words that are distinguished by one having a voiced and the other having a voiceless consonant.

The air passages above the larynx are known as the **vocal tract.** Figure 1.1 shows their location within the head (actually within my head, many years ago). The shape of the vocal tract is a very important factor in the production of

---

FIGURE 1.1   The vocal tract.

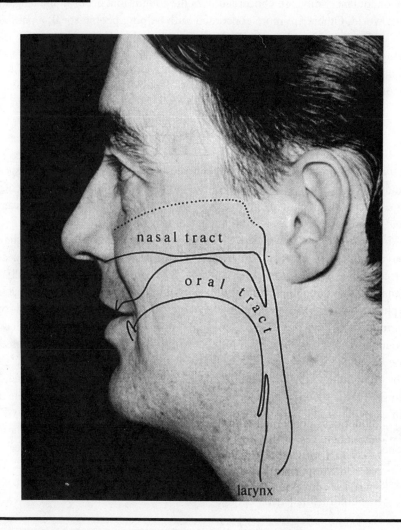

speech, and we will often refer to a diagram of the kind that has been superimposed on the photograph in Figure 1.1. Learn to draw the vocal tract by tracing the diagram in this figure. Note that the air passages that make up the vocal tract may be divided into the oral tract within the mouth and pharynx, and the nasal tract within the nose. The upper limit of the nasal tract has been marked with a dotted line since the exact boundaries of the air passages within the nose depend on soft tissues of variable size.

The parts of the vocal tract that can be used to form sounds are called articulators. The articulators that form the lower surface of the vocal tract often move toward those that form the upper surface. Try saying the word "capital" and note the major movements of your tongue and lips. You will find that the back of the tongue makes contact with the roof of the mouth for the first sound and then comes down for the following vowel. The lips come together in the formation of *p* and then come apart again in the vowel. The tongue tip comes up for the *t* and again, for most people, for the final *l*.

The names for the principal parts of the upper surface of the vocal tract are given in Figure 1.2. The upper lip and the upper teeth (notably the frontal incisors) are familiar enough structures. Just behind the upper teeth is a small protuberance that you can feel with the tip of the tongue. This is called the **alveolar ridge.** You can also feel that the front part of the roof of the mouth is formed by a bony structure. This is the **hard palate.** You will probably have to use a fingertip to feel further back. Most people cannot curl the tongue up far enough to touch the **soft palate,** or **velum,** at the back of the mouth. The soft palate is a muscular flap that can be raised to press against the back wall of the pharynx and shut off the nasal

FIGURE 1.2   The principal parts of the upper surface of the vocal tract.

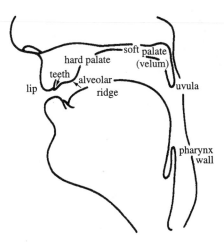

tract, preventing air from going out through the nose. In this case there is said to be a **velic closure.** This action separates the nasal tract from the oral tract so that the air can go out only through the mouth. At the lower end of the soft palate is a small appendage hanging down that is known as the uvula. The part of the vocal tract between the uvula and the larynx is the pharynx. The back wall of the pharynx may be considered to be one of the articulators on the upper surface of the vocal tract.

Figure 1.3 shows the lower lip and the specific names for different parts of the tongue that form the lower surface of the vocal tract. The tip and blade of the tongue are the most mobile parts. Behind the blade is what is technically called the front of the tongue: it is actually the forward part of the body of the tongue, and it lies underneath the hard palate when the tongue is at rest. The remainder of the body of the tongue may be divided into the center, which is partly beneath the hard palate and partly beneath the soft palate; the back, which is beneath the soft palate; and the root, which is opposite the back wall of the pharynx. The epiglottis is attached to the lower part of the root of the tongue.

Bearing all these terms in mind, say the word "peculiar" and try to give a rough description of the actions of the vocal organs during the consonant sounds. You should find that the lips come together for the first sound. Then the back and center of the tongue are raised. But is the contact on the hard palate or on the velum? (For most people, it is centered between the two.) Then note the position in the formation of the *l*. Most people make this sound with the tip of the tongue on the alveolar ridge.

Now compare the words "true" and "tea." In which word is the tongue contact further forward in the mouth? Most people make contact with the tip or blade of

---

FIGURE 1.3   The principal parts of the lower surface of the vocal tract.

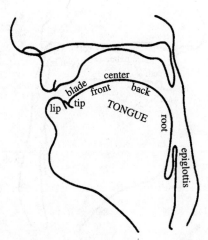

the tongue on the alveolar ridge when saying "tea," but slightly farther back in "true." Try to distinguish the differences in other consonant sounds, such as those in "sigh" and "shy" and those at the beginning of "fee" and "thief."

When considering diagrams such as those we have been discussing, it is important to remember that they show only two dimensions. The vocal tract is a tube, and the positions of the sides of the tongue may be very different from that of the center. In saying "sigh," for example, there is a deep hollow in the center of the tongue that is not present when saying "shy." We cannot represent this difference in a two-dimensional diagram showing just the midline of the tongue—a so-called mid-sagittal view. We will be relying on mid-sagittal diagrams of the vocal organs to a considerable extent in this book. But we should never let this simplified view become the sole basis for our conceptualization of speech sounds.

PLACES OF ARTICULATION

In order to form consonants, the airstream through the vocal tract must be obstructed in some way. Consonants can be classified according to the place and manner of this obstruction. The primary articulators that can cause an obstruction in most languages are the lips, the tongue tip and blade, and the back of the tongue. Speech gestures using the lips are called **labial** articulations; those using the tip or blade of the tongue are called **coronal** articulations; and those using the back of the tongue are called **dorsal** articulations.

If we do not need to specify the place of articulation in great detail, then the articulators for the consonants of English (and of many other languages) can be described using these terms. The word "topic," for example, begins with a coronal consonant; in the middle there is a labial consonant; and at the end a dorsal consonant. (Check this by feeling that the tip or blade of your tongue is raised for the first, coronal, consonant; your lips close for the second, labial, consonant; and the back of the tongue is raised for the final, dorsal, consonant.)

These terms, however, do not specify articulatory gestures in sufficient detail for many phonetic purposes. More specific places of articulation are indicated by the arrows going from one of the lower articulators to one of the upper articulators in Figure 1.4. Because there are so many possibilities in the coronal region, this area has been shown in more detail on the right of the figure. The principal terms for the particular types of obstruction required in the description of English are as follows:

1. **Bilabial**

    (Made with the two lips.) Say words such as "pie, buy, my" and note how the lips come together for the first sound in each of these words. Find a comparable set of words with bilabial sounds at the end.

| FIGURE 1.4 | A sagittal section of the vocal tract, showing the places of articulation that occur in English. The coronal region is shown in more detail on the right. |

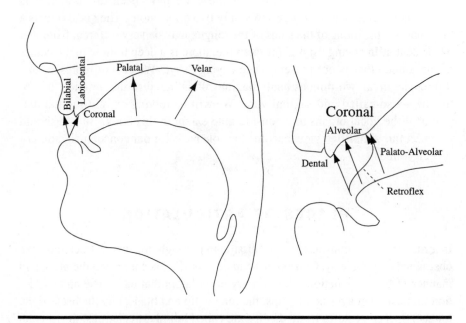

2. Labiodental

(Lower lip and upper front teeth.) Most people, when saying words such as "fie, vie," raise the lower lip until it nearly touches the upper front teeth.

3. Dental

(Tongue tip or blade and upper front teeth.) Say the words "thigh, thy." Some people (most speakers of American English) have the tip of the tongue protruding between the upper and lower front teeth; others (most speakers of British English) have it close behind the upper front teeth. Both these kinds of sounds are normal in English, and both may be called dental. If a distinction is needed, sounds in which the tongue protrudes between the teeth may be called **interdental.**

4. Alveolar

(Tongue tip or blade and the alveolar ridge.) Again there are two possibilities in English, and you should find out which you use. You may pronounce words such as "tie, die, nigh, sigh, zeal, lie" using the tip of the tongue or the blade of the tongue. Feel how you normally make the alveolar consonants in each of these words, and then try to make them in the other way. A good way to appreciate the difference between dental and alveolar sounds is to say "ten" and "tenth" (or "n" and "nth"). Which *n* is farther back? (Most people make the one in the first of each of these pairs of words on the alveolar ridge and the second as a dental sound with the tongue touching the upper front teeth.)

5. Retroflex

(Tongue tip and the back of the alveolar ridge.) Many speakers of English do not use retroflex sounds at all. But for some, retroflex sounds occur initially in words such as "rye, row, ray." Note the position of the tip of your tongue in these words. Speakers who pronounce *r* at the ends of words may also have retroflex sounds with the tip of the tongue raised in "ire, hour, air."

6. Palato-Alveolar

(Tongue blade and the back of the alveolar ridge.) Say words such as "shy, she, show." During the consonants, the tip of your tongue may be down behind the lower front teeth, or it may be up near the alveolar ridge, but the blade of the tongue is always close to the back part of the alveolar ridge. Because these sounds are made further back in the mouth than those in "sigh, sea, sew," they can also be called **post-alveolar.** You should be able to pronounce them with the tip or blade of the tongue. Try saying "shipshape" with your tongue tip up on one occasion and down on another. Note that the blade of the tongue will always be raised. You may be able to feel the place of articulation more distinctly if you hold the position while taking in a breath through the mouth. The incoming air cools the blade of the tongue and the back part of the alveolar ridge.

7. Palatal

(Front of the tongue and hard palate.) Say the word "you" very slowly so that you can isolate the consonant at the beginning. If you say this consonant by itself, you should be able to feel that the front of the tongue is raised toward the hard palate. Try to hold the consonant position and breathe inward through the mouth. You will probably be able to feel the rush of cold air between the front of the tongue and the hard palate.

8. Velar

(Back of the tongue and soft palate.) The consonants that have the farthest back place of articulation in English are those that occur at the end of "hack, hag, hang." In all these sounds, the back of the tongue is raised so that it touches the velum.

As you can tell from the descriptions of these articulations, the first two, bilabial and labiodental, can be classified as labial, involving at least the lower lip; the next four, dental, alveolar, retroflex, and palato-alveolar (post-alveolar), are coronal articulations, with the tip or blade of the tongue raised; and the last, velar, is a dorsal articulation, using the back of the tongue. Palatal sounds are sometimes classified as coronal articulations and sometimes as dorsal articulations, a point to which we shall return.

To get the feeling of different places of articulation, consider the consonant at the beginning of each of the following words: "fee, theme, see, she." Say these consonants by themselves. Are they voiced or voiceless? Now note that the place of articulation moves back in the mouth in making this series of voiceless consonants, going from labiodental, through dental and alveolar, to palato-alveolar.

THE ORO-NASAL PROCESS

Consider the consonants at the ends of "rang, ran, ram." When you say these consonants by themselves, note that the air is coming out through the nose. In the formation of these sounds, the point of articulatory closure moves forward, from velar in "rang," through alveolar in "ran," to bilabial in "ram." In each case, the air is prevented from going out through the mouth, but is able to go out through the nose because the soft palate, or velum, is lowered.

In most speech, the soft palate is raised so that there is a velic closure. When it is lowered and there is an obstruction in the mouth, we say that there is a nasal consonant. Raising or lowering the velum controls the oro-nasal process, the distinguishing factor between oral and nasal sounds.

MANNERS OF ARTICULATION

At most places of articulation there are several basic ways in which articulation can be accomplished. The articulators may close off the oral tract for an instant or a relatively long period; they may narrow the space considerably; or they may simply modify the shape of the tract by approaching each other.

STOP

(Complete closure of the articulators involved so that the airstream cannot escape through the mouth.) There are two possible types of stop.

Oral stop If, in addition to the articulatory closure in the mouth, the soft palate is raised so that the nasal tract is blocked off, then the airstream will be completely obstructed. Pressure in the mouth will build up and an **oral stop** will be formed. When the articulators come apart, the airstream will be released in a small burst of sound. This kind of sound occurs in the consonants in the words "pie, buy" (bilabial closure), "tie, dye" (alveolar closure), and "kye, guy" (velar closure). Figure 1.5 shows the position of the vocal organs in the bilabial stop in "buy."

FIGURE 1.5
FIGURE 1.5   The positions of the vocal organs in the bilabial stop in "buy."

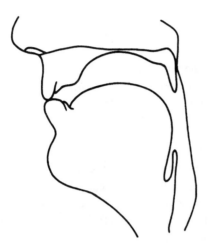

Nasal stop   If the air is stopped in the oral cavity but the soft palate is down so that it can go out through the nose, the sound produced is a **nasal stop.** Sounds of this kind occur at the beginning of the words "my" (bilabial closure) and "nigh" (alveolar closure) and at the end of the word "sang" (velar closure). Figure 1.6 shows the position of the vocal organs during the bilabial nasal stop in

FIGURE 1.6   The position of the vocal organs in the bilabial nasal stop in "my."

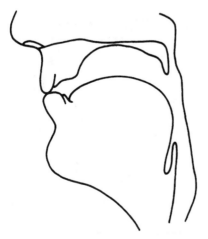

"my." Apart from the presence of a velic closure, there is no difference between this stop and the one in "buy"—shown in Figure 1.5. Although both the nasal sounds and the oral sounds can be classified as stops, the term **stop** by itself is almost always used by phoneticians to indicate an oral stop, and the term **nasal** is used to indicate a nasal stop. Thus the consonants at the beginnings of the words "day" and "neigh" would be called an alveolar stop and an alveolar nasal, respectively. Although the term *stop* may be defined so that it applies only to the prevention of air escaping through the mouth, it is commonly used to imply a complete stoppage of the airflow through both the nose and the mouth.

FRICATIVE

(Close approximation of two articulators so that the airstream is partially obstructed and turbulent airflow is produced.) The mechanism involved in making these slightly hissing sounds may be likened to that involved when the wind whistles around a corner. The consonants in "fie, vie" (labiodental), "thigh, thy" (dental), "sigh, zoo" (alveolar), and "shy" (palato-alveolar) are examples of fricative sounds. Figure 1.7 illustrates one pronunciation of the palato-alveolar fricative consonant in "shy." Note the narrowing of the vocal tract between the blade of the tongue and the back part of the alveolar ridge. The higher-pitched sounds with a more obvious hiss, such as those in "sigh, shy," are sometimes called **sibilants.**

| FIGURE 1.7 | The positions of the vocal organs in the palato-alveolar (post-alveolar) fricative in "shy." |

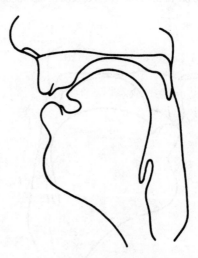

Approximant

(An articulation in which one articulator is close to another, but without the vocal tract being narrowed to such an extent that a turbulent airstream is produced.) In saying the first sound in "yacht," the front of the tongue is raised toward the palatal area of the roof of the mouth, but it does not come close enough for a fricative sound to be produced. The consonants in the word "we" (approximation between the lips and in the velar region) and, for some people, in the word "raw" (approximation in the alveolar region) are also examples of approximants.

Lateral (Approximant)

(Obstruction of the airstream at a point along the center of the oral tract, with incomplete closure between one or both sides of the tongue and the roof of the mouth.) Say the word "lie" and note how the tongue touches near the center of the alveolar ridge. Prolong the initial consonant and note how, despite the closure formed by the tongue, air flows out freely, over the side of the tongue. Because there is no stoppage of the air, and not even any fricative noises, these sounds are classified as approximants. The consonants in words such as "lie, laugh" are alveolar lateral approximants, but they are usually called just alveolar laterals, their approximant status being assumed. You may be able to find out which side of the tongue is not in contact with the roof of the mouth by holding the consonant position while you breathe inward. The tongue will feel colder on the side that is not in contact with the roof of the mouth.

Additional Consonantal Articulations

In this preliminary chapter, it will not be necessary to discuss all of the manners of articulation used in the various languages of the world—nor, for that matter, in English. But it might be useful to know the terms **trill** (sometimes called roll) and **tap** (sometimes called flap). Tongue-tip trills occur in some forms of Scottish English in words such as "rye" and "raw." Taps, in which the tongue makes a single tap against the alveolar ridge, occur in the middle of a word such as "pity" in many forms of American English.

The production of some sounds involves more than one of these manners of articulation. Say the word "cheap" and think about how you make the first sound. At the beginning, the tongue comes up to make contact with the back part of the alveolar ridge to form a stop closure. This contact is then slackened so that there is a fricative at the same place of articulation. This kind of combination of a stop immediately followed by a fricative is called an **affricate,** in this case a palato-alveolar (or post-alveolar) affricate. There is a voiceless affricate at the beginning and end of the word "church." The corresponding voiced affricate occurs at the beginning and end of "judge." In all these sounds the articulators (tongue tip or blade and alveolar ridge) come together for the stop; and then, instead of coming fully apart, they separate only slightly, so that a fricative is made at the same place of articulation. Try to feel these movements in your own pronunciation of these words.

To summarize, the consonants we have been discussing so far may be described in terms of five factors: (1) state of the vocal folds (voiced or voiceless); (2) place of articulation; (3) central or lateral articulation; (4) soft palate raised to form a velic closure (oral sounds) or lowered (nasal sounds); (5) manner of articulatory action. Thus the consonant at the beginning of the word "sing" is a (1) voiceless, (2) alveolar, (3) central, (4) oral, (5) fricative; and the consonant at the end of "sing" is a (1) voiced, (2) velar, (3) central, (4) nasal, (5) stop.

On most occasions it is not necessary to state all these five points. Unless a specific statement to the contrary is made, consonants are usually presumed to be central, not lateral, and oral rather than nasal. Consequently, points (3) and (4) may often be left out, so that the consonant at the beginning of "sing" is simply called a voiceless alveolar fricative. When describing nasals, point (4) has to be specifically mentioned and point (5) can be left out, so that the consonant at the end of "sing" is simply called a voiced velar nasal.

THE ARTICULATION OF VOWEL SOUNDS

In the production of vowel sounds, the articulators do not come very close together, and the passage of the airstream is relatively unobstructed. Vowel sounds may be specified in terms of the position of the highest point of the tongue and the position of the lips. Figure 1.8 shows the articulatory position for the vowels in "heed, hid, head, had, father, good, food." As you can see, in all these vowels the tongue tip is down behind the lower front teeth, and the body of the tongue is domed upward. Check that this is so in your own pronunciation. In the first four vowels, the highest point of the tongue is in the front of the mouth. Accordingly, these vowels are called **front vowels.** The tongue is fairly close to the roof of the mouth for the vowel in "heed," slightly less close for the vowel in "hid," and lower still for the vowels in "head" and "had." If you look in a mirror while saying the vowels in these four words, you will find that the mouth becomes progressively more open while the tongue remains in the front of the mouth. The vowel in "heed" is classified as a high front vowel, and the vowel in "had" as a low front vowel. The height of the tongue for the vowels in the other words is between these two extremes, and they are therefore called mid-front vowels. The vowel in "hid" is a mid-high vowel, and the vowel in "head" is a mid-low vowel.

Now try saying the vowels in "father, good, food." Figure 1.8 also shows the articulatory position for these vowels. In all three, the tongue is close to the upper or back surface of the vocal tract. These vowels are classified as **back vowels.** The

FIGURE 1.8   The positions of the vocal organs for the vowels in the words 1 heed, 2 hid, 3 head, 4 had, 5 father, 6 good, 7 food. The lip positions for vowels 2, 3, and 4 are in between those shown for 1 and 5. The lip position for vowel 6 is between those shown for 1 and 7.

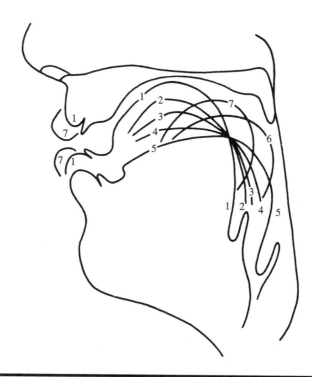

body of the tongue is highest in the vowel in "food" (which is therefore called a high back vowel), and lowest in the first vowel in "father" (which is therefore called a low back vowel). The vowel in "good" is a mid-high back vowel.

The position of the lips varies considerably in different vowels. They are generally closer together in the mid and high back vowels (as in "good, food"), though in some forms of American English this is not so. Look at the position of your lips in a mirror while you say just the vowels in "heed, hid, head, had, father, good, food." You will probably find that in the last two words there is a movement of the lips in addition to the movement that occurs because of the lowering and raising of the jaw. This movement is called lip rounding. It is usually most noticeable in the forward movement of the corners of the lips. Vowels may be described as being **rounded** (as in "who'd") or **unrounded** (as in "heed").

In summary, vowels can be described in terms of three factors: (1) the height of the body of the tongue; (2) the front–back position of the tongue; and (3) the degree of lip rounding. The relative positions of the highest points of the tongue are given

| FIGURE 1.9 | The relative positions of the highest points of the tongue in the vowels in 1 heed, 2 hid, 3 head, 4 had, 5 father, 6 good, 7 food. |

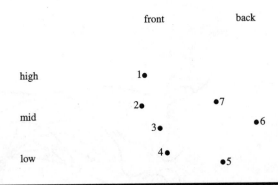

in Figure 1.9. Say just the vowels in the words given in the caption for this figure and check that your tongue moves in the pattern described by the points. It is very difficult to become aware of the position of the tongue in vowels, but you can probably get some impression of tongue height by observing the position of your jaw while saying just the vowels in the four words, "heed, hid, head, had." You should also be able to feel the difference between front and back vowels by contrasting words such as "he" and "who." Say these words silently and concentrate on the sensations involved. You should feel the tongue going from front to back as you say "he, who." You can also feel your lips becoming more rounded.

As you can see from Figure 1.9, the specification of vowels in terms of the position of the highest point of the tongue is not entirely satisfactory for a number of reasons. First, the vowels that are called high do not have the same tongue height. The back high vowel (point 7) is nowhere near as high as the front vowel (point 1). Second, the so-called back vowels vary considerably in their degree of backness. Third, as you can see by looking at Figure 1.8, this kind of specification disregards considerable differences in the shape of the tongue in front vowels and in back vowels. Furthermore, it does not take into account the fact that the width of the pharynx varies considerably with, and to some extent independently of, the height of the tongue in different vowels. We will discuss better ways of describing vowels in Chapters 4 and 9.

SUPRASEGMENTALS

Vowels and consonants can be thought of as the segments of which speech is composed. Together they form the syllables, which go to make up utterances.

Superimposed on the syllables are other features known as suprasegmentals. These include variations in stress and pitch. Variations in length are also usually considered to be suprasegmental features, although they can affect single segments as well as whole syllables.

Variations in stress are used in English to distinguish between a noun and a verb, as in "(an) insult" versus "(to) insult." Say these words yourself, and check which syllable has the greater stress. Then compare similar pairs, such as "(a) pervert, (to) pervert" or "(an) overflow, (to) overflow." You should find that in the nouns the stress is on the first syllable, but in the verbs it is on the last. Thus, stress can have a grammatical function in English. It can also be used for contrastive emphasis (as in "I want a *red* pen, not a black one"). Variations in stress are caused by an increase in the activity of the respiratory muscles (so that a greater amount of air is pushed out of the lungs) and in the activity of the laryngeal muscles (so that there is a significant change in pitch).

You can usually find where the stress occurs on a word by trying to tap with your finger in time with each syllable. It is much easier to tap on the stressed syllable. Try saying "abominable" and tapping first on the first syllable, then on the second, then on the third, and so on. If you say the word in your normal way you will find it easiest to tap on the second syllable. Many people cannot tap on the first syllable without altering their normal pronunciation.

Pitch changes due to variations in laryngeal activity can occur independently of stress changes. When they do, they can affect the meaning of the sentence as a whole. The pitch pattern in a sentence is known as the **intonation.** Listen to the intonation (the variations in the pitch of your voice) when you say the sentence "This is my father." Try to find out which syllable has the highest pitch and which the lowest. In most people's speech, the highest pitch will occur on the first syllable of "father" and the lowest on the second, the last syllable in the sentence. Now observe the pitch changes in the question "Is this your father?" In this sentence the first syllable of "father" is usually on a lower pitch than the last syllable. In English it is even possible to change the meaning of a sentence such as "That's a cat" from a statement to a question without altering the order of the words. If you substitute a mainly rising for a mainly falling intonation, you will produce a question spoken with an air of astonishment: "That's a *cat?*"

All the suprasegmental features are characterized by the fact that they must be described in relation to other items in the same utterance. It is the relative values of pitch, length, or degree of stress of an item that are significant. You can stress one syllable as opposed to another irrespective of whether you are shouting or talking softly. Children can also use the same intonation patterns as adults, although their voices have a higher pitch. The absolute values are never linguistically important. But they do, of course, convey information about the speaker's age, sex, emotional state, and attitude toward the topic under discussion.

EXERCISES

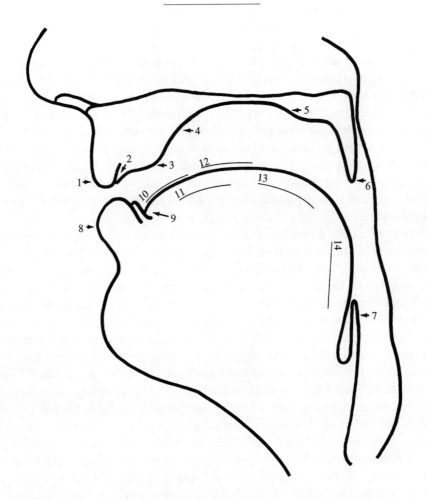

A Fill in the names of the vocal organs numbered in Figure 1.10 above.

1. lips
2. upper front teeth
3. alveolar ridge
4. hard palate
5. soft palate (velum)
6. uvular
7. pharynx

8. lower lips
9. lower front teeth
10. tongue tip
11. front of tongue
12. body/mid tongue
13. back of tongue
14. root of tongue

B Describe the consonants in the word "skinflint" using the following chart. Fill in all five columns, and put parentheses around the terms that may be left out, as shown for the first consonant.

	1 voiced or voiceless	2 place of articulation	3 central or lateral	4 oral or nasal	5 articulatory action
s	voiceless	alveolar	(central)	(oral)	fricative
k	voiceless	hard palate	central	oral	fricative
n	voiced	nasal	central	nasal	nasal
f	voiceless	dental	central	oral	fricative
l	voiced	alveolar	central	oral	liquid
t	voiceless	alveolar	central	oral	stop

C Figure 1.11a–g illustrates all the places of articulation we have discussed so far, except for retroflex sounds (which will be illustrated in Chapter 7). In the following spaces, state (1) the place of articulation and (2) the manner of articulation of each sound. In addition, give (3) an example of an English word beginning with the sound illustrated.

	(1) Place of articulation	(2) Manner of articulation	(3) Example
a	labial	lips come together	buy, my
b	dental	tongue tip between teeth	thy
c	alveolar	tongue tip / alveolar ridge	lilt
d	post alveolar	tongue blade / back of alve.	shy
e	velar	back of tongue / velum	Lach
f	retroflex	tongue tip / alveolar back of	"rye" Scottish
g	palatal	tongue / hard palate	you

FIGURE 1.11   Sounds illustrating all the places of articulation discussed so far, except for retroflex sounds.

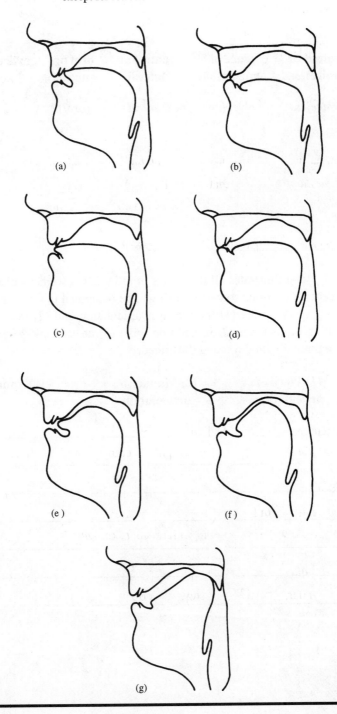

(a)

(b)

(c)

(d)

(e)

(f)

(g)

D Studying a new subject often involves learning a large number of technical terms. Phonetics is particularly difficult in this respect. Read over the definitions of the terms in this chapter, and then try the exercises that follow. Listen to the sounds of the words, and be careful not to be confused by spellings. Using a mirror may be helpful.

1. Circle the words that begin with a bilabial consonant:
   mat   gnat   sat   bat   rat   pat

2. Circle the words that begin with a velar consonant:
   knot   got   lot   cot   hot   pot

3. Circle the words that begin with a labiodental consonant:
   fat   cat   that   mat   chat   vat

4. Circle the words that begin with an alveolar consonant:
   zip   nip   lip   sip   tip   dip

5. Circle the words that begin with a dental consonant:
   pie   guy   shy   thigh   thy   high

6. Circle the words that begin with a palato-alveolar consonant:
   sigh   shy   tie   thigh   thy   lie

7. Circle the words that end with a fricative:
   race   wreath   bush   bring   breathe   bang
   rave   real   ray   rose   rough

8. Circle the words that end with a nasal:
   rain   rang   dumb   deaf

9. Circle the words that end with a stop:
   pill   lip   lit   graph   crab   dog   hide
   laugh   back

10. Circle the words that begin with a lateral:
    nut   lull   bar   rob   one

11. Circle the words that begin with an approximant:
    we   you   one   run

12. Circle the words that end with an affricate:
    much   back   edge   ooze

13. Circle the words in which the consonant in the middle is voiced:
    tracking   mother   robber   leisure   massive
    stomach   razor

14. Circle the words that contain a high vowel:
    sat   suit   got   meet   mud

15. Circle the words that contain a low vowel:

weed   wad   load   lad   rude

16. Circle the words that contain a front vowel:

gate   caught   cat   kit   put

17. Circle the words that contain a back vowel:

maid   weep   coop   cop   good

18. Circle the words that contain a rounded vowel:

who   me   us   but   him

E Define the consonant sounds in the middle of each of the following words as indicated in the example:

	Voiced or voiceless	**Place of articulation**	**Manner of articulation**
adder	*voiced*	*alveolar*	*stop*
father			
singing			
etching			
robber			
ether			
pleasure			
hopper			
selling			
sunny			
lodger			

F Complete the diagrams so as to illustrate the position of the vocal organs during the first consonants in each of the following words. If the sound is voiced,
schematize the vibrating vocal folds by a wavy line at the glottis. If it is voiceless, use a straight line.

Example:
mat

day

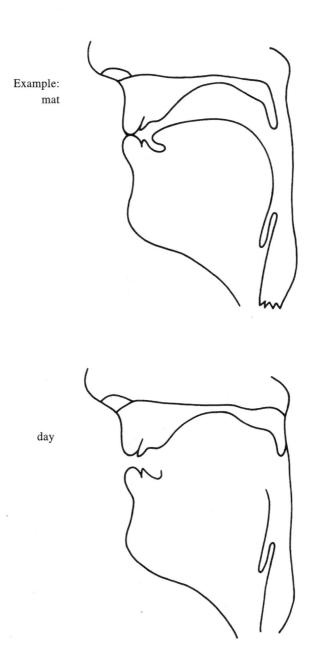

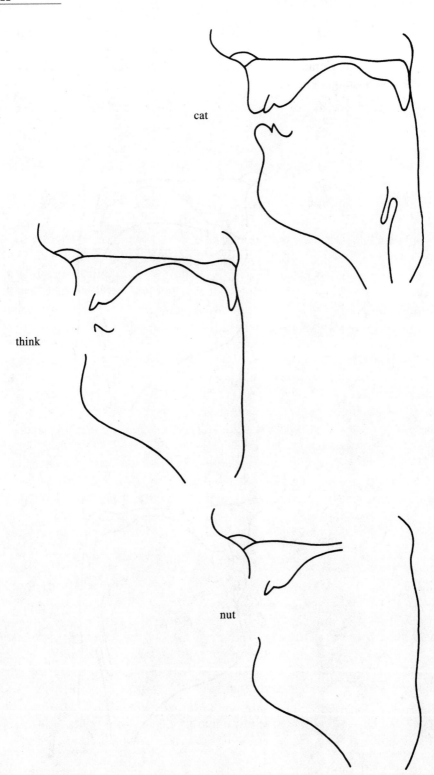

cat

think

nut

2

Phonology and Phonetic Transcription

Many people think that learning phonetics means simply learning to use phonetic transcription. But there is really much more to the subject than learning to use a set of symbols. A phonetician is a person who can describe speech, who understands the mechanisms of speech production and speech perception, and who knows how languages use these mechanisms. Phonetic transcription is no more than a useful tool that phoneticians use in the description of speech.

When phoneticians transcribe an utterance, they usually do so by noting how the sounds convey differences in meaning. For the most part, they concern themselves with describing only the significant articulations rather than the total set of movements of the vocal organs. For example, when saying the English word "tie," some people pronounce the consonant with the blade of the tongue against the alveolar ridge, others with the tip of the tongue. This kind of difference in articulation does not affect the meaning of the word and is not usually transcribed.

In order to understand what we transcribe and what we don't, it is necessary to understand the basic principles of phonology. **Phonology** is the description of the systems and patterns of sounds that occur in a language. It involves studying a language to determine its distinctive sounds and to find out which sounds convey a difference in meaning. Children have to do this when they are learning to speak. To begin with they might not realize that, for example, there is a difference between the consonants at the beginnings of words such as "white" and "right." Later they realize that these words begin with two distinct sounds. Eventually they learn to distinguish all the sounds that can change the meanings of words.

When two sounds can be used to differentiate words, they are said to belong to different **phonemes.** There must be a phonemic difference if two words (such as "white" and "right" or "cat" and "bat") differ in only a single sound. There are, however, small shades of sounds that cannot be used to distinguish words, such as the differences between the consonants at the beginning and end of the word "pop." For the first of these sounds, the lips must open and there must be a puff of air before the vowel begins. After the final consonant there may be a puff of air, but it is not necessary. In fact, you could say "pop" and never open your lips for hours, if it happened to be the last word you said before going to sleep. The sound at the end would still be a *p*. Both consonants in this word are voiceless bilabial stops. They are different, but the differences between them cannot be used to change the meaning of a word in English. They both belong to the same phoneme.

We cannot rely on the spelling to tell us whether two sounds are members of different phonemes. For example, if you think about the two words "key" and "car," you realize that they both begin with the same sound, despite the fact that one is spelled with the letter *k* and the other with the letter *c*. But this example also shows that there may be very subtle differences between members of a phoneme. The two words "key" and "car" do not begin with *exactly* the same sound. If you whisper just the first consonants in these two words, you can probably hear a difference; and you may be able to feel that your tongue touches the roof of your mouth in a different place. The two sounds at the beginning of "key" and "car" are slightly different, but it is not the kind of difference that changes the meaning of a word in English. They are both members of the same phoneme.

We noted other small changes in sounds that do not affect the meaning in Chapter 1, where we saw that the tongue is further back in "true" than in "tea," and the *n* in "tenth" is likely to be dental, whereas the one in "ten" is usually alveolar. In some cases the members of a phoneme are more different from one another. For example, most Americans (and many younger speakers of British English) have a *t* in the middle of "pity" that is very different from the *t* at the end of the word "pit." The one in "pity" sounds more like a *d*. Consider also the *l* in "play." You can say just the first two consonants in this word without any voicing, but you will still hear the *l* (try doing this). When you say the whole word "play" the *l* is typically voiceless, and very different from the one in "lay." Say the *l* at the beginning of "lay," and you'll hear that it is definitely voiced.

It follows from these examples that a phoneme is not a single sound but a name for a group of sounds. There is a group of *t* sounds and a group of *l* sounds that occur in English. It is as if you had in your mind an ideal *t* or *l,* and the ones that were actually produced were variations of it, which differed in small ways that did not affect the meaning of English words. These groups of sounds—the phonemes—are abstract units that form the basis for writing down a language systematically and unambiguously.

We often want to record all and only the variations between sounds that cause a difference in meaning. Transcriptions of this kind are called phonemic transcriptions. Languages that have been written down only comparatively recently (such as Swahili and most of the other languages of Africa) have a fairly phonemic spelling system. There is very little difference between a written version of a Swahili sentence and a phonemic transcription of that sentence. But because English pronunciation has changed over the centuries while the spelling has remained basically the same, phonemic transcriptions of English are different from written texts.

THE TRANSCRIPTION OF CONSONANTS

We can begin searching for phonemes by considering the contrasting consonant sounds in English. A good way is to find sets of words that rhyme. Take, for example, all the words that rhyme with "pie" and have only a single consonant at the beginning. A set of words, each of which differs from all the others by only one sound, is called a minimal set. The second column of Table 2.1 lists a minimal set of this kind. There are obviously many other words that rhyme with "pie," such as "spy, try, spry," but these words begin with sequences of two or more of the sounds already in the minimal set. Some of the words in the list begin with two consonant letters ("thigh, thy, shy"), but they each begin with a single consonant sound. "Shy," for example, does not contain a sequence of two consonant sounds in the way that "spy" and "try" do.

Some consonants do not occur in words rhyming with "pie." If we allow the names of the letters as words, then we can find a large set of consonants beginning words rhyming with "pea." A list of such words is shown in the third column of Table 2.1. (Speakers of British English will have to remember that in American English the name of the last letter of the alphabet belongs in this set rather than in the set of words rhyming with "bed.")

Even in this set of words, we are still missing some consonant sounds that contrast with others only in the middle or at the end of words. The letters *ng* often represent a single consonant sound that does not occur at the beginning of a word. You can hear this sound at the end of the word "rang," where it contrasts with other nasals in words such as "ram, ran." There is also a contrast between the consonants in the middle of "mission" and "vision," although there are very few pairs of words that are distinguished by this contrast in English. (One such pair in my English involves the name of a chain of islands—"Aleutian" versus "allusion.") Words illustrating these consonants are given in the fourth column of Table 2.1.

Most of the symbols in Table 2.1 are the same letters we use in spelling these words, but there are a few differences. One variation between spelling and phonetic usage occurs with the letter *c,* which is sometimes used to represent a [k] sound, as in "cup" or "bacon," and sometimes to represent an [s] sound, as in "cellar" or "receive." Two *c*'s may even represent a sequence of these sounds in the same word, as in "accent, access." A symbol that differs from the corresponding letter is [g], which is used for the sound "guy" and "guess" but never for the sound in "age" or the sound in the name of the letter *g.* A few other symbols are needed to supplement the regular alphabet. The phonetic symbols we will use are part of the set approved by the International Phonetic Association, a body founded in 1886 by a group of leading phoneticians from France, Germany, Britain, and Denmark. The complete set of IPA symbols is given in the chart in the inside covers of this book. It will be discussed in detail later in this book. Because we often need to talk about the symbols, the names that have been given to them are shown in the last column of Table 2.1.

TABLE 2.1		Symbols for transcribing English consonants. (Alternative symbols that may be found in other books are given in parentheses.) The last column gives the conventional names for the phonetic symbols in the first column.

p	pie	pea		lowercase *p*
t	tie	tea		lowercase *t*
k	kye	key		lowercase *k*
b	by	bee		lowercase *b*
d	dye	D		lowercase *d*
g	guy			lowercase *g*
m	my	me	ram	lowercase *m*
n	nigh	knee	ran	lowercase *n*
ŋ			rang	eng (or angma)
f	fie	fee		lowercase *f*
v	vie	V		lowercase *v*
θ	thigh			theta
ð	thy	thee		eth
s	sigh	sea	listen	lowercase *s*
z		Z	mizzen	lowercase *z*
ʃ (š)	shy	she	mission	esh (or long *s*)
ʒ (ž)			vision	long *z* (or yogh)
l	lie	lee		lowercase *l*
w	why	we		lowercase *w*
r (ɹ)	rye			lowercase *r*
j (y)		ye		lowercase *j*
h	high	he		lowercase *h*

Note also the following:

tʃ (tš)	chi(me)	chea(p)
dʒ (dž)	ji(ve)	G

The velar nasal at the end of "rang" is written with [ŋ], a letter *n* combined with the tail of the letter *g* descending below the line. Some people call this symbol "eng" and others "angma." The symbol [θ], an upright version of the Greek letter theta, is used for the voiceless dental fricative in words such as "thigh, thin, thimble, ether, breath, mouth." The symbol [ð], called "eth," is derived from an Anglo-Saxon letter. It is used for the corresponding voiced sound in words such as "thy, then, them, either, breathe." Both these symbols are ascenders (letters that go up from the line of writing rather than descending below it). The spelling system of the English language does not distinguish between [θ] and [ð]. They are both written with the letters *th* in pairs such as "thigh, thy."

The voiceless palato-alveolar (post-alveolar) fricative [ʃ] ("long *s*") in "shy, sheep, rash" is both an ascender and a descender. It is like a long, straightened *s* going both above and below the line of writing. The corresponding voiced symbol [ʒ] is like a long *z* descending below the line. This sound occurs in the middle of words such as "vision, measure, leisure" and at the beginning of foreign words such as the French "Jean, gendarme," and foreign names such as "Zsa Zsa."

In earlier editions of this book, the sound at the beginning of the word "rye" was symbolized by [ɹ], an upside-down letter *r*. As the two major dictionaries of American and British English pronunciation (see Further Reading) use a regular [r] for this sound, I have done so here.

It is unfortunate that different books on phonetics use different forms of phonetic transcription. This is not because phoneticians cannot agree on which symbols to use, but because different styles of transcription are more appropriate in one circumstance than in another. Thus in this book, where we are concerned with general phonetics, I have used the IPA symbol [j] for the initial sound in "yes, yet, yeast" because I wish to reserve the symbol [y] for another sound, the vowel in the French word "tu." Another reason for using [j] is that in many languages (German, Dutch, Norwegian, Swedish, and others) this letter is used in words such as "ja," which are pronounced with a sound that in our spelling system would be written with the letter *y*. Books that are concerned only with the phonetics of English often use [y] where this one uses [j]. Some books on phonetics also use [š] and [ž] in place of the IPA symbols [ʃ] and [ʒ], respectively.

There are also disagreements among texts on phonetics on how to transcribe sounds such as the first and last sounds in both "church" and "judge." I have taken the position that these sounds are each sequences of two other consonants and should be written [tʃ] and [dʒ]. They are like other words that begin or end with a sequence of two consonants that occur in other words such as "tray" and "adds."

You can see that a word such as "choose" might be said to begin with [tʃ] if you compare your pronunciation of the phrases "white shoes" and "why choose." In the first phrase, the [t] is at the end of one word and the [ʃ] at the beginning of the next; but in the second phrase, these two sounds occur together at the beginning of the second word. The difference between the two phrases is simply one of the timing of the articulations involved rather than the use of different articulations. Other pairs of phrases that demonstrate this point are "heat sheets" versus "he cheats" and "might shop" versus "my chop." There are no pairs of phrases illustrating the same point for the voiced counterpart [dʒ] found in "jar, gentle, age" because no English word begins with [ʒ].

Some other books on phonetics take the view that the sounds [tʃ] and [dʒ] (as in "church" and "judge") are really single units and are better transcribed with a single symbol, such as [č] and [ǰ]. This view has much to commend it, since the consonants [ʃ] and [ʒ] are not like other consonants such as [r] and [l]. Each of the latter pair of consonants can occur as the second element in many clusters (for example, in "priest, tree, cream, play, clay"). But [ʃ] and [ʒ] cluster only with [t] and [d], respectively. However, as this is a book on phonetics, it seems appropriate to use two symbols for the consonants in words such as "jay" and "age" to show that there are two elements in each of them, just as there are in other words containing consonant clusters, such as "tree" and "eats."

There is one minor matter still to be considered in the transcription of the consonant contrasts of English. In most forms of both British and American English, "which" does not contrast with "witch." Accordingly, both "why" and "we" in Table 2.1 are said to begin simply with [w]. But some speakers of English contrast pairs of words such as "which, witch; why, Wye; whether, weather." These speakers will have to transcribe the first of each of these pairs of words with an initial [h]. Note that phonetically the [h] is transcribed before [w] in that it is the first part of each of these words that is voiceless.

THE TRANSCRIPTION OF VOWELS

The transcription of the contrasting vowels (the vowel phonemes) in English is more difficult than the transcription of consonants for two reasons. First, accents of English differ more in their use of vowels than in their use of consonants. Second, authorities differ widely in their views of what constitutes an appropriate description of vowels.

Taking the same approach in looking for contrasting vowels as we did in looking for consonant contrasts, we might try to find a minimal set of words that differ only in the vowel sounds. We could, for example, look for monosyllables that begin with [h] and end with [d], and we could supplement this minimal set with other lists of monosyllables that contrast only in their vowel sounds. Table 2.2 shows four such sets of words.

We will consider one form of British and one form of American English. The major difference between the two is that speakers of American English pronounce [r] sounds after vowels, as well as before them, whereas in most forms of British English [r] can occur only before a vowel. American English speakers distinguish between words such as "heart" and "hot" not by making a difference in vowel quality (as I do, speaking a form of British English) but by pronouncing "heart" with an [r] and "hot" with the same vowel but without an [r] following it. In "here, hair, hire," these speakers may use vowels similar to those in "he, head, high," respectively, but in each case with a following [r]. Most speakers of British English distinguish these words by using different **diphthongs**—movements from one vowel to another within a single syllable.

Even within American English there are variations in the number of contrasting vowels that occur. Many Midwestern speakers and most Far Western speakers do not distinguish between the vowels in pairs of words such as "odd, awed" and "cot, caught." Some forms of American English make additional distinctions

| TABLE 2.2 | | Symbols for transcribing contrasting vowels in English. Column **1** applies to many speakers of American English, Column **2** to most speakers of British English. The last column gives the conventional names for the phonetic symbols in the second column, some of which are also accompanied by the length mark [:] or by [r]. |

1	**2**						
iː	iː	heed	he	bead	heat	keyed	lowercase *i*
ɪ	ɪ	hid		bid	hit	kid	small capital *I*
eɪ	eɪ	hayed	hay	bayed	hate	Cade	lowercase *e*
ɛ	ɛ	head		bed			epsilon
æ	æ	had		bad	hat	cad	ash
ɑːr	ɑː	hard		bard	heart	card	script *a*
ɑː	ɒ	hod		bod	hot	cod	(2) turned script *a*
ɔː	ɔː	hawed	haw	bawd		cawed	open *o*
ʊ	ʊ	hood				could	upsilon
oʊ	əʊ	hoed	hoe	bode		code	lowercase *o*
uː	uː	who'd	who	booed	hoot	cooed	lowercase *u*
ʌ	ʌ	Hudd		bud	hut	cud	turned *v*
ɝː	ɜː	herd	her	bird	hurt	curd	reversed epsilon
aɪ	aɪ	hide	high	bide	height		lowercase *a* (+ ɪ)
aʊ	aʊ		how	bowed		cowed	(as noted above)
ɔɪ	ɔɪ		(a)hoy	Boyd			(as noted above)
ɪr	ɪə		here	beard			(as noted above)
ɛr	ɛə		hair	bared		cared	(as noted above)
aɪr	aə	hired	hire				(as noted above)
Note also the following:							
ju	ju	hued	hue	Bude		cued	(as noted above)

not shown in Table 2.2. For example, some speakers (mainly from the East Coast) distinguish the auxiliary verb "can" from the noun "can," the latter being more diphthongal. But we will have to overlook these small differences in this introductory textbook.

There are several possible ways of transcribing the contrasting vowels in Table 2.2. The two principal forms that will be used in this book are shown in the first and second columns. The first column is suitable for many forms of American English and the second for many forms of British English. The two columns have been kept as similar as possible; as you will see in Chapter 4, I have tried to make the transcriptions compatible with those of well-known authorities on the phonetics of English.

As in the case of the consonant symbols, the vowel symbols in Table 2.2 are used in accordance with the principles of the IPA. Those symbols that have the same shape as ordinary letters of the alphabet represent sounds similar to the sounds these letters have in French or Spanish or Italian. Actually, the IPA usage of the vowel letters is that of the great majority of the world's languages when they are written with the Roman alphabet, including such diverse languages as Swahili, Turkish, and Navajo. The present spelling of English reflects the way it used to sound many centuries ago when it still had vowel letters with values similar to those of the corresponding letters in all these other languages.

One of the principal problems in transcribing English phonetically is that there are more vowel sounds than there are vowel letters in the alphabet. In a transcription of the English word "sea" as [siː], the [iː] represents a similar (but not identical) sound to that in the Spanish or Italian "si." But unlike Spanish and Italian, English differentiates between vowels such as those in "seat" and "sit" and "heed" and "hid." The vowels in "seat, heed" differ from those in "sit, hid" in two ways: they have a slightly different quality and they are longer. Because the vowels in "sit, hid" are somewhat like those in "seat, heed," they are represented by the symbol [ɪ], a small capital *I*. The difference in length is shown by the symbol [ː].

The vowels in words such as "hay, bait, they" are transcribed with a sequence of two symbols [eɪ], indicating that for most speakers of English these words contain a diphthong. The first element in this diphthong is similar to sounds in Spanish or Italian that use the letter *e,* such as the Spanish word for milk, which is written "leche" and pronounced [letʃe]. The second element in the English words "hay, bait, they" is [ɪ], the symbol used for transcribing the vowel in "hid."

Two symbols that are not ordinary letters of the alphabet, [ɛ] and [æ], are used for the vowels in "head" and "had," respectively. The first is based on the Greek letter epsilon, and the second on the letters *a* and *e* joined together. They may be referred to by the names epsilon and digraph.

Most Americans have the same vowel sound in the words "heart" and "hot" and can use one form of the letter *a.* They would transcribe these words as [hɑːrt] and [hɑːt], with the length mark [ː] indicating that it is a comparatively long vowel. But some East Coast Americans and speakers of British English who do not pronounce [r] sounds after a vowel distinguish between these words by the qualities of the vowels and have to use two different forms of the letter *a.* They would transcribe these words as [hɑːt] and [hɒt].

Most speakers of British forms of English, and many American speakers, distinguish between pairs of words such as "cot, caught; not, naught." The symbols [ɔː], an open letter *o* followed by a length mark, may be used in the second of each of these pairs of words and in words such as "bawd, bought, law." Many Midwestern and Far Western American speakers do not need to use this symbol in any of these words, as they do not distinguish between the vowels in words such as "cot" and "caught." They may, however, have different vowels in words such as "moss" and "morse," so that they, like many other Americans, would use the symbol [ɔː] when there is a following [r] sound.

Another special symbol is used for the vowel in "hood, could, good." This symbol [ʊ] may be thought of as a letter *u* with the ends curled out.

The vowel in "hoe, dough, code" is a diphthong. For most American English speakers, the first element is very similar to sounds that are written in Spanish, or Italian with a letter *o*. Many speakers of English from the southern parts of Britain use a different sound for the first element of the diphthong in these words (which we will symbolize with [ə], an upside down letter *e*). We will discuss this sound more fully in a later section. The final element of the diphthong in words such as "hoe, code" is somewhat similar to the vowel [ʊ] in "hood."

An upside down letter *v* [ʌ] is used for the vowel in words such as "bud, hut." This symbol is sometimes referred to by the name *wedge*.

Another symbol, [ɜː], a reversed form of the Greek letter epsilon followed by a length mark, is used for the sound in "pert, bird, curt," as pronounced by most speakers of British English and those speakers of American English who do not have an [r] in these words. In most forms of American English, the *r* is fully combined with the vowel, and the symbol [ɝ] is used. The little hook [˞] indicates the *r*-coloring of the vowel.

The next three words in Table 2.2 contain diphthongs composed of elements that have been discussed already. The vowel in "hide" [haɪd] begins with a sound between that of the vowel in "cat" [kæt] and that in "far" [fɑː(r)], and moves toward the vowel [ɪ] as in "hid" [hɪd]. The symbol [a] is used for the first part of this diphthong. The vowel in "how" [aʊ] begins with a similar sound but moves toward [ʊ] as in "hood." The vowel in "boy" [bɔɪ] is a combination of the sound [ɔ] as in "bawd" and [ɪ] as in "hid."

Most Americans pronounce the remaining words in Table 2.2 with one of the other vowels followed by [r], while most British English speakers have additional diphthongs in these words. In each case, the end of the diphthong is [ə], the same symbol we used for the beginning of the diphthong in "hoe" for most British English speakers. We will discuss this symbol further in the next paragraph. Some British English speakers also use a diphthong in words like "poor, cure" that can be transcribed as [ʊə]. Some people (myself included) have a diphthong [aə] in words such as "fire, hire." Others pronounce these words as two syllables (like "higher" and "liar"), transcribing them as [faɪə, haɪə].

The words in Table 2.2 are generally monosyllables. Consequently, none of them contains both stressed and unstressed vowels. By far the most common unstressed vowel is [ə], the one we noted at the end of the diphthongs in most forms of British English. It is often called by its German name, *schwa*. It occurs at the ends of words such as "sofa, soda" [ˈsoʊfə, ˈsoʊdə], in the middle of words such as "emphasis, deprecate" [ˈɛmfəsɪs, ˈdɛprəkeɪt], and at the beginnings of words such as "around, arise" [əˈraʊnd, əˈraɪz]. (In all these words, the symbol [ˈ] is a stress mark that has been placed before the syllable carrying the main stress. Stress should always be marked in words of more than one syllable.)

In British English, [ə] is usually the sole component of the "-er" part of words such as "father, brotherhood, simpler" [ˈfɑːðə, ˈbrʌðəhʊd, ˈsɪmplə]. In forms of American English with *r*-colored vowels, these words are usually [ˈfɑːðɚ, ˈbrʌðɚhʊd, ˈsɪmplɚ]. As with the symbol [ɝ], the small hook on [ɚ] symbolizes the *r*-coloring. Both [ə] and [ɚ] are very common vowels, [ə] occurring very frequently in unstressed monosyllables such as the grammatical function words "the, a, to, and, but." In connected speech these words are usually [ðə, ə, tə, ənd, bət].

Some of the other vowels also occur in unstressed syllables, but because of differences in accents of English, it is a little more difficult to say which vowel occurs in which word. For example, nearly all speakers of English differentiate between the last vowels in "Sophie" and "sofa" or "pity" and "patter." But some accents have the vowel [i] as in "heed" at the end of "Sophie, pity, only, corny." Others have [ɪ] as in "hid." Similarly, most accents make the vowel in the second syllable of "taxis" different from that in "Texas." Some have [i] and some have [ɪ] in "taxis." Nearly everybody pronounces "Texas" as [ˈtɛksəs]. (Note that in English the letter *x* often represents the sounds [ks].)

TRANSCRIPTION EXERCISES

Find the errors in the transcription of the consonant sounds in the following words. In each word there is one error, indicating an impossible pronunciation of that word for a native speaker of English of any variety. Circle this error, and write the correct symbol in the space provided after the word.

1. "strength"	[ˈstrɛŋgθ]	should be	[	]
2. "crime"	[ˈc̓raɪm]		[	]
3. "wishing"	[ˈwɪʃɪŋ]		[	]
4. "wives"	[ˈwaɪvs]		[	]
5. "these"	[ˈθiz]		[	]
6. "hijacking"	[ˈhaɪjækɪŋ]		[	]
7. "chipping"	[ˈtʃɪppɪŋ]		[	]
8. "yelling"	[ˈyɛlɪŋ]		[	]
9. "sixteen"	[ˈsɪxtiːn]		[	]
10. "thesis"	[ˈðisɪs]		[	]

Now try another ten words in which the errors are all in the vowels. Again, there is only one possible error; but because of differences in varieties of English, there are sometimes alternative possible corrections.

11. "man-made" [ˈmanmeɪd]   should be   [   ]

12. "football" [ˈfʊtbol]   [   ]

13. "tea chest" [ˈtiːtʃest]   [   ]

14. "tomcat" [ˈtomkæt]   [   ]

15. "tiptoe" [ˈtiptoʊ]   [   ]

16. "avoid" [æˈvɔɪd]   [   ]

17. "remain" [rəˈman]   [   ]

18. "roommate" [ˈrɔmmeɪt]   [   ]

19. "umbrella" [umˈbrɛlə]   [   ]

20. "manage" [ˈmænædʒ]   [   ]

Now correct the following words, again by circling the error and noting the correction. There is still only one per word, but it may be among the vowels, the consonants, or the stress marks.

21. "magnify" [ˈmægnifaɪ]   should be   [   ]

22. "traffic" [ˈtræfɪc]   [   ]

23. "simplistic" [ˈsɪmplɪstɪk]   [   ]

24. "irrigate" [ˈɪrɪgeɪt]   [   ]

25. "improvement" [ɪmˈprʊvmənt]   [   ]

26. "demonstrate" [ˈdɛmɑnstreɪt]   [   ]

27. "human being" [huːmən ˈbiːŋ]   [   ]

28. "appreciate" [əˈpreʃiːeɪt]   [   ]

29. "joyful" [ˈdʒɔyfʊl]   [   ]

Finally, transcribe the following words or phrases as you pronounce them, or as you think they should be pronounced in one of the well-known accents of English. Give a rough label for your accent or the one you have chosen to use (e.g., BBC English, Southern Californian, New York, London, Scottish), and try to make the transcription illustrate an ordinary conversational style. Do not use a reading pronunciation or one that you think ought to be used. Say the words aloud (or listen to someone else saying them) and notice how they are normally pronounced. Be careful to put in stress marks at the proper places.

accent _____

30. chocolate pudding

31. modern languages

32. impossibility

33. boisterous

34. youngster

35. another

36. diabolical

37. nearly over

38. red riding hood

39. inexcusable

CONSONANT AND VOWEL CHARTS

So far we have been using the consonant and vowel symbols mainly as ways of representing the contrasts that occur among words in English. But they can also be thought of in a completely different way. We may regard them as shorthand descriptions of the articulations involved. Thus [p] is an abbreviation for "voiceless bilabial stop" and [l] is equivalent to "voiced alveolar lateral approximant." The consonant symbols can then be arranged in the form of a chart as in Figure 2.1. The places of articulation are shown across the top of the chart, starting from the most forward articulation (bilabial) and going toward those sounds made in the back of the mouth (velar). The manners of articulation are shown on the vertical axis of the chart. By convention, the voiced–voiceless distinction is shown by putting the voiceless symbols to the left of the voiced symbols.

The symbol [w] is shown in two places in the consonant chart in Figure 2.1. This is because it is articulated with both a narrowing of the lip aperture, which makes it bilabial, and a raising of the back of the tongue toward the soft palate, which makes it velar. The symbol [h] does not appear anywhere on the chart. In English, [h] acts like a consonant, but from an articulatory point of view it is the voiceless counterpart of the surrounding sounds. It does not have a precise place of articulation, and its manner of articulation is similar to that of the vowels before and after it.

The symbols we have been using for the contrasting vowels may also be regarded as shorthand descriptions for different vowel qualities. There are problems in this respect, in that we have been using these symbols somewhat loosely, allowing them to have different values for different accents. But the general values can be indicated by a vowel chart as in Figure 2.2. The symbols have been placed within a quadrilateral, which shows the range of possible vowel qualities but does not show differences in length. Thus [i] is used for a high front vowel, [u] for a high back one, [ɪ] for a lower high front vowel, [e] for a raised mid-front vowel, [ɛ] for a lowered mid-front vowel, and so on.

| FIGURE 2.1 | A phonetic chart of the English consonants we have dealt with so far. Whenever there are two symbols within a single cell, the one on the left represents a voiceless sound. All other symbols represent voiced sounds. Note also the consonant [h], which is not on this chart, and the affricates [tʃ, dʒ], which are sequences of symbols on the chart. |

Place of articulation

Manner of articulation		bilabial	labio-dental	dental		alveolar	palato-alveolar	palatal	velar
nasal (stop)		m				n			ŋ
stop		p b				t d			k g
fricative			f v	θ ð	s z		ʃ ʒ		
(central) approximant		(w)				r		j	w
lateral (approximant)						l			

The simple vowel chart in Figure 2.2 shows only two of the dimensions of vowel quality, and (as we will see in later chapters) even these are not represented very accurately. Furthermore, Figure 2.2 does not show anything about the variations in the degree of lip rounding in the different vowels, nor does it indicate anything about vowel length. It does not show, for example, that in most circumstances [i] and [u] are longer than [ɪ] and [ʊ].

PHONOLOGY

At the beginning of this chapter we discussed another reason why it is only approximately true that in our transcriptions of English the symbols have the values shown in Figures 2.1 and 2.2. In the style of transcription we have been using so far, some of the symbols may represent different sounds when they occur in different contexts. For example, the symbol [t] may represent a wide variety of sounds. In "tap" [tæp] it represents a voiceless alveolar stop. But the

---

FIGURE 2.2   A vowel chart showing the relative vowel qualities represented by some of the symbols used in transcribing English. The symbols [e, a, o] occur as the first elements of diphthongs.

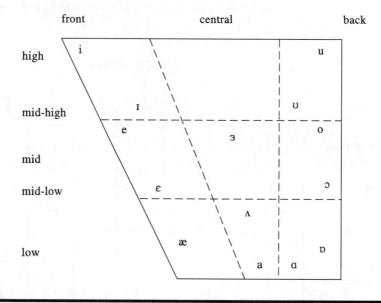

---

[t] in "eighth" [eɪtθ] may be made on the teeth, because of the influence of the following voiceless dental fricative [θ]. This [t] is more accurately called a voiceless dental stop, and we will later use a special symbol for transcribing it. In most forms of both British and American English, the [t] in "bitten" is accompanied by a glottal stop, and we will later be using a special symbol for this sound. As we saw, for most Americans and for many younger British English speakers, the [t] in "catty" [ˈkæti] symbolizes a voiced, not a voiceless, sound. All these different sounds are part of the / t / phoneme. Each of them occurs in a specific place—before [θ] or whatever may be the case—and none of them is different enough to change the meaning of a word in English. When saying them, what the speaker is trying to produce and what the listener hears is some form of / t /.

Similarly, other symbols represent different sounds in different contexts. The symbols [l] and [r] normally stand for voiced approximants. But in words such as "ply" [plaɪ] and "try" [traɪ] they represent voiceless sounds. Vowel sounds also vary. The [iː] in "heed" [hiːd] is usually very different from the [iː] in "heel" [hiːl].

Many of the variations we have been discussing can be described in terms of simple statements about regular sound patterns. Statements of this kind may be considered rules. In most forms of American English, for example, it is a rule that [t] becomes voiced not only in "catty," but on all occasions when it occurs between two vowels, the second of which is unstressed (for example, in "pity, matter, utter, divinity," etc.). In English of nearly all kinds, it is also a rule that whenever [t] occurs before a dental fricative, it is pronounced as a dental stop, so that we may use the special symbol [t̪]. The same is true of [d], as in "width" [wɪd̪ð], [n], as in "tenth" [tɛn̪θ], and [l], as in "wealth" [wɛl̪θ]. In all these cases, the mark [̪] may be added under the symbol in order to indicate that it represents a dental articulation.

When we describe the sound patterns that occur in English, we want to be able to say that in some sense there are always the same underlying sounds. But these underlying sounds may change depending on the context in which they occur. The phonology of a language is the set of rules that describe the changes in the underlying sounds, the abstract units called phonemes, defined at the beginning of this chapter. When we transcribe a word in a way that shows none of the details of the pronunciation that are predictable by phonological rules, we are making a phonemic transcription. Phonemic segments are usually placed between slanting lines. Thus we may say that the underlying phonemic segments in "ten" and "tenth" are / tɛn / and / tɛnθ /. But the phonetic segments that are actually pronounced are [tɛn] and [tɛn̪θ].

The variants of the phonemes that occur in detailed phonetic transcriptions are known as **allophones.** They are generated as a result of applying the phonological rules to the underlying phonemes. We have already discussed some of the rules that generate different allophones of the phoneme / t /. For example, we know that in most varieties of American English, / t / has a voiced allophone when it occurs between a stressed vowel and an unstressed vowel.

The transcription used in the first part of this chapter is not, strictly speaking, a simple phonemic transcription. The symbols in Tables 2.1 and 2.2 distinguish all the oppositions that occur in actual pronunciations of English words. But these are not the underlying segments. There are several ways in which we could change our notational system into a more abstract one that uses a simpler set of symbols.

One way would be not to show the differences in length between pairs of vowels. Our present transcription indicates the differences in both quality and length in the vowels in a pair or words such as "bead, bid" [biːd, bɪd] or "fool, full" [fuːl, fʊl]. But the differences in length are entirely predictable from the differences in quality. The symbols [i, u] can be said to represent long vowels, and the symbols [ɪ, ʊ] short vowels (perhaps with an additional stipulation that we have been tacitly assuming: [i] in unstressed position as in "happy" is not long). In this way we would eliminate the length mark [ː].

Alternatively, instead of not showing the length difference, we could regard the quality as predictable from the length and not show the quality difference. In this case, the vowel [i] would have the value appropriate for the vowel in "bead" when it occurred before a length mark as in [biːd]. But it would have the value appropriate for the vowel in "bid" when it occurred without a length mark, which would then be transcribed as [bid]. Remember that there is nothing sacred about the phonetic value of a symbol. Some phoneticians transcribe "bead, bid" as [biːd, bɪd] as I have been doing in this book so far, while others transcribe these same words as [biːd, bid]. Using the same principle, they might transcribe "cooed, could" not as [kuːd, kʊd], as I have done, but as [kuːd, kud]. Finally, "laid, led" would not be [leɪd, lɛd], but [leːd, led]. In this style of transcription, the differences in quality are treated as if they depended on the differences in length. The symbols / i / and / u / would be said to represent higher vowels when long, and the symbol / e / would be said to represent a diphthong in these circumstances. This style of transcription uses an additional symbol for length, but it more than compensates for that by eliminating the vowel symbols [ɪ, ɛ, ʊ].

We can now see why there are various possible ways of transcribing a language. Even if we consider only one particular accent of the language, it might be appropriate in some cases to symbolize one aspect of a contrast, such as the length, and in other cases to symbolize another, such as the quality. In addition, we may choose to make a transcription that shows only the underlying phonemes, or we may choose to represent some allophonic differences. Even if we are representing only the underlying phonemes in a particular accent of English, we may do so using only simple symbols, such as [r], or more unusual symbols, such as [ɹ], which convey more specific information on the phonetic quality. The term **broad transcription** is often used to designate a transcription that uses a simple set of symbols. Conversely, a **narrow transcription** is one that shows more phonetic detail, either just by using more specific symbols or by also representing some allophonic differences. The use of **diacritics,** small marks that can be added to a symbol to modify its value, is a means of increasing precision. One such diacritic is a small circle, [̥], that can be placed under a symbol to make it represent a voiceless sound, so that "ply" and "try," for instance, can be written [pl̥aɪ] and [tr̥aɪ]. Another useful diacritic is the mark [̪] beneath a consonant, which we have been using to indicate that the sound is dental and not alveolar.

Every transcription should be considered as having two aspects, one of which is often not explicit. There is the text itself, and at least implicitly there is a set of conventions for interpreting the text. These conventions are usually of two kinds. First, there are the conventions that ascribe general phonetic values to the symbols. It was with these conventions in mind that I said earlier that a symbol could be regarded as an approximate specification of the articulations involved. Second, there are the rules that specify the allophones that occur in different circumstances. Thus when I transcribe the word "peels" as [piːlz], I am assuming that the reader knows a number of the rules of English, including those that make / iː / somewhat lower and more central when it occurs before / l / and a final / z / voiceless toward the end.

On a few occasions, a transcription cannot be said to imply the existence of rules accounting for allophones. This is at least theoretically possible in the case of a narrow transcription so detailed that it shows *all* the rule-governed alternations among the sounds. A transcription that shows the allophones in this way is called a completely **systematic phonetic transcription.** In practice, it is difficult to make a transcription so narrow that it shows every detail of the sounds involved. On some occasions, a transcription may not imply the existence of rules accounting for allophones because, in the circumstances when the transcription was made, nothing was known about the rules. When writing down an unknown language or when transcribing a child or a patient not seen previously, one does not know what rules will apply. In these circumstances, the symbols indicate only the phonetic value of the sounds. This kind of transcription is called an **impressionistic transcription.**

EXERCISES

A Which of the two transcriptions below is the narrower?
"Betty cried as she left in the plane."

(a) [ˈbɛti ˈkraɪd əz ʃiː ˈlɛft ɪn ðə ˈpleɪn]

(b) [ˈbɛdi ˈkr̥aɪd əz ʃiː ˈlɛft ɪn̩ ðə ˈpl̥eɪn]

B State rules for converting the transcription in (a) into that in (b). Make your rules as general as possible, so that they cover not only this pair of transcriptions but also other similar sentences (for example, [t] → [d] when it occurs after a stressed vowel and before an unstressed vowel).

C Read the following passages in phonetic transcription. Both passages use a fairly broad style of transcription, showing few allophones. The first represents a form of British English of the kind I speak myself. The second represents an American pronunciation typical of a Midwestern speaker. By this time you should be able to read transcriptions of different forms of English, although you may have difficulty pronouncing each word exactly as it is represented. Nevertheless, read each passage several times and try to pronounce it as indicated. Take care to put the stresses on the correct syllables, and say the unstressed syllables with the vowels as shown. Note any differences between each transcription and your own pronunciation of the corresponding words.

British English

[ɪt ɪz ˈpɒsəbl tə træn'skraɪb fəˈnɛtɪklɪ ˈɛnɪ ˈʌtrəns, ɪn ˈɛnɪ ˈlæŋgwɪdʒ, ɪn ˈsɛvrəl ˈdɪfrənt ˈweɪz ˈɔl əv ðəm ˈjuːzɪŋ ði ˈælfəbɛt ənd kənˈvɛnʃnz əv ði ˈaɪ piː ˈeɪ. ðə ˈseɪm ˈθɪŋ ɪz ˈpɒsəbl wɪð ˈməʊst ˈʌðə ɪntəˈnæʃənl fəˈnɛtɪk ˈælfəbɛts. ə træn'skrɪpʃn wɪtʃ ɪz ˈmeɪd baɪ ˈjuːzɪŋ ˈlɛtəz əv ðə ˈsɪmpləst ˈpɒsəbl ˈʃeɪps, ənd ɪn ðə ˈsɪmpləst ˈpɒsɪbl ˈnʌmbə, ɪz ˈkɔːld ə ˈsɪmpl fəʊˈniːmɪk træn'skrɪpʃn.]

American English

[ɪf ðə 'nʌmbɚ əv 'dɪfrənt 'lɛdɚz ɪz 'mɔːr ðən ðə 'mɪnəməm æz dəˈfaɪnd əˈbʌv ðə trænˈskrɪpʃn wɪl 'nɑːt bi ə fəˈniːmɪk, bəd ən æləˈfɑːnɪk wʌn. 'sʌm əv ðə 'foʊniːmz, 'ðæd ɪz tə 'seɪ, wɪl bɪ rɛprəˈzɛntəd baɪ 'mɔːr ðən 'wʌn 'dɪfrənt 'sɪmbl̩. ɪn 'ʌðɚ 'wɝdz 'sʌm 'æləfoʊnz əv 'sʌm 'foʊniːmz wɪl bɪ 'sɪŋgld̩ 'aʊt fɚ 'rɛprəzɛnˈteɪʃn ɪn ðə trænˈskrɪpʃn, 'hɛns ðə 'tɝm æləˈfɑːnɪk.]

(Both these passages are adapted from David Abercrombie, *English Phonetic Texts* [Salem, NH: Faber & Faber, 1964].)

D Transcribe the following phrases as you pronounce them, or as you think they should be pronounced in one of the well-known accents of English using (a) a fairly broad transcription, and (b) a narrower transcription.

accent _____

"Please come home."

(a)

(b)

"He is going by train."

(a)

(b)

"The angry American."

(a)

(b)

"His knowledge of the truth."

(a)

(b)

"I prefer sugar and cream."

(a)

(b)

"Sarah took pity on the young children."

(a)

(b)

PERFORMANCE EXERCISES

As noted in the preface, it is extremely important to develop practical phonetic skills at the same time as you learn the theoretical concepts. One way to do this is to learn to pronounce nonsense words. You should also transcribe nonsense words that are dictated to you. By using nonsense words you are forced to listen to the sounds that are being spoken. Accordingly, you should find another student to work with, so that you can do the following exercises in pairs.

A Learn to say simple nonsense words. A good way is to start with a single vowel, and then add consonants and vowels one by one at the beginning. In this way you are always reading toward familiar material, rather than having new difficulties ahead of you. Make up sets of words such as the following:

zɑː

ɪˈzɑː

tɪˈzɑː

ˈætɪˈzɑː

ˈmætɪˈzɑː

ʌˈmætɪˈzɑː

tʌˈmætɪˈzɑː

B Choose an order in which to say the following "words" (for example, say the second word first, the fourth word next, and then the fifth, third, and first words). Write this order down as you dictate the words to your partner—whose task is, of course, to write down the order in which you have said them. Reverse roles and repeat the exercises. You may find it advisable to repeat each word twice.

spoken	**heard**
piːˈsuːz	
piːˈsuːs	
piːˈzuːs	
piːˈzuːz	
piːˈzuːʒ	

C Repeat this exercise with the following sets of words:

spoken	**heard**	**spoken**	**heard**
tɑːˈθɛð		ˈkiːpiːk	
tɑːˈθɛθ		ˈkɪpiːk	
tɑːˈðɛθ		ˈkiːpɪk	

spoken	heard	spoken	heard
taːˈðɛð		ˈkɪpɪk	
taːˈfɛð		ˈkɪpɪt	
ˈlæmæm		ˈmʌlʌl	
ˈlæmæn		ˈmʌɾʌl	
ˈlænæm		ˈmʌwʌl	
ˈlænæn		ˈnʌlʌl	
ˈlænæŋ		ˈnʌɾʌl	

D Look at the following nonsense words, and either say these to your partner or (preferably, since your partner has seen these words too) make up a set similar to them and say these instead. Your words can differ from the sample set in as many sounds as you like. But I suggest that you should not make them much longer at first. You will also find it advisable to write down your words and practice saying them for some time by yourself, so that you can pronounce them fluently when you say them to your partner.

ˈskaːnziːl

ˈbraɪgbluːzd

ˈdjɪŋsmæŋ

flɔɪʃˈθraɪðz

pjuːtˈpeɪtʃ

When you have finished saying each word several times and your partner has written the words down, compare notes. Try to decide whether any discrepancies were due to errors in saying the words or in hearing them. If possible, the speaker should try to illustrate discrepancies by pronouncing the word in both ways, saying, for example, "I said [ˈskaːnziːl] but you wrote [ˈskaːnsiːl]."

There is no one best way of doing ear training work of this kind. I find it helpful to look carefully at a person pronouncing an unknown word, then try to say the word myself immediately afterward, getting as much of it right as possible, but not worrying if I miss some things on first hearing. I then write down all that I can, leaving blanks to be filled in when I hear the word again. It seems important to me to get at least the number of syllables and the placement of the stress correct on first hearing, so that I have a framework in which to fit later observations.

Repeat this kind of production and perception exercise as often as you can. You should do a few minutes' work of this kind every day, so that you spend at least an hour a week doing practical exercises.

3

THE CONSONANTS
OF ENGLISH

This chapter will discuss the consonants of English in some detail, showing how they vary in different circumstances.

STOP CONSONANTS

Consider the difference between the words in the first column in Table 3.1 and the corresponding words in the second column. This opposition may be said to be between the set of voiceless stop consonants and the set of voiced stop consonants. But the difference is really not just one of voicing during the consonant closure, as you can see by saying these words yourself. Most people have very little voicing going on while the lips are closed during either "pie" or "buy." Both stop consonants are essentially voiceless. But in "pie," *after* the release of the lip closure, there is a moment of **aspiration,** a period of voicelessness after the stop articulation and before the start of the voicing for the vowel. If you put your hand in front of your lips while saying "pie," you can feel the burst of air that comes out during the period of voicelessness after the release of the stop.

In a narrow transcription, aspiration may be indicated by a small raised *h,* [ʰ]. Accordingly, these words may be transcribed as [pʰaɪ, tʰaɪ, kʰaɪ]. You may not be able to feel the burst of air in "tie, kye" because these stop closures are made well inside the mouth cavity. But listen carefully and notice that you can hear the period of voicelessness after the release of the stop closure in each of them. It is this interval that indicates the fact that the stop is aspirated. The major difference between the words in the first two columns is not that one has voiceless stops and the other voiced stops. It is that the first column has (voiceless) aspirated stops and the second column has (partially voiced) unaspirated stops. The amount of voicing in each of the stops [b, d, g] depends on the context in which it occurs. When it is in the middle of a sentence in which a voiced sound occurs on either side, voicing may occur throughout the stop closure. Most

TABLE 3.1		Words illustrating allophones of English stop consonants.		
1	**2**	**3**	**4**	**5**
pie	buy	spy	nap	nab
tie	die	sty	mat	mad
kye	guy	sky	knack	nag

speakers of English have no voicing during the closure of so-called voiced stops in sentence initial position.

You should be able to hear these differences (one of the main objects of this book is to teach you to become a phonetician by learning to listen very carefully), but you can also see them in computer produced waveforms. We will discuss acoustic analyses of sounds later in this book, but we can start studying simple waveforms here. Figure 3.1 is a record of the words "tie" and "die." It is quite easy to see the different segments in the sound wave. In the first word, "tie," there is a spike indicating the burst of noise that occurs when the stop closure is released, followed by a period of very small semirandom variations during the aspiration, and then a regular, repeating wave as the vocal folds begin to

FIGURE 3.1   The waveforms of the words "tie" and "die."

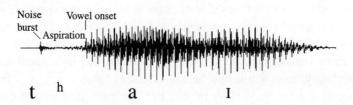

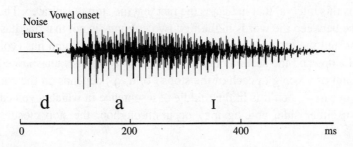

vibrate regularly for the vowel. In "die" there is no real spike at the beginning, just a somewhat irregular waveform before the start of the wave for the vowel. As you can see, the major difference between "tie" and "die" is the increase in time between the release of the stop and the start of the vowel. We will discuss this distinction further in Chapter 6.

Now consider the words in the third column of Table 3.1. Are the sounds of the stop consonants more like those in the first column or those in the second? As in many cases, English spelling is misleading, and they are in fact more like those in the second column. There is no opposition in English between words beginning with / sp / and / sb /, or / st / and / sd /, or / sk / and / sg /. English spelling uses *p, t, k,* but the stops that occur after / s / are really somewhere in between initial / p / and / b /, / t / and / d /, / k / and / g /, and usually more like the so-called voiced stops / b, d, g / in that they are completely unaspirated. Figure 3.2 shows the computer produced waveform in "sty." You can see the small variations in the waveform corresponding to the fricative / s /, followed by a straight line during the period in which there is no sound as there is a complete stop for the / t /. This is followed by a sound wave very similar to that of the / d / in Figure 3.1.

If you have access to a computer that can manipulate sounds and let you see the waveforms of words, you can verify this for yourself. Record words such as "spy, sty, sky, spill, still, skill," each said as a separate word. Now find the beginning and end of each / s /, and cut this part out. When you play the edited recordings to others and ask them to write down the words that they hear, they will almost certainly write "buy, die, guy, bill, dill, gill."

What about the differences between the words in the fourth and fifth columns of Table 3.1? The consonants at the end of "nap, mat, knack" are certainly voiceless. But if you listen carefully to the sounds at the end of the words "nab, mad,

---

FIGURE 3.2   The waveform of the word "sty."

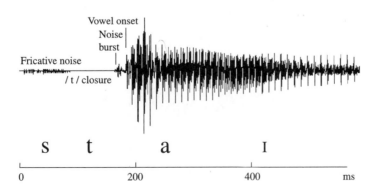

nag," you may find that the so-called voiced consonants / b, d, g / have very little voicing. Try saying these words separately. You can, of course, say each of them with the final consonant exploded and a short vowel-like sound resembling [ə] afterward. But it would be more normal to say each of them without exploding the final consonants. You could even say "cab" and not open the lips for a considerable period of time, if it were the last word of an utterance. In such circumstances it is quite clear that the final consonants are not fully voiced throughout the closure.

There is, however, a clear distinction between the words in the fourth and fifth columns. Say these words in pairs, "nap, nab; mat, mad; knack, nag," and try to decide which has the longer vowel. In these pairs, and in all similar pairs, such as "cap, cab; cat, cad; back, bag" the vowel is much shorter before the voiceless consonants / p, t, k / than it is before the voiced consonants / b, d, g /. The major difference between such pairs of words is in the vowel length, not in the voicing of the final consonants.

This length difference is very evident in Figure 3.3, which shows the waveforms of the words "mat" and "mad." The vowel in "mad" is almost twice as long as the vowel in "mat." You can also see small voicing vibrations during the / d / in "mad," but there is nothing noteworthy at the end of "mat" except the

| FIGURE 3.3 | The waveforms of the words "mat" and "mad." |

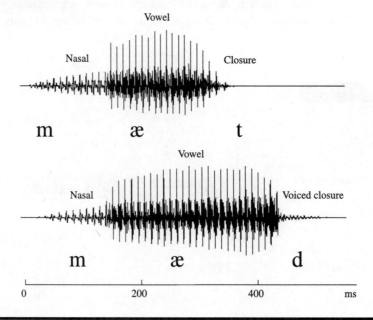

slightly irregular voicing at the time of the closure. We will return to this point later in this section.

Another way of comparing the length differences is to say short sentences such as "Take a cap now" and "Take a cab now." If you say both these sentences with a regular rhythm, you will find that the length of time between "Take" and "now" is about the same on both occasions. This is because the whole word "cap" is only slightly shorter than the whole word "cab." The vowel is much shorter in "cap" than in "cab." But the consonant / p / makes up for this by being slightly longer than the consonant / b /. It is a general rule of English (and of most other languages) that syllable final voiceless consonants are longer than the corresponding voiced consonants after this same vowel.

The phrases "Take a cap now" and "Take a cab now" also illustrate a further point about English stop consonants at the end of a word (or, in fact, at the end of a syllable). Say each of these phrases without a pause before "now." Do your lips open before the [n] of "now" begins, or do they open during the [n]? If they open before the [n], there will be a short burst of aspiration or a short vowel-like sound between the two words. But for most people, final stops are unexploded when the next word begins with a nasal. The same is true if the next word begins with a stop. The final [t] in "cat" is nearly always unexploded in phrases like "the cat pushed. . . ." In a narrow transcription we can symbolize the fact that a consonant is unexploded by adding a small raised mark [˺]. We could therefore transcribe the phrase as [ðə ˈkʰæt˺ ˈpʰʊʃt].

The same phenomenon occurs even within a word such as "apt" [æp˺t] or "act" [æk˺t]. Furthermore, across a word boundary the two consonants involved can even be identical, as in the phrase "white teeth." In order to convince yourself that there are two examples of / t / in this phrase, try contrasting it with "why teeth (are . . .)." Not only is the vowel in "white" much shorter than the vowel in "why" (because the vowel in "white" is in a syllable with a voiceless consonant at the end), but also the stop closure in "white teeth" is very much longer than the stop in the phrase with only one / t /. In "white teeth" there really are two examples of / t / involved, the first of which is unexploded.

Other languages do not have this rule. For example, it is a mark of speakers with an Italian accent (at least as caricatured in films and television) that they explode all their final stop consonants, producing an extra vowel at the end, as they normally would in their own language. Authors trying to indicate an Italian speaking English will write the sentence "It's a big day" as "It's a bigga day." They are presumably trying to indicate the difference between the normal [ɪts ə ˈbɪg˺ ˈdeɪ] and the foreign accent [ɪts ə ˈbɪgə ˈdeɪ].

It is interesting that words such as "rap, rat, rack" are all distinguishable, even when the final consonants are unexploded. The difference in the sounds must therefore be in the way that the vowels end—after all, the rest is silence. The consonants before and after a vowel always affect it, so that there is a slight but noticeable difference in its quality. Compare your pronunciation of words such as "pip, tit, kick." Your tongue tip is up throughout the word "tit," whereas in "pip" and "kick" it remains behind the lower front teeth. In "kick" it is the back of the tongue that is raised throughout the word, and in "pip" the lip gestures affect the entire vowel. The same is true for words with voiced consonants, such as "bib, did, gig." The consonant gestures are superimposed on the vowel in such a way that their effect is audible throughout much of the syllable.

The sounds [p, t, k] are not the only voiceless stops that occur in English. Many people also pronounce a glottal stop in some words. A glottal stop is the sound (or, to be more exact, the lack of sound) that occurs when the vocal folds are held tightly together. The symbol for it is [ʔ], which is similar to a question mark without the dot.

Glottal stops occur whenever one coughs. You should be able to get the sensation of the vocal folds being pressed together by making small coughing noises. Next, take a deep breath and hold it with your mouth open. Listen to the small plosive sound that occurs when you let the breath go. Now, while breathing out through your mouth, try to check and then release the breath by making and releasing a short glottal stop. Then do the same while making a voiced sound such as the vowel [ɑ]. Practice producing glottal stops between vowels, saying [ɑʔɑ] or [iʔi], so that you get to know what they feel like.

One of the most common occurrences of a glottal stop is in the utterance meaning "no," which is often spelled "uh-uh." If someone asks you a question, you can reply "no" by saying [ˈʔʌʔʌ]. Note that there is a contrast between the utterance meaning "no" and that meaning "yes" that is dependent on the presence of the glottal stop. If you had meant to say "yes," you might well have said [ˈʌhʌ]. We can tell that it is the glottal stop that is important in conveying the meaning by the fact that one could be understood equally well by using a syllabic consonant (shown by putting the mark [ˌ] under the consonant) instead of a vowel, and saying [ˈm̩hm̩] for "yes" and [ˈʔm̩ʔm̩] for "no." As long as there is a glottal stop between the two syllables, the utterance will mean "no," irrespective of what vowel or nasal is used.

Glottal stops frequently occur as allophones of / t /. Probably most Americans and many British speakers have a glottal stop followed by a syllabic nasal in words such as "beaten, kitten, fatten" [ˈbiːʔn̩, ˈkɪʔn̩, ˈfæʔn̩]. London Cockney also has a glottal stop between vowels as in "butter, kitty, fatter" [ˈbʌʔə, ˈkɪʔɪ, ˈfæʔə]. Many speakers in both countries have a glottal stop just before final voiceless stops in words such as "rap, rat, rack." Usually the articulatory gesture for the other stop is still audible, so these words could be transcribed [ræʔp, ræʔt, ræʔk]. When I recorded the word "mat" for Figure 3.3, I pronounced it as [mæʔt], with the glottal stop and the closure for [t] occurring almost simultaneously.

Practice producing words with and without a glottal stop. After you have some awareness of what a glottal stop feels like, try saying the words "rap, rat, rack" in several different ways. Begin by saying them with a glottal stop and a final release [ræʔpʰ, ræʔtʰ, ræʔkʰ]. Next, say them without a glottal stop and with the final stops unexploded [ræp̚, ræt̚, ræk̚]. Then say them with a glottal stop and a final unexploded consonant [ræʔp̚, ræʔt̚, ræʔk̚]. Finally, say them with a glottal stop and no other final consonant [ræʔ, ræʔ, ræʔ].

When a voiced stop and a nasal occur in the same word, as in "hidden," the stop is not released in the usual way. Both the [d] and the [n] are alveolar consonants. The tongue comes up and contacts the alveolar ridge for [d] and stays there for the nasal, which becomes syllabic [ˈhɪdn̩]. Consequently, as shown in Figure 3.4, the air pressure that is built up behind the stop closure is released through the nose by the lowering of the soft palate (the velum) for the nasal consonant. This phenomenon is known as **nasal plosion.** It is normally used in pronouncing words such as "sadden, sudden, leaden" [ˈsædn̩, ˈsʌdn̩, ˈlɛdn̩]. It is considered a mark of a foreign accent to add a vowel [ˈsædən, ˈsʌdən, ˈlɛdən]. Nasal plosion also occurs in the pronunciation of words with [t] followed by [n], as in "kitten" [ˈkɪtn̩], for those people who do not have a glottal stop instead of the [t].

It is worth spending some time thinking exactly how you and others pronounce words such as "kitten, button," in that it enables you to practice making detailed phonetic observations. There are a number of different possibilities.

FIGURE 3.4   Nasal plosion.

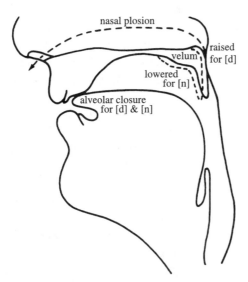

Most British and American English speakers make a glottal stop at the end of the vowel before making an alveolar closure. Then, while still maintaining the glottal stop, they lower the velum and raise the tongue for the alveolar closure. But which comes first? If they lower the velum before making the alveolar closure, there is only [ʔn] and no [t]. If they make the alveolar closure first, we could say that there is [ʔtn]; but there would not be any nasal plosion, as there would be no pressure built up behind the [t] closure. Nasal plosion occurs only if there is no glottal stop, or the glottal stop is released after the alveolar closure has been made and before the velum is lowered.

These are fairly difficult sequences to determine, but there are some simple things you can do to help you find out what articulations you use. First of all, find a drinking straw and something to drink. Put one end of the straw between your lips and hold the other end just below the surface of the liquid. Now say [ɑpɑ], and note how bubbles form during [p]. This is because pressure is built up behind your closed lips. Now push the straw slightly further into your mouth and say [ɑtɑ]. It will not sound quite right because the straw gets in the way of your tongue when it makes the alveolar closure. You may have to try different positions of the straw, but go on until you can see bubbles coming out, and convince yourself that pressure builds up behind the [t]. Now try saying "button." Of course there will be bubbles during the [b], but are there any at the end of the word, or do you have a glottal stop and no [t] behind which pressure builds up?

When two sounds have the same place of articulation, they are said to be **homorganic.** Thus the consonants [d] and [n], which are both articulated on the alveolar ridge, are homorganic. For nasal plosion to occur within a word, there must be a stop followed by a homorganic nasal. Only in these circumstances can there be pressure first built up in the mouth during the stop and then released through the nose by lowering the soft palate. Many forms of English do not have any words with a bilabial stop [p] or [b] followed by the homorganic nasal [m] at the end of the word. Nor in most forms of English are there any words in which the velar stops [k] or [g] are normally followed by the velar nasal [ŋ]. Consequently, both bilabial and velar nasal plosion are less common than alveolar nasal plosion in English. But when talking in a rapid conversational style, many people pronounce the word "open" as ['oʊpm̩], particularly if the next word begins with [m], as in "Open my door, please." Quite frequently when counting, people will pronounce "seven" as ['sɛbm̩], and I have also heard "something, captain, bacon" pronounced ['sʌmpm̩, 'kæpm̩, 'beɪkŋ̩]. You should try to pronounce all these words in these ways yourself.

A phenomenon similar to nasal plosion may take place when an alveolar stop [t] or [d] occurs before a homorganic lateral [l] as in "little, ladle" ['lɪtl̩, 'leɪdl̩]. The air pressure that is built up during the stop can be released by lowering the sides of the tongue; this effect is called **lateral plosion.** Say the word "middle" and note the action of the tongue. Many people (particularly British speakers) maintain the tongue contact on the alveolar ridge through both the stop and the lateral, releasing it only at the end of the word. Others (most Americans) pronounce a very short vowel in the second syllable. For those who have lateral plosion, no vowel sound occurs in the second syllables of "little, ladle." The final consonants in all these words are syllabic. There may also be lateral plosion in words such as "Atlantic," in which the [t] may be resyllabified so that it is at the beginning of the stressed, second syllable. We should also note that most Americans, irrespective of whether they have lateral plosion or not, do not have a voiceless stop in "little." There is a general rule in American English that whenever / t / occurs after a stressed vowel and before an unstressed syllable other than [n̩], it is changed into a voiced sound. For those Americans who have lateral plosion, this will be the stop [d].

This brings us to another important point about coronal stops and nasals. For many speakers, including most Americans, the consonant between the vowels in words such as "city, better, writer" is not really a stop but a quick tap in which the tongue tip is thrown against the alveolar ridge. This sound can be written with the symbol [ɾ] (instead of a [d] as I have been doing in similar words up till now) so that "city" can be transcribed as [ˈsɪɾi]. Many Americans also make this kind of tap when / d / occurs after a stressed vowel and before an unstressed vowel. As a result they do not distinguish between pairs of words such as "latter, ladder." But some maintain a distinction by having a shorter vowel in words such as "latter," which have a voiceless consonant in their underlying form. It is as if the statement that vowels are shorter before voiceless consonants had applied first, and then a later rule was applied changing [t] into [ɾ] when it occurred between a stressed and an unstressed syllable.

We can summarize the discussion of stop consonants by thinking of the possibilities that there are in the form of a branching diagram as shown in Figure 3.5. The first question to consider is whether the stop is released (exploded) or not. If it is released, then is it oral plosion or is the release due to the lowering of the velum, with air escaping through the nose, making it nasal plosion? If it is oral plosion, then is the closure in the mouth entirely removed, or is the articulation in the midline retained and one or both sides of the tongue lowered so that air escapes laterally? You should be able to produce words illustrating all these possibilities. For coronal stops, there is an additional point not shown in Figure 3.5, namely, is the [t] or [d] sound produced as a tap [ɾ]?

FRICATIVES

The fricatives of English vary less than the stop consonants, yet the major allophonic variations that do occur are in many ways similar to those of the stops. Earlier we saw that when a vowel occurs before one of the voiceless stops / p, t, k /, it is shorter than it would be before one of the voiced stops / b, d, g /. The

FIGURE 3.5   Stop consonant releases.

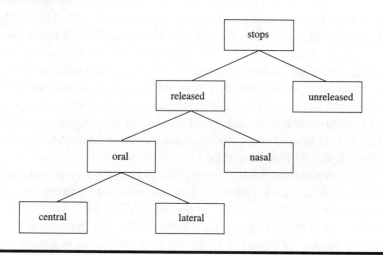

same kind of difference in vowel length occurs before voiceless and voiced fricatives. The vowel is shorter in the first word of each of the pairs "strife, strive" [straɪf, straɪv]; "teeth, teethe" [tiːθ, tiːð]; "rice, rise" [raɪs, raɪz]; and "mission, vision" ['mɪʃn̩, 'vɪʒn̩].

Stops and fricatives are the only English consonants that can contrast by being either voiced or voiceless. Consequently, we can revise our statement that vowels are shorter before voiceless stops than before voiced stops. Instead, we can say that vowels are shorter before all voiceless consonants than before all voiced consonants. In this way we can capture a linguistically significant generalization that would have been missed if our statements about English had included two separate statements, one dealing with stops and the other dealing with fricatives.

We also saw that a voiceless stop at the end of a syllable (as in "hit") is longer than the corresponding voiced stop (as in "hid"). Similarly, the voiceless fricatives are longer than their voiced counterparts in each of the pairs "safe, save" [seɪf, seɪv], "lace, laze" [leɪs, leɪz], and all the other pairs of words we have been discussing in this section. Again, because fricatives behave like stops, a linguistically significant generalization would have been missed if we had regarded each class of consonants completely separately.

Fricatives are also like stops in another way. Consider the degree of voicing that occurs in the fricative at the end of the word "ooze," pronounced by itself. In most pronunciations, the voicing that occurs during the final [z] does not last throughout the articulation but changes in the last part to a voiceless sound like [s]. In general, voiced fricatives at the end of a word, as in "prove, smooth, choose, rouge" [pruːv, smuːð, tʃuːz, ruːʒ] are voiced throughout their articulation only when they are followed by another voiced sound. In a phrase such as "prove it," the [v] is fully voiced because it is followed by a vowel. But in "prove two times two is four" or "try to improve," where the [v] is followed by a voiceless sound [t] or by a pause at the end of the phrase, it is not fully voiced.

Briefly stated, then, fricatives are like stops in three ways: first, stops and fricatives influence vowel length in similar ways—vowels before voiceless stops or fricatives are shorter than before voiced stops or fricatives; second, final voiceless stops and fricatives are longer than final voiced stops and fricatives; and third, the final stops and fricatives that are classified as voiced are not actually voiced throughout the articulation unless the adjacent sounds are also voiced. In addition, both these types of articulation involve an obstruction of the airstream. Because they have an articulatory feature in common and because they act together in phonological statements, we refer to fricatives and stops together as a natural class of sounds called **obstruents.**

However, fricatives do differ from stops in that they sometimes involve actions of the lips that are not immediately obvious. Try saying "fin, thin, sin, shin" [fɪn, θɪn, sɪn, ʃɪn]. There is clearly a lip action in the first word as it involves the labiodental sound [f]. But do your lips move in any of the other three words? Most people find that their lips move slightly in any word containing / s / ("sin, kiss") and quite considerably in any word containing / ʃ / ("shin, dish"), but that there is no lip action in words containing / θ / ("thin, teeth"). There is also lip movement in the voiced sounds corresponding to / s / and / ʃ /, namely / z / as in "zeal, zest" and / ʒ / in "leisure, treasure," but none in / ð /, as in "that, teethe."

The primary articulation in these fricatives is the close approximation of two articulators so that friction can be heard. The lip rounding is a lesser articulation in that the two articulators (the lower lip and the upper lip) approach one another but not sufficiently to cause friction. A lesser degree of closure by two articulators not involved in the primary articulation is called a secondary articulation. This particular one, in which the action of the lips is added to another articulation, is called labialization. The English fricatives / ʃ, ʒ / are strongly labialized, and the fricatives / s, z / are slightly labialized.

AFFRICATES

This is a convenient place to review the status of affricates in English. An affricate is simply a sequence of a stop followed by a homorganic fricative. Some such sequences, for example the dental affricate [tθ] as in "eighth" or the alveolar affricate [ts] as in "cats," have been given no special status in English phonology. They have been regarded just as consonant clusters comparable with those at the end of "lapse" and "sacks" (which are not affricates, as the stops and the fricatives are not homorganic). But, as we noted in the discussion of symbols for transcribing English, it is appropriate to regard the sequences [tʃ] and [dʒ] as different from other sequences of consonants. They are the only affricates in English that can occur at both the beginning and the end of words. In fact, even the other affricates that can occur at the end of words will usually do so only as the result of the formation of a plural or some other suffix as in "eighth." From the point of view of a phonologist considering the sound pattern of English, the palato-alveolar affricates are plainly single units.

NASALS

The nasal consonants of English vary even less than the fricatives. Nasals, together with [r, l], can be syllabic when they occur at the end of words. As we have seen, the mark [ˌ] under a consonant indicates that it is syllabic. (Vowels, of course, are always syllabic and therefore need no special mark.) In a narrow transcription, we may transcribe the words "sadden, table" as [ˈsædn̩, ˈteɪbl̩]. In most pronunciations, "prism, prison" can be transcribed [ˈprɪzm̩, ˈprɪzn̩], as these words do not usually have a vowel between the last two consonants. Syllabic consonants can also occur in phrases such as "Jack and Kate" [ˈdʒæk n̩ ˈkeɪt] and "not until" [nɑt n̩ˈtɪl].

The nasal [ŋ] differs from the other nasals in a number of ways. No English word can begin with [ŋ]. This sound can occur only within or at the end of a word, and even in these circumstances it does not behave like the other nasals. It can be preceded only by the vowels / ɪ, ɛ, æ, ʊ, ə, ɑ, ɔ /, and it cannot be syllabic (except in slightly unusual pronunciations, such as "bacon" [ˈbeɪkŋ̩], and phrases such as "Jack and Kate" mentioned previously).

One way to consider the different status of [ŋ] is that it is a sequence of the phonemes / n / and / g /. Looking at it this way, "sing" would be phonemically / sɪng / and "sink" would be / sɪnk /. There is a rule saying that / n / has the allophone [ŋ] whenever it occurs before / g / and / k /, turning [sɪng] into [sɪŋg] and [sɪnk] into [sɪŋk]. Another rule allows for the dropping of / g / (but not of / k /) whenever it occurs after [ŋ] at the end of either a word (as in "sing") or a stem followed by a suffix such as "-er" or "ing." In this way the / g / is dropped in "singer," which contains a suffix "-er," but is retained in "finger," in which the "-er" is not a suffix. This second rule would not apply in the case of some speakers from the New York area who make "singer" rhyme with "finger."

APPROXIMANTS

The voiced approximants are / w, r, j, l / as in "whack, rack yak, lack." The first three of these sounds are central approximants, and the last is a lateral approximant. The articulation of each of them varies slightly depending on the articulation of the following vowel. You can feel that the tongue is in a different position in the first sounds of "we" and "water." The same is true for "reap" and "raw," "lee" and "law," and "ye" and "yaw." Try to feel where your tongue is in each of these words.

These consonants also share the possibility of occurring in consonant clusters with stop consonants. The approximants / r, w, l / combine with stops in words such as "pray, bray, tray, dray, cray, gray, twin, dwell, quell, Gwen, play, blade, clay, glaze." The approximants are largely voiceless when they follow one of the voiceless stops / p, t, k / as in "play, twice, clay." This voicelessness is a manifestation of the aspiration that occurs after voiceless stops, which we discussed at the beginning of this chapter. At that time I introduced a small raised h symbol [ʰ], which could be used to show that the first part of the vowel was voiceless. When there is a consonant rather than a vowel immediately following the stop, we can use the diacritic [˳] to indicate that the consonant is voiceless. We can transcribe the words "play, twice, clay," in which there are approximants after initial voiceless plosives, as [pl̥eɪ, tw̥aɪs, kl̥eɪ]. The approximant / j / as in "you" [ju] can occur in similar consonant clusters, as in "pew, cue" [pj̥u, kj̥u] and, for speakers of British English, "tune" [tj̥un]. We will discuss the sequence [ju] again when we consider vowels in more detail.

Lip rounding is an essential part of / w /. Because there is a tendency for the articulations during one sound to anticipate those in the following sound, stops are slightly rounded when they occur in clusters in which / w / is the second element, as in "twice, dwindle, quick" [tw̥aɪs, ˈdwɪndl̩, kw̥ɪk]. We will discuss this phenomenon, which is known as anticipatory coarticulation, in a later section.

In many people's speech / r / also has some degree of lip rounding. Try saying words such as "reed" and "heed." Do you get some movement of the lips in the first word but not in the second? Note also whether you get anticipatory lip rounding so that the stops [t, d] are slightly rounded in words such as "tree, dream."

In most forms of British English, there is a considerable difference in the articulation of / l / before a vowel, as in "leaf" or "feeling," as compared with / l / before a consonant or at the end of a word, as in "field" or "feel." In most forms of American English, there is less distinction between these two kinds of / l /. Note the articulation of / l / in your own pronunciation. Try to feel where the tongue is during the / l / in "leaf." You will probably find that the tip is touching the alveolar ridge, and one or both sides are near the upper side teeth, but not quite touching. Now compare this articulation with the / l / in "feel." Most (but not all) speakers make this sound with the tongue tip touching the alveolar ridge. But in both British and American English the center of the tongue is pulled down and the back is arched upward as in a back vowel. If there is contact on the alveolar ridge, it is the primary articulation. The arching upward of the back of the tongue forms a secondary articulation, which we will call velarization. In most forms of American English, all examples of / l / are comparatively velarized, except, perhaps, those that are syllable initial and between high front vowels, as in "freely." In British English / l / is usually not velarized when it is before a vowel, as in "lamb" or "swelling," but it is velarized when word final or before a consonant, as in "ball" or "swelter."

The symbol for velarization is the mark [˜] through the middle of the symbol. Accordingly, a narrow transcription of "feel" would be [fiɫ]. In my own speech, the whole body of the tongue is drawn up and back in the mouth so that the tip of the tongue no longer makes contact with the alveolar ridge. Strictly speaking, therefore, this sound is not an alveolar consonant but more like some kind of back vowel in the speech of some English speakers.

Finally, we must consider the status of / h /. Earlier I suggested that English / h / is somewhat like the voiceless counterpart of the surrounding sounds. At the beginning of a sentence, / h / is like a voiceless vowel, but / h / can also occur between vowels in words or phrases like "behind the head." As you move from one vowel through / h / to another, the articulatory movement is continuous, and the / h / is signaled by a weakening of the voicing, which may not even result in a completely voiceless sound.

In many accents of English, / h / can occur only before stressed vowels or before the approximant / j / as in "hue" [hju]. Some speakers of English also sound / h / before / w /, so that they contrast "which" [hwɪtʃ] and "witch" [wɪtʃ]. The symbol [ʍ] (an inverted w) is sometimes used for this voiceless approximant. The contrast between / w / and / ʍ / is disappearing in most forms of English, so that in those dialects in which it occurs, [ʍ] is more likely to be found only in the less common words such as "whether" rather than in frequently used words such as "what."

RULES FOR ENGLISH CONSONANT ALLOPHONES

A good way of summarizing (and slightly extending) all that I have said about English consonants so far is to list a set of rules describing the allophones. These rules are simply *descriptions* of language behavior. They are not the kind of rules that prescribe what people ought to do. Like most phoneticians, I would not presume to set myself up as an arbiter of fashion and declare what constitutes "good" speech. To the extent that phonetics is part of an exact scientific discipline, I would like to be able to formalize my description of speech in terms of a set of precise statements. But these statements should be regarded as descriptive, not prescriptive, rules.

Some of the rules apply to all the consonants of English. One of the rules dealing with consonant length is the following:

(1) Consonants are longer when at the end of a phrase.

You can see the application of this rule by comparing the consonants in words such as "bib, did, don, nod." If you can, make a recording of these words, and then play the recording backward. Are the first two words the same backward and forward? Do the third and fourth words sound like each other when played in reverse?

Most of the rules apply to only selected groups of consonants, as in (2) through (18) as follows:

(2) Voiceless stops / p, t, k / are aspirated when they are syllable initial, as in words such as "pip, test, kick" [pʰɪp, tʰest, kʰɪk].

(3) Obstruents—stops and fricatives—classified as voiced (that is, / b, d, g, v, ð, z, ʒ /) are voiced through only a small part of the articulation when they occur at the end of an utterance (as the / v / in "Try to improve.") or before a voiceless sound (as the / d / in "add two").

(4) So-called voiced stops and affricates / b, d, g, dʒ / are voiceless when syllable initial, except when immediately preceded by a voiced sound.

(5) The approximants / w, r, j, l / are at least partially voiceless when they occur after initial / p, t, k /, as in "play, twin, cue" [pl̥eɪ, tw̥ɪn, kju].

(6) Voiceless stops / p, t, k / are unaspirated in words such as "spew, stew, skew."

(7) Voiceless stops and affricates / p, t, k, tʃ / are longer than the corresponding voiced stops and affricates / b, d, g, dʒ / when at the end of a syllable.

Words exemplifying this rule are "cap" as opposed to "cab" and "back" as opposed to "bag." Try contrasting these words in sentences, and you may be able to hear the differences more clearly.

(8) Stops are unexploded when they occur before another stop in words such as "apt" [æp̚t] and "rubbed" [rʌb̚d].

(9) In many accents of English, syllable final / p, t, k / are accompanied by a glottal stop, as in pronunciations of "tip, pit, kick" as [tɪʔp, pɪʔt, kɪʔk].

This rule does not apply to all varieties of English. Some people do not have any glottal stops in these circumstances, and others have glottal stops completely replacing some or all of the voiceless stops. In any case, even for those who simply add a glottal stop, the rule is not completely accurate as stated. Many people will have a glottal stop at the end of "cat" in phrases such as "that's a cat" or "the cat sat on the mat," but they will not have this allophone of / t / in "The cat is on the mat." An accurate statement would require my giving a much better account of what is meant by a syllable, but I cannot do this because it is not possible to give a phonetic definition of a syllable. We will return to this point in Chapter 10.

(10) In many accents of English, / t / is replaced by a glottal stop when it occurs before an alveolar nasal in the same word, as in "beaten" [ˈbiːʔn̩].

(11) Nasals are syllabic at the end of a word when immediately after an obstruent as in "leaden, chasm" ['lɛdn̩, 'kæzm̩].

Note that we cannot say that nasals become syllabic whenever they occur at the end of a word and after a consonant. The nasals in "kiln, film" are not syllabic in most accents of English. We can, however, state a rule describing the syllabicity of / l / by saying simply the following:

(12) The lateral / l / is syllabic at the end of a word when immediately after a consonant.

This rule summarizes the fact that / l / is syllabic not only after stops and fricatives (as in "paddle, whistle" ['pædl̩, 'wɪsl̩]), but also after nasals (as in "kennel, channel" ['kɛnl̩, 'tʃænl̩]). The only problem with this rule is what happens after / r /. It is correct for words such as "barrel" ['bærl̩], but it does not work in most forms of American English in words such as "snarl" [snɑrl], when / r / has to be considered as part of the vowel.

When it is not part of the vowel, / r / is like / l / in most forms of American English in that it, too, can be syllabic when it occurs at the end of a word and after a consonant, as in "sabre, razor, hammer, tailor" ['seɪbr̩, 'reɪzr̩, 'hæmr̩, 'teɪlr̩]. If we introduce a new term, **liquid,** which is used simply as a cover term for the consonants / l, r /, we may rephrase the statement in (12) and say:

(12a) The liquids / l, r / are syllabic at the end of a word when immediately after a consonant.

The next rule also applies more to American English than to British English. It accounts for the / t / in "fatty, data" ['fæɾi, 'dæɾə]. But note that these are not the only contexts in which these changes occur. This is not simply a change that affects / t / after a stressed vowel and before an unstressed one, in that / t / between two unstressed vowels (as in "divinity") is also affected. However, not all cases of / t / between vowels change in this way. The / t / in "attack" (i.e., before a stressed syllable) is voiceless, and / t / after another consonant (for example, in "hasty, captive") is also voiceless. Note also that most American English speakers have an articulatory gesture very like that in [ɾ] in words containing / d / and / n / in similar circumstances, such as "daddy, many." The first of these two words could well be transcribed ['dæɾi]. The second has the same sound, except that it is nasalized, so it could be transcribed ['mɛ̃ɾ̃i] in a narrow transcription. Nasalization is shown by the diacritic [˜] over a symbol. The following rule accounts for all these facts:

(13) Alveolar stops become voiced taps when they occur between two vowels, the second of which is unstressed.

Many speakers of American English require a similar rule to describe a sequence of an alveolar nasal followed by a stop. In words such as "painter, splinter," the / t / is lost and a nasal tap occurs. This has resulted in "winter" and "winner" and "panting" and "panning" being pronounced in the same way. For these speakers we can restate (13) this way:

(13a) Alveolar stops and alveolar nasal plus stop sequences become voiced taps when they occur between two vowels, the second of which is unstressed.

There is a great deal of variation among speakers with respect to this rule. Some make taps in familiar words such as "auntie" but not in less common words such as "Dante." Some make them only in fast speech. Try to formulate a rule in a way that describes your own speech.

(14) Alveolar consonants become dentals before dental consonants, as in "eighth, tenth, wealth" [eɪt̪θ, tɛn̪θ, wɛl̪θ]. Note that this rule applies to all alveolar consonants, not just stops, and it often applies across word boundaries, as in "at this" [æt̪ ðɪs].

In a more rapid style of speech, some of these dental consonants tend to be omitted altogether. Say these words first slowly and then more rapidly, and see what you do yourself.

It is difficult to give rules for when consonants get deleted, because this depends so much on the style of speech being used. Most people say "most people" as [ˈmoʊs ˈpipl̩] with no audible [t], and they produce phrases such as "sand paper" with no audible [d]. We could write this rule as follows:

(15) Alveolar stops are reduced or omitted when between two consonants.

Rule (15) raises an interesting point of phonetic theory. Note that I said "there may be no audible [d]," and "alveolar stops are reduced or omitted." However, the tongue tip gesture for the alveolar stop in "most people" may not be omitted but is just not audible because it is completely overlapped by the following labial stop. More commonly, it is partially omitted; that is to say, the tongue tip moves up for the alveolar stop but does not get to make a complete closure. When we think in terms of phonetic symbols, we can write [ˈmoʊs ˈpipl̩] or [ˈmoʊst ˈpipl̩]. But it is not really a question of whether the [t] is there or not. Part of the tongue tip gesture may have been made; but that is a fact that we have no way of symbolizing. Check this rule for yourself by thinking how you say phrases such as "best game" and "grand master." Say these and similar phrases with and without the alveolar stop. You may find the rule needs rewording to take into account all the contexts where alveolar stops may not appear in your speech.

Another rule is needed to account for the shortening effects that occur when two identical consonants come next to each other, as in "big game, top post." It is usually not true to say that one of these consonants is dropped: even in casual speech, most people would distinguish between "stray tissue, straight issue, straight tissue." (Try saying these in sentences such as "That's a stray tissue" and see for yourself.) But there clearly is a shortening effect that we can state as follows:

(16) A consonant is shortened when it is before an identical consonant.

We need rules stating not only where consonants are dropped and shortened, but also where they are added. Words such as "something" and "youngster" often are pronounced as [ˈsʌmpθɪŋ] and [ˈjʌŋkstə˞]. In a similar way, many people do not distinguish between "prince" and "prints," or "tense" and "tents." All these words are pronounced with a short voiceless stop between the nasal and the voiceless fricative. The insertion of a sound into the middle of a word is known as **epenthesis.**

(17) A homorganic voiceless stop may be inserted after a nasal before a
       voiceless fricative followed by an unstressed vowel in the same word.

Note that it is necessary to mention that the following vowel must be unstressed. Speakers who have an epenthetic stop in the noun "concert" do not usually have one in verbal derivatives such as "concerted" or in words such as "concern." Nothing need be said about the vowel before the nasal. Epenthesis may—like the [t] to [ɾ] change in rule (13)—occur between unstressed vowels. I have heard an inserted [t] in both "agency" and "grievances."

We can describe the more front articulation of / k / in "cap, kept, kit, key" [kæp, kɛpt, kɪt, ki] and of / g / in "gap, get, give, geese" [gæp, gɛt, gɪv, gis]. You should be able to feel the more front position of your tongue contact in the latter words of these series. The rule is as follows:

(18) Velar stops become more front as the following vowel in the same syl-
       lable becomes more front.

Finally, we need to note the difference in the quality of / l / in "life" [laɪf] and "file" [faɪɫ], or "clap" [klæp] and "talc" [tæɫk], or "feeling" [fiːlɪŋ] and "feel" [fiːɫ].

(19) The lateral / l / is velarized when after a vowel or before a consonant at
       the end of a word.

DIACRITICS

In this and the previous chapter we have seen how the transcription of English can be made more detailed by the use of diacritics, small marks added to a symbol to narrow its meaning. The six diacritics we have introduced so far are shown in Table 3.2. You should learn the use of these diacritics before you attempt any further detailed transcription exercises. Note that the nasalization diacritic is a small wavy line above a symbol, and the velarization diacritic is that same wavy line through the middle of a symbol. Nasalization is more common among vowels, which will be discussed in the next chapter.

TABLE 3.2		Some diacritics that modify the value of a symbol.			
̥h	Voiceless	w̥	l̥	kw̥ɪk, pl̥eɪs	"quick, place"
	Aspirated	tʰ	kʰ	tʰæp, kʰɪs	"tap, kiss"
̪	Dental	t̪	d̪	æt̪ ð̪ə, hel̪θ	"at the, health"
~	Nasalized	r̃	æ̃	mæ̃n	"man"
~	Velarized	ɫ		pʰɪɫ	"pill"
̩	Syllabic	n̩	l̩	'mɪʔn̩	"mitten"

EXERCISES

A The sequence of annotated diagrams that follows illustrates the actions that take place during the consonants at the end of the word "branch." Fill in the blanks.

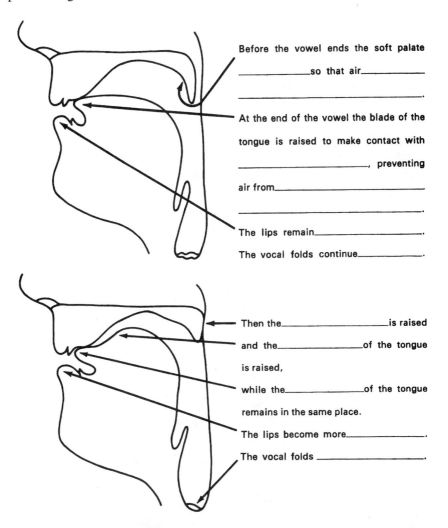

Before the vowel ends the soft palate _____so that air_____ _____.

At the end of the vowel the blade of the tongue is raised to make contact with _____, preventing air from_____ _____.

The lips remain_____.
The vocal folds continue_____.

Then the_____is raised and the_____of the tongue is raised, while the_____of the tongue remains in the same place.

The lips become more_____.

The vocal folds _____.

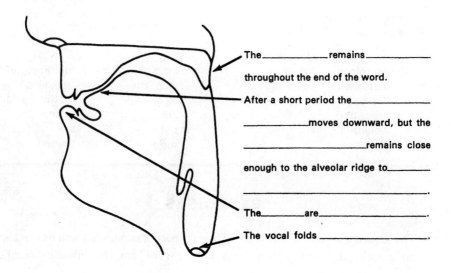

The_____remains_____
throughout the end of the word.
After a short period the_____
_____moves downward, but the
_____remains close
enough to the alveolar ridge to_____
_____.
The_____are_____.
The vocal folds _____.

B Annotate the following diagrams so as to describe the actions required for the consonants in the middle of the word "implant." Make sure that your annotations mention the action of the lips, the different parts of the tongue, the soft palate, and the vocal folds in each diagram. Try to make clear which of the vocal organs moves first in going from one consonant to another. The pronunciation illustrated is that of a normal conversational utterance; note the position of the tongue during the bilabial stop.

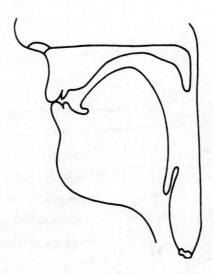

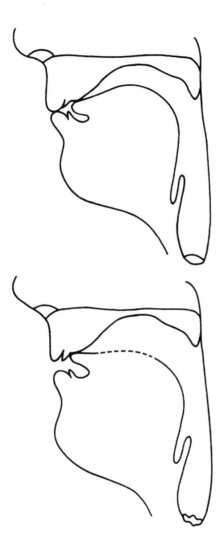

C Draw and annotate diagrams similar to those in the previous exercises, but this time illustrate the actions that occur in pronouncing the consonants in the middle of the phrase "thick snow." Make sure that you show clearly the sequence of events, noting what the lips, tongue, soft palate, and vocal folds do at each moment. Say the phrase over to yourself several times at a normal speed before you begin. Note especially whether the back of your tongue lowers before or after the tip of the tongue forms the articulation for subsequent consonants.

D As a transcription exercise, give a number of examples for each of rules (2) through (19) by making a narrow transcription of some additional words that fit the rules. Your examples should not include any words that have been transcribed in this book so far. Remember to mark the stress on words of more than one syllable.

Rule (2)　　　three examples (one for each voiceless stop)

_____　　_____　　_____

Rule (3)　　　seven examples (one for each voiced obstruent)

_____　　_____　　_____

_____　　_____　　_____

_____

Rule (4)　　　eight examples (two for each voiced stop or affricate)

_____　　_____

_____　　_____

_____　　_____

_____　　_____

Rule (5)　　　four examples (one for each approximant)

_____　　_____

_____　　_____

Rule (6)　　　three examples (one for each voiceless stop)

_____　　_____　　_____

Rule (7)　　　four contrasting pairs (one for each place of articulation)

_____　　_____

_____　　_____

_____　　_____

_____　　_____

Rule (8)　　　six examples (one for each voiced and voiceless stop)

_____　　_____　　_____

_____　　_____　　_____

Rule (9)　　　three examples (not necessarily from your own speech)

_____　　_____　　_____

Rule (10)   three examples (use three different vowels)

_____ _____ _____

Rule (11)   three examples (use at least two different nasals)

_____ _____ _____

Rule (12a)   six examples (three each with / l / and / r /)

_____ _____ _____

_____ _____ _____

Rule (13a)   six examples (two each with / t, d, n /, one being after an unstressed vowel)

_____ _____ _____

_____ _____ _____

Rule (14)   three examples (one each for / t, d, n /)

_____ _____ _____

Rule (15)   three examples (any kind)

_____ _____ _____

Rule (16)   three examples (any kind)

_____ _____ _____

Rule (17)   two examples (use two different nasals)

_____ _____ _____

Rule (18)   four examples (use four different vowels)

_____ _____

_____ _____

Rule (19)   two contrasting pairs (try to make them reversible words)

_____ _____

_____ _____

E   As a more challenging exercise, try to list two exceptions to some of these rules.

Rule (   ) _____

Rule (   ) _____

F Write a rule that describes the allophones of / h /.

_____

_____

_____

_____

PERFORMANCE EXERCISES

A Learn to produce some non-English sounds. First, in order to recall the sensation of adding and subtracting voicing while maintaining a constant articulation, repeat the exercise saying [ssszzzssszzz]. Now try a similar exercise, saying [mmmm̥m̥m̥mmmmm̥m̥m̥]. Make sure that your lips remain together all the time. During [m̥] you should be producing exactly the same action as when breathing out through the nose. Now say [m̥] in between vowels, producing sequences such as [am̥a, im̥i], and so on. Try not to have any gap between the consonant and the vowels.

B Repeat this exercise with [n, ŋ, l, r, w, j] learning to produce [ɑn̥ɑ, ɑŋ̊ɑ, ɑl̥ɑ, ɑr̥ɑ, ɑʍɑ, ɑj̊ɑ] and similar sequences with other vowels.

C Make sure that you can differentiate between the English words "whether, weather; which, witch," even if you do not normally do so. Say the following:

[hwɛðər]   "whether"

[wɛðər]   "weather"

[hwɪtʃ]   "which"

[wɪtʃ]   "witch"

D Learn to produce the following Burmese words. (You may for the moment neglect the tones, indicated by accents above the vowels.)

Voiced Nasals	Voiceless Nasals	Voiced Lateral	Voiceless Lateral
mâ "lift up"	m̥â "from"	la "moon"	l̥á "beautiful"
nă "pain"	n̥ă "nose"		
ŋâ "fish"	ŋ̊â "borrow"		

E Working with a partner, produce and transcribe _several_ sets of nonsense words. You should use slightly more complicated sets than previously. Make up your own sets on the basis of the illustrative set given here, including glottal stops, nasal and lateral plosion, and some combinations of English sounds that could not occur in English. Remember to mark the stress.

ˈkl̥ɑːntʃʊpsˈkweɪdʒ

ˈʒiːʒm̩ˈspobm̩

ˈtsɪʔɪˈbɛʔɪdl̩

mbuːˈtr̩ɪgŋ̩

ˈtwaɪbrɛʔɪp

F In order to increase your memory span in perceiving sounds, include some simpler but longer words in your production–perception exercises. A set of possible words is given here. You may find words such as the last two, which have eight syllables each, too difficult at the moment. But try to push your hearing ability to its limit. When you are listening to your partner dictating words, remember to try to (1) look at the articulatory movements; (2) repeat, to yourself, as much as you can immediately afterward; and (3) write down as much as you can, including the stress, as soon as possible.

ˈkiːpuːtuːˈpiːkiːtuː

ˈbɛgɪˈgɪdɛˈdɛdɪ

tr̩iːtʃɪʔiːtʃuːˈdruːdʒi

ˈriːlɛˈtolɛˈmɑnuˈdʊli

ˈfaɪθɪðiːˈvɔɪðuvuˈθiːfi

4

ENGLISH VOWELS

ENGLISH PHONETIC DICTIONARIES

As we saw in Chapter 2, the vowels of English can be transcribed in many different ways, partly because accents of English differ greatly in the vowels they use and partly because there is no one right way of transcribing even a single accent of English. The set of symbols used depends on the reason for making the transcription. If one is aiming to reduce English to the smallest possible set of symbols, then "sheep" and "ship" could be transcribed as [ʃiːp, ʃip]. If one were working on problems of computer speech recognition, one might choose to emphasize differences in vowel quality and write [ʃip, ʃɪp]. In a book such as this, in which we want to note that both length and quality differences occur, then [ʃiːp, ʃɪp] is the preferable transcription, despite the fact that vowel quality and vowel length are linked, and there is no need to mark both.

There is another reason why this style of transcription, introduced in Chapter 2, is the preferable one for this book. In previous editions it was hard to find anything that one could point to as a widely accepted, authoritative publication that transcribed both British and American English. Now there are some good reference books that specify pronunciations in both languages. One is an updated version of the dictionary produced by the English phonetician Daniel Jones, whose acute observations of English dominated British phonetics in the first half of the twentieth century. The current edition, *English Pronouncing Dictionary*, 15th ed. (Cambridge: Cambridge University Press) is familiarly known as EPD 15. It still bears Daniel Jones's name, but it has been completely revised by the new editors, Peter Roach and James Hartman, so that it now shows both British and American pronunciations. Another authoritative work is the *Longman Pronunciation Dictionary* (Harlow, U.K.: 2nd. ed. Pearson Education, 2000) by John Wells. This dictionary, which is familiarly known as LPD2, also gives the British and American pronunciations of more than 75,000 words. Professor John Wells holds the chair in phonetics at University College, London, previously held by Daniel Jones. He is clearly the leading authority on contemporary English pronunciation in all its forms—British, American, and other variants of the worldwide language. A third dictionary, *The Oxford Concise Dictionary of*

Pronunciation by Clive Upton, William Kretzschmar, and Rafal Konopka (Oxford: Oxford University Press, 2000), is due out at the same time as this book. It is slightly different from the other two dictionaries in that it gives a wider range of both British and American pronunciations and also uses a larger set of symbols, aiming to show more detail, using a more allophonic transcription than either of the other two dictionaries.

Everyone seriously interested in English pronunciation should be using one of these dictionaries. Each of them shows the pronunciations typically used by national newscasters—what we may regard as Standard American Newscaster English and Standard BBC English (often shortened to just American English and British English in this book). Of course, in neither country is there really a standard accent. In both countries there are some newscasters who have notable local accents. The dictionaries give what would be accepted as reasonable pronunciations for communicating in the two countries. They allow one to compare British and American pronunciations in great detail, noting, for example, that most British speakers pronounce "Caribbean" as [kærɪˈbiən], with the stress on the third syllable, whereas Americans typically say [kəˈrɪbiən], with the stress on the second syllable.

Ordinary American college dictionaries also provide pronunciations, but the symbols they use are not in accordance with the principles of the International Phonetic Association (IPA) and are of little use for comparative phonetic purposes. American dictionary makers sometimes say that they deliberately do not use IPA symbols because their dictionaries are used by speakers with different regional accents, and they want readers to be able to learn how to pronounce an unfamiliar word correctly in their own accents. But, as we have been observing, IPA symbols are often used to represent broad regions of sounds, and there is no reason why dictionary makers should not assign them values in terms of key words, just as they do for their ad hoc symbols.

Two of the three dictionaries we have been discussing, LPD and EPD 15, use virtually the same set of symbols, differing only in the way they transcribe the vowel in American English "bird"; LPD has[ɝ], whereas EPD 15 has [ɜr]. *The Oxford Concise Dictionary of Pronunciation* uses a slightly different set of symbols, but those symbols are readily interpretable within the IPA tradition. In this book I have kept to the style of transcription used in Wells's LPD with one exception, which is simply a typographical change: I have used [ɛ] in words such as "head, bed" instead of [e]. In later chapters we will be comparing vowels in other languages such as French and German, so we will need to use both [e] and [ɛ].

VOWEL QUALITY

In the discussion so far I have deliberately avoided making precise remarks about the quality of the different vowels. This is because, as I said in Chapter 1, the traditional articulatory descriptions of vowels are not very satisfactory. Try asking people who know as much about phonetics as you do to describe where the tongue is at the beginning of the vowel in "boy," and you will get a variety of responses. Can you describe where your own tongue is in a set of vowels?

It is difficult to give a meaningful answer to requests to describe the tongue position of a vowel in one's own speech. Very often people can only repeat what the books have told them, because they cannot find out for themselves where their tongue is. It is quite easy for a book to build up a set of terms that are not really descriptive but are in fact only labels. I started introducing terms of this kind for vowel qualities in Chapters 1 and 2 and will continue with this procedure here. But it is important for you to remember that the terms we are using are simply labels that describe how vowels sound in relation to one another. They are not absolute descriptions of the position of the body of the tongue.

Part of the problem in describing vowels is that there are no distinct boundaries between one type of vowel and another. When talking about consonants, the categories are much more distinct. A sound may be a stop or a fricative, but it cannot be halfway between the two. Vowels are different. It is perfectly possible to make a vowel that is halfway between a high vowel and a mid vowel. In theory (as opposed to what a particular individual can do in practice), it is possible to make a vowel at any specified distance between any two other vowels.

In order to appreciate the fact that vowel sounds form a continuum, try gliding from one vowel to another. Say [æ] as in "had" and then try to move gradually to [i] as in "he." Do not say just [æi], but try to spend as long as possible on the sounds in between them. If you do this correctly, you should pass through sounds that are something like [ɛ] as in "head" and [eɪ] as in "hay." If you have not achieved this effect already, try saying [æ-ɛ-eɪ-i] again, slurring slowly from one vowel to another.

Now do the same in the reverse direction, going slowly and smoothly from [i] as in "he" to [æ] as in "had." Take as long as possible over the in-between sounds. You should learn to stop at any point in this continuum so that you can make, for example, a vowel like [ɛ] as in "head," but slightly closer to [æ] as in "had."

Next, try going from [æ] as in "had" slowly toward [ɑ] as in "father." When you say [æ-ɑ], you probably will not pass through any other vowel of your own speech. But there is a continuum of possible vowel sounds between these two vowels. You may be able to hear sounds between [æ] and [ɑ] that are more like those used by other accents in "had" and "father." Some forms of Scottish English, for example, do not distinguish between the vowels in these words (or between "cam" and "calm"). Speakers with these accents pronounce both "had" and "father" with a vowel about halfway between the usual Midwestern American pronunciation of these two vowels. Some speakers of American English in the Boston area pronounce words such as "car, park" with a vowel between the more usual American vowels in "cam" and "calm." They do, however, distinguish the latter two words.

Last, in order to appreciate the notion of a continuum of vowel sounds, glide from [ɑ] as in "father" to [u] as in "who." In this case, it is difficult to be specific as to the vowels that you will go through on the way, because English accents differ considerably in this respect. But you should be able to hear that the movement from one of these sounds to the other covers a range of vowel qualities that have not been discussed so far in this section.

When you move from one vowel to another, you are changing the auditory quality of the vowel. You are, of course, doing this by moving your tongue and your lips; but, as we have noted, it is very difficult to say exactly how your tongue is moving. Consequently, because phoneticians cannot be very precise about the positions of the vocal organs in the vowels they are describing, they often simply use labels for the auditory qualities of the different vowels. The vowel [i] as in "heed" is called high front, meaning that it has the auditory quality high and the auditory quality front. Similarly, the vowel [æ] as in "had" has an auditory quality that may be called low front; and [ɛ] as in "head" sounds somewhere between [i] and [æ], but a little nearer to [æ], so we call it mid-low front. (Say the series [i, ɛ, æ] and check for yourself that this is true.) The vowel [ɑ] as in "father" is a low back vowel, and the vowel [u] in "who" is a high, fairly back vowel. The four vowels [i, æ, ɑ, u], therefore, give us something like the four corners of a space showing the auditory qualities of vowels, which may be drawn as in Figure 4.1.

None of the vowels has been put in an extreme corner of the space in Figure 4.1. It is possible to make a vowel that sounds more back than the vowel [u] that most people use in "who." You should be able to find this fully back vowel for yourself. Start by making a long [u], then round and protrude your lips a bit more. Now try to move your tongue back in your mouth while still keeping it

---

FIGURE 4.1   The vowel space.

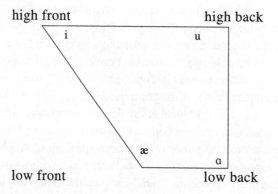

raised toward the soft palate. The result should be a fully back [u]. Another way of making this sound is to whistle the lowest note that you can, and then while retaining the same tongue and lip position, voice this sound. Again, the result will be an [u] sound that is farther back than the vowel in "who." Try saying [i] as in "heed," [u] as in "who," and then this new sound, which we may symbolize with an added underline [u̱]. If you say the series [i, u, u̱], you should be able to hear that [u] is intermediate between [i] and [u̱], but—for most speakers—much nearer [u̱].

Similarly, it is possible to make vowels with a more extreme quality than the usual English vowels [i, æ, ɑ]. If, for example, while saying [æ] as in "had," you lower your tongue or open your jaw slightly farther, you will produce a vowel that sounds relatively farther from [i] as in "heed." It will probably also sound a little more like [ɑ] as in "father."

Given a notion of an auditory vowel space of this kind, we can plot the relative quality of the different vowels. Remember that the labels high–low and front–back should not be taken as descriptions of tongue positions. They are simply indicators of the way one vowel *sounds* relative to another. The labels describe the relative auditory qualities, not the articulations.

Students of phonetics often ask why we use terms like high, low, back, and front if we are simply labeling auditory qualities and not describing tongue positions. The answer is that it is largely a matter of tradition. For many years phoneticians thought that they were describing tongue positions when they used these terms for specifying vowel quality. But there is only a rough correspondence between the traditional descriptions in terms of tongue positions and the actual auditory qualities of vowels. If you could take x-ray pictures that showed the position of your tongue while you were saying the vowels [i, æ, ɑ, u], you would find that the relative positions were not as indicated in Figure 4.1. But, as we will see in Chapter 8, if you use acoustic phonetic techniques to establish the auditory qualities, you will find that these vowels do have the relationships indicated in this figure.

At one time I thought of inventing new names to describe the auditory qualities. Other linguists have, in fact, used terms such as grave and acute instead of back and front in the description of vowels. But, for a variety of reasons, these terms did not become widely used, and it seems preferable to stick with the old terms high, low, back, and front, even though they are being used to describe auditory qualities rather than tongue positions.

Most of the vowels of a form of Standard American Newscaster English typical of many Midwestern speakers are shown in the upper part Figure 4.2. A comparable diagram of the vowels of British English as spoken by BBC newscasters is shown in the lower part of Figure 4.2. In both diagrams, the solid points represent the vowels that we are treating as monophthongs, and the lines represent the movements involved in the diphthongs. The symbols labeling the diphthongs are placed near their origins. There is a good scientific basis for placing the vowels as

| FIGURE 4.2 | The relative auditory qualities of some of the vowels of Standard American Newscaster English and of British (BBC newscaster) English. |

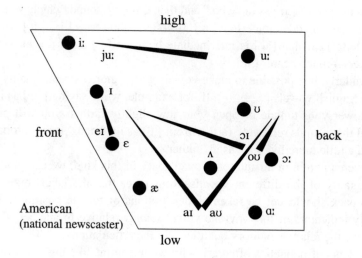

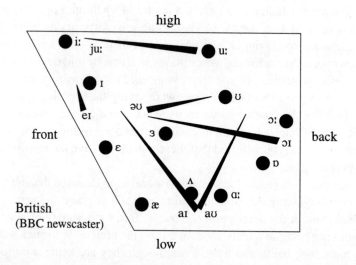

shown here. The positions of both monophthongs and diphthongs are not just the result of my own listening. The data are taken from the acoustic analyses of a number of authorities. We will return to this point in Chapters 8 and 9 when we discuss acoustic phonetics. Meanwhile, if you are able to listen to a speaker of Midwestern American English or BBC English, you should be able to hear that the relative vowel qualities are as indicated. Other varieties of English will differ in some respects, but you should find that in most accents the majority of the relationships are the same. We will note the cases in which there are substantial differences as we discuss the individual vowels.

Listen first of all to the vowels [iː, ɪ, ɛ, æ] as in "heed, hid, head, had." Do they sound as if they differ by a series of equal steps? Make each vowel about the same length (although in actual words they differ considerably), saying just [i, ɪ, ɛ, æ]. Now say them in pairs, first [i, ɪ], then [ɪ, ɛ], then [ɛ, æ]. In many forms of English, [i] sounds about the same distance from [ɪ] as [ɪ] is from [ɛ], and as [ɛ] is from [æ]. Some Eastern American speakers make a distinct diphthong in "heed" so that their [i] is really a glide starting from almost the same vowel as that in "hid." Other forms of English, for example, as spoken in the Midlands and the North of England, make a lower and more back vowel in "had," making it sound a little more like the [ɑ] in "father." This may result in the distance between [ɛ] and [æ] being greater than that between [ɛ] and [ɪ]. But speakers who have a lower [æ] may also have a slightly lower [ɛ], thus keeping the distances between the four vowels [i, ɪ, ɛ, æ] approximately the same.

The remaining front vowel in English is [eɪ] as in "hay." We will discuss this vowel after we have discussed some of the back vowels. The back vowels vary considerably in different forms of English, but no form of English has them evenly spaced like the front vowels. Say for yourself [ɑː, ɔː, ʊ, u] as in "father, author, good, food." As before, make each vowel about the same length, and say just [ɑ, ɔ, ʊ, u]. Consider pairs of vowels as you did the front vowels. Estimate the distances between each of these vowels, and compare them with those shown in Figure 4.2.

We have already noted that many Midwestern and Californian speakers do not distinguish [ɑː] and [ɔː] as in "cot" and "caught." They usually have a vowel intermediate in quality between the two points shown on the chart. On the other hand, most speakers of British English have an additional vowel in this area. They distinguish between the vowels [ɑː, ɒ, ɔː] as in "balm, bomb, bought." This results in a different distribution of the vowel qualities, as shown in the lower diagram in Figure 4.2. The additional vowel [ɒ] is more back and slightly more rounded than [ɑ].

The vowels [ʊ, u] as in "good, food" also vary considerably. Many speakers have a very unrounded vowel in "good" and a rounded but central vowel in "food." Look in a mirror and observe your own lip positions in these two vowels.

Both British and American English speakers have a mid-low central vowel [ʌ] as in "bud." In many forms of British English, this vowel may be a little lower than in American English. In this way it is distinct from the British English central vowel [ɜ] in "bird." The vowel in American English "bird" is not shown in the upper part of Figure 4.2 as it is distinguished from the vowel in "bud" by having r-coloring, which we will discuss later.

We must now consider the diphthongs shown in Figure 4.2. Each of these sounds involves a change in quality within the one vowel. As a matter of convenience, they can be described as movements from one vowel to another. The first part of the diphthong is usually more prominent than the last. In fact, the last part is often so brief and transitory that it is difficult to determine its exact quality. Furthermore, the diphthongs often do not begin and end with any of the sounds that occur in simple vowels.

As you can see from Figure 4.2, both of the diphthongs [aɪ, aʊ], as in "high, how," start from more or less the same low central vowel position, midway between [æ] and [ɑ] and, in BBC English, closer to [ʌ] than to any of the other vowels. (*The Oxford Concise Dictionary of Pronunciation* transcribes our [aɪ] as [ʌɪ] in British English.) Say the word "eye" very slowly and try to isolate the first part of it. Compare this sound with the vowels [æ, ʌ, ɑː] as in "bad, bud, father." Now make a long [ɑː] as in "father," and then say the word "eye" as if it began with this sound. The result should be something like some forms of New York or London Cockney English pronunciation of "eye." Try some other pronunciations, starting, for example, with the vowel [æ] as in "bad." In this case, the result is a somewhat affected pronunciation.

The diphthong [aɪ], as in "high, buy," moves toward a high front vowel, but in most forms of English it does not go much beyond a mid front vowel. Say a word such as "buy," making it end with the vowel [ɛ] as in "bed" (as if you were saying [baɛ]). A diphthong of this kind probably has a smaller change in quality than occurs in your normal pronunciation (unless you are one of the speakers from Texas or elsewhere in the South and Southwest who make such words as "by, die" into long monophthongs—[baː, daː]). Then say "buy," deliberately making it end with the vowel [ɪ] as in "bid." This vowel is usually slightly higher than the ending of this diphthong for many speakers of English. Finally, say "buy" with the vowel [i] as in "heed" at the end. This is a much larger change in quality than normally occurs in this word. But some speakers of Scottish English and Canadian English have a diphthong of this kind in words such as "sight," which is different from the diphthong that they have in "side."

The diphthong [aʊ] in "how" usually starts with a very similar quality to that at the beginning of "high." Try to say "owl" as if it started with [æ] as in "had," and note the difference from your usual pronunciation. Some speakers of the type of English spoken around London and the Thames estuary (often called Estuary English) have a complicated movement in this diphthong, making a sequence of qualities like those of [ɛ] as in "bed," [ʌ] as in "bud," and [u] as in "food." Say [ɛ-ʌ-u] in quick succession. Now say the phrase "how now brown cow" using a diphthong of this type.

The diphthong [eɪ] as in "hay" varies considerably in different forms of English. Some American English speakers have a diphthong starting with a vowel very like [ɛ] in "head" (as shown in the upper part of Figure 4.2). Most BBC English speakers and many Midwestern Americans have a smaller diphthong, starting closer to [ɪ] as in "hid." London and Estuary English has a larger diphthong, so that words such as "mate, take" sound somewhat like "might, tyke." Conversely, others (including many Scots) have a higher vowel, a monophthong that can be written [e]. Check your own pronunciation of "hay" and try to decide how it should be represented on a chart as in Figure 4.2.

The diphthong [oʊ] as in "hoe" may be regarded as the back counterpart of [eɪ]. In American English it is usually a movement in the high–low dimension, but in most forms of British English the movement is more in the front–back dimension, as you can see in Figure 4.2. Some British English speakers make this vowel start near [ɛ] and end a little higher than [ʊ]. Say each part of this diphthong and compare it with other vowels.

The remaining diphthong moving in the upward direction is [ɔɪ] as in "boy." Again, this diphthong does not end in a very high vowel. It often ends with a vowel similar to that in "bed." I might well have transcribed "boy" as [bɔɛ], if I had not been trying to keep the style of transcription used in this book as similar as possible to other widely used transcriptions.

The last diphthong, [ju] as in "cue," differs from all the other diphthongs in that the more prominent part occurs at the end. Because it is the only vowel of this kind, many books on English phonetics do not even consider it as a diphthong; they treat it as a sequence of a consonant followed by a vowel and symbolize it by [ju] (or [yu], in the case of books not using the IPA system of transcription). I have considered it to be a diphthong because of the way it patterns in English. Historically, it is a vowel, just like the other vowels we have been considering. Furthermore, if it is not a vowel, then we have to say that there is a whole series of consonant clusters in English that can occur before only one vowel. The sounds at the beginning of "pew, beauty, cue, spew, skew" and (for most speakers of British English) "tune, dune, sue, Zeus, new, lieu, stew" occur only before / u /. There are no English words beginning with / pje / or / kjæ /, for example. In stating the distributional properties of English sounds, it seems much simpler to recognize / ju / as a diphthong and thus reduce the complexity of the statements one has to make about the English consonant clusters.

The only common stressed vowel of American English not shown in Figure 4.2 is [ɝː] as in "sir, herd, fur." This vowel does not fit on the chart because it cannot be described simply in terms of the features high–low, front–back, and rounded–unrounded. The vowel [ɝː] can be said to be *r-colored*. It involves an additional feature called **rhotacization.** Just like high–low and front–back, the feature rhotacization describes an auditory property, the r-coloring, of a vowel. When we describe the height of a vowel, we are saying something about how it sounds rather than something about the tongue position necessary to produce it. Similarly, when we describe a sound as a rhotacized vowel, we are saying something about how it sounds. In most forms of American English, there are both stressed and unstressed rhotacized vowels. The transcription for the phrase "my sister's bird" in most forms of American English would be [maɪ ˈsɪstɚz ˈbɝːd].

Rhotacized vowels are often called retroflex vowels, but there are at least two distinct ways in which the r-coloring can be produced. Some speakers have the tip of the tongue raised, as in a retroflex consonant, but others keep the tip down and produce a high bunched tongue position. These two gestures produce a very similar auditory effect. X-ray studies of speech have shown that in both these ways of producing a rhotacized quality there is usually a constriction in the pharynx caused by retraction of the part of the tongue below the epiglottis.

The most noticeable difference among accents of English is in whether they have r-colored vowels or not. In many forms of American English, rhotacization occurs when vowels are followed by [r], as in "beard, bared, bard, board, poor, tire, hour." Accents that permit some form of [r] after a vowel are said to be **rhotic.** The rhotacization of the vowel is often not so evident at the beginning of the vowel, and something of the quality of the individual vowel remains. But in "sir, herd, fur" the whole vowel is rhotacized (which is why I prefer LPD2 ['bɝd], rather than EPD 15 ['bɜrd]). Insofar as the quality of this vowel can be described in terms of the features high–low and front–back, it appears to be a mid-central vowel such as [ɜ] with added rhotacization.

Rhotic accents are the norm in most parts of North America. They were prevalent throughout Britain in Shakespeare's time and still occur in the West Country, Scotland, and other regions distant from London. Shortly after it became fashionable in the Southeast of England to drop post-vocalic / r /, this habit spread to areas of the United States in New England and parts of the South. These regions are now nonrhotic to various degrees. Try to find a speaker of English with an accent that is the opposite of your own—rhotic or nonrhotic as the case may be. Listen to the speaker's vowels in words such as "mirror, fairer, surer, poorer, purer" and compare them with your own.

Standard BBC English is not rhotic and has diphthongs (not shown in Figure 4.2) going from a vowel near the outside of the vowel space toward the central vowel [ə]. In words such as "here" and "there," these are transcribed [ɪə] and [ɛə]. Some speakers have a long [ɛː] instead of [ɛə], particularly before [r] as in "fairy, bearing." Some people have a centering diphthong [ʊə] in words such as "poor," but this is probably being replaced in most nonrhotic accents of British English by [ɔː]. We also noticed in Chapter 2 that some speakers have a centering diphthong (though we did not call it that at the time) in "hire, fire," which are [haə, faə].

UNSTRESSED SYLLABLES

In all forms of English, the symbol [ə], which is not shown in Figure 2.2, may be used to specify a range of mid-central vowel qualities. As we saw in Chapter 2, vowels of this sort occur in grammatical function words, such as "to, the, at" [tə, ðə, ət]. They also occur at the ends of the words "sofa, China"

[ˈsoʊfə, ˈtʃaɪnə] and, for most British speakers, "better, farmer" [ˈbɛtə, ˈfɑːmə]. In American English the vowel at the end of words with the "-er" spelling is usually [ɚ], a very similar quality, but with added r-coloring. As the vowel chart in Figure 4.2 represents a kind of auditory space, vowels near the outside of the chart are more distinct from one another than vowels in the middle, and differences in vowel quality become progressively reduced among vowels nearer the center. The symbol [ə] may be used to designate many vowels that have a **reduced vowel** quality.

We will be considering the nature of stress in English in the next chapter, but we can note here that vowels in unstressed syllables do not necessarily have a completely reduced quality. All the English vowels can occur in unstressed syllables in their full (unreduced) forms. Many of them can occur in three forms, as shown in Table 4.1. In this table, the vowel to be considered is in boldface. The words in the first column illustrate the full forms of the vowels. The second column gives an example of the same unreduced vowel in an unstressed syllable. The last column illustrates the same underlying vowel as a reduced vowel. For many people, the reduced vowels in this last column are all very similar. Some accents have slightly different qualities in some of these words, but still within the range of a mid-central vowel that can be symbolized by [ə]. Others have [ɪ] in some of these words, such as "recitation," or a high-central vowel, which

TABLE 4.1	Examples of vowels in stressed and unstressed syllables and in reduced syllables. The boldface type shows the vowel under consideration.

	Stressed Syllable	Unstressed Syllable	Reduced Syllable
iː	depr**e**ciate	cr**e**ate	depr**e**cate
ɪ	impl**i**cit	s**i**mplistic	impl**i**cation
eɪ	expl**ai**n	ch**ao**tic	expl**a**nation
ɛ	all**e**ge	t**e**mpestuous	all**e**gation
æ	emph**a**tic	f**a**ntastic	emph**a**sis
ɑː, ɒ	dem**o**nstrable	pr**o**gnosis	dem**o**nstration
ɔː	c**au**se	c**au**sality	
oʊ, əʊ	inv**o**ke	v**o**cation	inv**o**cation
ʊ	h**oo**dwink	neighborh**oo**d	
uː	ac**ou**stic	ac**ou**stician	
ʌ	confr**o**nt	**u**mbrella	confr**o**ntation
ɚː, ɜː	conf**ir**m	v**er**bose	conf**ir**mation
aɪ	rec**i**te	c**i**tation	rec**i**tation
aʊ	dev**ou**t	**ou**tsider	
ɔɪ	expl**oi**t	expl**oi**tation	
juː	comp**u**te	comp**u**tation	circ**u**lar

may be symbolized by [ɨ]—a symbol that is sometimes called "barred i." Say all these words yourself and find out which vowels you have.

There are some widely applicable rules of English relating the pronunciation of the words in the first column to that of the words in the third column. Consequently, we are able to say that the same underlying vowels occur in the words in the first and third columns. If we were making a high level phonological transcription, we could transcribe the vowels in the different columns with the same symbols and allow the rules to make it clear that different allophones occurred. Thus we could transcribe "emphatic" as / ɛmfætɪk / and "emphasis" as / ɛmfæsɪs /, as long as we also have a rule that assigns the stress and makes / æ / into [ə] in the second word.

The rules accounting for the allophones are very general in the sense that they account for thousands of similar alternations among English words. But they are also very complicated. They have to account for the blanks in the third column, which show that some vowels can be completely reduced but others cannot. There is, for example, a completely reduced vowel in "explanation, demonstration, recitation," but not, for most people, in the very similar words "exploitation, computation." As you can also see from an examination of Table 4.1, some vowels, such as [ʊ, uː], do not fit into this scheme of alternations in the same way as the other vowels. Because the rules are so complicated, we will not use transcriptions showing the underlying forms of English in this elementary textbook. Instead, we will continue to use [ə] or [ɪ] in reduced syllables.

Most British and some American English speakers have a vowel more like [ɪ] in suffixes such as "-ed, -(e)s" at the ends of words with alveolar consonants such as "hunted, houses" ['hʌntɪd, 'haʊzɪz]. For these speakers, both vowels in "pitted" ['pɪtɪd] have much the same quality. A reduced vowel more like [ʊ] may occur in the suffix "-ful" as in "dreadful" ['drɛdfʊl], but for many people this is just a syllabic [l̩], ['drɛdfl̩].

TENSE AND LAX VOWELS

The vowels of English can be divided into what may be called **tense** and **lax** sets. These terms are really just labels that are used to designate two groups of vowels that behave differently in English words. There are phonetic differences between the two groups, but they are not simply a matter of "tension." To some extent the differences between the two sets are due to facts in the history of English that are still represented in the spelling. The tense vowels occur in the words with a final, so-called silent *e* in the spelling (e.g., "mate, mete, kite, cute"). The lax vowels occur in the corresponding words without a silent *e*: "mat, met, kit, cut." In addition, the vowel in "good," which, for reasons connected with the history of English, has no silent *e* partner, is also a member of the lax set. This spelling based distinction is, however, only a rough indication of the difference between the two sets. It is better exemplified by the data in Table 4.2.

TABLE 4.2		The distribution of tense and lax vowels in stressed syllables in American English.				

Tense Vowels	Lax Vowels	Most Closed Syllables	Open Syllables	Syllables Closed by [r]	Syllables Closed by [ŋ]	Syllables Closed by [ʃ]
iː		beat	bee	beer		(leash)
	ɪ	bit			sing	wish
eɪ		bait	bay			
	ɛ	bet		bare	length	fresh
	æ	bat			hang	crash
ɑː		hot	pa	bar		slosh
ɔː		bought	saw	bore	long	(wash)
oʊ		boat	low	(boar)		
	ʊ	good				push
uː		boot	boo	poor		
	ʌ	but			hung	crush
aɪ		bite	buy	fire		
aʊ		bout	bough	hour		
ɔɪ		void	boy	(coir)		
ju		cute	cue	pure		

The difference between the two sets can be discussed in terms of the different kinds of syllables in which they can occur. Table 4.2 shows some of the restrictions for one form of American English. The first column of words illustrates a set of **closed syllables**—those that have a consonant at the end. All of the vowels can occur in these circumstances. The next column shows that in **open syllables**—those without a consonant at the end—only a restricted set of vowels can occur.

None of the vowels [ɪ, ɛ, æ, ʊ, ʌ] as in "bid, bed, bad, good, bud" can appear in stressed open syllables. This is the set of vowels that may be called lax vowels as opposed to the tense vowels in the other words. In order to characterize the differences between tense and lax vowels, we can consider some of them in pairs, each pair consisting of a tense vowel and the lax vowel that is nearest to it in quality. Three pairs of this kind are [iː, ɪ] as in "beat, bit"; [eɪ, ɛ] as in "bait, bet"; and [uː, ʊ] as in "boot, foot." In each of these pairs, the lax vowel is shorter, lower, and slightly more centralized than the corresponding tense vowel. There are no vowels that are very similar in quality to the remaining two lax vowels in most forms of American English, [æ] as in "hat, cam" and [ʌ] as in "hut, come." But both of these low lax vowels are shorter than the low tense vowel [ɑː] as in "spa." Speakers of most forms of British English have an additional lax vowel. They have the tense vowel [ɑː] as in "calm, car, card" in both open and closed syllables; and they also have a lax vowel [ɒ] as in "cod, common, con" [kɒd, ˈkɒmən, kɒn], which occurs only in closed syllables.

The fifth column in Table 4.2 shows the vowels that can occur in syllables closed by / r / in American English. There is no contrast between a tense vowel and the lax vowel nearest to it in quality in a syllable closed by / r /. Consequently, as often happens in contexts in which there is no opposition between two sounds, the actual sound produced is somewhere between the two. (We have already observed another example of this tendency. We saw that after / s / at the beginning of a word, there is no contrast between / p / and / b /, or / t / and / d /, or / k / and / g /. Consequently, the stops that occur in words such as "spy, sty, sky" are in between the corresponding voiced and voiceless stops; they are unaspirated, but they are never voiced.)

I put the words "boar" and "coir" in parentheses in this column because for many people [oʊ] and [ɔɪ] do not occur before / r /. The word "coir" [kɔɪr], which is the only word I have heard pronounced with [ɔɪr], is not in many people's vocabulary; and many people make no difference between "bore" and "boar." But some speakers do contrast [ɔː] and [oʊ] in these two words, or in other pairs such as "horse" and "hoarse."

The next column shows the vowels that occur before [ŋ]. In these circumstances, again, there is no possible contrast between tense and lax vowels. But, generally speaking, it is the lax vowels that occur. However, many younger Americans pronounce "sing" with a vowel closer to that in "beat" rather than to that in "bit." And in some accents, "length" is regularly pronounced with virtually the same vowel as that in "bait" rather than that in "bet"; in others, it is pronounced with the vowel in "bit." The pronunciation of "long" varies. It is [lɑːŋ] or [lɔːŋ] in most forms of American English and [lɒŋ] in most forms of British English. Several other changes are true of vowels before all nasals in many forms of American English. For example, [æ] may be considerably raised in "ban, lamb" as compared with "bad, lab." In many accents, "pin, pen" and "gym, gem" are not distinguished.

The last column shows that there are similar restrictions in the vowels that can occur before [ʃ]. By far the majority of words ending in / ʃ / have lax vowels for most speakers, although some accents (e.g., that used in parts of Indiana) have [iː] in "fish" (making it like "fiche") and [uː] in "push" and "bush." In my own speech, the only words containing the tense vowel / iː / before / ʃ / are "leash, fiche, quiche." Some speakers have tense vowels in a few new or unusual words such as "creche, gauche," which may be [kreɪʃ, goʊʃ]. The pronunciation of "wash" varies in much the same way as that of "long." Both [wɑːʃ] and [wɔːʃ] occur in American English.

RULES FOR ENGLISH VOWEL ALLOPHONES

We can conclude this chapter as we did the previous one—by considering some rules that apply to vowels. The first concerns vowel length:

(1) A given vowel is longest in an open syllable, next longest in a syllable closed by a voiced consonant, and shortest in a syllable closed by a voiceless consonant.

If you compare words such as "sea, seed, seat" or "sigh, side, site," you will hear that the vowel is longest in the first word in each set, next longest in the second, and shortest in the last. You can see an example of part of this rule in Figure 3.3, which showed the waveforms of the words "mat" and "mad." Because some vowels are inherently longer than others, we have to restrict rule (1) to a vowel of a given quality. On many occasions the so-called short vowel in "bid" may be longer than the so-called long vowel in "beat."

Even when we are considering the same vowel in syllables with the same consonants, there may be a difference in vowel length. Stressed syllables are longer than the corresponding unstressed syllables. Compare words such as "below" and "billow." You will find that the vowel [oʊ] in the stressed syllable in the first word is longer than the same vowel in the second word, where it occurs in an unstressed syllable. We will therefore have a rule:

(2) Other things being equal, vowels are longer in stressed syllables.

We still had to hedge this rule with the phrase "other things being equal," as there are other causes of variation in vowel length. Another kind of length variation is exemplified by sets of words such as "speed, speedy, speedily." Here the vowel in the stressed syllable gets progressively shorter as a result of adding extra syllables in the same word. The reasons for this phenomenon will be dealt with in the next chapter. Here we will simply state the following:

(3) Other things being equal, vowels are longest in monosyllabic words, next longest in words with two syllables, and shortest in words with more than two syllables.

We should also add a statement about unstressed vowels, which may become voiceless in words such as "potato, catastrophe." For some people, this happens only if the following syllable begins with a voiceless stop; but for many (including myself), it also happens in a normal conversational style in words such as "permission, tomato, compare." One wording of this rule would be as follows:

(4) A reduced vowel may be voiceless when it occurs after a voiceless stop (and before a voiceless stop).

The parenthesized phrase could be omitted for many people.

A further extension of this rule would allow for completely voiceless syllables when the unstressed vowel follows a voiceless stop cluster with / r /, as in "*pre*paratory, spec*tro*graph, in*tro*duction." What about clusters with / l /, such as "re*pli*cate, com*pli*cate"? Some people make some of these syllables voiceless as well.

Other rules can be used to specify the changes due to the vowel being influenced by the following consonant. The most obvious is that vowels tend to become nasalized before nasal consonants. In a word such as "ban," the soft palate often lowers for the nasal considerably before the tongue tip rises to make the articulatory contact. As a result, much of the vowel is nasalized. As we saw in the previous chapter, nasalization is shown by the diacritic [˜] over a symbol. In a narrow transcription; "ban" might be transcribed [bæ̃n]. We can make the following general statement:

(5) Vowels are nasalized in syllables closed by a nasal consonant.

The degree of nasalization in a vowel varies extensively. Many people will have the velum lowered throughout a syllable beginning and ending with a nasal, such as "man," making the vowel fully nasalized.

Finally, we must note the allophones produced when vowels occur in syllables closed by / l /. Compare your pronunciation of / iː / in "heed" and "heel," of / eɪ / in "paid" and "pail," and [æ] in "pad" and "pal." In each case, you should be able to hear a noticeably different vowel quality before the velarized [ɫ]. All the front vowels become considerably retracted in these circumstances. It is almost as if they became diphthongs with an unrounded form of [ʊ] as the last element. In a narrow transcription, we could transcribe this element so that "peel, pail, pal" would be [pʰiʊɫ, pʰeʊɫ, pʰæʊɫ]. Note that I omitted the usual second element of the diphthong [eɪ] in order to show that in these circumstances the vowel moved from a mid-front to a mid-central rather than to a high-front quality.

Back vowels, as in "haul, pull, pool," are usually less affected by the final [ɫ] because they already have a tongue position similar to that of [ɫ]. But there is often a great difference in quality in the vowels in "hoe" and "hole." As we have seen, many speakers of British English have a fairly front vowel as the first element in the diphthong [əʊ]. This vowel becomes considerably retracted before / ɫ / at the end of the syllable. You can observe the change by comparing words such as "holy," where there is no syllable final [ɫ], and "wholly," where the first syllable is closed by [ɫ].

The exact form of the rule for specifying vowel allophones before [ɫ] will vary from speaker to speaker. But, so that we can include a rule in our set summarizing some of the main allophones of vowels in English, we may say the following:

(6) Vowels are retracted before syllable final [ɫ].

Some speakers have a similar rule that applies to vowels before / r /, as in "hear, there," which might be [hiᵊr, ðeᵊr]. Note again how / l, r / may act together in rules, as we found when discussing consonants in rule (12a) in the preceding chapter.

Again, let me emphasize that these rules roughly specify only some of the major aspects of the pronunciation of English. They do not state everything about English vowels that is rule governed, nor are they completely accurately formulated. There are problems, for example, in saying exactly what is meant by a word or a syllable, and it is possible to find both exceptions to these rules and additional generalizations that can be made.

EXERCISES

A Put your own vowels in this chart, using a set of words such as that given in Table 2.2. Listen to each vowel carefully and try to judge how it sounds relative to the other vowels. You will probably find it best to say each vowel as the middle vowel of a three-member series, with the vowels in the words above and below forming the first and last vowels in the series. In the case of the diphthongs, you should do this with both the beginning and the ending points.

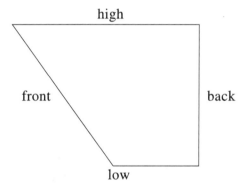

B Try to find a speaker with an accent different from your own (or perhaps a foreigner who speaks English with an accent) and repeat Exercise A, using this blank chart.

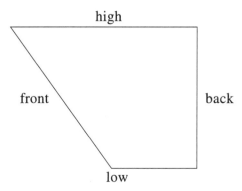

C List words illustrating the occurrence of vowels in syllables closed by / p /. Do not include names of foreign origin. You will find that some vowels cannot occur in these circumstances.

iː

ɪ

eɪ

ɛ

æ

ɑː

ɔː

oʊ

ʊ

uː

ʌ

aɪ

aʊ

ɔɪ

D Considering only the vowels that *cannot* occur in syllables closed by / p / as in Exercise C, give words, if possible, illustrating their occurrence in syllables closed by the following consonants.

/ b /

/ m /

/ f /

/ t /

/ n /

/ l /

/ s /

/ z /

/ k /

/ g /

E Which vowel occurs before the smallest number of consonants? Also, which class of consonants occurs after the largest number of vowels? (Define the class in terms of the place of articulation at which these consonants are made.)

F Look at Table 4.1. Find additional examples illustrating the relationship between the words in the first and third columns. Transcribe each pair of words as shown here for the vowel / iː /.

vowel	**stressed syllable**	**reduced syllable**
iː	secrete [səˈkriːt]	secretive [ˈsiːkrətɪv]
ɪ		
eɪ		
ɛ		
æ		
ɑː or ɒ		
oʊ		
aɪ		

G Make up and transcribe a sentence containing at least eight different vowels.

H Give a number of examples for each of rules (1) through (6) by making a transcription of some additional words that fit the rules. Your examples should not include any words that have been transcribed in this book so far. Remember to mark the stress on words of more than one syllable.

Rule (1)   three examples (one for each syllable)

_____   _____   _____

Rule (2)   two pairs of examples (each showing words differing principally in stress)

_____   _____

_____   _____

Rule (3)   two sets of examples (each containing a one-syllable, a two-syllable and a three-syllable word, with the first, stressed syllable remaining constant)

_____   _____   _____

_____   _____   _____

Rule (4)   four examples

_____   _____   _____

_____

Rule (5)   four examples (use different vowels and different nasals)

_____   _____

_____   _____

Rule (6)   two sets of examples, each containing a contrasting pair of words

_____   _____

_____   _____

PERFORMANCE EXERCISES

A Learn to produce only the first part of the vowel [eɪ] as in "hay." Try saying this sound in place of your normal diphthong in words such as "they came late." Similarly, learn to produce a mid-high back vowel [o], and say it in words that you have been transcribing with the diphthong [oʊ], such as "Don't go home."

B Incorporate [e] and [o] in nonsense words for production and perception exercises. These words might also now include the voiceless sounds [m̥, n̥, ŋ̊, w̥, j̊]. Remember to practice saying the words by yourself, so that you can say them fluently to your partner. Start with easy words such as the following:

maˈŋɑ

n̥eme

ˈŋ̊ɑle

ˈmoʔi

ˈl̥ele

Then go on to more difficult words like these:

heˈm̥ɑn̥e

ˈŋambm̥bel̥

'spoʔetn̩ʔɔɪ

'wo̥θʃoˈɾesfi

'tlepɾidʒiˈkuʒ

C Again working with a partner, write the numbers 1 through 5 somewhere on a vowel chart as, for example, shown in the chart below. Now say vowels corresponding to these numbered positions in nonsense monosyllables, saying, for example, something like [dub]. Your partner should try to plot these vowels on a blank chart. When you have pronounced five words, compare notes, and then discuss the reasons for any discrepancies between the two charts. Then reverse roles and repeat the exercise.

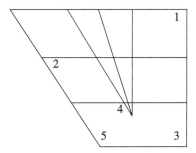

D Repeat Performance Exercise C with as many different partners as you can. It is difficult to make perceptual judgments of the differences among vowels, but you should be able to find a rough consensus.

E In addition to nonsense words of the kind given in Performance Exercise B, continue practicing with words to increase your auditory memory span. Say each word only two or three times. Remember that you should be spending at least one hour a week on production and perception exercises.

θeˈmifeˈðim̩e

'serapoˈsɑpofiˈpos

moˈpretepleteˈki

n̥ɑˈkotoˈtɑkpoto

lɑˈkimitiˈnoneʔe

5

ENGLISH WORDS AND SENTENCES

STRONG AND WEAK FORMS

The form in which a word is pronounced when it is considered in isolation is called its **citation form.** At least one syllable is fully stressed and has no reduction of the vowel quality. But in connected speech, many changes may take place. Some smaller words such as "and, to, him" may be considerably altered. They will usually be completely unstressed, the vowel may be reduced to [ə] or may disappear altogether, and one or more of the consonants may be dropped or altered. Thus "and" in its reduced form may be pronounced as [ənd] or [ən] or [n]. Try to pronounce it in these three different ways in a phrase such as "bread and butter."

Many words are like "and" in that they seldom maintain their citation form in conversational speech. These words may be said to have two different forms of pronunciation. There is a **strong form,** which occurs when the word is stressed, as in sentences such as "I want money *and* happiness, not money *or* happiness." There is also a **weak form,** which occurs when the word is in an unstressed position. Table 5.1 lists a number of common English words that have strong and weak forms.

Several of the words in Table 5.1 have more than one weak form. Sometimes, as in the case of "and," there are no clear rules as to when one as opposed to another of these forms is likely to occur. After a word ending with an alveolar consonant, I have a tendency to drop the vowel and say [n̩] or [n̩d] in phrases such as "cat and dog" or "his and hers." But this is far from invariable.

For some words, however, there are rules that are nearly always applicable. The alternation between "a" [ə] before a consonant and "an" [ən] before a vowel is even recognized in the spelling. Similar alternations occur with the words "the, to," which are [ðə, tə] before consonants and are often [ðiː, tuː] or [ðɪ, tʊ] before vowels. Listen to your own pronunciation of these words in the sentence, "The [ðə] man and the [ðɪ] old woman went to [tə] Britain and to [tʊ] America." The two examples of "the" will often be pronounced differently. It should be noted, however, that there is a growing tendency for younger American English speakers to use the form [ðə] in all circumstances, even before a

| TABLE 5.1 | Strong and weak forms of some common English words. More than five times as many could easily have been listed. |

Word	Strong Form	Weak Form	Example of a Weak Form
a	eɪ	ə	a cup [ə ˈkʌp]
and	ænd	ənd, n̩d, ən, n̩	you and me [ˈjuː ən ˈmiː]
as	æz	əz	as good as [əz ˈɡʊd əz]
at	æt	ət	at home [ət ˈhoʊm]
can	kæn	kən, kn̩	I can go [aɪ kn̩ ˈɡoʊ]
has	hæz	həz, əz, z, s	he's left [hɪz ˈlɛft]
he	hi	i, hɪ, ɪ	will he go? [wɪl ɪ ˈɡoʊ]
must	mʌst	məst, məs, ms̩	I must sell [aɪ ms̩ ˈsɛl]
she	ʃi	ʃɪ	did she go? [ˈdɪd ʃɪ ˈɡoʊ]
that	ðæt	ðət	he said that it did [hɪ ˈsɛd ðət ɪt ˈdɪd]
to	tuː	tʊ, tə	to Mexico [tə ˈmɛksɪkoʊ]
would	wʊd	wəd, əd, d	it would do [ˈɪt əd ˈduː]

vowel. If a glottal stop is inserted before words beginning with a vowel (another growing tendency in American English), then the form [ðə] is even more likely to be used.

Some of the words in Table 5.1 are confusing in that the same spelling represents two words with different meanings (two homonyms). Thus the spelling "that" represents a demonstrative pronoun in a phrase such as "that boy and the man," but it represents a relative pronoun in "he said that men were better." Only the relative pronoun has a weak form. The demonstrative "that" is always pronounced [ðæt]. Similarly, when "has" indicates past tense, it may be [z], as in "she's gone," but it is [həz] or [əz] when it indicates possession, as in "she has nice eyes."

There is another way in which words can be affected when they occur in connected speech. As you already know, sounds are often affected by adjacent sounds—for example, the [n] in "tenth" is articulated on the teeth because of the following dental fricative [θ]. Similar effects commonly occur across word boundaries, so that in phrases such as "in the" and "on the" the [n] is realized as a dental [n̪] because of the following [ð].

When one sound is changed into another because of the influence of a neighboring sound, there is said to be a process of **assimilation.** There is an assimilation of [n] to [n̪] because of the [ð] in the phrase "in the." Anticipatory coarticulation is by far the most common cause of assimilations in English. But perseverative assimilations do occur, for example, in the pronunciation of the phrase "it is" [ɪt ɪz] as "it's" [ɪts] as a result of the perseveration of the voicelessness of [t].

There is, of course, nothing slovenly or lazy about using weak forms and assimilations. Only people with artificial notions about what constitutes so-called good speech could use adjectives such as these to label the kind of speech I have been describing. Weak forms and assimilations are common in the speech of every sort of speaker in both Britain and America. Foreigners who make insufficient use of them sound stilted.

STRESS

A stressed syllable is usually produced by pushing more air out of the lungs in one syllable relative to others. A stressed syllable thus has greater respiratory energy than neighboring unstressed syllables. It may also have an increase in laryngeal activity. Stress can always be defined in terms of something a speaker does in one part of an utterance relative to another.

It is difficult to define stress from a listener's point of view. A stressed syllable is often, but not always, louder than an unstressed syllable. It is usually, but not always, on a higher pitch. The most reliable thing for a listener to detect is that a stressed syllable frequently has a longer vowel than that same vowel would be if it were unstressed. But this does not mean that all long vowels are necessarily stressed. The second and third vowels in "radio," for example, are comparatively long, but they do not have the extra push of air from the lungs that occurs on the first vowel. Conversely, the vowels in the first syllables of "Russia" and "hit man" are comparatively short, but they have extra respiratory energy and so are felt to be stressed.

Stress can always be correlated with something a speaker does rather than with some particular acoustic attribute of the sounds, Consequently, you will find that the best way to decide whether a syllable is stressed is to try to tap out the beat as a word is said. This is because it is always easier to produce one increase in muscular activity—a tap—exactly in time with an existing increase in activity. When as listeners we perceive the stresses that other people are making, we are probably putting together all the cues available in a particular utterance in order to deduce the motor activity (the articulations) we would use to produce those same stresses. It seems as if listeners sometimes perceive an utterance by reference to their own motor activities. When we listen to speech, we may be considering, in some way, what we would have to do in order to make similar sounds.

Stress has several different functions in English. In the first place, it can be used simply to give special emphasis to a word or to contrast one word with another. As we have seen, even a word such as "and" can be given a contrastive stress. The contrast can be implicit rather than explicit. For example, if someone else says, or if I had even thought that someone else might possibly say

    'John or 'Mary should 'go

I might, without any prior context actually spoken, say

    'I think 'John *and* 'Mary should 'go.

Another major function of stress in English is to indicate the syntactic relationships between words or parts of words. There are many noun–verb oppositions, such as "an 'insult, to in'sult; an 'overflow, to over'flow; an 'increase, to in'crease." In all these pairs of words, the noun has the stress on the first syllable and the verb has it on the last. The placement of the stress indicates the syntactic function of the word.

Similar oppositions occur in cases where two word phrases form compounds, such as "a 'walkout, to 'walk 'out; a 'put-on, to 'put 'on; a 'pushover, to 'push 'over." In these cases, there is a stress only on the first element of the compound for the nouns but on both elements for the verbs. Stress also has a syntactic function in distinguishing between a compound noun, such as "a 'hot dog" (a form of food), and an adjective followed by a noun, as in the phrase "a 'hot 'dog" (an overheated animal). Compound nouns have a single stress on the first element, and the adjective plus noun phrases have stresses on both elements.

Many other variations in stress can be associated with the grammatical structure of the words. Table 5.2 exemplifies the kind of alternations that can occur. All the words in the first column have the main stress on the first syllable. When the noun-forming suffix "-y" occurs, the stress in these words shifts to the second syllable. But as you can see in the third column, the adjectival suffix "-ic" moves the stress to the syllable immediately preceding it, which in these words is the third syllable. If you make a sufficiently complex set of rules, it is possible to predict the location of the stress in the majority of English words. There are very few examples of lexical items such as "differ" and "defer" that have the same syntactic function (they are both verbs) but different stress patterns. "Billow" and "below" is another pair of words that illustrates that differences in stress are not always differences between nouns and verbs.

DEGREES OF STRESS

In some longer words, it might seem as if there is more than one degree of stress. For example, say the word "multiplication" and try to tap on the stressed syllables. You will find that you can tap on the first and the fourth syllables of "'multipli'cation." The fourth syllable seems to have a higher degree of stress.

TABLE 5.2	English word stress alternations.	
ˈ__ _ __	_ ˈ__ __	__ _ˈ__ _
diplomat	diplomacy	diplomatic
photograph	photography	photographic
monotone	monotony	monotonic

The same is true of other long words such as "'magnifi'cation" and "'psycho-lin'guistics." But this apparently higher degree of stress on the later syllable only occurs when the word is said in isolation or at the end of a phrase. Try saying a sentence such as "The 'psycholin'guistics 'course was 'fun." If you tap on each stressed syllable, you will find that there is no difference between the first and fourth syllables of "psycholinguistics." If you have a higher degree of stress on the fourth syllable in "psycholinguistics," this word will be given a special emphasis, as though you were contrasting some other psychology course with a psycholinguistics course. The same is true of the word "magnification" in a sentence such as "The de'gree of 'magnifi'cation de'pends on the 'power of the 'lens." The word "magnification" will not have a larger stress on the fourth syllable as long as you do not break the sentence into two parts and leave this word at the end of the first phrase.

Why does it seem as if there are two degrees of stress in a word when it occurs at the end of a phrase or when it is said alone—which is, of course, at the end of a phrase? The answer is that in these circumstances another factor is present. As we will see in the next section, the last stressed syllable in a phrase often accompanies a peak in the intonation. In longer words containing two stresses, the apparent difference in the levels of the first and the second stress is really due to the superimposition of an intonation pattern. When these words occur within a sentence in a position where there are no intonation effects, then there are no differences in the stress levels.

A lower level of stress may also seem to occur in some English words. Compare the words in the two columns in Table 5.3. The words in both columns have the stress on the first syllable. The words in the first column might seem to have a second, weaker, stress on the last syllable as well, but this is not so. The words in the first column differ from those in the second by having a full vowel in the final syllable. This vowel is always longer than the reduced vowel—usually [ə]—in the final syllable of the words in the second column. The result is that there is a difference in the rhythm of the two sets of words. This is due to a difference in the vowels that are present; it is not a difference in stress. There is not

TABLE 5.3	Three-syllable words exemplifying the difference between an unreduced vowel in the final syllable (first column) and a reduced vowel in the final syllable (second column).

'multiply	'multiple
'regulate	'regular
'copulate	'copula
'circulate	'circular
'criticize	'critical
'minimize	'minimal

a strong increase in respiratory activity on the last syllable of the words in the first column. Both sets of words have increases in respiratory activity only on the first syllable.

In summary, we can note that the syllables in an utterance vary in their degrees of prominence, but these variations are not all associated with what we want to call stress. A syllable may be especially prominent because it accompanies a peak in the intonation. We will say that syllables of this kind have a tonic stress. Given this, we can note that English syllables are either stressed or unstressed. If they are stressed, they may or may not be the tonic stress syllables that carry the major pitch change in the tone group. If they are unstressed, they may or may not have a reduced vowel. These relationships are shown in Figure 5.1.

As an aid to understanding the difference between these processes, consider the set of words "explain, explanation, exploit, exploitation." If each of these words is said in its citation form, as a separate tone group, the set will be pronounced as shown here (using a schematic representation of the intonation peak):

Intonation Peak	↑	↑	↑	↑
Stress	ex'plain	'expla'nation	ex'ploit	'exploi'tation
Segments	[ɪkspleɪn	ɛkspləneɪʃən	ɪksplɔit	ɛksplɔiteɪʃən]

Another way of representing some of these same facts is shown in Table 5.4. This table shows just the presence (+) or absence (−) of an intonation peak (a tonic accent), a stress, and a full vowel in each syllable in these four words. Considering first the stress (in the middle row), note that the two-syllable words are marked [+ stress] on the second syllable, and the four-syllable words are marked [+ stress] on both the first and third syllables.

FIGURE 5.1   Degrees of prominence of different syllables in a sentence.

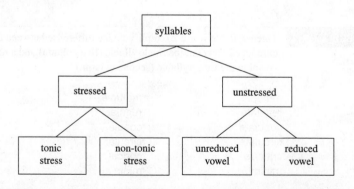

TABLE 5.4	The combination of stress, intonation, and vowel reduction in a number of words.			
	explain	**explanation**	**exploit**	**exploitation**
tonic accent	– +	– – + –	– +	– – + –
stress	– +	+ – + –	– +	+ – + –
full vowel	– +	+ – + –	– +	+ + + –

As you can see by comparing the middle row with the top row, the last [+ stress] syllable in each word has been marked [+ tonic accent]. There is a [+] in the third row if the vowel is not reduced. Note that the difference between "explanation" and "exploitation" is that the second syllable of "explanation" has a reduced vowel but this syllable in "exploitation" has a full vowel. As we saw in the previous chapter, there are a number of vowels that do not occur in reduced syllables. Furthermore, the actual phonetic quality of the vowel in a reduced syllable varies considerably from dialect to dialect. I have transcribed the first vowel in "explain" as [ɪ] because that is the form I use. But other dialects may have [ə] or some other quality.

Some other books do not make the distinctions described here, maintaining instead that there are several levels of stress in English. The greatest degree of stress is called stress level one, the next is level two, the next level is three, a lower level still is level four, and so on. Note that in this system a smaller degree of stress has a larger number.

You can easily convert our system into a multilevel stress system by adding the number of [+] marks on a syllable in a table of the sort just used and subtracting this number from four. If there are three [+] marks, it is stress level one; if two, stress level two; if one, stress level three; and if none, it is stress level four. Try this for yourself with the data in Table 5.4. Writing the stress levels as superscripts after the vowels, you will find that "explanation" and "exploitation" are "e^{2}xpla^{4}na^{1}tio^{4}n" (a pattern of 2414) and "e^{2}xploi^{3}ta^{1}tio^{4}n" (a pattern of 2314).

I personally do not consider it useful to think of stress in terms of a multilevel system. Descriptions of this sort are not in accord with the phonological facts. But as it is so commonly said that there are many levels of stress in English, I thought I should explain how these terms are used. In this book, however, we will continue to regard stress as something that either does or does not occur on a syllable in English, and we will view vowel reduction and intonation as separate processes.

We can sometimes predict by rules whether a vowel will be reduced to [ə] or not. For example, we can formalize a rule stating that [ɔɪ] never reduces. But other cases are usually a matter of how recently the word came into common use. Factors of this sort seem to be the reason why there are reduced vowels at the end of "postman," "bacon," and "gentleman," but not at the end of "mailman," "moron," and "superman."

SENTENCE STRESS

The stresses that can occur on words sometimes become modified when the words are part of sentences. The most frequent modification is the dropping of some of the stresses. There is a stress on the first syllable of each of the words "Mary, younger, brother, wanted, fifty, chocolate, peanuts" when these words are said in isolation. But there are normally fewer stresses when they occur in a sentence such as "Mary's younger brother wanted fifty chocolate peanuts." Tap with your finger at each stressed syllable while you say this phrase in a normal conversational style. You will probably find it quite natural to tap on the first syllables marked with a preceding stress mark in "'Mary's younger 'brother wanted 'fifty chocolate 'peanuts." Thus the first syllables of "younger," "wanted," and "chocolate" are pronounced without stresses (but with their full vowel qualities).

The same kind of phenomenon can be demonstrated with monosyllabic words. Say the sentence "The big brown bear ate ten white mice." It sounds unnatural if you put a stress on every word. Most people will say "The 'big brown 'bear ate 'ten white 'mice." As a general rule, English tries to avoid having stresses too close together. Very often, stresses on alternate words are dropped in sentences where they would otherwise come too near one another.

The tendency to avoid having stresses too close together may cause the stress on a polysyllabic word to be on one syllable in one sentence and on another in another sentence. Consider the word "clarinet" in "He had a 'clarinet 'solo" and in "He 'plays the clari'net." The stress is on the first or the third syllable, depending on the position of the other stresses in the sentence. Similar shifts occur in phrases such as "'Vice-president 'Jones" versus "'Jones, the vice-'president." Numbers such as "14, 15, 16" are stressed on the first syllable when counting, but not in phrases such as "She's 'only six'teen." Read all these phrases with the stresses as indicated and check that it is natural to tap on the stressed syllables. Then try tapping on the indicated syllables while you read the next paragraph.

'Stresses in 'English 'tend to re'cur at 'regular 'intervals of 'time. (') It's 'often 'perfectly 'possible to 'tap on the 'stresses in 'time with a 'metronome. (') The 'rhythm can 'even be 'said to de'termine the 'length of the 'pause between 'phrases. (') An 'extra 'tap can be 'put in the 'silence, (') as 'shown by the 'marks with'in the pa'rentheses. (')

Of course, not all sentences are as regular as those in the preceding paragraph. I said that stresses *tend* to recur at regular intervals. It would be quite untrue to say that there is always an equal interval between stresses in English. It is just that English has a number of processes that act together to maintain the rhythm.

I have already mentioned two of these processes. First, we saw that some words that might have been stressed are nevertheless often unstressed so as to prevent too many stresses coming together. Thus, to give another example, both "wanted" and "pretty" are stressed in "She 'wanted a 'pretty 'parrot," but they may not be in "My 'aunt wanted 'ten pretty 'parrots." Second, we saw that some words have variable stress; compare "the 'unknown 'man" with "the 'man is un'known."

We can also consider some of the facts mentioned in the previous chapter as part of this same tendency to reduce the variation in the interval between stresses. We saw that the vowel in "speed" is longer than that in "speedy," and this in turn is longer than that in "speedily." This can be interpreted as a tendency to minimize the variation in the length of words containing only a single stress, so that adjacent stresses remain much the same distance apart.

Taking all these facts together, along with others that will not be dealt with here, it is as if there were a conspiracy in English to maintain a regular rhythm. However, this conspiracy is not strong enough to completely override the irregularities caused by variations in the number and type of unstressed syllables. In a sentence such as "The 'red 'bird flew 'speedily 'home," the interval between the first and second stresses will be far less than that between the third and fourth. Stresses tend to recur at regular intervals. But the sound pattern of English does not make this an overriding necessity, adjusting the lengths of syllables so as to enforce complete regularity. The interval between stresses is affected by the number of syllables within the stress group, by the number and type of vowels and consonants within each syllable, and by other factors such as the variations in emphasis that are given to each word.

INTONATION

Listen to the pitch of the voice while someone says a sentence. You will find that it is changing continuously. The difference between speaking and singing is that in singing you hold a given note for a noticeable length of time and then jump to the pitch of the next note. But when one is speaking, there are no steady-state pitches. Throughout every syllable in a normal conversational utterance, the pitch is going up or down. (Try talking with steady-state pitches and notice how odd it sounds.)

The intonation of a sentence is the pattern of pitch changes that occurs. The part of a sentence over which a particular pattern extends is called an **intonational phrase.** A short sentence forming a single intonational phrase is shown in (1). The line above the sentence shows the pitch changes that occurred when this sentence was produced by a speaker of American English (see Sources at the end of the book for details). The positioning of the individual words above this line gives an indication of their relative timing. The sentence is shown below the line in ordinary spelling, but with IPA stress marks added and one syllable preceded by an asterisk. Within the intonational phrase, each stressed syllable has a minor pitch increase; but there is usually a single syllable that stands out because it carries the major pitch change. A syllable of this kind is called the **tonic syllable** and will be marked in this section by an asterisk. In sentence (1), the first syllable of "area" is the tonic syllable, and, as you can see, it has the greatest pitch change. Each of the stress syllables is accompanied by a small increase in pitch, but the major pitch movement starts on the first syllable of the last word.

(1)

We 'know a 'man in our *area

The tonic accent usually occurs on the last stressed syllable in a tone group. But it may occur earlier, if some word requires emphasis.

(2)

We 'know a *millionaire in our 'area

The pitch changes that start on the tonic syllable may be continued on the following syllables. In the previous examples, the fall in pitch continues (but at a slower rate and with a small increase on the stressed syllable) until the end of the sentence.

Sometimes there are two or more intonational phrases within an utterance. When this happens the first one ends in a small rise, which we may call a continuation rise. It indicates that there is more to come, the speaker has not yet completed the utterance.

(3)

I *worry when I'm a 'way, ‖ *know ing you're un 'well

The beginning of a new intonational phrase may be marked, as in (3), by ‖. The pitch changes that begin on the tonic syllable in the first intonational phrase continue only until the beginning of the next phrase.

There is no syntactic unit exactly corresponding to an intonational phrase. When speaking slowly in a formal style, a speaker may choose to break a sentence up into a large number of phrases. The way in which a speaker breaks up a sentence depends largely on what that person considers to be the important information points in the sentence. An intonational phrase is a unit of information rather than a syntactically defined unit. It is only in rapid conversational style that there is likely to be one intonational phrase per sentence.

It is also usually impossible to predict which syllable will be the tonic syllable in an intonational phrase. Again, it depends on what the speaker considers to be important. In general, new information is more likely to receive a tonic accent than material that has already been mentioned. The topic of a sentence is less likely to receive the tonic accent than the comment that is made on that topic. Thus, if I were telling someone about lions, I might say:

(4)

A   'lion   is   a   * mammal

In this case, the topic of the sentence is a lion, and the comment on that topic is that it is a mammal. But if I were discussing mammals, and considering all the animals that fitted into that category, I might say:

(5)

A   *lion   is   a   'mammal

Various pitch changes are possible within the tonic accent. In sentences (1) through (5) the intonation may be simply described as having a falling contour, except for the continuation rise in the middle of (3). Another possibility is that the tonic syllable is the start of an upward glide of pitch. This kind of pitch change, which we will refer to as a rising contour, is typical in questions requiring the answer "yes" or "no," such as:

(6)

Will   you   'mail   me   my   *money?

As with falling contours, the syllable that starts the rising contour is not necessarily the last stressed syllable in an intonational phrase. It occurs earlier in:

(7)

Will   you   *mail   me   my   'money?

Now consider what you do in questions that cannot be answered "yes" or "no," such as:

(8)

'when   will   you   'mail   my   *money?

Of course, there are many possible ways of saying this sentence. But probably the most neutral is with a falling contour starting on the final stressed syllable. Questions that begin with *wh*–question words, such as "where, when, who, why, what," are usually pronounced with a falling intonation.

As we saw in (3), a small rising intonation occurs in the middle of sentences, a typical circumstance being at the end of a clause, as, to give another example, in:

(9) When you are *winning ‖ I will run a *way

A list of items also has a continuation rise:

(10) We knew 'Anna 'Lenny 'Mary and *Nora

Note that yes–no questions can nearly always be reworded so that they fit into this pattern:

(11) Will you mail me my money, or not?

It is useful to distinguish between two kinds of rising intonation. In the one, which typically occurs in yes–no questions, there is a large upward movement of pitch. In the other, the continuation rise that usually occurs in the middle of sentences, there is a smaller upward movement. These two intonations are often used contrastively. Thus, if there is a low rising intonation on an utterance, it means that there is something more to come. I might have a slightly rising intonation in:

(12) Yes

(13) Go on

These are the kinds of utterances one makes when listening to someone telling a story. They mean, "I hear you; please continue." If I have a larger rise in pitch and say:

(14) Yes

(15) Go on

it means, "Did you say 'Yes'?" or "Did you say 'Go on'?" It should be noted, however, that people are not entirely consistent in the way they use this difference in intonation.

Both rising and falling intonations can occur within the same tonic accent. If you tell me something that surprises me, I might have a distinct fall on the tonic syllable followed by a rise on the remainder of the intonational phrase:

(16) Your *mom will 'marry a 'law yer?

There are also distinct intonation patterns that one can use when addressing or calling someone. If I am answering a question such as "Who is that over there?" I will have a falling intonation over much of my pitch range, as shown in (17). However, if I am trying to attract someone's attention, I might use a falling intonation, but with only half the range of the full fall, as in (18). Calling to someone in this way can even be done as a chant, with comparatively steady pitches after the first rise, as in (19).

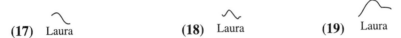

(17) Laura   **(18)** Laura   **(19)** Laura

We can sum up many differences in intonation by referring to the different ways in which a name can be said, particularly if the name is long enough to show the pitch curve reasonably fully. In curves (20) through (24), I have included dotted lines showing part of a pitch scale, so as to make comparisons easier. (It is actually an octave, 100 Hz to 200 Hz.) These curves show different pronunciations of the name "A'melia" (not written along the curve, as in the previous examples). (20) is a simple statement, equivalent to "Her name is Amelia." (21) is the question, equivalent to "Did you say Amelia?" (22) is the form with the continuation rise, which might be used when addressing Amelia, indicating that it is her turn to speak. (23) is a question expressing surprise, equivalent to "Was it really Amelia who did that?" Lastly, (24) is the form for a strong reaction, reprimanding Amelia.

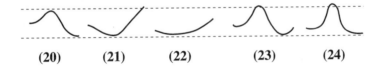

(20)   **(21)**   **(22)**   **(23)**   **(24)**

TARGET TONES

We have been considering intonation in terms of tunes that apply over whole sentences or phrases, but there are a number of other ways in which intonation can be described. Instead of considering the shape of the curve over a whole phrase, we could describe the intonation in terms of a sequence of high (H) and low (L) target pitches. When people talk they aim to make either a high or low pitch on a stressed syllable and to move upward or downward as they go into or come away from this target. One system for representing pitch changes of this kind is known as **ToBI,** standing for Tone and Break Indices. In this system, target tones H* and L* (called H star and L star) are typically written on a line (called a tier) above the segmental symbols, and put immediately above the stressed syllables. A high tone, H*, can be preceded by a closely attached low pitch, written L + H*, so that the listener hears a sharply rising pitch. Similarly

L* can be followed by a closely attached high pitch, L* + H, so that the listener hears a scoop upward in pitch after the low pitch at the beginning of the stressed syllable. Sometimes a stressed syllable can be high but nevertheless contain a small step down of the pitch. This is known as High plus downstepped High, and written H + !H*, with the exclamation mark indicating the small downstep in pitch. In special circumstances, to be discussed at the end of this section, a downstepped high syllable, !H*, can itself be a pitch accent. There are therefore six possibilities, shown in Table 5.5, that can be regarded as the possible pitch accents that occur in English.

The last pitch accent in a phrase is called the nuclear pitch accent. The ToBI system allows the phrase to be marked by an additional tone after the nuclear pitch accent. This tone, called the phrase accent, is written H– (H minus) or L– (L minus). Finally there is a boundary tone, which is marked H% or L%, depending on whether the phrase ends on a rising or falling pitch. In this framework all English intonations consist of a sequence of tones formed as shown in Table 5.5. As you can see exemplified by the first two columns, there may or may not be a number of pitch accents on stressed syllables before the nuclear pitch accent. The third column shows the nuclear pitch accents, one of which must always be present in a phrase. The part of the intonational phrase after the nuclear pitch accent must be high or low, and there must be a high or low boundary tone.

The ToBI system also allows us to transcribe the strength of the boundary between words by means of a number. This is called a Break Index giving the name ToBI (To and Break Indices) to this transcription system. If there is no

TABLE 5.5	The ToBI system for characterizing English intonations. Each intonational phrase (tone group) must have one item from each of the last three columns, and it may also have additional pitch accents marked on other stressed syllables, as shown in the first two (or could be more) columns. The parenthesized accent, (!H*), will be explained at the end of this section.

Optional Pre-Nuclear Pitch Accents on Stressed Syllables	Nuclear Pitch Accent	Phrase Accent	Boundary	Tone
H*	H*	H*		
L*	L*	L*		
L + H*	L + H*	L + H*	L–	H%
L* + H	L* + H	L* + H		
H + !H*	H + !H*	H + !H*	H–	L%
(!H*)	(!H*)	(!H*)		

break, as, for example, in "you're" (which is usually identical with "your"), the Break Index can be marked as 0. This is a useful way of showing that a phrase such as "to Mexico" is usually pronounced as if it were a single word—there's no added break in "to Mexico" as compared with "tomorrow." Intervals between words are classified as having Break Index 1 (although, to my mind, there is usually nothing that can be called a break between words). Higher levels of break indices show, roughly speaking, greater pauses. A Break Index of 3 is usual between clauses that form intermediate intonational phrases, and a Break Index of 4 occurs between larger intonational phrases, such as whole sentences.

The last five intonation curves we considered would be transcribed in a ToBI transcription as follows (without indicating the Break Indices, which would always be a 4 at the end of each of these utterances):

(20) A'melia. Simple statement in response to "What is her name?"	Tone tier Segmental tier	[H* L–L%] [ə m iː l iː ə]
(21) A'melia? A question, equivalent to "Did you say Amelia?"	Tone tier Segmental tier	[L* H–H%] [ə m iː l iː ə]
(22) A'melia— Addressing Amelia, indicating that it is her turn to speak.	Tone tier Segmental tier	[L* L–H%] [ə m iː l iː ə]
(23) A'melia!? A question indicating surprise.	Tone tier Segmental tier	[L + H* L–H%] [ə m iː l iː ə]
(24) A'melia!! A strong reaction, reprimanding Amelia.	Tone tier Segmental tier	[L + H* L–L%] [ə m iː l iː ə]

The ToBI transcription for (20), [H* L– L%], is typical of a simple statement with only one stressed syllable receiving a pitch accent. The part of the phrase after the nuclear accent is low, and the phrase ends with a low boundary tone. Similarly, the transcription for (21), [L* H– H%], is a typical tune for a question that can be answered by "yes" or "no," which ends with a fairly large pitch rise. At the end of the next phrase, (22), there is a smaller rise of the kind that occurs in an unfinished utterance, or in a list of words such as we exemplified in (10), ". . . Anna, Lenny, Mary and . . . ." The way in which ToBI separates the large pitch rise in (21) —the question rise—from the smaller rise in (22)—the continuation rise—is by making the phrase tone L–, so that (22) has the tune [L* L– H%] instead of [L* H– H%] as in (21). The low phrase tone prevents the final high boundary from being so high. The stressed syllables of the final two tunes begin with an L, ensuring that the H* indicates a sharp rise from a low pitch. Thus in (23) we have [L + H* L– H%], with a low phrase tone and a small pitch rise at the end, much as in (22). Finally (24), [L + H* L– L%], is like (23) in beginning with a strong rise, but it ends with a low boundary tone.

The simple statements, questions, and other intonations that we discussed earlier can be transcribed in a similar way.

(1) We know a 'man in our 'area.
Simple statement.

Tone tier	[	H*	H*L–L%]
Segmental tier	[wiː nou ə mæn m ɑːr eriə		]

(6) Will you 'mail me my 'money?
Simple yes–no question.

Tone tier	[	H*	L*H–H%]
Segmental tier	[wɪl juː meɪl miː maɪ mʌni		]

(9) When you are 'winning, 'I will run a'way.
Two clauses with a Break Index 4.

Break Index	[	1 1 1	4 1	1	1	4]		
Tone tier	[	H*L–H%H*		H*LL%]				
Segmental tier	[wen juː ɑː wɪnɪŋ	aɪ wɪl rʌn əweɪ]						

The Break Indices are shown in (9). At the end of the first intonational phrase there is a continuation rise represented by L– H%, and a break index 4. All the words are closely joined together, so in each case the Break Index is 1.

Finally we must consider how to transcribe another fact about English intonation (which also applies to many other languages). The pitch in most sentences has a tendency to drift down. Earlier, when discussing stress, we considered the sentence "Mary's younger 'brother wanted 'fifty chocolate 'peanuts," with stresses on alternate words, "Mary's," " brother," "fifty," and "peanuts." If you say this sentence with these stresses, you will find that there is an H* pitch accent on each of the stressed syllables, but each of these high pitches is usually a little lower than the preceding high pitch. This phenomenon is known as **downdrift.** We can represent this in the transcription by marking the H* pitch accents as being downstepped, a notion that was mentioned earlier in connection with a fall from a high pitch within a syllable. In Table 5.5 we used a small raised exclamation mark, !. We can indicate that each of the H* tones is a little lower than the preceding one by transcribing them as **downstepped** highs, ! H*, in the tone tier for this sentence:

[H* !H* !H* !H* L–L%]
(25) Mary's younger brother wanted fifty chocolate peanuts.

Note that successive H* pitch accents do not have to be downstepped. If I had wanted to put a very slight emphasis on "brother," indicating that it was Mary's younger brother, not her younger sister, who had this peculiar desire, then I could have made the downstepping begin at "fifty" and said:

[H* H* !H* !H* L–L%]
(26) Mary's younger brother wanted fifty chocolate peanuts.

The ToBI system is a way of characterizing English intonation in terms of a limited set of symbols—a set of six possible pitch accents including a downstep mark, two possible phrase accents, two possible boundary tones, and four possible Break Indices, going from 1 (close connection) to 4 (a boundary between intonation phrases). It was designed specifically for English intonations, but, with a few modifications, it may be appropriate for other languages as well.

EXERCISES

A List the strong and weak forms of ten words not mentioned in this chapter. For each word, transcribe a short utterance illustrating the weak form (as in Table 5.1).

Word	Strong Form	Weak Form	Example of Weak Form
_____	_____	_____	_____
_____	_____	_____	_____
_____	_____	_____	_____
_____	_____	_____	_____
_____	_____	_____	_____
_____	_____	_____	_____
_____	_____	_____	_____
_____	_____	_____	_____
_____	_____	_____	_____
_____	_____	_____	_____

B Give two new examples of each of the following kinds of assimilations, one of the examples involving a change within a word, the other involving a change across word boundaries. (Even if you yourself do not say assimilations of the kind illustrated, make up plausible examples. I myself have heard all the examples given.)

A change from an alveolar to a bilabial consonant.

input	[ɪmpʊt]	*Saint Paul's*	[sm̩ˈpɔːlz]
_____	_____	_____	_____

A change from an alveolar consonant to a dental consonant.

tenth	[tɛn̪θ]	*In this*	[ɪn̪ ðɪs]
_____	_____	_____	_____

A change from an alveolar consonant to a velar consonant.

synchronous   [ˈsɪŋkrənəs]   *within groups*   [wɪðˈɪŋ gruːps]

————————— ————————— ————————— —————————

A change from a voiceless consonant to a voiced consonant.

catty   [ˈkædi]   *sit up*   [sɪˈdʌp]

————————— ————————— ————————— —————————

C Give five more examples of assimilation. Choose examples as different as possible from any that have been given before.

—————————————   [—————————————]

—————————————   [—————————————]

—————————————   [—————————————]

—————————————   [—————————————]

—————————————   [—————————————]

D Make up pairs of phrases or sentences that show how each of the following words can have two different stress patterns.

Example: continental
It's a ˈcontinental ˈbreakfast.
She's ˈvery contiˈnental.

afternoon

—————————————————————————————————

—————————————————————————————————

artificial

—————————————————————————————————

—————————————————————————————————

diplomatic

—————————————————————————————————

—————————————————————————————————

absentminded

_____

_____

New York

_____

_____

E Fill in plus and minus signs so as to indicate which syllables in the following table have tonic accents, which have stress, and which have full vowels. You may find it useful to refer back to Table 5.4.

	computation	**compute**	**inclination**	**incline** (verb)
tonic accent				
stress				
full vowel				

F About 100 years ago, the following words had stress as shown. Some of them still do for some people. But many of them (in my speech, all of them) are stressed differently nowadays. Transcribe these words and show the stress on each of them in your own speech. Then state a general rule describing this tendency for the position of the stress to change to a particular syllable.

an'chovy _____

ab'domen_____

'applicable _____

'controversy_____

'nomenclature _____

tra'chea _____

eti'quette _____

re'plica_____

va'gary_____

blas'phemous_____

a'cumen _____

Rule: _____

_____

G List three more sets of words showing the stress alternations of the kind shown in Table 5.2.

'photograph   pho'tography   photo'graphic

_____   _____   _____

_____   _____   _____

_____   _____   _____

H Indicate the stress and intonation patterns that might occur in the situations described for the following utterances. Draw curves indicative of the pitch rather than using ToBI symbols.

1. "Can you pass me that book?" (said politely to a friend)

2. "Where were you last night?" (angry father to daughter)

3. "Must it be typewritten?" (polite question)

4. "Who is the one in the corner?" (excitedly, to a friend)

5. "He's very nice . . ." (but I don't like him)

I Make a segmental transcription and also show the Tone Tier with a ToBI transcription of the following utterances for which the pitch curves have been drawn in this chapter.

(2) We know a millionaire in our area.

(4) A lion is a mammal.

(5) A lion is a mammal.

(7) Will you mail me my money?

(8) When will you mail me my money?

(10) We knew Anna, Mary, Lenny, and Nora.

PERFORMANCE EXERCISES

A Pronounce the following phrases exactly as they have been transcribed, with all the assimilations and elisions. (Each of these transcriptions is a record of an utterance that I have actually heard in normal conversations between educated speakers.)

"What are you doing?"	[ˈwɑdʒəˈduɪn]
"I can inquire."	[ˈaɪkŋ ŋ ˈkwaɪə]
"Did you eat yet?"	[ˈdʒitjɛʔ]
"I don't believe him."	[aɪˈdoʊmbəˈliːvɪm]
"We ought to have come."	[wiˈɔːtʃˈkʌm]

B Working with a partner, try to transcribe the intonation of a few sentences. You may find it difficult to repeat a sentence over and over again with the same intonation. If you do, try to work from a tape recording. In any case, write down the sentence and the intonation you intend to produce. Practice saying it in this way before you say it to your partner.

C Take turns saying nonsense words such as those shown below, transcribing them, and comparing transcriptions.

ʃkeɪʒdʒˈminʒe

ˈʔɑŋkliθuntθ

sfeˈeʔɛm̩ɑ

grɔɪpstˈbraɪgz

D Also make up lists of words for improving your memory span. These words are more difficult if the stress is varied and if the sounds are mainly of the same class (stops, front vowels, voiceless fricatives, etc.).

tipeˈkiketiˈpe

θɔɪˈsaɪθaʊˈfɔɪʃaʊθaʊ

ˈmonɑŋuˈŋonɔmɑ

woˈʔɔɪlaʊrɑˈrɔlojɔ

bəbdɪgˈbɛdgɪbdɛdˈbɛbdəd

6

AIRSTREAM MECHANISMS AND PHONATION TYPES

In order to describe the various languages of the world, we need to consider the total range of the phonetic capabilities of humans. There are several ways in which the sets of terms that we have been using to describe English must now be enlarged. In the first place, all English sounds are initiated by the action of lung air going outward; other languages may use additional ways of producing an airstream. Second, all English sounds can be categorized as voiced or voiceless; in some languages, additional states of the glottis are used. This chapter surveys the general phonetic categories needed to describe the airstream mechanisms and phonation types that occur in other languages. Subsequent chapters will survey other ways in which languages differ.

AIRSTREAM MECHANISMS

Air coming out of the lungs is the source of power in nearly all speech sounds. When this body of air is moved, we say that there is a **pulmonic airstream mechanism.** The lungs are spongelike tissues within a cavity formed by the rib cage and the diaphragm. When the diaphragm (a dome-shaped muscle) contracts, it enlarges the lung cavity so that air flows into the lungs. The air can be pushed out of the lungs by a downward movement of the rib cage or an upward movement of the diaphragm, resulting from a contraction of the abdominal muscles.

In the description of most sounds, we take it for granted that the pulmonic airstream mechanism is the source of power. But in the case of stop consonants, other airstream mechanisms may be involved. Stops that use only an egressive, or outward-moving, pulmonic airstream are called **plosives.** Stops made with other airstream mechanisms will be specified by other terms.

In some languages, speech sounds are produced by moving different bodies of air. If you make a glottal stop, so that the air in the lungs is contained below the glottis, then the air in the vocal tract itself will form a body of air that can be moved. An upward movement of the closed glottis will move this air out of the mouth. A downward movement of the closed glottis will cause air to be sucked into the mouth. When either of these actions occurs, there is said to be a **glottalic airstream mechanism.**

An egressive glottalic airstream mechanism occurs in many languages. Hausa, the principal language of Northern Nigeria, uses this mechanism in the formation of a velar stop that contrasts with the voiceless and voiced velar stops [k, g]. The movements of the vocal organs are shown in Figure 6.1. These are estimated, not drawn on the basis of x-rays.

As far as I can tell, in Hausa the velar closure and the glottal closure are formed at about the same time. Then, when the vocal folds are tightly together, the larynx is pulled upward, about 1 cm. In this way it acts like a piston, compressing the air in the pharynx. The compressed air is released by lowering the back of the tongue while the glottal stop is maintained. This produces a sound with a quality different from that in an English [k]. Very shortly after the release of the velar closure, the glottal stop is released and the voicing for the following vowel begins.

Stops made with a glottalic egressive airstream mechanism are called **ejec-tives.** The diacritic indicating an ejective is an apostrophe [’] placed after a symbol. The Hausa sound I have just described is a velar ejective, symbolized [k’], as in the Hausa word for "song" [wák’àː]. (The accents over the vowels indicate significant pitches, which we will disregard for the moment.) Other languages have ejectives made at other places of articulation. Some languages also

---

FIGURE 6.1   The sequence of events that occurs in a glottalic egressive velar stop [k’].

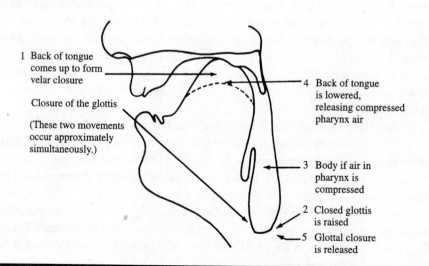

1 Back of tongue comes up to form velar closure

Closure of the glottis

(These two movements occur approximately simultaneously.)

4 Back of tongue is lowered, releasing compressed pharynx air

3 Body if air in pharynx is compressed

2 Closed glottis is raised

5 Glottal closure is released

use this mechanism in the production of fricatives as well as stops. Of course, a fricative made in this way can continue only for a short length of time, as there is a comparatively small amount of air that can be moved by raising the closed glottis. Ejectives of different kinds occur in a wide variety of languages, including American Indian languages, African languages, and languages spoken in the Caucasus. Table 6.1 gives examples of ejectives and contrasting sounds made with a pulmonic airstream mechanism in Lakhota, an American Indian language. The sounds of Lakhota differ from those of English in many ways in addition to having contrastive ejectives. We will discuss the unfamiliar symbols in this table later in this book.

Some people make ejectives at the ends of words in English, particularly in sentence final position. I have heard people say words such as "bike" with a glottal stop accompanying the final [k]. If the velar stop is released while the glottal stop is still being held, a weak ejective may be heard. See if you can superimpose a glottal stop on a final [k] and produce an ejective. Now try to make a slightly more forceful ejective stop. By now you should be fully able to make a glottal stop in a sequence such as [aʔa], so the next step is to learn to raise and lower the glottis. You can recognize what it feels like to raise the glottis by singing a very low note and then moving to the position for singing the highest note that you possibly can. If you do this silently, you will find it easier to concentrate on feeling the muscular sensations involved. It will also help you to realize what you are doing if you put your fingers on your throat above the larynx so that you can feel the movements. Repeat (silently) this sequence—low note, very high note—until you have thoroughly experienced the sensation of raising your glottis. Now try to make this movement with a closed glottis. There will, of course, be no sounds produced by these movements alone.

The next step is to learn to superimpose this movement on a velar stop. Say the sequence [ɑk]. Then say this sequence again, very slowly, holding your tongue in the position for the [k] closure at the end for a second or so. Now say it again, and while maintaining the [k] closure, do three things: (1) make a glottal stop; (2) if you can, raise your larynx; and (3) release the [k] closure while

TABLE 6.1	Contrasts involving ejective stops in Lakhota. An ejective mechanism is shown by a following apostrophe.		
Ejective	p'o "foggy"	t'uʃɛ "at all costs"	k'u "to give"
Voiceless Unaspirated	paɣõ t̪a "mallard"	t̪uwa "who"	kah "that"
Voiceless + Velar Fricative	pˣa "bitter"	t̪ˣawa "own"	kˣant̪a "plum"

maintaining the glottal stop. Don't worry about step 2 too much. The important thing to concentrate on is having a glottal stop and a velar closure going on at the same time and then releasing the velar closure *before* releasing the glottal stop. The release of the velar closure will produce only a very small noise, but it will be an ejective [k'].

Next, try to produce a vowel after the ejective. This time start from the sequence [ɑkɑ]. Say this sequence slowly, with a long [k] closure. Then, during this closure, make a glottal stop and raise the larynx. Then release the [k] closure while still maintaining the glottal stop. Finally, release the glottal stop and follow it with a vowel. You should have produced something like [ɑk'ʔɑ]. When this sequence becomes more fluent, so that there is very little pause between the release of the velar closure and the release of the glottal stop, it can be considered simply an ejective followed by a vowel—[ɑk'ɑ]. There is, of course, still a glottal stop after the release of the velar stop and before the vowel, but unless it is exceptionally long, we may consider it to be implied by the symbol for the ejective.

Another way of learning to produce an ejective is to start from the usual American (and common British) pronunciation of "button" as [ˈbʌʔn̩]. Try starting to say "button" but finishing with another vowel [ʌ] instead of the nasal [n]. If you make sure that you do include the glottal stop form of / t /, the result will probably be [ˈbʌʔtʌ]. If you say this slowly, you should be able to convert it first into [ˈbʌʔt'ʔʌ], then into [ˈbʌt'ʌ], and finally, altering the stress, into [bʌˈt'ʌ].

You should eventually be able to produce sequences such as [p'ɑ, t'ɑ, k'ɑ] and perhaps [tʃ'ɑ, s'ɑ] as well. Practice producing ejectives before, after, and between a wide variety of vowels. You should also try to say the Lakhota words in Table 6.1. But if you find ejectives difficult to produce, don't worry. Many people take years to learn to say them. Just keep practicing.

It is also possible to use a downward movement of the larynx to suck air inward. Stops made with an ingressive glottalic airstream mechanism are called **implosives.** In the production of implosives, the downward moving larynx is not usually completely closed. The air in the lungs is still being pushed out, and some of it passes between the vocal folds, keeping them in motion so that the sound is voiced. Figure 6.2 shows the movements in a voiced bilabial implosive of a kind that occurs in Sindhi (an Indo-Aryan language spoken in India and Pakistan). Implosives sometimes occur as allophones in English, particularly in emphatic articulations of bilabial stops as in "absolutely *billions* and *billions*."

In all the implosives I have measured, the articulatory closure—in this case, the lips coming together—occurs first. The downward movement of the glottis, which occurs next, is like that of a piston that would cause a reduction of the pressure of the air in the oral tract. But it is a leaky piston in that the air in the lungs continues to flow through the glottis. As a result, the pressure of the air in the oral tract is not affected very much. (In a plosive [b] there is, of course, an increase in

FIGURE 6.2   Estimated sequence of events in a Sindhi bilabial implosive [ɓ].

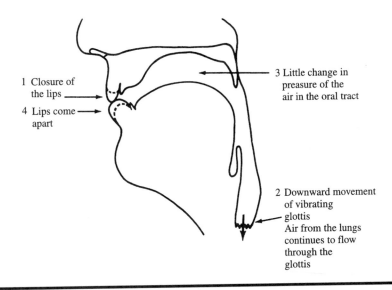

1 Closure of
the lips

4 Lips come
apart

3 Little change in
preasure of the
air in the oral tract

2 Downward movement
of vibrating
glottis
Air from the lungs
continues to flow
through the
glottis

the pressure of the air in the vocal tract.) When the articulatory closure is released, there is neither an explosive nor, in a literal sense, an implosive action. Instead, the peculiar quality of the sound arises from the complex changes in the shape of the vocal tract and in the vibratory pattern of the vocal folds.

In many languages, such as Sindhi and several African and American Indian languages, implosives contrast with plosives. However, in some languages (for example, Vietnamese), implosives are simply variants (allophones) of voiced plosives and not in contrast with those sounds. The top line of Table 6.2 illustrates implosives in Sindhi. The symbols for implosives have a small hook on the top of the regular symbol. For the moment, we will consider only the first and last columns in Table 6.2, which illustrate [ɓ] and [ɠ], the bilabial and velar implosives respectively, in the first row, contrasting with the regular plosives [b] and [g] in the second row. Sindhi has additional places of articulation illustrated in the second, third, and fourth columns, which we will consider in Chapter 7. The lower rows in the table illustrate phonation types that we will consider later in this chapter.

I do not know any simple way of teaching people to make implosives. Some people can learn to make them just by imitating their instructor; others can't. (I, incidentally, was one of the latter group. I did not learn to make implosives until nearly the end of a year studying phonetics.) The best suggestion I can make is to start from a fully voiced plosive. Say [aba], making sure that the voicing continues throughout the closure. Now say this sequence slowly, making the closure

TABLE 6.2		Contrasts involving implosives and plosives with different phonation types in Sindhi.		
ɓəni		ɗɪnu	ɟ̢ətu	ɠənʊ
"field"		"festival"	"illiterate"	"handle"
bənu	dəru	ɖoru	ɟətu	gunu
"forest"	"door"	"you run"	"illiterate"	"quality"
pənu	təru	ʈənu	cətu	kənu
"leaf"	"bottom"	"ton"	"to destroy"	"ear"
pʰənu	tʰəru	ʈʰəɟu	cʰətu	kʰə ɳ ʊ
"snake hood"	(district name)	"thug, cheat"	"crown"	"you lift"
bʱanu	dʱəru	ɖʱəɟu	ɟʱətu	gʱənɪ
"manure"	"trunk"	"bull"	"a grab"	"excess"

last as long as you can while maintaining strong vocal fold vibrations. Release the closure (open the lips) *before* the voicing stops. If you put your fingers on your throat above the larynx while doing this, you will probably be able to feel the larynx moving down during the closure.

There are straightforward mechanical reasons why the larynx moves down in these circumstances. In order to maintain voicing throughout a [b], air must continue to flow through the glottis. But it cannot continue to flow for very long because, while the articulatory position of [b] is being held, the pressure of the air in the vocal tract is continually increasing. In order to keep the vocal folds vibrating, the air in the lungs must be at an appreciably higher pressure than the air in the vocal tract so that there is a pressure drop across the glottis. One of the ways of maintaining the pressure drop across the glottis is to lower the larynx and thus increase the space available in the vocal tract. Consequently, there is a natural tendency when saying a long [b] to lower the larynx. If you try to make a long, fully voiced [b] very forcibly, but open your lips before the voicing stops, you may end up producing implosive [ɓ]. You can check your progress in learning to produce implosives by using a straw in a drink. Hold a straw immersed in a liquid between your lips while you say [ɑɓɑ]. You should see the liquid move upward in the straw during the [ɓ].

Historically, languages seem to develop implosives from plosives that have become more and more voiced. As I mentioned earlier, in many languages, voiced implosives are simply allophones of voiced plosives. Often, as in Vietnamese, these languages have voiced plosives that have to be fully voiced in order to keep them distinct from two other sets of plosives that we will discuss in the next section. In languages such as Sindhi, for which we have good evidence of the earlier stages of the language, we can clearly see that the present implosives grew out of older voiced plosives in this way; and the present contrasting voiced plosives are due to later influences of neighboring languages.

There is one other airstream mechanism that is used in a few languages. This is the mechanism that is used in producing **clicks,** such as the interjection expressing disapproval that novelists write "tut-tut" or "tsk-tsk." Another type of click is commonly used to show approval or to signal horses to go faster. Yet another click in common use is the gentle, pursed-lips type of kiss that one might drop on one's grandmother's cheek. Clicks occur in words (in addition to interjections or nonlinguistic gestures) in several African languages. Zulu, for example, has a number of clicks, including one that is very similar to our expression of disapproval.

The easiest click to start studying is the gentle-kiss-with-pursed-lips type. In a language that uses bilabial clicks of this sort, the gesture is not quite the same as that used by most people making a friendly kiss. The linguistic gesture does not involve puckering the lips. They are simply compressed in a more grim manner. Make a "kiss" of this type. Say this sound while holding a moistened finger lightly along the lips. You should be able to feel that air rushes into the mouth when your lips come apart. Note that while you are making this sound, you can continue to breathe through your nose. This is because the back of the tongue is touching the velum, so that the air in the mouth used in making this sound is separated from the airstream flowing in and out of the nose.

Now say the click expressing disapproval, the one that authors sometimes write "tsk-tsk" or "tut-tut" when they wish to indicate a click sound; they do not, of course, mean [tɪsk tɪsk] or [tʌt tʌt]. Say a single click of this kind and try to feel how your tongue moves. The positions of the vocal organs in the corresponding Zulu sound are shown in Figure 6.3. At the beginning of this sound, there are both dental and velar closures. As a result, the body of air shown in the dark shaded area in Figure 6.3 is totally enclosed. When the back and central parts of the tongue move down, this air becomes rarefied. A click is produced when this partial vacuum is released by lowering the tip of the tongue. The IPA symbol for a dental click is [|], a single vertical stroke.

Movement of the body of air in the mouth is called a **velaric airstream mechanism.** Clicks are stops made with an ingressive velaric airstream mechanism (as shown in Figure 6.3). It is also possible to use this mechanism to cause the airstream to flow outward by raising the tongue and squeezing the contained body of air, but this latter possibility is not actually used in any known language.

The sound described in Figure 6.3 is a dental click. If the partial vacuum is released by lowering the side of the tongue, a lateral click—the sound sometimes used for encouraging horses—is produced. The phonetic symbol is [‖], a pair of vertical strokes. Clicks can also be made with the tip (*not* the blade) of the tongue touching the posterior part of the alveolar ridge. The phonetic symbol for a click of this kind is [!], an exclamation point. These three possibilities all occur in Zulu and in the neighboring language Xhosa. Some of the aboriginal South African languages, such as Nama and !Xóõ, have an even wider variety of click articulations. !Xóõ, spoken in Botswana, is one of the few languages that

| FIGURE 6.3 | The sequence of events in a dental click. Initially, both the tip and the back of the tongue are raised, enclosing the small pocket of air indicated by the dark shading. When the center of the tongue moves down, the larger, slightly shaded cavity is formed. Then the tip moves down to the position shown by the dashed line, and, a little later, the back of the tongue comes down to the position shown by the dashed line. |

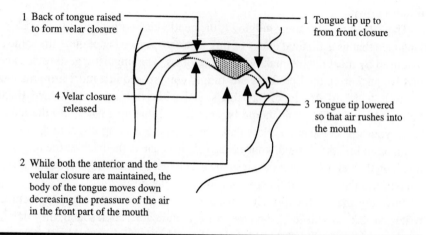

1 Back of tongue raised to form velar closure

1 Tongue tip up to from front closure

4 Velar closure released

3 Tongue tip lowered so that air rushes into the mouth

2 While both the anterior and the velular closure are maintained, the body of the tongue moves down decreasing the preassure of the air in the front part of the mouth

have bilabial clicks—a sort of thin, straight lips, kiss sound, for which the symbol is [ʘ].

In the production of click sounds, there is a velar closure, and the body of air involved is in front of this closure (that is, in the front of the mouth). Consequently, it is possible to produce a velar sound with a glottalic or pulmonic airstream mechanism while a click is being made. You can demonstrate this for yourself by humming continuously while producing clicks. The humming corresponds to a long [ŋ], a voiced velar nasal. We may symbolize the co-occurrence of a nasal and a click by writing a tie bar [⌢] over the two symbols. Thus a dental click and a velar nasal would be written [ŋ͡ǀ]. In transcribing click languages, the tie bar is usually left off, and simultaneity is assumed.

Even if the soft palate is raised so that air cannot flow through the nose, the pulmonic airstream mechanism can still be used to keep the vocal folds vibrating for a short time during a click. When the back of the tongue is raised for a click and there is also a velic closure, the articulators are in the position for [g]. A voiced dental click of this kind is therefore a combination of [g] and [ǀ] and may be symbolized [gǀ] (omitting the tie bar).

At this point, we should note that, strictly speaking, the transcription of clicks always requires a symbol for both the click itself and for the activity that can be associated with the velar closure. We transcribed the voiced click with a [g] plus the click symbol, and the nasalized click with [ŋ] plus the click symbol. We should also transcribe the voiceless click with [k] plus the click symbol. It is perhaps not necessary for a beginning student in phonetics to be able to produce all sorts of different clicks in regular words. But you should be able to produce at least a simple click followed by a vowel. Try saying [kǀ] followed by [ɑ]. Make a vowel as soon after the click as possible, so that it sounds like a single syllable [kǀɑ] (using the convention that regards the [k] and the click as simultaneous, as if there were a tie bar).

As a more challenging exercise, learn to produce clicks between vowels. Start by repeating [kǀɑ] a number of times, so that you are saying [kǀɑkǀɑkǀɑ]. Now say dental, post-alveolar, and lateral clicks in sequences such as [ɑkǀɑ, ɑk!ɑ, ɑkǁɑ]. Make sure that there are no pauses between the vowels and the clicks. Now try to keep the voicing going throughout the sequences, so that you produce [ɑgǀɑ, ɑg!ɑ, ɑgǁɑ]. Last, produce nasalized clicks, perhaps with nasalized vowels on either side [ɑŋǀɑ, ɑŋ!ɑ, ɑŋǁɑ] (again with the nasal being simultaneous with the click). Repeat with other vowels.

The spelling system regularly used in books and newspapers in Zulu and Xhosa employs the letters c, q, x for the dental, post-alveolar and lateral clicks for which we have been using the symbols[ǀ, !, ǁ], respectively. The name of the language Xhosa should therefore be pronounced with a lateral click at the beginning. The h following the x indicates a short burst of aspiration following the click. Try saying the name of the language with an aspirated lateral click at the beginning. Table 6.3 shows a set of contrasting clicks in Xhosa. Nearly all the words in this table are infinitive forms of words, which is why they begin with the prefix [ukú].

TABLE 6.3	Contrasts involving clicks in Xhosa. The rows differ in phonation types, as will be discussed later in this chapter.		
	Dental	**Post-Alveolar**	**Lateral**
Voiceless Unaspirated Velar Plosive	ukúkǀola "to grind fine"	ukúk!oɓa "to break stones"	úkǁolo "peace"
Voiceless Aspirated Velar Plosive	úkukǀʰóla "to pick up"	ukúk!ʰola "perfume"	ukúkǁʰóa "to arm oneself"
Murmured Velar Plosive	úkugǀôɓa "to be joyful"	ukúg!oba "to scoop"	ukúgǁoba "to stir up mud"
Voiced Velar Nasal	ukúŋǀoma "to admire"	ukúŋ!ola "to climb up"	ukúŋǁliɓa "to put on clothes"
Murmured Velar Nasal	ukúŋǀola "to be dirty"	ukúŋ!ala "to go straight"	ukúŋǁóŋǁa "to lie on back, knees up"

| TABLE 6.4 | | The principal airstream processes. | | | |

Airstream	Direction	Brief Description	Specific Name for Stop Consonant	Examples	Vocal Folds
Pulmonic	egressive	lung air pushed out under the control of the respiratory muscles	plosive	p t k, b d g	voiceless or voiced
Glottalic	egressive	pharynx air compressed by the upward movement of the closed glottis	ejective	p' t' k'	voiceless
Glottalic	ingressive	downward movement of the vibrating glottis; pulmonic egressive airstream may also be involved	implosive	ɓ ɗ ɠ	usually voiced by pulmonic airstream
Velaric	ingressive	mouth air rarefied by backward and downward movement of the tongue	click	ǀ ! ‖ ⊙	combine with pulmonic airstream

Table 6.4 summarizes the principal airstream mechanisms. Note that pulmonic sounds can be voiced or voiceless. Glottalic egressive sounds—ejectives—are always voiceless. Glottalic ingressive sounds—implosives—are nearly always voiced by being combined with a pulmonic egressive airstream, but voiceless glottalic ingressive sounds (voiceless implosives) have been reported in one or two languages. Velaric ingressive sounds (clicks) may be combined with pulmonic egressive sounds so that the resulting combination can be voiced or voiceless. These combinations can also be oral or nasal.

STATES OF THE GLOTTIS

So far we have been considering sounds to be either voiceless, with the vocal folds apart, or voiced, with them nearly together so that they will vibrate. But in fact the **glottis** (which is defined as the space between the vocal folds) can assume a number of other shapes. Some of these glottal states are important in the description of other languages.

Photographs of four states of the glottis are shown in Figure 6.4. These photographs were taken by placing a small mirror at the back of the mouth, so that it

FIGURE 6.4   Four states of the glottis.

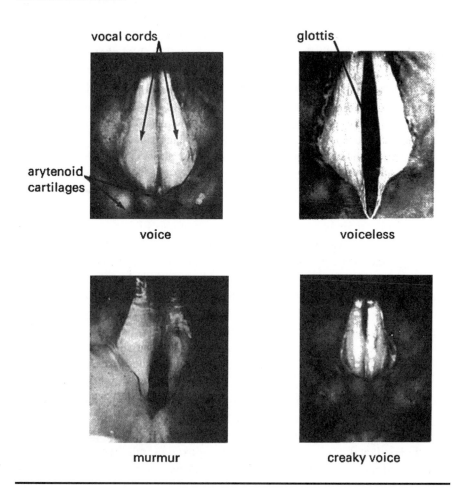

vocal cords

glottis

arytenoid cartilages

voice

voiceless

murmur

creaky voice

was possible to look straight down the pharynx toward the larynx. The top of the picture is toward the front of the neck, the lower part toward the back. The vocal folds are the white bands running from back to front in each picture. Their position can be adjusted by the movements of the **arytenoid cartilages**, which are underneath the small protuberances visible in the lower part of the pictures.

In a voiced sound, the vocal folds are close together and vibrating, as in the first photograph. In a voiceless sound, as in the second photograph, they are pulled apart. This position will produce a completely voiceless sound if there is little or no airflow through the glottis, as in the case of a voiceless fricative or an unaspirated stop. But if there is considerable airflow, as in an *h*-like sound, the vocal folds will be set vibrating while remaining apart. In this way they produce what is called **breathy voice,** or **murmur.** I have labeled the second photograph "voiceless" because this is the usual position in voiceless fricatives. But in an intervocalic [h] as in "ahead," the vocal folds are in a very similar position. In these circumstances they will produce breathy voice, vibrating loosely, so they appear to be simply flapping in the airstream. The third photograph shows another kind of breathy voice. In this sound, the vocal folds are apart between the arytenoid cartilages in the lower (posterior) part of the photograph. They can still vibrate, but at the same time a great deal of air passes out through the glottis.

Murmured sounds occur in English in the pronunciation of / h / in between vowels as in "ahead, behind." In most of the speakers of English I have been able to observe, the / h / in these words is made with the vocal folds slightly apart along their entire length, but still continuing to vibrate as if they were waving in the breeze. The term *voiced h* is sometimes used for this sound, but it is somewhat confusing as there is certainly no voicing in the usual sense. The term *murmured h* is preferable. The symbol for this sound is [ɦ].

Learn to distinguish between the murmured sound [ɦ] as in "aha" and the voiceless sound [h] as at the beginning of an English word such as "heart." The murmured sound is like a sigh produced while breathing heavily. Take a deep breath and see how long you can make first [ɦ] and then [h]. In the voiceless sound [h], the air from the lungs escapes very rapidly, so that this sound cannot be prolonged to any great extent. But you can make the murmured sound [ɦ] last much longer, as the flow of air from the lungs is slowed down by the vibrating vocal folds. Note that [ɦ] can be said on a range of different pitches.

Now say [ɦ] before a vowel. When you say [ɦɑ], you will probably find that the breathiness extends into the vowel. But try to make only the first part of the syllable breathy and produce regular voicing at the end. Finally, try to produce the sequence [ɦɑ] after a stop consonant. Murmured stops of this kind occur in Hindi and in many other languages spoken in India. These sounds will be discussed more fully in the next section; but we can note here that in murmured stops the murmur occurs only during the release of the stop. There must be a comparatively high rate of flow of air out of the lungs to produce murmur, and this cannot happen during the stop closure.

It is fairly easy to produce the required flow rate during a vowel. Some languages contrast plain and murmured vowels. Table 6.5 shows pairs of words in Gujarati, another language spoken in India. Murmured vowels are indicated by a dieresis (two dots) below the symbol. This diacritic can be used to show murmur or breathy voice on other sounds, such as nasals, which occur in a number of languages.

In **creaky voice,** which is the other state of the glottis illustrated in Figure 6.4, the arytenoid cartilages are tightly together, so that the vocal folds can vibrate only at the anterior end (the small opening at the top of the photograph). Note that the vocal folds appear to be much shorter in this photograph. This is partly because the posterior portion at the bottom of the photograph is not visible when

TABLE 6.5	Murmured vowels in Gujarati.		
Breathy		**Plain**	
ka̤n	"krishna"	kan	"ear"
mɛ̤l	"palace"	mɛl	"dirt"
pɔ̤r	"down"	pɔr	"last year"
ʃɛ̤r	"city"	ʃɛr	"pound"
ba̤r	"outside"	bar	"twelve"

the arytenoid cartilages are pulled together. But it is also the case that in creaky voice the folds are not stretched from front to back as they are on higher pitches. It is not possible to make accurate measurements of the lengths of the vibrating folds in these photographs, as the glottis is at varying distances from the camera, but this probably accounts for only a small proportion of the variation in length apparent in the photographs. Creaky voice is a very low-pitched sound that occurs at the ends of falling intonations for some speakers of English. You can probably learn to produce it by singing the lowest note that you can—and then trying to go even lower. Creaky-voiced sounds may also be called **laryngealized.**

In some languages, laryngealization is used to distinguish one sound from another. Hausa and many other Chadic languages of Northern Nigeria distinguish between two palatal approximants. One has regular voicing, rather like the English sound at the beginning of "yacht," and the other has creaky voice. The IPA diacritic to indicate creaky voice is [˷] placed under the symbol. Hausa orthography uses an apostrophe (') before the symbol for the corresponding voiced sound, thus contrasting y and 'y. The Hausa letters y and 'y correspond to IPA [j] and [j̰]. Try differentiating between the laryngealized and nonlaryngealized sounds in the Hausa words "'ya'ya" (children) and "yaro" (boy).

A slightly more common use of laryngealization is to distinguish one stop from another. Hausa and many other West African languages have voiced stops [b, d] contrasting with laryngealized stops [ɓ, ɗ]. In these sounds, the creaky voice is most evident not during the stop closure itself but during the first part of the following vowel. Similar sounds occur in some American Indian languages.

VOICE ONSET TIME

We saw earlier that the terms *voiced* and *voiceless* refer to the state of the glottis during a given articulation. We also saw that the terms *aspirated* and *unaspirated* refer to the presence or absence of a period of voicelessness during and after the release of an articulation. The interval between the release of a closure and the start of the voicing is called the **Voice Onset Time** (usually abbreviated as VOT).

The easiest way to visualize VOT is by reference to the waveform of a sound. This is the technique we used in Chapter 3 to discuss the differences between "tie" and "die." The VOT is measured in milliseconds (ms) from the spike indicating the release of the stop closure to the start of the oscillating line indicating the vibrations of the vocal folds in the vowel. If the voicing begins during the stop closure (i.e., before the release), the VOT has a negative value.

The top part of Figure 6.5 shows the waveforms of the first parts of three of the Sindhi words in Table 6.2: [dəru] "door," [təru] "bottom," [tʰəru] (name of a district). The dashed line indicates the moment of release of the stop. There is a time scale centered on that moment at the bottom of the figure. In the waveform for [də] at the top of the figure there is voicing throughout the closure, the

---

FIGURE 6.5 Waveforms showing stops with different degrees of voicing and aspiration.

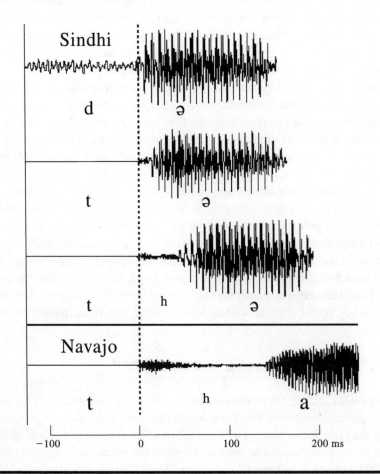

release, and the vowel. This is a fully voiced stop that has a negative VOT of
−130 ms.

In the next waveform, [tə], there are no voicing vibrations during the closure
(before the dashed line). This is, therefore, a voiceless stop. The voicing starts
very shortly after the closure, the VOT being less than 20 ms, making this an
unaspirated stop. In order to produce this stop, the vocal folds are apart during
the whole of the closure period but are close together at the moment of release
of the closure, so that voicing starts as soon as there is sufficient airflow through
the glottis. In the middle of the closure, the vocal folds might be in a position
similar to that shown in the second photograph in Figure 6.4.

The third waveform, [tʰə], shows an aspirated stop, with a VOT of about 50
ms. In producing this sound, the vocal folds are apart during the stop closure and
the glottis is still open at the moment of the release of the stop closure.

There is a continuum of possible voice onset times. Some languages, such as
Sindhi, have very fully voiced stops with a large negative VOT. Others, such as
English, have little or no voicing during the closure, unless the stop is preceded
by a sound in which the vocal folds are already vibrating, in which case the
vibration may continue through the closure. Similarly languages vary in the
VOT they use for aspirated stops. In the Sindhi example in the third row in Figure 6.5 it is only 50 ms. In Navajo, as shown in the last row in Figure 6.5, aspirated stops have a VOT of about 150 ms. When producing a strongly aspirated
stop such as this, the maximum opening of the vocal folds will be much larger
than that shown in the second photograph in Figure 6.4. The maximum opening
will occur at about the moment of release of the stop closure. In general, the
degree of aspiration (the amount of lag in the voice onset time) will depend on
the degree of glottal aperture during the closure. The greater the opening of the
vocal folds during a stop, the longer the amount of the following aspiration.

Different languages choose different points along the VOT continuum in
forming oppositions among stop consonants. This point is illustrated in Figure
6.6, in which some of the possibilities that occur in different languages are
shown with reference to a scale going from most aspirated (largest positive
VOT) at the top to most voiced (largest negative VOT) at the bottom. The
Navajo aspirated stops, shown in the first column, have a very large VOT that is
quite exceptional. Navajo does not have a bilabial stop series, but for all the
other languages the positions shown on the scale correspond to bilabial stops. As
you can see, also in the first column, a normal value for the VOT of English
stressed initial / p / would be between 50 and 60 ms. English initial / b /, at the
bottom of the first column, may have a VOT of about 10 ms, but, as indicated by
the dashed line, it may be less, and even slightly negative. After an initial / s /,
English / p / will have a VOT much like English initial / b /.

Other languages make the contrast between phonemes such as / p, t, k / and
/ b, d, g / in initial position with very different VOTs. Navajo contrasts initial
/ k / with a / g / that is far from voiced; it has a VOT of over 40 ms. As this sound

FIGURE 6.6	Differences in Voice Onset Time in different languages on a scale going from most voiced (largest negative VOT) to most aspirate (largest positive VOT).

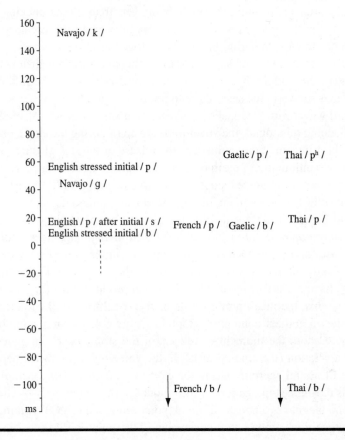

is completely voiceless, it might be better to say that the contrast in Navajo is between / kʰ / and / k /, rather than between / k / and / g /. However, both ways of transcribing Navajo are perfectly valid. As we saw in Chapter 2, you can make a broad transcription that shows the phonemic contrasts in a language using the simplest possible symbols, or you can make a narrow transcription that shows the phonetic detail. As long as the broad transcription is accompanied by a statement that specifies how it should be interpreted, it is equally accurate. The choice of symbol depends in part on the reason for making the transcription. In broad transcriptions of English, it is sufficient just to use / b, p /. But if one wants to show more phonetic detail, one can specify that the phoneme / b / is a completely voiceless [b̥] in, for instance, "That boy" [ˈðæʔtb̥ɔɪ] in my English. Similarly, one might want to show phonetic details such as the aspirated / p / that occurs in "pie" [pʰaɪ] or the unaspirated / p / in "spy" [spaɪ].

The second column in Figure 6.6 shows how the sounds of French line up with those of English and Navajo. The voiced stops in French (and Spanish, Italian and many other languages) are nearly always fully voiced. The length of the voicing varies, depending on the length of the closure, which is why I added an arrow alongside French / b /. Voiceless stops in these languages are unaspirated, making French / p / similar to English initial / b /.

French / p / is even more like Gaelic / b /, which is virtually never voiced, even between vowels. The Gaelic opposition between / b / and / p / is, in a narrow phonetic transcription, / p / versus / pʰ /. In the Gaelic spoken in the Outer Hebrides of Scotland, the VOT of / pʰ / is around 65 ms, nothing like as long as that in Navajo, but longer than that in English.

Some languages contrast three different voice onset times. Thai has voiced, voiceless unaspirated, and aspirated stops, as shown in the final column in Figure 6.6. Words illustrating these contrasts in Thai are given in Table 6.6. As in the case of French, the voiced stops are fully voiced, with the duration of the voicing depending on the length of the stop closure.

Many languages spoken in India, such as Hindi and Sindhi, have not only the three possibilities that occur in Thai, but also murmured stops as well. After the release of the closure, there is a period of breathy voice or murmur before the regular voicing starts. Some illustrative Hindi words are given in Table 6.7. The breathy voice release of these stops is indicated by [ʰ], a raised hooked letter h. The Sindhi words in the last row of Table 6.2 also illustrate breathy voiced stops. As shown in the tables, in addition to the breathy voiced stops, both Sindhi and Hindi also contrast stops with three different voice onset times.

Figure 6.7 shows the waveforms of the Hindi dental stops in the second row of Table 6.7. There is voicing during the stop closure of [d̪] (in the top line), but not during the stops in the second and third lines. The second line has a voiceless unaspirated [t̪] with a VOT of about 20 ms. The third line has an aspirated [t̪ʰ], with a VOT of almost 100 ms. In the fourth line, the [d̪ʰ] has voicing during the closure followed by a waveform that has some of the appearance of voicing—a wavy line—but also has noise superimposed on it. This is breathy voicing. It is

TABLE 6.6	Stops in Thai.			
Voiced	bâ: "crazy"	d̪à: "curse"		
Voiceless Unaspirated	pâ: "aunt"	ta: "eye"	tɕaːn "dish"	ka: "crow"
Voiceless Aspirated	pʰâ: "cloth"	tʰâ: "landing place"	tɕʰaːm "bowl"	kʰa: "remain in"

TABLE 6.7	Stops in Hindi.			
	Voiceless Unaspirated	**Voiceless Aspirated**	**Voiced**	**Breathy Voiced**
Bilabial	pal	pʰal	bal	bɦal
	"take care of"	"knife blade"	"hair"	"forehead"
Dental	t̪al	t̪ʰal	d̪al	d̪ɦal
	"beat"	"plate"	"lentil"	"knife"
Retroflex	ʈal	ʈʰal	ɖal	ɖɦal
	"postpone"	"wood shop"	"branch"	"shield"
Post-Alveolar Affricate	t̠ʃʌl	t̠ʃʰʌl	dʒʌl	dʒɦʌl
	"walk"	"deceit"	"water"	"glimmer"
Velar	kan	kʰan	gan	gɦan
	"ear"	"mine"	"song"	"bundle"

difficult to say how long this breathy voiced aspiration lasts, as it shades into the regular voicing for the vowel. During this breathy voicing the vocal folds are drawn into loose vibrations and do not come fully together.

The difference between voiceless unaspirated, aspirated, and murmured stops (the last three rows in Figure 6.7) is largely a matter of the size and timing of the opening of the vocal folds. In voiceless unaspirated stops, the maximum opening of the glottis (which is not very great) occurs during the stop closure. In (voiceless) aspirated stops, the glottal opening is larger and occurs later, near the moment of release of the stop closure. In murmured stops, the glottal opening is similar in size to that in voiceless unaspirated stops, but it occurs later, during the release of the closure. Because there is a rapid flow of air through the vocal folds at this time, the vocal folds vibrate while remaining slightly apart, thus producing breathy voice.

Learn to produce a series of sounds with different voice onset times. Start by producing fully voiced stops [b, d, g]. See how long you can make the voicing continue during each of these sounds. You will find that you can make it last longer during [b] than during [d] or [g] because in [b] there is a fairly large space above the glottis. Air from the lungs can flow through the glottis for a relatively longer period of time before the pressure above the glottis begins to approach that of the air in the lungs. The vocal folds can be kept vibrating throughout this period. But in [g] there is only a small space above the glottis into which air can flow, so that the voicing can be maintained only briefly. Languages often fail to have fully voiced velar stops. Note that Thai does not have a voiced stop contrasting with a voiceless unaspirated stop at this place of articulation.

When you can produce fully voiced stops satisfactorily, try saying voiceless unaspirated [p, t, k]. You may find it easiest to start with words like "spy, sty, sky." Say these words very slowly. Now say words like them, but without the initial [s].

FIGURE 6.7   Waveforms showing the VOT of the stops in Hindi.

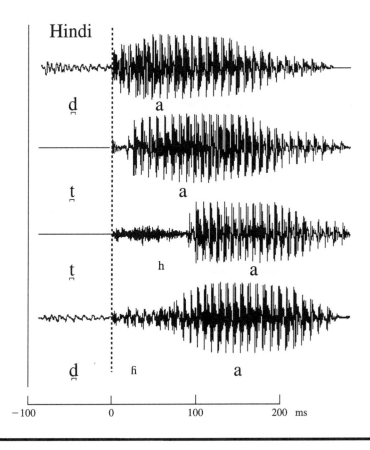

You will have less difficulty in making aspirated stops, because they occur in most forms of English—in words such as "pie" [pʰaɪ] and "tie" [tʰaɪ]. But do try pronouncing all of the Thai and Hindi words in Tables 6.6 and 6.7.

SUMMARY OF GLOTTAL ACTIONS

The vocal folds are involved in many different kinds of actions. They are used in the production of implosives and ejectives and in forming different phonation types. These two types of activities are often not clearly separable. The implosives of some forms of Hausa are as likely to be marked by creaky voice as by a downward movement of the glottis, and Zulu has weak ejectives that could well be considered simply as glottal stops superimposed on plosives. Consequently it

TABLE 6.8	The principal actions of the glottis.	
Glottal Stop	Vocal folds together	ʔ
Ejective	Vocal folds together and moving upwards	p', t', k', s'
Implosives	Vocal folds moving downward, sometimes closed	ɓ̥, ɗ̥, ɠ̥
	Usually nearly closed vocal folds moving downward with regular vibrations or creaky voice	ɓ, ɗ, ɠ
Creaky Voice	Vocal folds held tightly together posteriorly, but vibrating (usually at a low rate) anteriorly	b̰, d̰, a̰, ḛ
(Modal) Voice	Regular vibrations of the vocal folds	b, d (in French), a, e
Breathy Voice (Murmur)	Vocal folds vibrating without coming fully together	a̤, e̤
	Often during a stop release	bɦ, dɦ
Voiceless	Vocal folds apart	p, t, k, s m̥, n̥
Aspirated	Vocal folds apart during the release of an articulation	pʰ, tʰ, kʰ, sʰ

is convenient to summarize all these activities in a single table. Table 6.8 shows the principal actions of the glottis.

EXERCISES

A Label the following diagram so as to show the sequence of events involved in producing a voiced alveolar implosive.

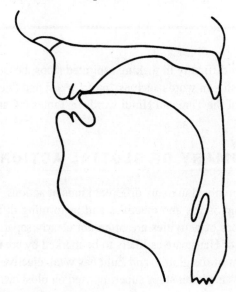

B Complete the following diagram so as to show the positions of the vocal organs in producing[ŋ͡]. Add labels so that the sequence of events is clear.

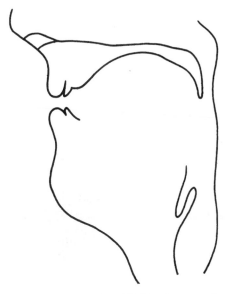

C Measure (to the nearest 10 ms) the VOT in the waveforms of the stops in "a pie, a buy, a spy."

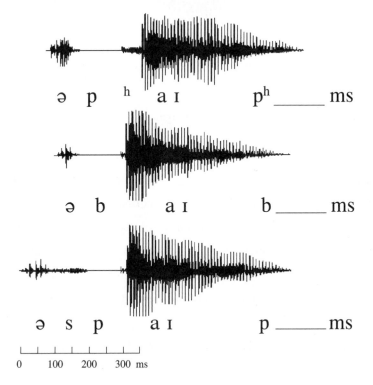

ə p ͪ a ɪ   pʰ_____ ms

ə b   a ɪ   b_____ ms

ə s p a ɪ   p _____ms

0   100   200   300 ms

D Put a narrow transcription above the waveform of the phrase, "He started to tidy it." The phrase has been split during the closure of the [t] in "to." The location of the [d] in "tidy" is also shown. Measure (to the nearest 10 ms) the VOT in the waveforms of the stops.

First stop in "started" _____ ms.

Second stop in "started" _____ ms.

Stop in "to" _____ ms.

First stop in "tidy" _____ ms.

Second stop in "tidy" _____ ms.

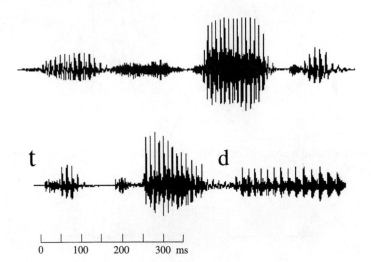

E Fill in the blanks in the following passage.

There are three principal airstream mechanisms: the _____ airstream mechanism, the _____ airstream mechanism, and the _____ airstream mechanism. In normal utterances in all the languages of the world, the airstream is always flowing outward if the _____ airstream mechanism is involved. Stops made with this mechanism are called _____. The only mechanism that is used in some languages to produce some sounds with inward going air and some sounds with outward going air is the _____ airstream mechanism. Stops made with this mechanism acting ingressively are called _____.

Stops made with this mechanism acting egressively are called _____.

The mechanism that is used in language to produce sounds only with inward going air is the _____ airstream mechanism. Stops made with this mechanism are called_____.

 Stops may vary in their voice onset time. In this respect, [b, d, g] are _____ stops, [p, t, k] are_____ stops, and [pʰ, tʰ, kʰ] are _____ stops. The stops [bʱ, dʱ, gʱ], which occur in Hindi, are called _____ stops. The stops [ɓ, ɗ], which occur in African languages such as Hausa, are called _____stops.

PERFORMANCE EXERCISES

A large number of non-English sounds were discussed in this chapter. About the same number of additional sounds will be considered in the next chapter. Beginning with the following exercises, you should spend more time doing practical phonetic work. Try to double the time you spend doing work of this kind. If possible, you should spend about twenty minutes a day working with a partner reviewing the material in the chapter and going through the following exercises.

A Review the different types of phonation. Start by simply differentiating voiced and voiceless sounds, saying:
(1) [aaaɑ̥ɑ̥aaaɑ̥ɑ̥]
Now add breathy-voiced (murmured) sounds to the sequence:
(2) [aaaɑ̤ɑ̤ɑ̥ɑ̥]
Next, add creaky-voiced (laryngealized) sounds:
(3) [ɑ̰ɑ̰aaaɑ̤ɑ̤ɑ̥ɑ̥]
Then make the sequence begin with a glottal stop:
(4) [ʔɑ̰ɑ̰aaaɑ̤ɑ̤ɑ̥ɑ̥]
Finally, practice saying this sequence in the reverse order:
(5) [ɑ̥ɑ̥ɑ̤ɑ̤aaaɑ̰ɑ̰ʔ]

B Try to go in one smooth movement through all these states of the glottis, saying the following fairly quickly:
(1) [ʔɑ̰aɑ̤ɑ̥]
and the reverse sequence:
(2) [ɑ̥ɑ̤aɑ̰ʔ]

C Repeat Exercises A and B slowly, quickly, reversed, and so on, with other articulations, for example:

(1) [ʔmmm̥m̥]

(2) [ʔnnn̥n̥]

(3) [ʔŋŋŋ̥ŋ̥]

(4) [ʔ lll̥ l̥]

(5) [ʔ i i i̥ i̥]

D Try to superimpose breathy voice (murmur) onto intervocalic consonants, saying:

[am̤a, an̤a, al̤a]

Do not worry if the breathy voice is also evident on the adjacent vowels.

E Now try adding breathy voice to stops. The release of the closure should be followed by a period of murmur extending into the vowel:

[abɦa, adɦa, agɦa]

F Similarly, add creaky voice (laryngealization) to intervocalic consonants, saying:

[am̰a, an̰a, al̰a]

G Then produce stops with creaky voice (laryngealization):

[ab̰a, ad̰a, ag̰a]

Again, do not worry if the creaky voice is most evident in the adjacent vowels.

H Say [aba], making sure that you have a fully voiced intervocalic stop. Now repeat this sequence a number of times, each time increasing the length of the consonant closure. Try to make the consonant closure as long as you can while maintaining the voicing.

I Repeat Exercise H with the sequences [ada] and [aga].

J Produce long, fully voiced stops before vowels: [ba, da, ga]. Make sure that there is a velic closure and that you are *not* saying [mba, nda, ŋga] but are correctly saying a long, fully voiced, oral stop.

K Produce voiceless unaspirated stops before vowels: [pa, ta, ka]. You may find it helpful to imagine that there is a preceding [s] as in "spar, star, scar."

L Say a series of stops with more aspiration than usual: [pʰa, tʰa, kʰa]. Make sure that there is a really long period of voicelessness after the release of the closure and before the start of the vowel.

M Practice saying sequences of voiced, voiceless unaspirated, and aspirated plosives: [bɑ, pɑ, pʰɑ], [dɑ, tɑ, tʰɑ], and [gɑ, kɑ, kʰɑ].

N Try to produce as many intermediate stages as you can in each of these series. You should be able to produce each series with

(1) a long, fully voiced stop.

(2) a slightly less long, partially voiced stop.

(3) a completely voiceless, but unaspirated, stop.

(4) a slightly aspirated stop.

(5) a strongly aspirated stop.

O Practice these exercises until you are certain that you can reliably produce a distinction between at least (1) voiced, (2) voiceless unaspirated, and (3) aspirated stops at each place of articulation.

P Extend this series by beginning with a laryngealized stop and ending with a murmured stop. Say:

(1) b̰ɑ	(2) d̰ɑ	(3) g̰ɑ
bɑ	dɑ	gɑ
pɑ	tɑ	kɑ
pʰɑ	tʰɑ	kʰɑ
bʱɑ	dʱɑ	gʱɑ

Q Incorporate all these sounds into simple series of nonsense words. If you are making up your own series to say to someone else, do not make them too difficult. Try saying something like the following:

(1) ˈtemɑs	(2) ˈbɛkɑl	(3) ˈgodeŋ
ˈdemɑs	ˈbʱɛgɑl	ˈgʱoteŋ
ˈtʰemɑs	ˈpʰɛkʰɑl	ˈkoteŋ
ˈd̰emɑs	ˈb̰egɑl	ˈkʰod̰eŋ
ˈdʱemɑs	ˈpɛbʱɑl	ˈgodʱeŋ

R Review the description of ejectives. When making an ejective, you should be able to *feel* that you (1) make an articulatory closure (for example, bringing your lips together), (2) make a glottal stop (feel that you are holding your breath by closing your glottis), (3) raise the larynx (place your fingers on your throat to feel this movement), (4) release the articulatory closure (open your lips), and (5) release the glottal closure (let go of your breath).

S If you cannot produce the sequences [p'ɑ, t'ɑ, k'ɑ], reread the section on ejectives in hope of finding some useful hints that might help you.

T Review the description of voiced implosives. Starting from a fully voiced stop, try to feel the downward movement of your larynx. Try to say [ɓa, ɗa, ɠa].

U Review the description of clicks. Try to say a voiceless version of each click between vowels [akǀa, akǃa, akǁa], then a voiced version [agǀa, agǃa, agǁa], and finally a nasalized version [aŋǀa, aŋǃa, aŋǁa].

V Incorporate all these sounds into simple series of nonsense words such as:

ˈpʼetag	ˈgopetʼ	ˈkǀoko
ˈdedak	ˈtipʼuk	ˈkʼokǀo
ˈpetʼak	ˈbaʄod	ˈɓekǁa
ˈɓedag	ˈɗukapʼ	ˈkakǀo
ˈkʼebap	ˈtʼeduʄ	ˈtʼikǀi

7

PLACE AND MANNER OF ARTICULATION

There is a wide variety of consonants in the languages of the world. The places of articulation employed in speaking English do not represent all of the possibilities. Different manners of articulation also occur in other languages. This chapter will consider the place and manner of articulation of a number of different consonants.

PLACES OF ARTICULATION

Many of the possible places of articulation that are used in the languages of the world were defined in Chapter 1. Figure 7.1, which is similar to Figure 1.4, shows three additional places that will be discussed. The terms for all the places of articulation are not just names for particular locations on the roof of the mouth. As is indicated by the numbered arrows, each term specifies two things: first, the part of the upper surface of the vocal tract that is involved, and second, the articulator on the lower surface that is involved.

A large number of non-English sounds can be found in other languages, but the majority of them involve using different manners of articulation at the same places of articulation as in English. We will illustrate this point by considering how each place of articulation is used in English and other languages for making stops, nasals, and fricatives. The numbers in the following paragraphs refer to the numbered arrows in Figure 7.1.

(1) English has bilabial stops and nasals [p, b, m] but no bilabial fricatives. When these fricatives do occur in English, they are simply allophones of the labiodental sounds [f, v]. But in some languages (for example, Ewe of West Africa), bilabial fricatives contrast with labiodental fricatives. The symbols for the voiceless and voiced bilabial fricatives are [ɸ, β]. These sounds are pronounced by bringing the two lips nearly together, so that there is only a slit between them. In Ewe, the name of the language itself is [èβè], whereas the word for "two" is [èvè]. Try to pronounce these contrasting words yourself. Note

FIGURE 7.1   Places of articulation.

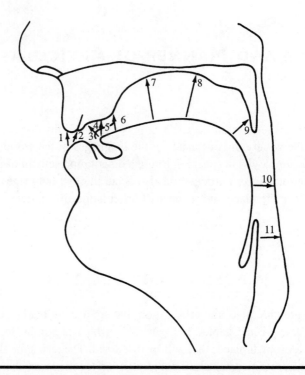

also the contrast between voiceless bilabial and labiodental fricatives in the Ewe words [éɸá], "he polished," and [éfá], "he was cold."

We should also note here some other labial sounds not shown in Figure 7.1. A few Austronesian languages spoken in Vanuatu have **linguo-labials** in which the tongue touches the upper lip. V'enen Taut has nasals, stops, and fricatives made in this way. The diacritic for indicating a linguo-labial articulation is [˷], a shape like a seagull, placed under the coronal symbol. The V'enen Taut for "breadfruit" is [t̼atei], and for "stone" is [nað̼at].

(2) Many languages are like English in having the labiodental fricatives [f, v]. But probably no language has labiodental stops or nasals except as allophones of the corresponding bilabial sounds. In English, a labiodental nasal, [ɱ], may occur when / m / occurs before / f /, as in "emphasis" or "symphony." Say these words in a normal conversational style and see if your lower lip ever contacts your upper lip during the nasal.

Some languages have affricates in which the bilabial stop is released into a labiodental fricative. Practice these sounds by learning to say the German words "Pfanne" [ˈpfanə] (bowl) and "Pflug" [pfluk] (plough).

(3) Most speakers of both British and American English have dental fricatives [θ, ð] but no dental stops, nasals, or laterals except allophonically, before [θ, ð], as in "eighth, tenth, wealth" [eɪt̪θ, tɛn̪θ, wɛl̪θ]. Many speakers of French, Italian, and other languages typically have dental stops, nasals, and laterals. In these languages [t̪, d̪, n̪] are not just coarticulated allophones that occur only before [θ, ð] as in English. However there is a great deal of individual variation in the pronunciation of these consonants in all these languages. Around one third of Californian English speakers (the only regional accent for which I have seen reliable data) have dental stops; and many French speakers have alveolar rather than dental consonants—well over half of them in the case of the lateral / l /. Say words such as "tip, dip, nip, lip," and try to feel where your tongue touches the roof of the mouth.

Some languages, such as Malayalam, a Dravidian language spoken in Southern India, contrast dental and alveolar consonants. Examples of contrasting Malayalam nasals are shown in Table 7.1.

(4) Alveolar stops, nasals, and fricatives all occur in English and in many other languages. They need no further comment here.

(5) Retroflex stops, nasals, and fricatives do not occur in most forms of English. The outstanding exception is the English spoken in India. Retroflex sounds are made by curling the tip of the tongue up and back so that the underside touches or approaches the back part of the alveolar ridge. The symbols used by the IPA for retroflex sounds include [ʈ, ɖ, ɳ]. Remember that, just as dental is a separate place of articulation that can be symbolized by adding [̪] to the alveolar symbol, so also retroflex is considered to be a separate *place* of articulation. This is a somewhat confusing notion in that the term retroflex specifies a particular gesture of the tongue, and one might imagine that it describes how a sound is made (its manner of articulation) rather than where it is made (its place of articulation). But in fact retroflex is a place of articulation like dental and alveolar. At each of these places of articulation it is possible to produce stops,

TABLE 7.1	Contrasts involving bilabial, dental, alveolar, retroflex, palatal, and velar places of articulation in Malayalam, illustrating the necessity for six points of articulation. Dental articulations are indicated by a subscript of the form [̪].

Bilabial	Dental	Alveolar
kʌmmi	pʌn̪n̪i	kʌnni
"shortage"	"pig"	"first"

Retroflex	Palatal	Velar
kʌɳɳi	kʌɲɲi	mʌŋŋi
"link in chain"	"boiled rice & water"	"faded"

nasals, fricatives, and sounds made with other manners of articulation. As we saw in Tables 6.2 and 6.7, Sindhi and Hindi contrast several types of retroflex stops, and Malayalam (Table 7.1) contrasts three coronal places of articulation: dental, alveolar, and retroflex. In addition, Malayalam has bilabial, palatal, and velar sounds, so that it contrasts nasals at six places of articulation, all of which are exemplified in Table 7.1.

Because a retroflex consonant is made with the under surface of the tip of the tongue touching or near the back of the alveolar ridge, the blade (the upper surface of the tip) of the tongue is usually a considerable distance from the roof of the mouth. As a result, the tongue is somewhat hollowed, as shown in the diagram of a retroflex fricative [ṣ] in Figure 7.2. Try making this sound yourself. Start with [s] in which the tip of the tongue is raised toward the front part of the alveolar ridge. Now, while maintaining the fricative noise, slowly slide the tip of the tongue back, curling it up as you move it backward. You will be producing a consonant [ṣ], which sounds something like [ʃ], although the articulatory position is different. (See (6) for discussion of the articulatory position of [ʃ].)

When you have learned to say [ṣ], try adding voice so that you produce [ẓ]. Alternate the voiced and voiceless sounds [sssẓẓẓsssẓẓẓ]. Next, still with the tip of the tongue curled up and back in this position, make the stops [ṭa,ḍa]. Notice how the stops affect the quality of the following vowel, giving it a sort of

---

FIGURE 7.2 The articulation of the retroflex fricative [ṣ]. The dashed lines indicate the position of the sides of the tongue.

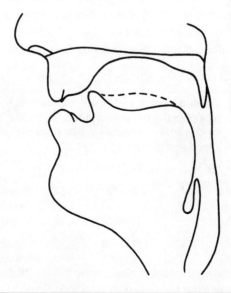

r-coloring at the beginning. Now produce the corresponding nasal [ɳ]. Learn to say all these sounds before and after different vowels. Finally, try to say the Malayalam words in Table 7.1. Retroflex stops and nasals occur in many of the major languages of India, and retroflex fricatives are not at all uncommon. They vary somewhat in the degree to which the tip of the tongue is curled backward. In Hindi and other languages of Northern India, retroflex sounds often have the tip of the tongue only slightly behind the most prominent part of the alveolar ridge, much as indicated in Figure 7.2. In Malayalam and other languages spoken in the South of India, the tip is curled further back, so that the underside of the tip of the tongue touches the roof of the mouth.

(6) The palato-alveolar sounds [ʃ, ʒ] differ from retroflex sounds in the part of the tongue involved. In palato-alveolar sounds, the upper surface of the tip of the tongue is near the roof of the mouth. In addition, the front of the tongue is slightly domed, as opposed to being hollowed. Compare Figure 1.7, which shows the position of the vocal organs in the palato-alveolar fricative [ʃ] as in "shy," with Figure 7.2. Note that in both [ʂ] and [ʃ] the maximum constriction of the vocal tract occurs near the back of the alveolar ridge. But these two sounds are said to have different places of articulation, because the terms specifying place of articulation designate both what part of the roof of the mouth is involved and what part of the tongue is involved. In retroflex sounds the underside of the tip of the tongue forms the articulation, but in palato-alveolar sounds the articulation is made by the upper surface of the tip of the tongue.

Another way of distinguishing between retroflex and palato-alveolar sounds is to call them all post-alveolar and name, in addition, the part of the tongue involved. Sounds made with the tip of the tongue may be called **apical,** and those made with the blade may be called **laminal.** Then the term retroflex is exactly equivalent to apical post-alveolar, and palato-alveolar is equivalent to laminal post-alveolar.

There are advantages in introducing the terms apical and laminal in that they may also apply at other places of articulation. Dental sounds may be made with the tip or the blade of the tongue, and so may alveolar sounds. With the use of these extra terms we can distinguish between the apical dental stops that occur in Hindi and the laminal dental stops that occur in French. In Australian aboriginal languages, the difference between apical and laminal sounds is often very important.

In English, the only palato-alveolar sounds are the fricatives and affricates [ʃ, ʒ, tʃ, dʒ]. In other languages, such as French and Italian, there are nasals made in either the same or a very similar position. These nasals are often, arbitrarily, considered to be palatal sounds. No language that I know of makes a distinction between a palato-alveolar nasal and a palatal nasal.

The IPA chart puts palato-alveolars into the post-alveolar column. In a section labeled "other symbols" it also mentions **alveolo-palatals** and provides the symbols [ɕ, ʑ]. These symbols are used for voiceless and voiced fricatives in Polish and Chinese. They are are similar to [ʃ, ʒ], but have considerable raising of the front of the tongue. They are also made in the post-alveolar region.

(7) Palatal sounds can be defined as being made with the front of the tongue approaching or touching the hard palate, and with the tip of the tongue down behind the lower front teeth. There is no clear-cut distinction between these sounds and palato-alveolar sounds. The only true palatal in English is / j /, which is usually an approximant but may be allophonically a voiceless fricative in words such as "hue." The symbol for a voiceless palatal fricative is [ç], so this word may be transcribed phonemically as / hju / and phonetically as [çu]. Voiceless palatal fricatives occur as allophones of [x] (discussed in 8) in German in words such as "ich" [ɪç], meaning "I," and "nicht" [nɪçt], meaning "not."

Say [ç] as in "hue" and then try to prolong this sound. Add voice so that you make a fricative something like the [j] as in "you," but with the front of the tongue nearer the hard palate. The symbol [ʝ], a curly tailed *j*, is used for a voiced palatal fricative. Say [ççç ʝ ʝ ʝ ç ç ç ʝ ʝ ʝ], making sure that the tip of the tongue is down behind the lower front teeth. Now change the fricative [ç] into a stop by raising the front of the tongue still more, while keeping the tip of the tongue down. The symbols for voiceless and voiced palatal stops are [c, ɟ]. Say sequences such as [aca] and [aɟa], making sure that the front of your tongue touches the hard palate, but the tip of the tongue is down. Then try making similar sequences with a palatal nasal (for which the symbol is [ɲ], reminding one of [n] and [j] combined).

Palatal nasals occur in several languages, including French, Italian, Spanish, and many non-Indo-European languages. Try saying French words such as "agneau" [aɲo] (lamb) and Spanish words such as "Señor" [seɲor] (Mr.).

Palatal stops are slightly less common than palatal nasals. They occur, for example, in the Akan languages of Ghana. Because of the shape of the roof of the mouth, the contact between the front of the tongue and the hard palate often extends over a fairly large area. As a result, the formation and release of a palatal stop is often not as rapid as in the case of other stops, and they tend to become affricates.

(8) Velar stops and nasals [k, g, ŋ] occur in English. But unlike other languages such as German, we no longer have velar fricatives. They are not, however, hard to make. Starting from a syllable such as [ak], build up pressure behind the velar closure, and then lower the tongue slightly. The result will be a voiceless velar fricative, which we write as [x]. The symbol for the corresponding voiced sound is [ɣ]. As with other fricatives, learn to say [xxxɣɣɣxxx]. Then produce sequences such as [axa, exe, oɣo, ɛɣɛ].

Examples of words in other languages containing velar fricatives are Lakhota, as shown in Table 6.1; German "Achtung" [ʔaxtʊŋ] (warning), "Bach" [bax] (Bach; proper name); and Spanish "jamás" [xaˈmas] (never), "ojo" [ˈoxo] (eye), "pago" [ˈpaɣo] (I pay), "diga!" [ˈdiɣa] (speak!). The Spanish [ɣ] is often not very fricative and more like an approximant. It may be more accurately transcribed using the symbol for a voiced velar approximant, which is [ɰ]. The part of the tongue involved in making velar sounds, the back of the tongue, is sometimes called the **dorsum;** these sounds are referred to as dorso-velar sounds.

(9) Uvular sounds are made by raising the back of the tongue toward the uvula. They do not occur at all in most forms of English. But in French a voiced uvular fricative—[ʁ]—is the common form of *r* in words such as "rouge" [ʁuʒ] (red) and "rose" [ʁoz] (rose). The voiceless uvular fricative, [χ], also occurs in French as an allophone of / ʁ / after voiceless stops, as in "lettre" [lɛtχ] (letter). French differs from English in that it often has perseverative assimilations in which, for example, the voicelessness of one sound continues on through the following sound.

Uvular stops, written [q, ɢ], and nasals, written [ɴ], occur in Eskimo, Aleut, and other American Indian languages. Table 7.2 illustrates contrasts between uvular and velar stops and palato-alveolar affricates in Quechua, an American Indian language widely spoken in Bolivia, Chile, and Peru. Note that Quechua has voiceless unaspirated plosives, aspirated plosives, and ejectives.

One way of learning to produce uvular sounds is to start from a voiceless velar fricative [x]. While making this sound, slide your tongue slightly further back in your mouth so that it is close to the uvula. The result will be the voiceless uvular fricative [χ]. Learn to make this sound before and after vowels, in sequences such as [aχa, oχo, uχu]. You will find it easier to use back vowels at first; then go on to sequences such as [eχe, iχi]. Next, add voice to this sound, saying [χχχʁʁʁχχχʁʁʁ]. Practice saying [ʁ] before and after vowels. Try saying the French words cited in the first paragraph of this section.

Once you have mastered the pronunciation of uvular fricatives, try changing them into uvular stops. Say [aχa], then make a stop at the same place of articulation, saying [aqa]. Now produce a voiced uvular stop [aɢa] and a uvular nasal [aɴa]. Practice all these sounds before and after different vowels.

(10) Pharyngeal sounds are produced by pulling the root of the tongue back toward the back wall of the pharynx. Many people cannot make a stop at this position. Furthermore, it would be literally impossible to make a pharyngeal

TABLE 7.2	Contrasts involving stops in Quechua.	
Palato-Alveolar	**Velar**	**Uvular**
tʃaka	kujuj	qaʎu
"bridge"	"to move"	"tongue"
tʃʰaka	kʰujuj	qʰaʎu
"large ant"	"to whistle"	"shawl"
tʃ'aka	k'ujuj	q'aʎu
"hoarse"	"to twist"	"tomato sauce"

nasal, for closure at that point would prevent the airstream from coming through the nose. But pharyngeal fricatives, shown by the symbols [ħ, ʕ], can be made, and they do in fact occur in Semitic languages such as Arabic. The Arabic word for "bath" is [ħammaam], for "uncle," [ʕamm]. The voiced pharyngeal fricative [ʕ] usually has a great deal of laryngealization (creaky voice), perhaps because the necessary constriction in the pharynx also causes a constriction in the larynx. For many speakers there is little or no actual friction, so that these sounds may be more like approximants than fricatives.

(11) Epiglottal sounds are produced with a constriction that is even deeper in the throat than that in pharyngeal sounds. The root of the epiglottis and the lowest part of the pharynx just above the larynx form the constriction. Some speakers of Arabic actually use epiglottal rather than pharyngeal articulations in the words described in the preceding paragraph. Neither Arabic nor any of the other Semitic languages distinguish between pharyngeal and epiglottal fricatives; but some of the languages of the Caucasus contrast these two possibilities.

At a first stage in learning phonetics, it is sufficient to be able to produce either pharyngeal or epiglottal fricatives. If you try to constrict your pharynx as much as possible, you will probably be doing so by retracting the epiglottis. Try to produce the voiceless sound [ħ]. Now, if you can, produce this sound before a vowel. Next, try to make the voiced sound [ʕ], not worrying if it turns out to have creaky voice. Produce these sounds in the Arabic words cited earlier.

Before finishing this section on places of articulation, we must note that some sounds involve the simultaneous use of two places of articulation. The English approximant [w] has both an approximation of the lips (making it a bilabial sound) and of the back of the tongue and the soft palate (making it a velar sound). Sounds that involve these two articulations are called **labial velars,** or **labiovelars.**

Yoruba, Ewe, Tiv, and many other languages spoken in West Africa have labial velar stops. Some of the languages spoken in this area also have labial velar nasals. As in the case of nasal and voiced clicks, we symbolize two co-occurring articulations with a tie bar joining two symbols. The Yoruba for "arm" is [ak͡pá] and for "adult" is [àg͡bà]. In these words, the two closures occur almost simultaneously.

There is another complication in the production of these sounds in Yoruba and in most West African languages that have labial velar stops or nasals. During the labial and velar closures, the back of the tongue sometimes moves slightly farther back, creating a slight suction effect as in a click. Thus the stops [k͡p, g͡b] and the nasal [ŋ͡m] often have a weak velaric ingressive mechanism, so they might be classified as voiceless or voiced or nasal bilabial clicks. One of the best ways of learning to say these sounds is to start by making a bilabial click (a kissing sound, but with the lips being simply compressed and not puckered) in between vowels. Say [a](kiss)[a] at first slowly, and then as fast as you can. Then weaken the suction component of the kiss, so that you are making little

TABLE 7.3	Symbols for nasals, stops, and fricatives. As in all consonant charts, when there are two symbols within a single cell, the one on the left indicates a voiceless sound.

	Bilabial	Labiodental	Dental	Alveolar	Retroflex	Palato-Alveolar	Palatal	Velar	Uvular	Pharyngeal	Labial Velar
Nasal	m	ɱ	n̪	n	ɳ		ɲ	ŋ	N		ŋ͡m
Stop	p b		t̪ d̪	t d	ʈɖ		c ɟ	k g	q ɢ		k͡p g͡b
Fricative	ɸ β	f v	θ ð	s z	ʂ ʐ	ʃ ʒ	ç ʝ	x ɣ	χ ʁ	ħ ʕ	

more than a labial velar articulation between vowels. The result should be a labial velar stop much as in the Yoruba word [ak͡pá], "arm."

This is a convenient place to review all the places of articulation we have discussed so far. Table 7.3 is a consonant chart showing the symbols for all the nasals, stops, and fricatives that have been mentioned, except for the epiglottal consonants. Check that you know the values of all these symbols.

MANNERS OF ARTICULATION

STOPS

We can begin our consideration of the different manners of articulation that occur in the languages of the world by reviewing what has been said already about stop consonants. Table 7.4 illustrates a number of different types of stops, most of which have been discussed earlier in this book. The first seven possibilities were discussed in Chapter 6. Make sure that you understand all these terms and know what all these stops sound like, even if you cannot make them all yourself.

The only comment on the first seven sounds that it is necessary to add here—where they are all listed together—is that no language distinguishes between (5), an implosive [ɓ], and (6), a laryngealized (creaky-voiced) [b̰]. Certain languages have the one sound, and other languages have the other sound. In a few languages, both sounds occur as allophones or as free variants of the same phoneme. They have not been found in contrast with one another.

Stops with nasal release, the eighth possibility listed in Table 7.4, were discussed in relation to English in Chapter 3. Nasal plosion occurs in English at the ends of words such as "hidden, sudden." In some languages, however, it can occur at the beginning of a word. Try to say the Russian word for "bottom," which is [dno].

| TABLE 7.4 | Examples of stop consonants. |

Description	Symbol	Example	
1. voiced	b	bənʊ	(Sindhi "forest")
2. voiceless unaspirated	p	pənʊ	(Sindhi "leaf")
3. aspirated	pʰ	pʰənʊ	(Sindhi "snake hood")
4. murmured (breathy)	bʰ	bʰənənu	(Sindhi "lamentation")
5. implosive	ɓ	ɓəni	(Sindhi "field")
6. laryngealized (creaky)	b̰	b̰á:b̰è	(Hausa "quarrel," *vb.*)
7. ejective	k'	k'à:k'a:	(Hausa "how")
8. nasal release	dn	dno	(Russian "bottom")
9. prenasalized	nd	ndizi	(Swahili "banana")
10. lateral release	tɬ	tɬàh	(Navajo "oil")
11. ejective lateral release	tɬ'	tɬ'ée?	(Navajo "night")
12. affricate	ts	tsaɪt	(German "time")
13. ejective affricate	ts'	ts'áal	(Navajo "cradle")

The next possibility listed in Table 7.4 is the prenasalized stop [nd], which is in some senses the reverse of a nasally released stop. In a prenasalized stop, the oral closure—in this case the alveolar closure—is formed first, while the soft palate is lowered. Then there is a short nasal consonant, after which the soft palate is raised so that there is a stop. This stop is released by removing the oral closure (in this case by lowering the tongue tip) while the soft palate remains raised. Prenasalized stops occur in many African languages. Additional words for practice are given in Table 7.5. When you try to make these sounds, be careful not to make the initial nasal component into a separate syllable. Make it as short as possible.

Stops with lateral release (see (10) in Table 7.4) were also discussed in relation to their occurrence in English (for example, in "little, ladle"). In other languages, they too can occur initially in a word. Sometimes, as indicated by (11) in Table 7.4, laterally released stops can occur with an ejective airstream mechanism. On these occasions, the stop closure for [t] is formed, the glottalic egressive (ejective) airstream mechanism is set in motion, and then the stop is released laterally by lowering the sides of the tongue.

| TABLE 7.5 | Prenasalized stops in Margi, a language spoken in Northern Nigeria. |

mpà	"fight"	mbà	"tie"
ntà	"split"	ndàl	"throw"
ntsàntsà	"shouted"	ndzɔ̀ndzɔ̀ʔbʊ	"covered"
ntʃà	"point at"	ndʒà	"open wide"
ɲcàhʊ	"break"	ɲɟárí	"leave"

The only affricates that can occur initially in most forms of English are [tʃ, dʒ]. Some dialects (for example, London Cockney) have a slightly affricated stop of a kind that might be written [tˢ] in words such as "tea" [tˢəi]. Alveolar affricates also occur in German, as shown in (12) in Table 7.4. Remember that German has a bilabial affricate [pf], as in "Pflug" [pfluk] (plough). Affricates can also occur with an ejective airstream mechanism. Example (13) in Table 7.4 is from an American Indian language, Navajo, which in addition to the ejective [ts'], also has the affricate [ts] made with a pulmonic airstream mechanism as in German.

NASALS

We will now consider the other manners of articulation that are used in the languages of the world. There is little more that need be said about nasals. We have already seen that, like stops, they can occur voiced or voiceless (for example, in Burmese). But as voiceless nasals are comparatively rare, they are symbolized simply by adding the voiceless diacritic [̥] under the symbol for the voiced sound. There are no special symbols for voiceless nasals.

FRICATIVES

There are two ways to produce the rough, turbulent flow that occurs in the airstream during a fricative. It may be just the result of the air passing through a narrow gap, as in the formation of [f]. Or it may be due to the airstream first becoming speeded up by being forced through a narrow gap and then being directed over a sharp edge, such as the teeth, as in the production of [s]. Partly because there are these two possible mechanisms, the total number of different fricatives that have been observed is larger than the number of stops or the number of nasals. In Table 7.3, there are ten pairs of fricative symbols, in comparison with seven pairs of stop symbols and seven nasal symbols.

So far, we have classified fricatives as being voiced or voiceless and as being made at a number of different places of articulation. But we can also subdivide fricatives in accordance with their manner of production. Some authorities have divided fricatives into those such as [s], in which the tongue is grooved so that the airstream comes out through a narrow channel, and those such as [θ], in which the tongue is flat and forms a wide slit through which the airflows. Unfortunately, not enough is known about fricatives to be sure how this distinction should be applied in all cases. It is also clearly irrelevant for fricatives made with the lips and the back of the tongue.

A slightly better way of dividing fricatives is to separate them into groups on a purely auditory basis. Say the English voiceless fricatives [f, θ, s, ʃ]. Which two have the loudest high pitches? You should be able to hear that [s, ʃ] differ from [f, θ] in this way. The same kind of difference occurs between the voiced fricatives [z, ʒ] and [v, ð]. The fricatives [s, z, ʃ, ʒ] are called **sibilant** sounds. They have more acoustic energy—that is, greater loudness—at a higher pitch than the other fricatives.

The sound patterns that occur in languages often arise because of auditory properties of sounds. We can divide fricatives into sibilant and nonsibilant sounds only by reference to auditory properties. We need to divide them into these two groups to show how English plurals are formed. Consider words ending in fricatives, such as "cliff, moth, kiss, dish, church, dove, lathe, maze, rouge, judge." Which of these words add an extra syllable in forming the plural? If you say them over to yourself, you will find that they are all monosyllables in the singular. But those that end with one of the sounds [s, ʃ, z, ʒ]—that is, with a sibilant fricative or an affricate containing a sibilant fricative—become two syllables in the plural. It seems as though English does not favor two sibilant sounds together. It breaks them up by inserting a vowel before adding a sibilant suffix to words ending in sibilants.

TRILLS, TAPS, AND FLAPS

Even in the case of a very short trill where there is only a single contact with the roof of the mouth, the movement is different from that in what is sometimes called a tap, or a flap. In a **trill,** the tip of the tongue is set in motion by the current of air. A **tap** or a **flap** is caused by a single contraction of the muscles so that one articulator is thrown against another. It is often just a very rapid articulation of a stop.

It is useful to distinguish between taps and flaps. In a tap, the tip of the tongue simply moves up to contact the roof of the mouth in the dental or alveolar region and then moves back to the floor of the mouth along the same path. In a flap, the tip of the tongue is first curled up and back in a retroflex gesture and then strikes the roof of the mouth in the post-alveolar region as it returns to its position behind the lower front teeth. The distinction between taps and flaps is thus to some extent bound up with what might be called a distinction in place of articulation. Flaps are typically retroflex articulations, but it is possible to make the articulatory gesture required for a flap at other places of articulation. The tongue can be pulled back and then, as it is flapped forward, made to strike the alveolar ridge or even the teeth, making alveolar or dental flaps. Flaps are distinguished from taps by the direction of the movement—from back to front for flaps, as opposed to up and down for taps—rather than by the exact point of contact.

Some forms of American English have both taps and flaps. Taps occur as the regular pronunciation of / t, d, n / in words such as "latter, ladder, tanner." The flap occurs in words that have an r-colored vowel in the stressed syllable. In "dirty" and "sorting," speakers who have the tongue bunched or retracted for the r-colored vowel will produce a flap as they move the tongue forward for the non-r-colored vowel.

Trills are rare in most forms of English. The stage version of a Scottish accent with trilled / r / is not typical of most Scots. In Scottish English / r / is more likely to be pronounced as a tap. The American pronunciation of "petal" with a voiced alveolar tap in the middle will sound to a Scotsman from Edinburgh like his regular pronunciation of "pearl."

The distinction between trills and different kinds of taps and flaps is much more important in other languages. But before this point can be illustrated, we must review the symbols that can be used for different types of "r" sounds. In a broad transcription, they can all be transcribed as / r /. But in a narrower transcription, this symbol may be restricted to voiced alveolar trills. An alveolar tap may be symbolized by the special symbol [ɾ], and the post-alveolar (retroflex) flap by [ɽ]. The approximant that occurs in many people's pronunciation of / r / may be symbolized by [ɹ], an upside-down r. If it is important to show that this sound is particularly retroflex, the symbol [ɻ] may be used. Most speakers of American English do not have a retroflex approximant, but for those who do [ɻ] is an appropriate symbol in a narrow transcription. All these symbols are shown in Table 7.6.

As illustrated in Table 7.6, Spanish distinguishes between a trill and a tap in words such as "perro" [pero] (dog) and "pero" [peɾo] (but). Similar distinctions also occur in some forms of Tamil, a language of South India. This language, like Hausa (Nigeria), may also distinguish between an alveolar and a retroflex flap. Trills may also have accompanying friction, as in the Czech example in Table 7.6, which uses the IPA diacritic [˔] meaning raised (and thus more fricative).

TABLE 7.6	Specific symbols for types of *r* and for bilabial trills. Note the use of [*] as a special symbol that can be defined and used when there is no prescribed symbol.

r	voiced alveolar trill	[pero]	(Spanish "dog")
ɾ	voiced alveolar tap	[peɾo]	(Spanish "but")
ɽ	voiced retroflex flap	[báɽà:]	(Hausa "servant")
ɹ	voiced alveolar approximant	[ɹɛd]	(English "red")
ɻ	voiced retroflex approximant	[ɻɛd]	(some American-English "red")
ř	voiced alveolar fricative trill	[řɛk]	(Czech "rivers")
ʀ	voiced uvular trill	[ʀuʒ]	(Provençal-French "red")
ʁ	voiced uvular fricative or approximant	[ʁuʒ]	(Parisian-French "red")
ʙ	voiced bilabial trill	[mʙulim]	(Kele "your face")
*	voiced labiodental flap	[bá*ú]	(Margi "flying away")

Learning to make a trill involves placing the tongue, very loosely, in exactly the right position so that it will be set in vibration by a current of air. The easiest position seems to be with the tongue just behind the upper front teeth and very lightly touching the alveolar ridge. If you get the tongue in just the right position and relaxed, you can blow across the top of it, setting it vibrating in a voiceless trill. Many people find it easier to start with a voiceless trill, and then add voicing once they can make steady vibrations. The jaw should be fairly closed, leaving a space of 5 mm between the front teeth. Check this by inserting the top of a pencil between your teeth and then removing it before making the sound. The problem experienced by most people who fail to make trills is that the blade of the tongue is too stiff.

Most people can learn to produce a voiced tap in words such as "Betty" (which would then be transcribed as [ˈbɛɾi]). You should also be able to produce a retroflex flap. As we have seen, many speakers of American English use this type of articulation in sequences such as "herding," in which the tongue is curled up and back after the r-colored vowel, and then strikes the back part of the alveolar ridge as it moves down during the consonant.

When you have mastered all these sounds, try saying them in different contexts. You might also learn to say voiced and voiceless trills, taps, and flaps. Try varying the place of articulation, producing both dental and post-alveolar trills and flaps. Some languages (Malayalam, spoken in South India) contrast alveolar and dental trills. The word for "room" in this language is [ʌrʌ], whereas the word for "half" is [ʌr̪ʌ].

The tongue tip is not the only articulator that can be trilled. Uvular trills occur in some dialects of French, although, as we have noted already, most forms of French have a uvular fricative in words such as "rose" [ʁoz]. The symbol for a uvular trill is [ʀ]. There is no symbol to distinguish between uvular fricatives and approximants. Both sounds are symbolized by [ʁ].

Trills involving the lips occur in a few languages. The IPA symbol for these sounds is a small capital [ʙ] (just as a small capital [ʀ] is used for a uvular trill). In Kele and Titan, two languages spoken in Papua New Guinea, bilabial trills occur in a large number of words. The Titan for "rat" is [mʙulei]. To pronounce the first part of this word you need to hold the lips loosely together while making [m] and then blow the lips apart. Some people find it easier to trill the lips than the tongue tip. If you are having difficulty making an alveolar trill [r], see if you can get the sensation of making a trill by making a bilabial trill [ʙ].

I have also heard a labiodental flap—in Margi, of Northern Nigeria—in which the lower lip is drawn back inside the upper teeth and then allowed to strike against them in passing back to its normal position. There is no IPA symbol for this sound. I have included this rare sound so as to demonstrate how to symbolize a sound for which there is no IPA symbol. In all such cases, it is possible to use an asterisk and define it, as I have done in Table 7.6.

LATERALS

In Chapter 1, we regarded the term lateral as if it specified a manner of articulation in a way comparable to other terms such as fricative, stop, or approximant. But this is really an oversimplification. The central-lateral opposition can be applied to all these manners of articulation, producing a lateral stop and a lateral fricative as well as a lateral approximant, which is by far the most common form of lateral sound. The only English lateral phoneme is / l /, with, at least in British English, allophones [l] as in "led" [lɛd] and [ɫ] as in "bell" [bɛɫ]. In most forms of American English there is not such a large difference between syllable initial and syllable final / l /. In all forms of English the air flows freely without audible friction, making this sound a voiced alveolar lateral approximant. It may be compared with the sound [ɹ] in "red" [ɹɛd], which is for many people a voiced alveolar central approximant. Laterals are usually presumed to be voiced approximants, unless a specific statement to the contrary is made.

Try subtracting and adding voice while saying an English [l] as in "led." You will probably find that the voiceless lateral you produce is a fricative, not an approximant. When the vocal folds are apart, the airstream flows more rapidly, so that it produces a fricative noise in passing between the tongue and the side teeth. The symbol for this sound is [ɬ], so in alternating the voiced and voiceless sounds you will be saying [llllɬɬllllɬɬ]. It is possible to make a nonfricative voiceless lateral, but you will find that to do this you will have to move the side of the tongue farther away from the teeth. The alternation between a voiced and a voiceless lateral approximant may be symbolized [llllḷḷḷllllḷḷḷ].

It is also possible to make a voiced lateral that is a fricative. Try doing this by starting from an ordinary [l], as in "led," and then moving the sides of your tongue slightly closer to your teeth. You may find it easier to produce this sound by starting from the voiceless alveolar lateral fricative described in the previous paragraph and then adding the voicing, but making sure that you keep the fricative component.

To summarize, there are four lateral sounds under discussion: voiced alveolar lateral approximant, [l]; voiced alveolar lateral fricative, [ɮ]; voiceless alveolar lateral approximant, [l̥]; and voiceless alveolar lateral fricative, [ɬ]. No language uses the difference between the last two sounds contrastively. But some languages make a phonemic distinction between three of the four possibilities. Zulu, for example, has words such as [lòndá] "preserve"; [ɮùɮá] "roam loose"; and [ɬòɬá] "prod." Voiceless lateral fricatives can also be exemplified by Welsh words such as [ɬan] "church" and [ˈkəlɛɬ] "knife."

The distinction between a central and a lateral articulation can be applied to other manners of articulation in addition to approximants and fricatives. Trills are always centrally articulated, but flaps can be made with either a central or a lateral articulation. If, when making [ɾ] or [ɽ], you allow the airstream to flow over the sides of the tongue, you will produce a sound that is intermediate in quality between those sounds and [l]. This will be a voiced alveolar or retroflex lateral flap. The symbol for either of these possibilities is [ɺ]. A sound of this kind sometimes occurs in languages such as Japanese that do not distinguish between / r / and / l /. But some African languages, for example, Chaga, spoken in East Africa, make a phonemic distinction among all three of these sounds.

The central-lateral distinction can in some senses be said to apply to stops as well. English stops with lateral plosion, as in "little, ladle," can, of course, be considered to be sequences of stop plus lateral. But the Navajo sound [tɬ'], in which the ejective airstream mechanism applies to both the stop and the lateral, is appropriately called a lateral ejective. Similarly, we clearly want to distinguish between the central and lateral clicks [!] and [‖].

Having seen that the central-lateral distinction can apply to a number of different manners of articulation, we must now consider whether it applies to several different places of articulation. Here the limitations are obvious. Generally speaking, laterals are made with the tip, blade, or front of the tongue. They may be either dental (as in Malayalam and other Indian languages), alveolar (as in English), retroflex (also in Malayalam and other Indian languages), or palatal (as in Italian). Velar laterals do occur in a few languages spoken in Papua New Guinea, but they are so uncommon that we will not consider them here. The symbols for voiced retroflex and palatal laterals are [ɭ] and [ʎ], respectively. Try saying Italian words such as "famiglia" [faˈmiʎʎa] (family) and "figlio" [ˈfiʎʎo] (son). In both of these words, the lateral sound is doubled in that it acts as the final consonant for one syllable as well as the first consonant of the next syllable. Note that some forms of Spanish distinguish between [ʎ] and the similar sounding sequence [lj] in words such as "pollo" [ˈpoʎo] (chicken) and "polio" [ˈpoljo] (polio). See if you can make this distinction. If you are feeling ambitious, you might also try making the palatal lateral ejective in the Zulu word [cʎ'ècʎ'á], which means "tattoo."

SUMMARY OF MANNERS OF ARTICULATION

Table 7.7 presents a summary of the manners of articulation we have been discussing. Note that the terms central and lateral have been placed separately, to indicate that they can be used in conjunction with many of the terms in the upper part of the table. This table also lists many of the symbols that were mentioned in the latter part of this chapter. You should be sure that you can pronounce each of them in a variety of contexts.

The only consonants that we have not considered in detail in this chapter are approximants. Alveolar approximants—both central [ɹ] and lateral [l]—have

TABLE 7.7	Manners of articulation.	
Phonetic Term	**Brief Description**	**Symbols**
Nasal (Stop)	Soft palate lowered so that air flows out through the nose; complete closure of two articulators	m, n, ŋ, and so on
(Oral) Stop	Soft palate raised, forming a velic closure; complete closure of two articulators	p, b, t, and so on
Fricative	Narrowing of two articulators so as to produce a turbulent airstream	f, v, θ, and so on
Approximant	Approximation of two articulators without producing a turbulent airstream	w, j, l, ɹ, and so on
Trill	An articulator set in vibration by the airstream	r, R, ʙ
Tap	Tongue tip hitting the roof of the mouth; a single movement in a trill	ɾ
Flap	One articulator striking another in passing	ɽ, ɺ
Lateral	With a central obstruction, so that air passes out at the side	l, ɬ, ɭ, ʎ, ʟ
Central	Articulated so that air passes out the center	s, ɹ, w, and so on

been discussed. But sounds such as [w, j] as in "wet, yet" have not. Approximants of the latter kind are sometimes called semivowels, or glides. It will be more appropriate to discuss them after we have considered the nature of vowels more fully. But in order to describe vowels, we must first leave the field of articulatory phonetics and consider some of the basic principles of acoustic phonetics.

A more complete summary of the terms required so far for describing consonants is given in the first exercise that follows. Note that in order to define a consonant fully, you may need to say up to eight things about it: (1) What is the airstream mechanism; (2) what is the direction of the airstream; (3) what is the state of the glottis; (4) what part of the tongue is involved; (5) what is the primary place of articulation; (6) is it central or lateral; (7) is it oral or nasal; and (8) what is the manner of articulation? As we will see in Chapter 9, consonants may be even more complicated; so that in addition to stating the primary place of articulation, it may also be necessary to mention so-called secondary articulations, such as added lip rounding.

EXERCISES

The following table lists most of the terms required for classifying consonants. Make sure you know the meaning of all these terms.

(1)	**(2)**	**(3)**	**(4)**	**(5)**
Airstream	**Direction**	**Glottis**	**Tongue**	**Place**
pulmonic	egressive	voiced	apical	bilabial
glottalic	ingressive	voiceless	laminal	labiodental
velaric		murmured	(neither)	dental
		laryngealized		alveolar
		closed		retroflex
				palato-alveolar
				palatal
				velar
				uvular
				pharyngeal
				labial velar

(6)	**(7)**	**(8)**
Centrality	**Nasality**	**Manner**
central	oral	stop
lateral	nasal	fricative
		approximant
		trill
		flap
		tap

A Give a full description of the following sounds.

[b] _____

[tʰ] _____

[t'] _____

[ɬ] _____

[!] _____

[ʀ] _____

B List five combinations of terms that are impossible.

_____

_____

_____

_____

_____

C If we overlook secondary articulations such as rounding, most consonants can be specified by using one term from each of these eight columns. But, in addition to the affricates [tʃ, dʒ], one of the consonants listed in the chapter on transcription cannot be specified in this way. Which consonant is this? How can this deficiency be remedied?

_____

_____

D Still without considering secondary articulations and affricates, what sounds mentioned in this chapter cannot be specified by taking one term from each of the eight columns?

_____

_____

PERFORMANCE EXERCISES

This chapter, like the previous chapter, introduced many non-English sounds. During this part of the course, it is important to do as much practical work as time will allow. But do not try to go too fast. Make sure that you have thoroughly mastered the performance exercises at the end of Chapter 6 before going on to do the exercises that follow. Note that there are no performance exercises at the end of Chapter 8, so that you can allow more time for the exercises here and at the end of Chapter 6.

A Learn to produce voiceless stops before [ɑ] at a number of different places of articulation. Begin by making a clearly interdental stop, [t̪ɑ], with the tongue tip between the teeth. Next, make a very retroflex stop, [ʈɑ], with the tongue tip curled back and up toward the hard palate. Now try to make as many stops as you can with tongue positions between these two extremes. Using the diacritics [ˌ] and [ˍ] to mean more forward and more retracted, a series of this kind could be symbolized [t̪ɑ, t̪ɑ, t̪ɑ, tɑ, t̠ɑ, ʈɑ, ʈɑ]. Try to feel different articulatory positions such as these.

B Repeat Exercise A using a voiced stop:
[d̪ɑ, d̪ɑ, d̪ɑ, dɑ, d̠ɑ, ɖɑ, ɖɑ]

C Repeat Exercise A using a nasal:
[n̪ɑ, n̪ɑ, n̪ɑ, nɑ, n̠ɑ, ɳɑ, ɳɑ]

D Repeat Exercise A using a voiceless sibilant fricative of the [s] type. Note that it is perfectly possible to make a sibilant dental fricative [s̪], but a true interdental sibilant is not possible.

[s̪ɑ, s̪ɑ, sɑ, s̪ɑ, s̪ɑ, s̪ɑ]

E Repeat this exercise using a voiced sibilant fricative of the [z] type. Say:

[z̪ɑ, z̪ɑ, zɑ, z̪ɑ, z̪ɑ, z̪ɑ]

F Make a series of voiceless fricative articulations with the tongue tip down. Start with a palato-alveolar fricative [ʃ] with the blade of the tongue. (Be careful it is not made with the tip of the tongue up, which may be your normal articulation of this sound.) Next, move the point of articulation backward by raising the front of the tongue, so that you produce a palatal fricative [ç]. Then move the articulation farther back, producing first [x] and then [χ]. Finally, pull the tongue root back so that you produce a pharyngeal fricative [ħ]. Try to move in a continuous series, going through all the articulations:

[ʃ, ç, x, χ, ħ]

G Say these fricatives before vowels:

[ʃɑ, çɑ, xɑ, χɑ, ħɑ]

H Repeat Exercise F with the corresponding voiced sounds, producing the series:

[ʒ, ʝ, ɣ, ʁ, ʕ]

I Say these fricatives before vowels:

[ʒɑ, ʝɑ, ɣɑ, ʁɑ, ʕɑ]

J After you are fully aware of the positions of the tongue in all these fricatives, try saying some of the corresponding voiceless stops. There is no significant difference between palato-alveolar and palatal stops, and pharyngeal stops do not occur, so just say:

[cɑ, kɑ, qɑ]

K Repeat Exercise J with the voiced stops:

[ɟɑ, gɑ, ɢɑ]

L Repeat Exercise J with the voiced nasals:

[ɲɑ, ŋɑ, ɴɑ]

M Consolidate your ability to produce sounds at different places of articulation. Produce a complete series of nasals between vowels:

[ɑmɑ, ɑn̪ɑ, ɑnɑ, ɑɳɑ, ɑɲɑ, ɑŋɑ, ɑɴɑ]

N Produce a series of voiceless stops between vowels:

[ɑpɑ, ɑt̪ɑ, ɑtɑ, ɑʈɑ, ɑcɑ, ɑkɑ, ɑqɑ]

O Produce a series of voiced stops between vowels:
[αbα, αd̪α, αdα, αɖα, αɟα, αgα, αɢα]

P Produce a series of voiceless fricatives between vowels:
[αɸα, αfα, αθα, αsα, αʂα, αʃα, αçα, αχα, αχα, αhα]

Q Produce a series of voiced fricatives between vowels:
[αβα, αvα, αðα, αzα, αʐα, αʒα, αjα, αɣα, αʁα, αʕα]

R Repeat all these exercises using other vowels.

S Review the pronunciation of trills, taps, flaps, and similar sounding approximants. Say:
[αrα, αɾα, αɽα, αɹα, αʀα, αʁα]

T Some of these sounds are more difficult to pronounce between high vowels.
Say:
[iri, iɾi, iɽi, iɹi, iʀi, iʁi]

U Make sure that you can produce contrasting lateral sounds. Say:
[lα, ɮα, ɬα, ɭα, ʎα, tlα, tɬ'α, dlα]

V Repeat Exercise U with other vowels.

W Incorporate all these sounds into simple series of nonsense words, such as the
following:

ʁeˈsaʔi	taˈŋoʒe	ˈpʼexonu
ˈɬupez̧o	ˈbeɾeɬa	doʔeˈɗo
fiɣoˈca	βinoˈɟe	ʂeˈʃetʼe
koˈriɖo	ʀeˈʎaxa	ˈɢeheɹu
ˈɲeqeɸu	ˈɮaɲexo	moˈɓale

Remember that you should look at as well as listen to anyone saying ear-
training words.

8

ACOUSTIC PHONETICS

So far, we have been describing speech sounds mainly by stating how they are made, but it is also possible to describe them in terms of what we can hear. The way in which we hear a sound depends on its acoustic structure. In an introductory discussion of phonetics, there is no need to go into too much detail concerning the acoustic nature of speech sounds, but it is important to understand the basic principles involved, because we want to be able to describe the acoustics of speech for many reasons. Linguists and speech pathologists need to explain why certain sounds are confused with one another. They can also give better descriptions of some sounds (such as vowels) by describing their acoustic structure rather than by describing the articulatory movements involved. A knowledge of acoustic phonetics is also helpful for understanding how computers synthesize speech and how speech recognition works (topics that are addressed more fully in my book *Vowels and Consonants*). Furthermore, it is normally impossible to obtain photographs or x-rays showing what the speaker is doing. If we want to analyze speech we have to work from a recording. We can get more information than is available from merely listening to a recording by making acoustic analyses of the sounds.

We can hear that sounds with the same length can differ from one another in three ways. They can be the same or different in (1) pitch, (2) loudness, and (3) quality. Thus two vowel sounds may have exactly the same pitch and loudness but might differ in that one might be [e] and the other [o]. On the other hand, they might have the same vowel quality but differ in that one was said on a higher pitch than the other or that one of them was spoken more loudly. In this chapter, we will discuss each of these three aspects of speech sounds and consider the techniques of experimental phonetics that may be used for recording them.

SOUND WAVES

Sound consists of small variations in air pressure that occur very rapidly one after another. These variations are caused by actions of the speaker's vocal organs that are (for the most part) superimposed on the outgoing flow of lung air.

Thus in the case of voiced sounds, the vibrating vocal folds chop up the stream of lung air so that pulses of relatively high pressure alternate with moments of lower pressure. In fricative sounds, the airstream is forced through a narrow gap so that it becomes turbulent, with irregularly occurring peaks of pressure. The same principles apply in the production of other types of sounds.

Variations in air pressure in the form of sound waves move through the air somewhat like the ripples on a pond. When they reach the ear of a listener, they cause the eardrum to vibrate. A graph of a sound wave is very similar to a graph of the movements of the eardrum.

Figure 8.1 shows the variations in air pressure that occur during a small part of my pronunciation of the vowel [ɑ], as in "father." The vertical axis represents air pressure (relative to the normal surrounding air pressure), and the horizontal axis represents time (relative to an arbitrary starting point). As you can see, the major peaks in air pressure recur about every .01 seconds (that is, every one-hundredth of a second). This is because on this particular occasion, my vocal folds were vibrating approximately one hundred times a second. The smaller variations in air pressure that occur within each one-hundredth of a second period are due to the way air vibrates when the vocal tract has the particular shape required for the vowel [ɑ].

The waveforms of speech sounds can be readily observed on a computer. If we want to look at details of variations in the air pressure that occur as a result of two or three vibrations of the vocal folds, we can make pictures similar to Figure 8.1. But if we want to observe a longer phrase, we can compress the time scale and produce pictures such as that in Figure 8.2. The lower part of this figure is the waveform of the phrase "Jane, Pat, and John." (The upper part of the figure

| FIGURE 8.1 | The waveform during a short period (a little over two vocal fold vibrations) in my pronunciation of [ɑ], as in "caught." |

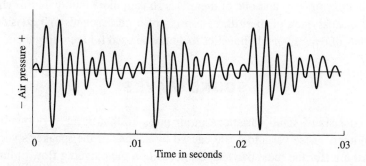

is a pitch record, which we will discuss later.) It is usually difficult to look at the waveform of an utterance and say what sounds occurred. However, the manner of articulation is often clear, and if one knows what has been said, one can look at the waveform and see at which point one manner of articulation changed into another. At the beginning of the utterance in Figure 8.2, there is a small spike followed by some very small random variations in air pressure. This is the affricate [dʒ] at the beginning of "Jane." Following this there are a number of vertical lines, corresponding to the pulses produced by the vibrating vocal folds in the vowel [eɪ]. It is difficult to say where the vowel ends and the nasal consonant begins, but the silence corresponding to the closure for [p] is clearly visible, as is the small burst of noise following the closure release and the subsequent aspiration. The vowel [æ] in "Pat" has regular vocal fold pulses (the vertical lines) that get further apart at the end as a creaky voice glottal stop occurs before the [t] closure. The word "and" was pronounced simply as a syllabic [n̩]. The [dʒ] in "John" has a very short closure, followed by a noisy waveform. As we saw in Chapter 6, English voiced stops (and affricates) are distinguished by having a negligible Voice Onset Time (VOT), rather than by voicing during the closure. Finally the vowel in "John" has regular vocal fold pulses.

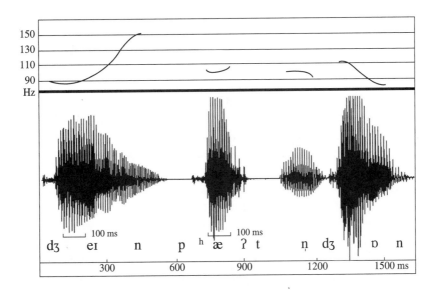

FIGURE 8.2   Acoustic records of the phrase "Jane, Pat, and John." The upper part of the figure shows the fundamental frequency (pitch). The waveform, with a narrow phonetic transcription, is below it. At the bottom there is a time scale.

PITCH AND FREQUENCY

As we saw in Chapter 1, the pitch of a sound depends on the rate of vibration of the vocal folds. In a sound with a high pitch, there is a higher frequency of vibration than in a sound with a low pitch. Because each opening and closing of the vocal folds causes a peak of air pressure in the sound wave, we can estimate the pitch of a sound by observing the rate of occurrence of the peaks in the waveform. To be more exact, we can measure the frequency of the sound in this way. **Frequency** is a technical term for an acoustic property of a sound—namely, the number of complete repetitions (cycles) of variations in air pressure occurring in a second. The unit of frequency measurement is the Hertz, usually abbreviated as Hz. If the vocal folds make 220 complete opening and closing movements in a second, we say that the frequency of the sound is 220 Hz. The frequency of the vowel [ɑ] shown in Figure 8.1 was 100 Hz as the vocal fold pulses occurred every 10 milliseconds (one hundredth of a second).

The **pitch** of a sound is that auditory property that enables a listener to place it on a scale going from low to high, without considering its acoustic properties. In practice, when a speech sound goes up in frequency, it also goes up in pitch. For the most part, at an introductory level of the subject, the pitch of a sound may be equated with its fundamental frequency, and, indeed, some books do not distinguish between the two terms, using pitch for both the auditory property and the physical attribute.

It is possible to determine the frequency of a sound by counting the peaks of air pressure in a record of its waveform. Near the bottom at the left of Figure 8.2, above the transcription, there is a bar indicating 100 milliseconds (one tenth of a second). As you can see, there were almost nine pulses of the vocal folds during this interval. In one second there would be almost 90 pulses. You can check your understanding of what is meant by frequency by trying to estimate the frequency of the vocal fold pulses in the waveform of the vowel in "Pat." (You should find that it is about 100 Hz.)

Looking at the peaks in the waveform is a very time-consuming way to determine the frequency of the vocal fold vibrations in an utterance. Fortunately, computer systems will provide graphical displays corresponding to the pitch. As well as the waveform, Figure 8.2 shows the output of the PCquirer/Macquirer program (from SciConRD), which determines the fundamental frequency at each moment in an utterance. You can see that the pitch goes up at the end of the first two words and falls throughout the last word. As we saw in Chapter 5, this is a typical intonation pattern for a list of items in English.

All the intonation curves shown in Chapter 5 are redrawn versions of pitch curves of the kind shown in Figure 8.2. You may have noticed a somewhat odd fact about the sentences used as illustrations of different intonations: they contained almost no voiceless sounds and hardly any voiced stops or fricatives. This is because voiceless sounds have no vocal fold pulses and therefore no pitch. Voiced stops and fricatives also perturb the smooth pitch curve.

Voiced sounds have a regular waveform of the kind that you hear as having a recognizable pitch. In voiceless sounds, the variations in air pressure are caused by the smooth flow of the airstream being interrupted by being forced through a narrow channel or directed over irregular surfaces. In the sound waves that are produced, there are usually more rapid (and therefore higher frequency) variations in air pressure than occur during voiced sounds. For a male voice, the frequency of the vocal fold vibrations in speech may be between 80 and 200 Hz. A woman's voice may go up to about 400 Hz. The predominant frequencies in voiceless sounds are usually above 2,000 Hz.

LOUDNESS AND INTENSITY

In general, the **loudness** of a sound depends on the size of the variations in air pressure that occur. Just as frequency is the acoustic measurement most directly corresponding to the pitch of a sound, so acoustic intensity is the appropriate measure corresponding to loudness. The **intensity** is proportional to the average size, or amplitude, of the variations in air pressure. It is usually measured in decibels (abbreviated as dB) relative to the amplitude of some other sounds. Technically, to get the dB difference one has to compare the power ratio, where the power is defined as the square of the mean amplitude (the mean variation in air pressure). The difference in dB is 10 times the common logarithm of the power ratio of the two sounds or 20 times the log of the amplitude ratio. The human ear can hear (perhaps tolerate would be a better word) a range of about 120 dB, although if you persist in listening to sounds 110 to 120 dB above the quietest sound you can hear you will soon go deaf, as many rock musicians have found out. When one sound has an intensity 5 dB greater than another, then it is approximately twice as loud. A change in intensity of 1 dB is a little more than the just noticeable difference in loudness.

Figure 8.3 shows the waveform of the phrase "We saw three dogs" and underneath it a record of the intensity in dB. Intensity is always a relative measure—one sound has an intensity of so many dB more or less than another. The zero point in Figure 8.3 is arbitrarily taken to be the level recorded for the silence (actually the quiet room noise) at the beginning and end of the utterance. The vowels in "We" and "see" have a level of about 34 dB above this. The vowels in "saw" and "dogs" have intensities about 10 dB greater still, making them well over twice as loud. The two fricatives, [s] and [θ], are much lower, [s] having a mean of about 17 dB and [θ] being about 13 dB above the base line. Generally, vowels such as [ɑ] and [ɔ], in which the mouth is more open, are about 5 dB greater than vowels such as [i] and [u], assuming all these vowels have been

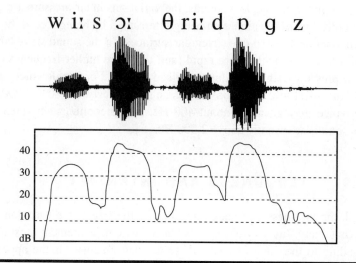

The waveform of the phrase "We saw three dogs;" underneath it is a record of the intensity in dB.

said with an equal degree of stress. In this particular phrase, the words "saw" and "dogs" were stressed, so their vowels have an even higher intensity. In any utterance, the actual intensity of a segment will depend on many factors, such as its position in the sentence, the degree of stress on each word, and the personal characteristics of the speaker.

ACOUSTIC MEASUREMENTS

The frequency (pitch) record in Figure 8.2 has been calibrated with scales in Hz, and the intensity record in Figure 8.3 has been calibrated in dB. One of the objectives of any science is to be able to measure the things that are being described so that they can be expressed in terms of valid, reliable, and significant numbers that other people can check. A valid number is one that truly measures the thing that you say you are measuring. Thus, technically speaking, a measurement of frequency in Hz is not a valid measurement of the pitch unless we can show that frequency measurements are related to how people perceive pitch. In fact, experiments on the perception of pitch have shown that within the range of pitches used by both male and female voices, a change in frequency is directly related to a change in pitch. A pitch change from 100 to 300 Hz is perceived as being the same (within small limits) as one from 300 to 500 Hz, so we can regard frequency as being equivalent to pitch when discussing the pitch of the voice. At frequencies above 1,000 Hz equal increases in frequency are not perceived as equal increases in pitch. The interval from 1,000 to 2,000 Hz is judged to be more like the interval between 2,000 and 4,000 Hz, a doubling of the frequency. The relation between pitch and frequency has been derived experimentally and used to form the **Bark scale.** Equal distances along the Bark scale correspond to equal changes in pitch. The mathematical relation between Hz and Bark is fairly complex (see Sources at the end of the book). Later in this chapter we will use it (in a computer program) to plot the frequencies of complex sounds in a way that reflects the difference in pitch between them. However, when dealing simply with the pitch of the voice, a straightforward linear plot of the frequency is sufficient.

The relation between acoustic intensity and loudness is also nonlinear, but fortunately only slightly so. For all practical purposes we can consider differences in loudness to be simply related to differences in intensity, reported in dB. As we noted earlier, each increase of 5 dB corresponds to a doubling of the perceived loudness.

Acoustic records are useful for studying various kinds of phonetic problems. Records of the waveform and the intensity provide a good way of studying variations in length. Figure 8.4 illustrates records of four sentences of the form "Say _____ now." These sentences allow us to study the relative lengths of the segments in the words "pat, pad, bad, spat." Each word has been said in the same frame "Say _____ now" so as to make sure that the differences are not due to variations in the rate of utterance. If the words "say" and "now" are about the same on each occasion, then we can assume that the speaker was talking at a constant rate. Furthermore, if the words had been said simply as a list of items, then almost certainly the last one would have been longer and with a falling intonation pattern (as in the phrase "Jane, Pat, and John" in Figure 8.2). Even when reading a list of sentences such as those in Figure 8.3, it is difficult not to make the last one longer. If you are getting someone else to read a list of words or sentences that you are going to measure, it is often a good idea to add one or two extra items at the end which you simply disregard when you make the relevant measurements.

The first utterance in Figure 8.4 has been segmented so that you can measure the duration of each item. Of course, I have made no attempt to split either of the diphthongs [eɪ] or [aʊ] into two elements. It would be meaningless to do so, since they are both single vowels with continuously changing qualities. The fact that each of them is written with two separate symbols does not mean that each contains two distinct elements.

You should now try to segment the other utterances in Figure 8.4 in a similar way. How much longer is the vowel in "pad" than that in "pat?" Is the [t] in "pat" longer or shorter than the [d] in "pad?" Note that the [b] closure in the

FIGURE 8.4 Waveforms of "Say pat now; say pad now; say bad now; say spat now." Only the first of these phrases has been segmented. You should try to segment the other three phrases yourself.

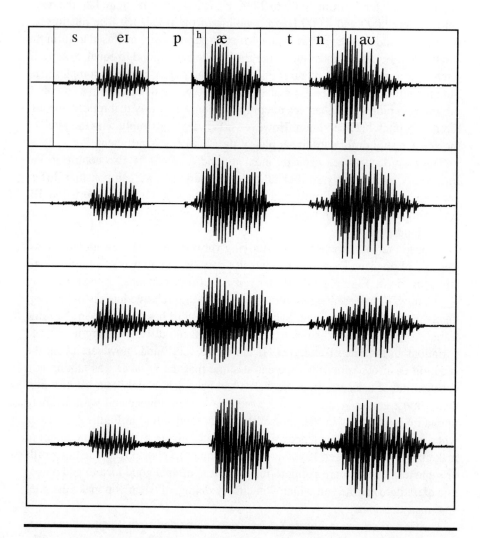

third utterance is voiced throughout, but is it longer or shorter than the [p] closure in "pat?" Is the [p] in "spat" aspirated, or does the voicing start immediately after the release of the consonant? Is the vowel in "spat" longer than the vowel in "pat?"

Now consider the two utterances in Figure 8.5. Both of them contain the sentence "Bonny told Peter she'd plans to leave," spoken by a British English speaker. Try to segment these two utterances. Look for the [n] in the middle of

FIGURE 8.5 Waveform and pitch records of "Bonny told Peter she'd plans to leave," said in two different ways.

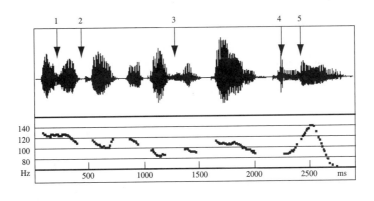

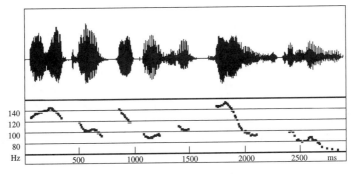

"Bonny," evident as a decrease in the energy between the two vowels, marked (1) in the sentence in the upper part of the figure. Now find the silence, (2), for the aspirated stop at the beginning of "told." You should be able to find the silence for the stop at the beginning of "Peter" (which has not been marked). Remember that British speakers usually have a voiceless stop in the middle of "Peter," so you can also find another period of silence for the [t]. The [ʃ] is represented by a random pattern, marked (3), followed by the regular voicing vibrations for the short vowel in "she'd." The silence for the [p] of "plans" is clear, but it is virtually impossible to make a phonetic transcription showing all the separate segments of "plans." In the sentence in the upper part of the figure, the word "to" is pronounced with considerable aspiration and there are only a couple of voicing vibrations for the vowel (4). There is an abrupt decrease in the amplitude for the [l], and then the long vowel in "leave" starts at arrow (5). The sentence in the lower part of the figure has a slightly longer vowel in "to" and then the same sort of change in the pattern for [l] before the vowel. In neither case is the final [v] easily distinguished.

This sentence can be said in two different ways. It could mean "Bonny told Peter she had some drawings she was going to leave (for him to look at)." Or it could mean "Bonny told Peter that she had intentions to leave (the house)." Try to read the sentence in these two different ways, and notice how the intonation patterns differ. In the one meaning, the major pitch fall is likely to be on "plans," in the other, the fall will be on "leave." The frequency curve makes it quite clear that in the lower sentence Bonny is talking about architectural drawings.

ACOUSTIC ANALYSIS OF VOWELS

In the first part of this chapter, I described how differences in pitch and loudness can be recorded. Now we must consider the differences in quality. A set of vowel sounds provides a suitable starting point, since vowels can all be said on the same pitch and with the same loudness.

The quality of a sound such as a vowel depends on its overtone structure. Putting this another way, we can say that a vowel sound contains a number of different pitches simultaneously. There is the pitch at which it is actually spoken, and there are the various overtone pitches that give it its distinctive quality. We distinguish one vowel from another by the differences in the overtones.

Normally, one cannot hear the separate overtones of a vowel as distinguishable pitches. The only sensation of pitch is the note on which the vowel is said, which depends on the rate of vibration (the frequency) of the vocal folds. But there are circumstances in which the characteristic overtone structure of each vowel can be heard. Try saying the vowels [i, ɪ, ɛ, æ, ɑ, ɔ, ʊ, u] as in the words "heed, hid, head, had, hod, hawed, hood, who'd," but say all of them as long vowels. Now whisper these vowels. In a whispered sound, the vocal folds are not vibrating, and there is no regular pitch of the voice. Nevertheless, when you whisper these vowels you can hear that they form a series of sounds on a continuously descending pitch. What you are hearing is one of the overtones that characterize the vowels. This particular overtone is highest for [i] and probably lowest for [ɔ] or [ʊ, u], with the other vowels falling in between. Now try whistling a very high note and then the lowest note that you can. You will find that for the high note you have to have your tongue in the position for [i]—but, of course, with the lips rounded, as in the vowel in the French word "tu"—and for the low note your tongue and lips are in the [u] position. Again, intermediate notes would have the tongue positions of the other vowels in the series. From all this it seems as if there is some kind of high pitch associated with [i], and a low pitch associated with [u].

Another way of removing or minimizing the auditory effect of the vocal fold frequency is to say the vowels in a very low, creaky voice. It is easiest to produce this kind of voice with a vowel such as [æ] or [ɑ]. Some people can produce a creaky-voice sound in which the rate of vibration of the vocal folds is so low that you can hear the individual pulsations.

Try saying just the four vowels [i, ɪ, ɛ, æ] as in the words "heed, hid, head, had" in a creaky voice. You should be able to hear a change in pitch, although, in one sense, the pitch of all of them is just that of the low creaky voice. In this series of vowels, there is a clearly audible overtone that steadily increases in pitch by approximately equal steps with each vowel. Now say the four vowels [ɑ, ɔ, ʊ, u] as in "hod, hawed, hood, who'd" in a creaky voice. These four vowels have an overtone with a steadily decreasing pitch.

There is another way in which it is possible to hear the pitch of this overtone. Make a vowel such as [æ], and then make a glottal stop while retaining the same tongue position. Now flick a finger against your throat just above the larynx. You should hear a dull hollow note corresponding to the pitch of the overtone. Try making another vowel position and hear how the pitch changes. If you tilt your head slightly backward so that the skin of the neck is stretched, you may be able to hear this sound somewhat better. But be careful to maintain a vowel position and not to raise the back of the tongue against the soft palate. If you check a complete set of vowel positions [i, ɪ, e, ɛ, æ, ɑ, ɔ, ʊ, u] with this technique, you should hear the pitch go up for the first four vowels and down for the second four vowels, just as it does in creaky voice.

Summarizing what I have said about acoustic quality so far, vowels are largely distinguished by two characteristic pitches associated with their overtones. One of them (actually the higher of the two) goes downward throughout most of the series [i, ɪ, e, ɛ, æ, ɑ, ɔ, o, u]. The other goes up for the first four vowels and then down for the next four. These characteristic overtones are called the **formants** of the vowels, the lower of the two being called the first formant and the higher the second formant. Actually, there is another characteristic overtone, the third formant, which is also present, but there is no simple way of demonstrating its pitch. Higher formants may also be evident, but we will not consider them until later in this chapter.

It is possible to analyze sounds so that we can measure the actual frequencies of the formants. We can then represent them graphically as in Figure 8.6. This figure gives the average of a number of authorities' values of the frequencies of the first three formants in eight American English vowels. Try to see how your own vowels compare with these. Do you have a much larger jump in the pitch of the second formant (which you hear when whispering) between [ɛ] and [æ] as compared with [ɪ] and [ɛ]? Do you distinguish between "hod" and "hawed" in terms of their formant frequencies?

The formants that characterize different vowels are the result of the different shapes of the vocal tract. Any body of air, such as that in the vocal tract or that in a bottle, will vibrate in a way that depends on its size and shape. If you blow across the top of an empty bottle, you can usually produce a low-pitched note. If you partially fill the bottle with water so that the volume of air is smaller,

FIGURE 8.6
The frequencies of the first three formants in eight American English vowels.

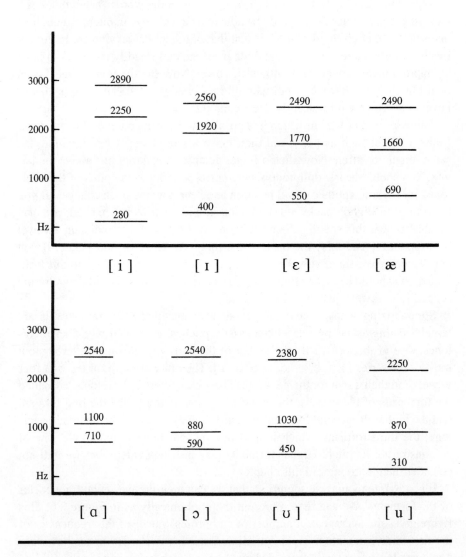

you will be able to produce a note with higher pitch. Smaller bodies of air, like smaller piano strings or smaller organ pipes, produce higher pitches. In the case of vowel sounds, the vocal tract has a complex shape so that the different bodies of air produce a number of overtones.

The air in the vocal tract is set in vibration by the action of the vocal folds. Every time the vocal folds open and close, there is a pulse of air from the lungs.

These pulses act like sharp taps on the air in the vocal tract, setting the resonating cavities into vibration so that they produce a number of different frequencies, just as if you were tapping on a number of different bottles at the same time. Irrespective of the rate of vibration of the vocal folds, the air in the vocal tract will resonate at these frequencies as long as the position of the vocal organs remains the same. A vowel has its own characteristic auditory quality, which is the result of the specific variations in air pressure due to its vocal tract shape being superimposed on the fundamental frequency produced by the vocal folds.

There is nothing particularly new about this way of analyzing vowel sounds. The general theory of formants was stated by the great German scientist Hermann Helmholtz almost 150 years ago. Even earlier, in 1829, the English physicist Robert Willis had said, "A given vowel is merely the rapid repetition of its peculiar note." We would nowadays say that it is the rapid repetition (corresponding to the vibrations of the vocal folds) of its peculiar two or three notes (corresponding to its formants). Willis was one of the first people to make an instrumental analysis of the acoustic structure of speech. But the notion of a single formant (actually the second formant) had been observed several centuries earlier. In about 1665, Isaac Newton wrote in his notebook: "The filling of a very deepe flaggon with a constant streame of beere or water sounds ye vowells in this order w, u, ω, o, a, e, i, y." He was about twelve years old at the time. (The symbols are the best matches to the letters in Newton's handwriting in his notebook, which is in the British Museum. We can only guess at what he had in mind, but most of them might well have something like their IPA values.) Fill a deep narrow glass with water (or beer!) and see if you can hear something like the second formant in the vowels [u, o, ɔ, ɑ, æ, ɛ, e, i] as the glass fills up.

It is difficult to hear the formants—the overtones that distinguish vowels—when you say them all on the same pitch. There are, however, computer programs that can analyze sounds and show their separate components. The display that is produced is called a **spectrogram,** in which time runs from left to right, the frequency of the components is shown on the vertical scale, and the intensity of each component is shown by the darkness. It is thus a display that shows, roughly speaking, dark bands for each of the groups of overtone pitches in a sound.

Figure 8.7 is a set of spectrograms of an American English speaker saying the words "heed, hid, head, had, hod, hawed, hood, who'd." Because the higher frequencies of the human voice have less energy, the higher frequencies have been given added emphasis. If they had not been boosted in this way, the higher formants would not have been visible. The time scale along the bottom of the picture shows intervals of 100 ms, so you can see that these words differ in length. The words were actually said one after another, but they have been put in separate frames as there was no point showing the blank spaces between them. The vertical scale goes up to 4,000 Hz, which is sufficient to show the component frequencies of vowels. Because the formants have greater relative intensity,

| FIGURE 8.7 | A spectrogram of the words "heed, hid, head, had, hod, hawed, hood, who'd" as spoken by a male speaker of American English. The locations of the first three formants are shown by arrows. |

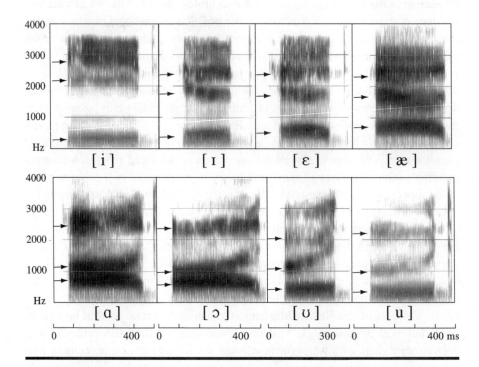

shown by the darkness of the mark, they can be seen as dark horizontal bars. The location of the first three formants in each vowel are indicated by arrows.

There is a great deal of similarity between Figures 8.6 and 8.7. Figure 8.6 is like a schematic spectrogram of the isolated vowels. Figure 8.7 differs in that it represents a particular American English speaker rather than the mean of a number of speakers of American English. It also shows the effects of the consonant at the end of the word (which we will discuss later), and the slightly diphthongal character of some of the vowels. Note, for example, that the vowel [ɪ] starts with a higher second formant, and that the vowel [ʊ] has a large upward movement of the second formant. There is also a small downward movement of the second formant at the end of [æ], indicating diphthongization of this vowel, that we will note further when discussing consonants. In addition, there are some extra horizontal bars corresponding to higher formants that are not linguistically significant. The exact position of the higher formants varies a great deal from speaker to speaker. They are not uniquely determined for each speaker, but they certainly are indicative of a person's voice quality.

Figure 8.8 shows spectrograms of my form of British English. It is similar to Figure 8.7, but not exactly the same both because of the differences in accent and because of the individual differences. My head is larger than that of the American English speaker, so all my formants are slightly lower. My vowels are less diphthongal—they have longer steady states.

Whenever the vocal folds are vibrating, there are regularly spaced vertical lines, close together, on the spectrogram. During a vowel, the vertical lines are visible throughout a large part of the spectrogram. Each vertical line in the vowels is the result of the momentary increase of acoustic energy due to a single movement of the vocal folds. We have seen that it is possible to observe the pulses in a record of the waveform and from this to calculate the pitch. It is equally possible to measure the pitch from observations of the vertical striations on spectrograms. When they are close together, the pitch must be higher than when they are farther apart. At the bottom left of Figure 8.8, below the baseline but just above the symbol for [ɒ], there are two small lines, 100 ms apart. Within this tenth of a second you can see that there are between eight and nine

FIGURE 8.8   A spectrogram of the words "heed, hid, head, had, hod, hawed, hood, who'd" as spoken in a British accent. The locations of the first three formants are shown by arrows.

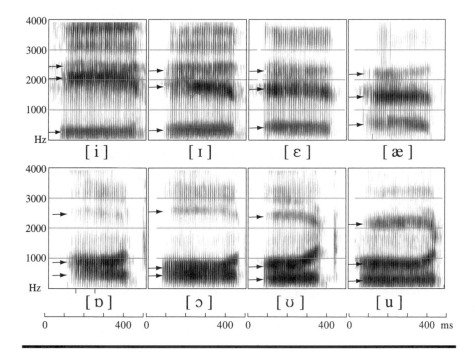

vertical striations in the vowel formants. The vocal folds must have been vibrating at about 85 Hz. This is not the best way of using spectrograms to determine the pitch. As we will see, it is possible to make another kind of spectrographic record that gives a better picture of the variations in pitch.

The traditional articulatory descriptions of vowels are related to the formant frequencies. We can see that the first formant frequency (indicated by the lowest of the three arrows in the frame for each vowel) increases as the speaker moves from the high vowel in "heed" to the low vowel in "had." In these four vowels the first formant frequency goes up as the vowel height goes down, both for the American English speaker in Figure 8.7 and for my vowels in Figure 8.8. In the four vowels in the bottom rows of Figures 8.7 and 8.8, the first formant frequency decreases as the speaker goes from the low vowel in "hod" to the high vowel in "who'd." Again in these vowels, the first formant frequency is inversely related to vowel height. We can also see that the second formant frequency is much higher for the front vowels in the top row than it is for the back vowels in the bottom row in each figure. But the correlation between the second formant frequency and the degree of backness of a vowel is not as good as that between the first formant frequency and the vowel height. The second formant frequency is considerably affected by the degree of lip rounding as well as vowel height.

We can see some of these relationships when we plot the formant frequencies given in Figure 8.6 along axes as shown in Figure 8.9. Because the formant frequencies are inversely related to the traditional articulatory parameters, the axes have been placed so that zero frequency would be at the top right corner of the figure rather than at the bottom left corner, as is more usual in graphical representations. In addition, the frequencies have been arranged in accordance with the bark scale, mentioned earlier, in which perceptually equal intervals of pitch are represented as equal distances along the scale. As a further refinement, because the second formant is not as prominent as the first formant (which, on average, has 80% of the energy in a vowel), the second formant scale is not as expanded as the first formant scale. (Remember that in Figures 8.7 and 8.8, and in all the spectrograms in this book, the darkness scale does not correspond directly to the acoustic intensity of each sound. The higher frequencies have been given added emphasis so as to make them more visible.)

On this kind of plot, [i] and [u] appear at the top left and right of the graph, and [æ] and [ɑ] are at the bottom, with all the other vowels in between. Consequently, this arrangement allows us to represent vowels in the way that we have become accustomed to seeing them in traditional articulatory descriptions.

In the preceding paragraphs, I have been careful to refer to the correlation between formant frequencies and the *traditional* articulatory descriptions. This is because, as we noted in Chapter 1, traditional articulatory descriptions are not entirely satisfactory. They are often not in accord with the actual articulatory

FIGURE 8.9	A formant chart showing the frequency of the first formant on the ordinate (the vertical axis) plotted against the second formant on the abscissa (the horizontal axis) for eight American English vowels. The scales are marked in Hz, arranged at Bark scale intervals.

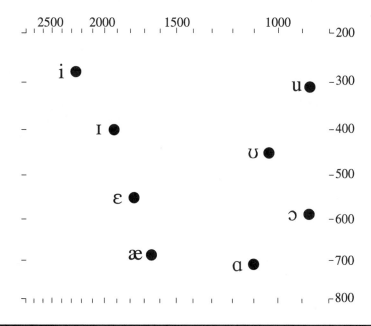

facts. For well over a hundred years, phoneticians have been describing vowels in terms such as high versus low and front versus back. There is no doubt that these terms are appropriate for describing the relationships between different vowel qualities, but to some extent phoneticians have been using these terms as labels to specify acoustic dimensions rather than as descriptions of actual tongue positions. As G. Oscar Russell, one of the pioneers in x-ray studies of vowels, said, "Phoneticians are thinking in terms of acoustic fact, and using physiological fantasy to express the idea."

There is no doubt that the traditional description of vowel "height" is more closely related to the first formant frequency than to the height of the tongue. The so-called front–back dimension has a more complex relationship to the formant frequencies. As we have noted, the second formant is affected by both backness and lip rounding. We can eliminate some of the effects of lip rounding by considering the second formant in relation to the first. The degree of backness is best related to the difference between the first and the second formant frequencies. The closer they are together, the more back a vowel sounds.

Formant charts are now commonly used to represent vowel qualities. In order to consolidate acoustic notions about vowels, you should now try to represent the vowels in Figures 8.7 and 8.8 in terms of a formant chart. I have provided arrows that mark what I take to be the formants that characterize these vowels. Measure these frequencies in terms of the scale on the left of each figure. Make a table listing the first and second formant frequencies and plot the vowels. A blank chart is provided in Figure 8.10.

FIGURE 8.10 A blank formant chart for showing the relation between vowels. Using the information in Figures 8.7 and 8.8, plot the frequency of the first formant on the ordinate (the vertical axis) and the second formant on the abscissa (the horizontal axis).

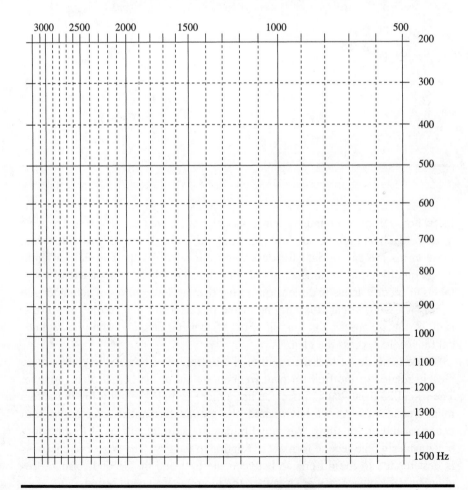

ACOUSTIC ANALYSIS OF CONSONANTS

The acoustic structure of consonants is usually more complicated than that of vowels. In many cases, a consonant can be said to be a particular way of beginning or ending a vowel, and during the consonant articulation itself there is no distinguishing feature. Thus there is virtually no difference in the sounds during the actual closures of [b, d, g], and absolutely none at all during the closures of [p, t, k], for at these moments there is only silence.

Each of the stop sounds conveys its quality by its effect on the adjacent vowel. We have seen that during a vowel such as [æ], there will be formants corresponding to the particular shape of the vocal tract. These formants will be present as the lips open in a syllable such as [bæ]. They will have frequencies corresponding to the particular shape that occurs at the moment that the lips come apart. As the lips come farther apart and the vocal tract shape changes, the formants will move correspondingly. Closure of the lips causes a lowering of all the formants. Consequently, the syllable [bæ] will begin with the formants in a lower position and will be distinguished by their rapidly rising to the positions for [æ]. Similarly, in the syllable [æb], the formants in [æ] will descend as the lip closure is formed. In an alveolar or velar stop the tongue has a particular position that affects the formants. Whichever stop is formed or released, there will be a particular shape of the vocal tract that will be characterized by particular formant frequencies.

When you say "bib" or "bab," for example, the tongue will be in the position for the vowel even when the lips are closed at the beginning of the word. Consequently the formant frequencies at the beginning of "bib" will not be exactly the same as those at the beginning of "bab." Nevertheless the formants will have a different origin from those in "did" or "dad," because the vocal tract shapes associated with these these stops are different. The apparent point of origin of the formant for each place of articulation is called the **locus** of that place of articulation.

Figure 8.11 shows spectrograms of the words "bab, dad, gag," as spoken by the American English speaker who produced the vowels in Figure 8.7. In each case he said the word "a" [ə] in front so as to make the voicing during the consonant visible. (I have also made the spectrogram rather darker than usual for the same reason.) You can see the faint voicing striations near the baseline above each of the symbols [b, d, g]. At the beginning of each of these syllables they are less evident than at the end. Evidence of voicing near the baseline during a consonant closure is called a **voice bar.**

In all three words the first formant rises from a low position. This is simply a mark of a stop closure and does not play a major part in distinguishing one place of articulation from another. What primarily distinguishes these three stops is the onsets and offsets of the second and third formants. The onsets are marked

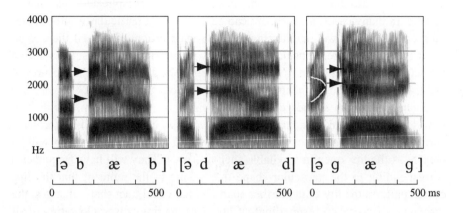

FIGURE 8.11   A spectrogram of the words "a bab, a dad, a gag."

by arrows in Figure 8.11. At the beginning of the word "bab" the second and third formants have a lower frequency than they do at the beginning of the word "dad." The second formant is noticeably rising for the initial [b] from a comparatively low locus. At the end of this word the fall is not so evident because of the diphthongization of this vowel. There is, however, a distinct decrease in the frequency of the third formant. In the word "dad," both the second and the third formants are fairly steady at the beginning. At the end of the word the third formant frequency is steady, not falling as it was before [b], and there is a noticeable increase in the second formant, after the lowering due to the diphthongization. In "gag" the most noticeable feature is the narrowing of the distance between the second and third formants. The raising effect on the second formant persists throughout the vowel, so that this vowel is no longer a diphthong. The second and third formants have been marked by white lines in the syllable [ə] before "gag." It is almost as if they were going to a common point. This coming together of the second and third formants is very characteristic of velar consonants.

The corresponding voiceless stops [p, t, k] are illustrated in Figure 8.12, in the words "Pam, tan, kang." There is, of course, no word "kang;" it is just the first part of the word "kangaroo." Again the word "a" [ə] has been put in front of each of these syllables. The release of the aspirated stops is marked by a sharp spike corresponding to the onset of a burst of noise. This noise has a comparatively random pattern, mainly in the upper frequencies. The burst for [p] in "Pam" has the lowest frequency. For both [t] and [k] the noise extends above the 4,000 Hz shown in the spectrogram, as we will see in later figures. The highest frequencies are actually in the [t] burst rather than the [k]. If you whisper a

| FIGURE 8.12 | A spectrogram of the words "a Pam, a tan, a kang." The arrows indicate the oral closures forming the nasal consonants. |

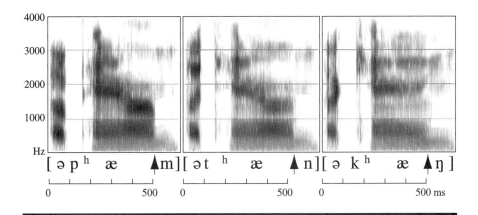

sequence of consonants [t, t, t, k, k, k, p, p, p] in that order, [t, k, p], you can hear that the highest pitch is associated with [t], the next with [k], and the lowest with [p]. You can also hear that [t] is the loudest, [k] next, and [p] is the least loud. The intensity of the [p] burst is sometimes so low that there is hardly any evidence of a sharp spike in the spectrogram. The formant transitions after voiceless aspirated stops take place during the period of aspiration and are therefore not as apparent in Figure 8.12 as they are after the voiced stops in Figure 8.11. However, you can see the upward movements of the second and third formants during the aspiration (above the [ʰ]) in "Pam." In addition, the transitions into the stops from the vowels before them are easily visible. The second and third formants are falling at the end of [ə] before [p], the second formant is rising, and the third is almost level before [t], and, most distinctive of all, the second and third formants are coming together before [k].

The nasal consonants [m, n, ŋ] are also illustrated in Figure 8.12. A clear mark of a nasal (or, as we will see, a lateral) consonant is an abrupt change in the spectrogram at the time of the formation of the articulatory closure, indicated by an arrow just before the nasal symbols in Figure 8.12. Each of the nasals has a formant structure similar to that of a vowel, except that the bands are fainter and are in particular frequency locations that depend on the characteristic resonances of the nasal cavities. In nasal consonants, there is usually a very low first formant centered at about 250 Hz. The location of the higher formants varies, but generally there is a large region above the first formant with no energy. This speaker has a second, rather faint, nasal formant just below 2,000 Hz. The difference between each of the nasals is often determinable from the different formant transitions that occur at the end of each vowel. There is a decrease in the second formant of the vowel before [m] and formants two and three are coming together before the velar nasal at the end of "kang." But the place cues are sometimes not very clear.

Figure 8.13 shows the words "fie, thigh, sigh, shy," illustrating the voiceless fricatives. The frequency scale for these spectrograms has been increased to 8,000 Hz, as the highest frequencies in speech occur during fricatives. In [s] sounds, the random noise extends well beyond the upper limits of even this spectrogram. The spectrogram of the first word, "fie," shows the diphthong that occurs in each of these words. The second and third formants in this diphthong start close together in the position for a low central vowel. They then move apart so that at the end of the diphthong they are in locations similar to those in [ɪ] in Figure 8.7. As the formant pattern for the diphthong is the same in "fie, thigh, sigh, shy," only the first part has been shown for the last three words.

All these sounds have random energy distributed over a wide range of frequencies. In [f] and [θ] the pattern is much the same. What distinguishes these two words is the movement of the second formant into the following vowel, marked by arrows in the figure. There is very little movement in [f], but in [θ] the second formant starts at around 1,200 Hz and moves down. Because the differences between these two sounds are so small, they are often confused in noisy circumstances, and they have fallen together as one sound in some accents of English, such as London Cockney, which does not distinguish between "fin" and "thin."

FIGURE 8.13   A spectrogram of the words "fie, thigh, sigh, shy." The frequency scale goes up to 8,000 Hz in this figure. The arrows mark the onsets of the second formant transitions. Only the first word is shown in full. The second part of the diphthong has been deleted for the other words.

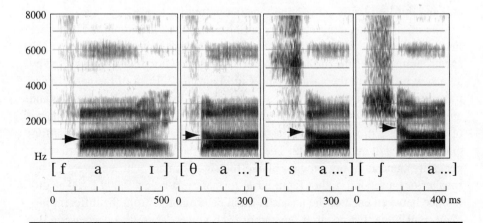

The noise in [s] is centered at a high frequency, between 5,000 and 6,000 Hz in Figure 8.13. In [ʃ] it is lower, extending down to about 2,500 Hz. Both [s] and [ʃ] have a comparatively large acoustic intensity and hence produce darker patterns than [f] or [θ]. They are also marked by distinctive formant transitions. The apparent origin (the locus) of the second formant transition increases throughout the four words "fie, thigh, sigh, shy," so that in the "shy" it is in a position comparable with its location in the vowel [ɪ] and falls considerably.

The voiced fricatives corresponding to [f, θ, s, ʃ] do not contrast at the beginnings of words. Accordingly Figure 8.14 shows [v, ð, z, ʒ] in between vowels. These voiced fricatives have patterns similar to their voiceless counterparts, but with the addition of the vertical striations indicative of voicing. The fricative component of [v] in "ever" is even fainter than the [f] in "face" and is really only visible at the start of the following vowel. The vertical striations due to voicing are apparent throughout the articulation. The same is true of [ð] in "whether." As with their voiceless counterparts, [f, θ], it is the formants in the adjacent vowels that distinguish these words. In this figure, both these fricatives are preceded by [ɛ] and followed by [ɚ]. The second formants are much higher around [ð] than around [v].

The fricative energy in the higher frequencies is very apparent in [z] and [ʒ]. There is a faint voice bar in [z], but in [ʒ] the voicing is hard to see. There are only a few vertical striations due to voicing in the 6,000 to 8,000 Hz range at the beginning of the fricative noise. The formant transition from [z] into the vowel [ɚ] is level, but that from [ʒ] falls considerably. This last word, "pleasure," also enables us to see what happens when an aspirated stop such as [p] is followed by an approximant such as [l]. Most of the [l] is voiceless, audible only by the effect it has on the [p] burst and the aspiration noise.

FIGURE 8.14   A spectrogram of "ever, weather, fizzer, pleasure."

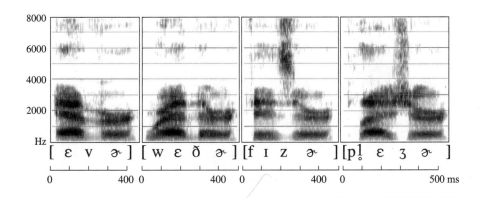

The last set of English consonants to consider are the lateral and central aproximants, [l, r, w, j]. Figure 8.15 shows these sounds in the words "led, red, wed, yell." All these voiced approximants have formants not unlike those of vowels. The initial lateral in the first word has formants with center frequencies of approximately 250, 1,100, and 2,400 (low intensity), which change abruptly in intensity at the beginning of the vowel. As we noted earlier, a marked change in the formant pattern is characteristic of voiced nasals and laterals. At the end of a word, as in "yell" in Figure 8.14, there may be a less marked change. A final lateral may have little or no central contact, making it not really a lateral but a back unrounded vowel. A formant in the neighborhood of 1,100 or 1,200 Hz is typical of most initial laterals for most speakers.

The second word in Figure 8.15 illustrates the approximant [r] in "red." (Remember that in the broad transcription of English used in this book, the symbol [r] is used for the approximant [ɹ].) The most obvious feature of this kind of [r] is the very low frequency of the third formant. In this example, its origin (above the symbol [r]) is around 1,600 Hz, only just above the second formant, which also rises for this front vowel. There is a great deal of similarity between "red" and the third word, "wed," which is why young children sometimes have difficulty learning to distinguish them. The approximant [w] also starts with a low position of all three formants, but this time it is the second formant that has the sharpest rise. The movements of the formants for [w] are like those in a movement away from a very short [u] vowel. Finally, the movements of the formants for [j], as in "yell" or "yes," are like those in a movement away from a very short [i] vowel. Both [w] and [j] are appropriately called semivowels.

I hope that the vagueness of many of the remarks in the preceding paragraphs has led you to realize that the interpretation of sound spectrograms is often not

---

FIGURE 8.15   A spectrogram of "led, red, wed, yell."

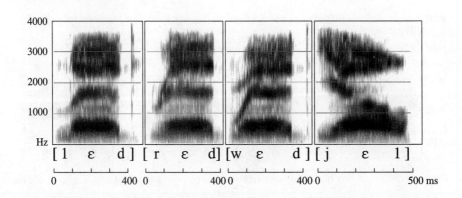

all straightforward. The acoustic correlates of some articulatory features are summarized in Table 8.1. But in a book such as this it is impossible to give a completely detailed account of the acoustics of speech. The descriptions that have been given should be regarded as rough guides rather than accounts of in-variable structures that can always be seen in spectrograms. When any of the segments described occurs in a different phonetic context, it may have a very different acoustic structure.

All the words illustrated in spectrograms so far were spoken in a fairly dis-tinct way. In connected speech, as in the remainder of the spectrograms illustrat-ing this chapter, many of the sounds are more difficult to distinguish. Before reading the next paragraph, transcribe the segments in Figure 8.16, given the in-formation that the utterance was "She came back and started again," as spoken by the speaker who produced the vowels in Figure 8.7.

Looking at the segments one at a time, we can see that the initial [ʃ] sound is similar to that in "shy" in Figure 8.12. The frequency scale is not as extended as that in Figure 8.12 (so that more attention can be paid to the vowel formants), but it is quite easy to see that this is [ʃ], not [s] as in segment (12), which has a higher frequency. The second segment, [i], has second and third formant fre-quencies that are a little lower than in this speaker's vowel in Figure 8.7. At the

TABLE 8.1	Acoustic correlates of consonantal features. Note: These descriptions should be regarded only as rough guides. The actual acoustic correlates depend to a great extent on the particular combination of articulatory features in a sound, and on the neighboring vowels.

Voiced	Vertical striations corresponding to the vibrations of the vocal folds.
Bilabial	Locus of both second and third formants comparatively low.
Alveolar	Locus of second formant about 1,700–1,800 Hz.
Velar	Usually high locus of the second formant. Common origin of second and third formant transitions.
Retroflex	General lowering of the third and fourth formants.
Stop	Gap in pattern, followed by burst of noise for voiceless stops or sharp beginning of formant structure for voiced stops.
Fricative	Random noise pattern, especially in higher frequency regions, but dependent on the place of articulation.
Nasal	Formant structure similar to that of vowels but with nasal formants at about 250, 2,500, and 3,250 Hz.
Lateral	Formant structure similar to that of vowels but with formants in the neighborhood of 250, 1,200, and 2,400 Hz. The higher formants are considerably reduced in intensity.
Approximant	Formant structure similar to that in vowels, usually changing.

FIGURE 8.16   A spectrogram of "She came back and started again."

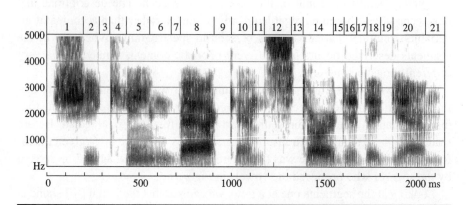

end of segment (2) the second and third formants come together for the velar stop [k] that forms segment (3). This stop is followed by a burst of aspiration, marked as segment (4) before the onset of the vowel. The vowel in "came," (5), is a diphthong, [eɪ], with a faint additional formant around 1,100 Hz, associated with the nasalization of the vowel. At the end of the bilabial nasal (6), there is a short [b] closure (7), in which the voicing is just barely visible. The upward transitions after the bilabial stop at the beginning of [æ] (8) in "back" are much more evident. There is no difficulty in seeing the coming together of the second and third formants before the velar stop [k] (9). There is only a short period of aspiration, not given a separate segment number, followed by a transition, the coming apart of the second and third formants, before a neutral vowel, [ə] (10). This is followed by an alveolar nasal [n] (11).

The [s] (12) in "started" is followed by a short [t], (13) which is only slightly aspirated (as is normal for [t] whenever it occurs after [s] in English). The falling second formant into the vowel, [ɑ] (14) is typical of the transition from [t] into [ɑ]. The low third formant for the last part of segment (14) is associated with the r-coloring. Approximately the last half of the vowel is rhotacized. The stop in (15) has a voice bar, and could symbolized by [ɾ] in a narrow phonetic transcription. For many people, including this speaker, past tense "-ed" forms after an alveolar stop have a fairly high second formant and a low first formant. I would transcribe the vowel in segment (16) as [ɪ] rather than [ə]. Segment (17), like segment (15), is a tap [ɾ]. The vowel in segment (18) is also [ɪ]; unstressed vowels before velar consonants are often [ɪ] rather than [ə]. The velar stop [ɡ] in segment (19) is clearly marked by the coming together of the second and third formants in the vowels on either side of it. The final syllable in "again" has a fairly low vowel—formant one is about as high as it is in segment

(8), the vowel [æ] in "back." Segment (20) could be transcribed as [ɛ] or [æ]. Segment (21) is the final nasal [n].

Now you should try segmenting a more difficult utterance. Figure 8.17 shows a spectrogram of my saying, "I should have thought spectrograms were unreadable." This phrase was spoken in a normal, but rapid, conversational style. This time, instead of marking the separate segments, I have simply placed evenly spaced lines above the spectrogram, so that I can refer to particular places. Try to write a transcription below these lines. Make sure that the symbols you write correctly indicate how the phrase was actually pronounced, rather than how you might say it.

When given a problem like this, it is always best to find the obvious things first. The voiceless fricatives [s] and [ʃ] stand out from other sounds, so begin by trying to find the [ʃ] in "should" and the [s] in "spectrograms." The [ʃ] is at (3) and the [s] is between (9) and (10). You can now start at the beginning and find the vowel [aɪ] in the first word. It is below (1) and (2), ending where the [ʃ] begins. You know that the [s] in "spectrograms" is between (9) and (10), so the vowel in "thought" must be at (7), with the [t] after it at (8). What happens before the vowel in "thought" and after the [ʃ] in "should?" Is there any voicing in any of the segments between these sounds? It seems as if the whole of the phrase "should have" was pronounced without any voicing. There must be a [t] at (4) and an [f] and a [θ] at (6). A narrow transcription of the phrase "I should have thought" is [aɪʃtf ˈθɔt].

Now go on from the [s] in "spectrograms," bearing these points in mind. Try to transcribe "spectrograms were unreadable," remembering that some of the

---

FIGURE 8.17   A spectrogram of "I should have thought spectrograms were unreadable," spoken in a normal, but rapid, conversational style (British English).

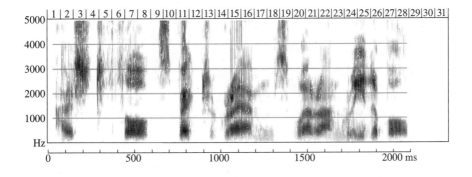

sounds you might have expected to be voiced might be voiceless. When you have done this, read the next paragraph.

As you might expect, there is no aspiration after the [p] in "spectrograms," which is between (10) and (11). The vowel [ɛ] at (11) is very short, but you can see the coming together of the second and third formants for the [k] at (12). The [t] is also at (12) and is highly aspirated, so that the following [r] is almost completely voiceless (and hence in a narrow transcription [ɹ̥]). There is virtually no voicing in the short [ə] at (13). The velar stop [g] at (14) is released into [ɹ], easily located by the lowering of the third and fourth formants. The vowel [æ] at (15–16) is followed by a long [m], with its faint formants occupying most of (17) and (18). The fricative at the end of this word, below (18–19), appears to be voiceless. I would transcribe it as [z̥] rather than [s] because of its lack of intensity.

One of the next most identifiable points is the drop in the third formant below (21) at the end of the word "were," showing that on this occasion I did pronounce the [ɹ] in this word. This is normal for most speakers of British English when the next word begins with a vowel. The [w] at the beginning of this word, at (20), is distinguishable by the low second formant. The syllable [ʌn] of "unreadable" is below (22) and (23). The lowering of the third formant at (24) marks the beginning of the syllable "read," the high vowel [i] at (25) having a low first formant and a high second formant. The very short [d] and [ə] at (25–26) are followed by a comparatively long [b] at (26–27), and the final syllabic [l̩] at (27–28) looks like a back vowel.

If you want a more difficult exercise in interpreting sound spectrograms, look at Figure 8.18, and see if you can say what it is. It is an ordinary English sentence

---

FIGURE 8.18   A spectrogram of an English sentence as described in the text.

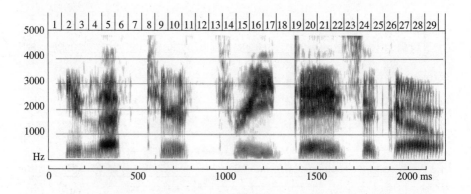

spoken by the American English speaker who said the vowels in Figure 8.7. You will find it hard to determine the whole sentence, but some segments are quite easy. For example, what must be there when the third formant is below 2,000 Hz, near (14–15)? Can you see a distinctive pattern of the second and third formants at (26), and perhaps also at (24–25)?

At the beginning, below (1), there is a small fricative noise near 3,000 Hz. Then at (2) there is a vowel that might be [i] or [ɪ]. A sharp break in the pattern is followed at (3) by a segment with faint formants at about 250, 1,300, and 1,400 Hz. This break must indicate a nasal or a lateral, with a lateral being the more probable here. If you look at Figure 8.7 you will see that the vowel at (5) is something like [æ] or [ɛ]. This is followed by a fricative at (6) that could only be [θ] or [f]. At (7) there is a voiceless stop [p], [t], or [k], with the aspiration at (8) being strong and high frequency, making it most likely [t]. The vowel at (9) is again either [i] or [ɪ], judging by the first two formants. But you can also see that the third formant is low at (10), indicating r-coloring.

As there seems to be a pause after (10), we can stop there for a moment and write out our possible transcription choices:

(1)	(2)	(3)	(4)	(5)	(6)	(7)	(8)	(9)	(10)
?	i	l		æ	θ	t	ʰ	ɪ	r
		ɪ	n, m, ŋ	ɛ	f	k, p		i	

Can you make a path through these possible choices? The second syllable could be "laugh" or "laughed" or "left," making a possible phrase "He laughed" or "He left." What was actually said was "He left here," but it would be very difficult to get this. You should, however, get segments such as those listed here.

Now look at the last part of the sentence in Figure 8.18, which is a bit easier. There is a fricative at (13–14) that is [θ] or [f], followed by a low third formant at (15) indicating [ɹ], and then a vowel at (16–17) in which the first formant is lower and the second formant is higher than anywhere else in the sentence, making it clearly [i]. This gives us the syllable "free" or "three." You can see a little bit of voicing near the baseline at (17–18) during what is presumably a voiced stop. The intensity of the burst, the high frequency energy, and the level formants at the onset of the vowel all suggest that this is [d]. The vowel at (20–21) is long and almost as high (first formant low) and front (second formant high) as the preceding vowel, making it probably [eɪ]. Segment (23) is clearly a fricative looking like [s], but, because of its lack of intensity, it may be [z] with voicing too faint to be seen. There is a very short vowel at (24), and a good rule for such vowels is to regard them as [ə]. The consonant at (25–26) must be a velar stop. The final long vowel at (27–29) is a diphthong, ending in a back vowel (low second formant) like [ʊ].

Putting this last part together we have the following:

(13–14)	(15)	(15–16)	(17–18)	(20–21)	(23)	(24)	(25–26)	(27–29)
f	ɹ	i	d	eɪ	s	ə	g	... ʊ
θ			b		z		k	

Read these possible transcriptions and you may be able to find a path that gives you the whole sentence: "He left here—three days ago."

Try another of these sentences on your own. Figure 8.19 is a spectrogram of the American English speaker. The utterance was a normal English sentence, containing no proper nouns. As before, many of the sounds occur in new combinations, which means that they have slightly different patterns. But if you start with the more obvious sounds, and use your knowledge of possible English words, you should be able to succeed. Many users of the earlier editions of this book have already done so.

The spectrograms that have been used to illustrate this chapter so far are called wide-band spectrograms. They are very accurate in the time dimension. They show each vibration of the vocal folds as a separate vertical line and indicate the precise moment of a stop burst with a vertical spike. But they are less accurate in the frequency dimension. There are usually several component frequencies present in a single formant, all of them being lumped together in one wide band on the spectrogram.

It is a fact of physics that one can know either fairly precisely when a sound occurred or, to a comparable degree of accuracy, what its frequency is. This should be intuitively clear when you recall that knowing the frequency of a sound involves observing the variations in air pressure over a period of time. This period of time has to be long enough to ensure observations of a number of repetitions

---

FIGURE 8.19   A spectrogram of an ordinary English sentence containing no names (British accent).

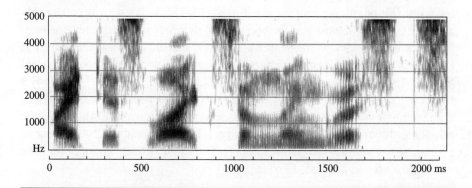

of the variations of air pressure. You can either know that a pulse from the vocal folds has happened (producing the vertical voicing striation in all the spectrograms we have considered so far), or, if the piece of the sound wave being analyzed contains two or three pulses of the vocal folds, we can tell how far apart they are and hence know the frequency.

Spectrograms that are more accurate in the frequency dimension (at the expense of accuracy in the time dimension) are called narrow-band spectrograms. Figure 8.20 shows both wide- and narrow-band spectrograms of the question "Is Pat sad, or mad?" In the wide-band spectrogram, there are sharp spikes at the release of each stop, for example, for the [d] at the end of the utterance. The spikes are smeared in the time dimension in the narrow-band spectrogram. But the frequencies that compose each formant are visible.

When the vocal folds vibrate, they produce what are called harmonics of their fundamental frequency of vibration. Harmonics are vibrations at whole-number multiples of the fundamental frequency. Thus when the vocal folds are vibrating

FIGURE 8.20 Wide-band (upper part of the figure) and narrow-band (lower part) spectrogram of the question "Is Pat sad, or mad?" The fifth, tenth, and fifteenth harmonics have been marked by white squares in two of the vowels.

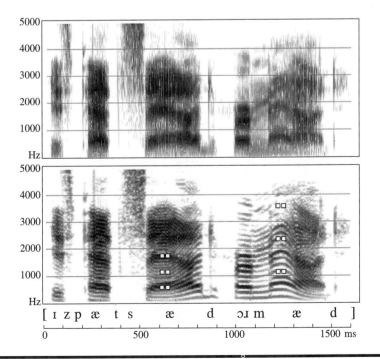

at 100 Hz, they produce harmonics at 200, 300, 400 Hz, and so on. In a given vowel, the particular harmonics that are evident are those that correspond to the resonances of the vocal tract shape occurring in that vowel. I have put two small white squares in the middle of the fifth, tenth, and fifteenth harmonics in the middle of the vowels in "sad" and "mad." The vocal folds are vibrating at about 118 Hz in "sad," so the fifth harmonic has a frequency of $5 \times 118 = 590$ Hz, the tenth harmonic a frequency of 1,180 Hz, and the fifteenth harmonic a frequency of 1,770 Hz. The first formant is formed by the fifth and sixth harmonics, and the main components of the second formant are the fourteenth and fifteenth harmonics. Compare this with the vowel in "mad," which has very similar formants, both being examples of the / æ / phoneme. Near the beginning of the last word the third harmonic is the main component of the first formant and the eighth harmonic the main component of the second formant. As we have noted, the quality of a vowel sound depends on the frequencies of the formants. But the pitch depends on the fundamental frequency, which is determined by the rate of vibration of the vocal folds.

In women's voices, which usually have a higher pitch, the formants are sometimes more difficult to locate precisely. Figure 8.21 show spectrograms of a female speaker of American English saying the same set of vowels as those of the male speaker in Figure 8.7. Even though these spectrograms have been made with considerable care, choosing the most appropriate degree of narrowness of the spectrogram to best show the formant frequencies, the harmonics still interfere with the display of the formants. Notice, for example, the change in vowel quality in the vowel [ʊ], which appears as a series of steps as different harmonics become available to make up the formant. In a narrow band spectrogram it is even more difficult to locate the centers of the formants when the fundamental frequency is high.

Narrow-band spectrograms are obviously useful for determining the intonation—or tone—of an utterance. One can do this by looking at the fundamental frequency itself, but when this goes from, say, 100 to 120 Hz, the frequency of the tenth harmonic will go from 1,000 to 1,200 Hz, which is much easier to see. The actual pitch—or, to be more exact, the fundamental frequency—at any moment will be one-tenth that of the tenth harmonic. As we saw earlier in this chapter (and also in Chapter 5), computers can analyze speech to give a good record of the fundamental frequency (the pitch). But most fundamental frequency routines make occasional errors when the pitch is too low or when the vocal folds are not vibrating regularly. In these cases, a narrow-band spectrographic analysis can be very useful.

We may now summarize the kinds of information that can and cannot be obtained from spectrograms. The most reliable measurements will be those of the length of the segments, for which purpose spectrograms are often even better

FIGURE 8.21 A spectrogram of the words "heed, hid, head, had, hod, hawed, hood, who'd" as spoken by a female speaker of American English. The locations of the first three formants are shown by arrows.

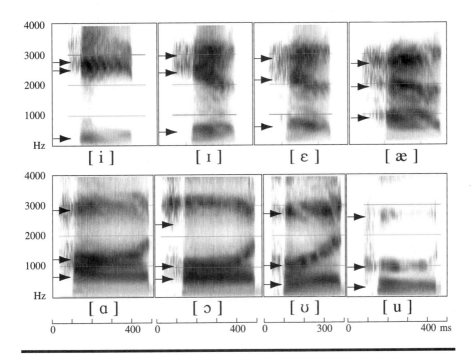

than waveforms. Differences among vowels, nasals, and laterals can be seen on spectrograms, whereas it may be impossible to see these differences in the waveforms.

Spectrograms are usually fairly reliable indicators of relative vowel quality. The frequency of the first formant certainly shows the relative vowel height quite accurately. The second formant reflects the degree of backness quite well, but there may be confusions due to variations in the degree of lip rounding.

It is also possible to tell many things about the manner of articulation from spectrograms. For example, one can usually see whether a stop has been weakened to a fricative, or even to an approximant. Affrication of a stop can be seen on most occasions. Trills can be separated from flaps and voiced from voiceless sounds. One can also observe the relative rates of movement of different articulations.

Spectrograms cannot be used to measure degrees of nasalization, nor are they much help in differentiating between adjacent places of articulation. For studying these aspects of speech, other techniques are more useful.

INDIVIDUAL DIFFERENCES

The last subject that must be dealt with in this chapter is differences among individual speakers. This is important for several reasons. First, anyone working in phonetics should be able to form an opinion as to the extent of idiosyncratic qualities in an individual's voice. Second, one must know how to discount purely individual features in an acoustic record if one is to measure features that are linguistically significant. This is an important matter for anyone interested in computer speech recognition. If we all spoke with exactly the same voice quality then recognizing the patterns of individual words would be much easier. Computer speech recognition has to disregard individual differences and report just the words that have been spoken. Third, spectrograms have become used in forensic situations.

Spectrograms of a person's voice are sometimes called "voice-prints," and they are said to be as individual as fingerprints. This is a greatly exaggerated claim. If it were true it would be very useful. Banks would be able to verify a depositor's identity over the telephone, and the police would be able to make a positive identification of criminals whose conversations had been recorded. Some individual characteristics are recorded in spectrograms. The position of the fourth and higher formants in most vowels is indicative of a speaker's voice quality rather than the linguistic aspects of the sounds. Similarly, the exact locations of the higher formants in nasals depend to a great extent on individual physiological characteristics of the speaker.

There are also a number of features observable on spectrograms that indicate a speaker's speech habits and are not language dependent. For example, there is a great deal of individuality in the length and type of aspiration that occurs after initial voiceless stops. The rate of transition of the formants after voiced stops also varies from one individual to another.

Nobody knows how many individuals share similar characteristics. There are occasions when one can say that the voice on a particular recording is *probably not* the same as the voice on some other recording, and times when one can say that the voice on a recording *could* be the same as the voice on another. Speaker identification using spectrographic evidence has been used in a number of criminal cases. My best guess at the moment, based on studies reported in the literature, my own examination of thousands of spectrograms, and appearances in a large number of court cases, is that an expert may be wrong about one time in twenty in making a positive identification of an unknown voice on a recording. In my view, it is completely irresponsible to say, as I have heard witnesses testify in court, "The voice on the recording is that of the accused and could be that of no other speaker."

Individual variation is also important from a general phonetic point of view. In summarizing the uses of spectrograms, I was careful to say that spectrograms showed *relative* vowel quality. It is clearly true that one can use spectrograms such as that in Figure 8.18 to tell that the speaker has a higher vowel in "three" than in the beginning of the vowel in "here." One can also use formant plots such as that in Figure 8.9 to show that the average American English vowel in "who'd" is farther forward than that in "hawed." But it is not so easy to say if the vowel in a given word as pronounced by one speaker is higher or lower than that of another speaker.

In general, when two different speakers pronounce sets of vowels with the same phonetic quality, the relative positions of these vowels on a formant chart will be similar, but the absolute values of the formant frequencies will differ from speaker to speaker. Figure 8.22 shows the formants for the vowels in "heed, hid, head, had. hod, hood, who'd" as pronounced by two speakers of Californian English. The Californian English of most university students does not distinguish between "hod" and "hawed" or between "cot" and "caught," so it was possible to show only seven of the eight vowels in Figure 8.7. The relative positions of the vowels in each set are similar, but the absolute values are different.

FIGURE 8.22   A formant chart showing some of the vowels of two speakers of Californian English. The frequency of the first formant is plotted on the ordinate (the vertical axis), and the difference between the frequencies of the second and first formants is plotted on the abscissa (the horizontal axis).

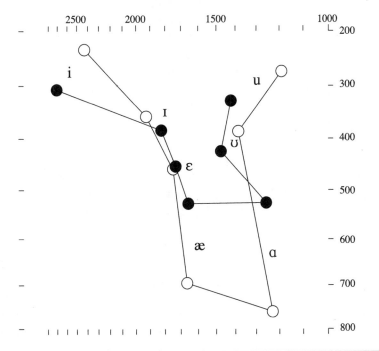

There is no simple technique that will enable one to average out the individual characteristics so that a formant plot will show only the phonetic qualities of the vowels. The simplest way to deal with this problem is probably to regard the average frequency of the fourth formant as an indicator of the individual's head size, and then express the values of the other formants as percentages of the mean fourth formant frequency. But this possibility is not open when the fourth formant frequencies have not been reported for the sets of vowels that are being compared. An alternative method is to assume that each set of vowels is representative of the complete range of a speaker's vowel qualities. Then we can express the formant frequency of each vowel in terms of the total range of that formant in that speaker's voice. This method will minimize differences between extreme vowels, falsely assuming that all speakers of all languages pronounce [i, ɑ, u] in much the same way as one another. Phoneticians do not really know how to compare acoustic data on the sounds of one individual with those of another. We cannot write a computer program that will accept any individual's vowels as input, and output a narrow phonetic transcription. If we could solve this problem, we might be able to isolate the individual characteristics of a person's voice so that a "voice-print" would really be as distinctive as a fingerprint.

Much of the work of the applied phonetician today is concerned with computer speech technology and directed toward improving speech synthesis systems. The greatest challenges in the field of speech synthesis are concerned with improvements in intonation and rhythm. Synthetic speech often sounds unnatural because the intonation is too stereotyped. In order to get the correct pitch changes, one must know the speaker's attitude to the world in general and to the topic under discussion. In addition, the syntax of the utterance must be taken into account, as well as various higher level pragmatic considerations, such as whether the word or a synonym of it has been used in a previous sentence. The rhythm of the sentence depends not only on all the segmental influences that were discussed in earlier parts of this book, but also on the particular emphasis that the speaker wishes to convey at that moment. If we are going to make synthetic speech lively and interesting, we have to develop computer programs that are very linguistically sophisticated, and can also simulate human emotions.

Speech recognition systems are largely the province of engineers, but phoneticians also play a part. For a long time, we have been able to use computers to distinguish single words, such as the digits zero through nine. More recently, several systems have been developed that can recognize limited sets of words in task-specific situations, in which the computer can structure the dialogue. For example, in an airline reservations system, the computer can ask, "Which day of the month do you wish to travel? At what time? On what airline? To what airport?" For each of these questions there is only a limited set of possible answers. Computers can do all this and more, with sufficient accuracy for commercial purposes. But they cannot as yet serve as court reporters, producing an accurate written transcript of ordinary speech as spoken by people with a wide range of accents and different personal characteristics.

EXERCISES

A Put a transcription of the segments in the phrase "Please pass me my book" above the waveform that follows. Draw lines showing the boundaries between the segments.

B The following spectrogram shows the phrase "Show me a spotted hyena." Put a transcription above it, and show the segment boundaries. In places where there are no clear boundaries (as in the first part of "hyena") draw dashed lines.

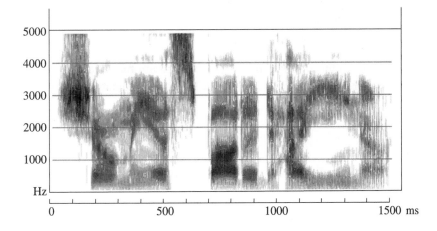

C In the following spectrogram, the segments have been delimited, some with dashed lines as they do not have sharp boundaries. In each of the spaces above the spectrogram write a symbol for a sound that has the same manner of articulation as that segment. Those for the first segment have been filled in as examples. A few other segments that are particularly difficult to determine have also been filled in.

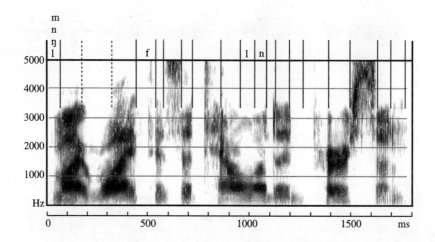

The spectrogram is an ordinary English sentence, containing no names, so obviously the third possibility shown for the first segment could not be correct, as no English sentence could begin with [ŋ]. Bearing in mind what sequences of sounds are possible in English, write as many words or syllables as you can. This is a true statement.

D Look at the sentence in Figure 8.19, a spectrogram for which the text is not given. Say as much as you can about the different segments.

9

VOWELS AND VOWEL-LIKE ARTICULATIONS

In previous chapters we saw that there are three main aspects of vowel quality: (1) vowel height, which is inversely proportional to the frequency of the first formant; (2) backness, which is proportional to the difference between the frequencies of the second and first formants; and (3) the degree of lip rounding, an articulatory feature that has complex acoustic correlates. This chapter will discuss these three features in greater detail and will also consider some additional, less prominent, features of vowel quality.

Figure 4.2 in Chapter 4 shows the relative auditory qualities of the English vowels and diphthongs. As I mentioned at that time, the precise locations of the points in this diagram reflected acoustic measurements, not mere auditory impressions. It can, therefore, be considered to be a formant chart, similar to that shown in Figure 9.1. Some of the acoustic measurements were the formant frequencies reported in the previous chapter. They were supplemented by measurements of the formant frequencies of the other vowels and diphthongs, all taken from published sources. (For bibliographical details, see the section on sources at the end of the book.)

Most phoneticians would agree that Figure 9.1 is a fairly accurate reflection of both the way in which American English vowels have traditionally been described as well as the way in which listeners perceive the relative auditory qualities. During the discussion of this diagram in Chapter 4, you probably made up your own mind on the extent to which it agrees with your own perception of the relative distance between vowels. But remember that if it seems inaccurate to you, this may be because your accent is not identical with the form of American English represented in the figure.

CARDINAL VOWELS

When describing the vowels that occurred on a particular occasion, one may not have access to measurements of the formant frequencies. Phoneticians who want to describe the vowels of a certain dialect or of a certain speaker often have to

---

FIGURE 9.1   A combined acoustic and auditory representation of some of the vowels of American English. (Compare Figures 4.2 and 8.9.)

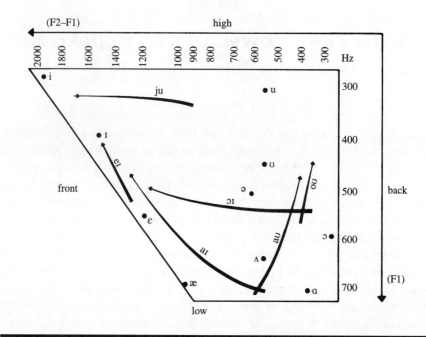

rely on their auditory abilities. They plot the vowels on a vowel chart, so that anybody knowing about vowel charts can see where the points are and can infer the quality of the vowels they are describing.

If a vowel chart is to be truly interpretable, the vowels on it must be plotted with reference to certain fixed points. These points must be known to both the people originally plotting the vowels and to the people who are going to interpret their descriptions. The space within a vowel chart represents a continuum of possible qualities. Before I can convey anything to you by telling you that a certain vowel is halfway (or a third of the way) between one vowel and another, I must be certain that we both know the exact quality of the vowels that act as reference points. There are several ways in which known fixed points can be provided.

In the first place, we can rely on the fact that a vowel chart shows the limits of possible vowel quality. Thus a point in the extreme upper left corner of the chart represents a vowel with the highest and most front quality possible. If the tongue were moved higher or more forward, a palatal consonant would be produced. A vowel in the extreme lower right corner represents the lowest and most back quality possible. Further movement of the tongue would produce a pharyngeal consonant. Similarly, the points in the other two corners of the diagram represent extreme qualities. We would have some fixed reference point if I could rely on the fact that you and I both know the sound of the highest and most front possible vowel, the lowest and most back possible vowel, and so on.

This use of a vowel chart is quite satisfactory for the description of vowels that are near the corners of the possible vowel area. But it does not provide enough fixed points for the description of other vowels. Recognizing this problem, the British phonetician Daniel Jones proposed a series of eight **cardinal vowels,** evenly spaced around the outside of the possible vowel area and designed to act as fixed reference points for phoneticians. In no case is the quality of a cardinal vowel exactly the same as that of an English vowel. It can happen that a particular language may have a vowel that is virtually identical with a cardinal vowel. Several of the vowels of a conservative form of Parisian French vowels are very similar. But by definition the cardinal vowels are arbitrary reference points.

Two of the cardinal vowels are defined in articulatory terms. Cardinal vowel (1) is produced with the lips spread and the tongue as high and far forward as possible without causing audible friction. It is therefore something like the vowel [i], but with a more extreme quality. The symbol for it is also [i].

The other cardinal vowel that is defined in articulatory terms is cardinal vowel (5). This vowel is made with the lips in a neutral position—neither spread nor rounded—and with the tongue as low and as far back as possible. Accordingly, it is something like some forms of the American English vowel [ɑː] as in "father, hot" or the British English vowel [ɒ] as in "hot." The American [ɑː], however, is not usually made with the tongue as far back as possible, and the British [ɒ] usually has slight lip rounding. The symbol for cardinal vowel (5) is [ɑ].

Try to make cardinal vowels (1) and (5) in accordance with these descriptions. Remember to have your lips fully spread when saying [i]. Make sure that your tongue is so close to the roof of the mouth that you would produce a voiced palatal fricative [ʝ] if you raised it any higher. Similarly, when producing [ɑ], make sure that the tongue is pulled so far down and back in the mouth that you are almost producing a voiced pharyngeal fricative [ʕ] (not to be confused with a glottal stop, which is [ʔ]).

Cardinal vowels (2), (3), and (4) are defined as front vowels that form a series of auditorily equidistant steps between numbers (1) and (5). As we saw in the previous chapter, the acoustic definition of front vowels is that the distance between formant one and formant two is as great as possible. We can also specify in acoustic terms what is meant by auditorily equidistant steps. It implies that when these five vowels are plotted on a formant chart of the kind we have been discussing, they will be represented by points that are equal distances apart. (There are some complications in this respect that we will discuss later.)

Cardinal vowels (6), (7), and (8) are defined as vowels that continue on from number (5), with the same size steps as in the first part of the series, but that are in the case of these vowels as back as possible (that is, with as small a distance as possible between formants one and two). In order to continue with these same size steps, the back vowels have to become not only increasingly higher but also increasingly more rounded. As a result, cardinal vowel (8) is in fact the highest, most back, most rounded possible vowel—even though it is not defined in this way.

The symbols for cardinal vowels (2), (3), and (4) are [e, ɛ, a], respectively. The symbols for cardinal vowels (6), (7), and (8) are [ɔ, o, u]. Most of these vowels have qualities something like those of the English vowels we have been symbolizing in a similar way. In accordance with the principles of the IPA, the symbols chosen for most of the English vowels are those of the nearest cardinal vowels. The major exception is the vowel in "fat," which, following the tradition of many English-speaking phoneticians, has been symbolized by [æ] rather than [a].

The cardinal vowel system has been extensively used by phoneticians in the description of a wide variety of languages. There are, however, a number of difficulties in this respect. First, as Daniel Jones said in *An Outline of English Phonetics* (London: Heffer, 1957): "The values of the cardinal vowels cannot be learned from written descriptions; they should be learned by oral instruction from a teacher who knows them." It was for this reason that I did not suggest that you try to produce a complete series of cardinal vowels immediately after reading the descriptions given previously. If you have access to a recording of the cardinal vowels and if there is someone who can listen critically to your imitations of them, then it is possible to learn to produce them with a fair degree of accuracy. Recordings of cardinal vowels are available on the Web at the address mentioned in the Preface to this edition.

A second problem with the cardinal vowel system is the notion of auditory equidistance between the vowels. The traditional description of the cardinal vowels arranges them on a plot as shown in Figure 9.2, in which the points are not equidistant. Cardinal vowels (5), (6), (7), and (8) are much closer together than (1), (2), (3), (4), and (5). This plot is somewhat in agreement with the notion that vowel height corresponds inversely to the frequency of formant one and backness corresponds to the distance between formant two and formant one. The line on the left-hand side of the figure slants because the degree of the distance between formants one and two decreases in going from [i] to [ɑ]. It is comparatively straight on the right-hand side because the distance between the first two formants is much the same for these vowels; both formant one and formant two go steadily down from [ɑ] to [u].

Another problem with the cardinal vowel system is that there has been a great deal of confusion over whether vowels are being described in terms of tongue height or in terms of acoustic properties. Many phoneticians—and many textbooks on phonetics—talk about diagrams such as Figure 9.2 as if they specified the highest point of the tongue. The distance between the points representing the back vowels is therefore said to be less because the movements of the tongue are said to be less (which is not actually true). The differences in auditory quality are presumed to be the same in both front and back vowels, despite the supposed

FIGURE 9.2   The cardinal vowels.

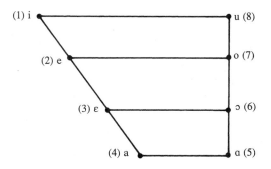

smaller movements of the tongue in back vowels, because back vowels also have increasing lip rounding. But diagrams such as Figures 9.1 and 9.2 do not really specify the position of the highest point of the tongue. Figure 9.3 shows the relative positions of the highest point of the tongue in a set of cardinal vowels, and these positions form an outline very different from that in Figure 9.2. The

FIGURE 9.3   The highest points of the tongue as shown in a published set of x-rays of cardinal vowels (see Sources). The outline of the upper surface of the vocal tract is not clear on the x-rays and is, therefore, estimated.

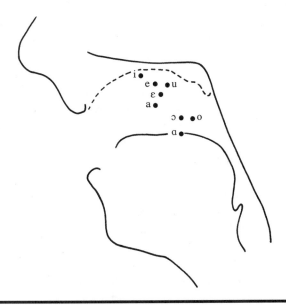

same point can be made by referring to Figures 1.8 and 1.9, which show the articulatory positions of some of the vowels in Figure 9.1. The position of the highest point of the tongue is not a valid indicator of vowel quality. I have tried to avoid describing vowels in terms of tongue height, using instead the term vowel height—meaning an auditory quality that can be specified in acoustic terms rather than in articulatory terms.

Despite all these problems, the cardinal vowel system has worked fairly successfully. It allowed the vowels of a large number of languages and dialects to be described with far greater precision than any other method. The descriptions may have been said in the past to be descriptions of tongue height, but in fact phoneticians had all along been making very accurate judgments of the frequency of the first formant and the distance between the frequencies of the second and first formants. It is now becoming more common to describe vowels simply in terms of their formant frequencies. But the ability to make auditory judgments in terms of a set of reference vowels is still a necessary skill for any phonetician.

SECONDARY CARDINAL VOWELS

The cardinal vowels have increasing degrees of lip rounding, [i] having spread lips, [ɑ] a neutral lip position, and [u] being fully rounded. If we consider vowels to be specifiable in terms of three dimensions, this implies that the cardinal vowels fall on a plane in this three-dimensional space, as shown in Figure 9.4. Most of the vowels of English would also fall on this plane, although for many speakers of American English, [ʊ] is a back vowel that is comparatively unrounded and would therefore be nearer the back of the diagram.

As an aid in the description of vowels with different degrees of lip rounding, there is a series of secondary cardinal vowels numbered (9) through (16). These vowels differ from the eight primary cardinal vowels in having an opposite amount of lip rounding. Cardinal vowel (9) is defined as a vowel with the same tongue position as cardinal vowel (1), but with closely rounded lips. Cardinal vowels (10) through (16) have the same tongue positions as cardinal vowels (2) through (8), but continually decreasing—instead of increasing—lip rounding. Cardinal vowel (16), therefore, is an unrounded version of cardinal vowel (8).

Figure 9.5 shows the symbols for these vowels, together with some additional symbols for central vowels. The symbols [ɨ] and [ʉ] are used for unrounded and rounded vowels midway between cardinal vowels (1) and (8). The symbol [ə] is not defined in terms of cardinal vowels but is used, as we have seen, for a range of mid-central vowels. In addition, note that the symbol [ʌ], which is the symbol for an unrounded cardinal vowel (6), is often used for a lowered mid-central vowel.

Even if you cannot make a complete set of the primary cardinal vowels, you should try to make some of the secondary cardinal vowels. Practice rounding

FIGURE 9.4   A three-dimensional representation of the vowel space, showing
that the cardinal vowels fall on a plane that cuts across the space.

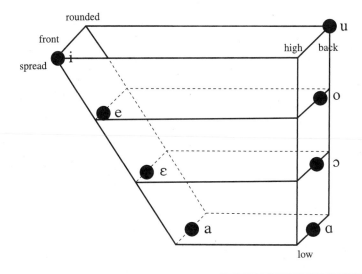

and unrounding your lips while saying cardinal vowel (1), so that you say [iy iy
iy]. Make sure that you maintain an absolutely constant tongue position and
move only your lips. Next, repeat this exercise with cardinal vowel (2) or some
similar vowel of the [e] type. Remember that the rounding for [ø] is not as
close as that for [y]. Last, try unrounding cardinal vowel (8), producing [uɯ
uɯ uɯ]. The usual difficulty here is in maintaining a sufficiently back tongue

FIGURE 9.5   The symbols for some secondary cardinal vowels and some central
vowels.

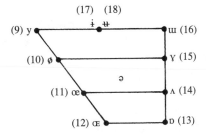

position, as most dialects of English do not have a very back variety of [u]. Note also that the secondary cardinal vowels that you learn to produce by doing these exercises are arbitrary reference points and not necessarily the same as the vowels in any particular language. However, the vowels [y] and [ø] are fairly similar to the French front rounded vowels that occur in "tu" [ty] (you) and "peu" [pø] (small).

Distances on an appropriately scaled vowel chart are similar to auditory distances for vowels in the plane of the cardinal vowels. But this is not so for vowels with degrees of rounding that are unlike those of the nearest cardinal vowels. Front vowels that are rounded or back vowels that are unrounded will be misplaced on a chart if we rely simply on acoustic criteria. The degree of rounding is an independent dimension that must be stated separately from the degree of height (the inverse of the first formant) and the degree of backness (the distance between formant two and formant one). The perspective of the vowel space in Figure 9.4 was chosen so as to reflect the formant frequencies of the secondary cardinal vowels as much as possible. A secondary cardinal vowel [y] will have a lower formant two, bringing it more to the right on the figure, and secondary cardinal vowel [ɯ] will have a higher formant two, bringing it more to the left. But the first formant of each of these vowels is much the same as the corresponding primary cardinal vowel.

VOWELS IN OTHER ACCENTS AND OTHER LANGUAGES

For those who do not know the cardinal vowels, an alternative method of describing vowels is to use as reference points the vowels of a particular dialect of a language that is known to both the person making the description and the person reading the description. This is what I have been trying to do in reference to the vowels of American English as shown in Figure 9.1. If you and I both know what these vowels sound like, then the points on Figure 9.1 provide good reference points. When I remark, for example, that in some forms of Scottish English the vowel in "sacks" is only a little lower than the American English [ε] vowel, then you should be able to pronounce this word in this particular way.

Any language will serve to provide known reference points. For example, when teaching English as a second language, one might use the vowels of the first language of the students as reference points for comparison with the dialect of English that one is trying to teach. If a chart of the vowels of this language is not available, then the instructor's first step should be to make one. This will involve comparing the vowels of this language with the vowels of some language known to the instructor for which there is a chart available.

Fortunately, there are published descriptions of the auditory quality of the vowels in a large number of languages. There are also several sets of acoustic measurements available. We can now make precise statements about many accents of English by reference to the average formant frequencies of groups of speakers. The accent of American English represented in Figure 9.1 is fairly conservative, typical perhaps of elderly newscasters. The first two formants of a group of university students in California are shown in Figure 9.6. We have already noted that this accent does not contrast the vowels in "cot" and "caught"—they are both [ɑː]. Now we can see that younger Californians have a higher vowel (lower first formant) in [eɪ] than in [ɪ]. The high back vowels seem more front in that they have a higher second formant. In the case of the vowel [ʊ] as in "good," this is largely a matter of unrounding. This vowel is often pronounced with spread lips.

Another change is going on in a number of northern cities in the United States, such as Pittsburgh and Detroit. As you can see from Figure 9.7, in this accent [æ] has raised (formant one has decreased) so that is very close to [ɛ]. The back vowels have a lower second formant, making them all further back than in Californian English. This accent does distinguish [ɑː] and [ɔː].

| FIGURE 9.6 | A plot of the first two formants of the vowels of a group of Californian English speakers. |

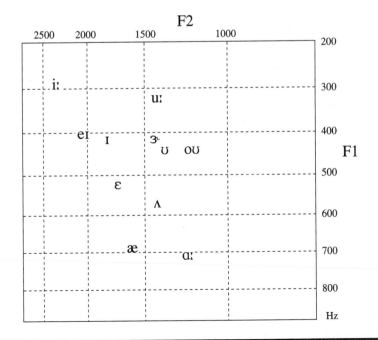

| FIGURE 9.7 | A plot of the first two formants of the vowels of (U.S.) Northern Cities English. |

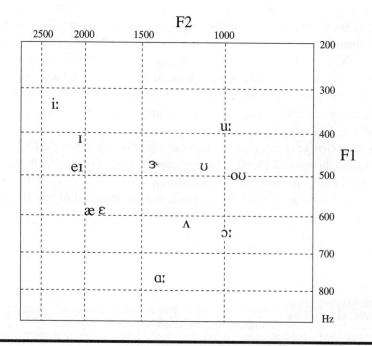

Finally among accents of English, consider the vowels in Figure 9.8, which are the mean of a group of BBC English speakers. The main feature to be noted here is the distinction between the three back vowels [ɑː] as in "father, cart," [ɒ] as in "bother, cot," and [ɔː] as in "author, caught." Note also that [ʌ] has a very low position in comparison with most forms of American English. British English speakers distinguish the vowel [ʌ] in "cut" from the vowel [ɜ] in "curt" (which does not have any r-coloring) mainly by the frequency of the first formant.

Next we will consider the vowels of three other languages for which acoustic measurements are available. Vowel charts for all three languages are shown in Figure 9.9. The sources for the data are listed at the end of the book.

Spanish has a very simple system, contrasting only five vowels. Note that the symbols used in broad transcriptions of Spanish are [i, e, a, o, u]. Obviously, these symbols do not have the same values in Spanish as they do in English or in descriptions of cardinal vowels.

Japanese also has a set of five vowels. In a broad phonetic transcription, these might also have been transcribed [i, e, a, o, u]. But in a narrower transcription that reflects the phonetic quality of the vowels more accurately, the high back

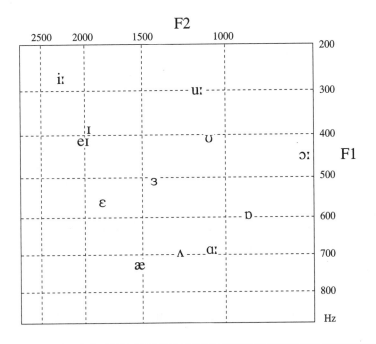

FIGURE 9.8   A plot of the first two formants of BBC English.

vowel could be transcribed as [ɯ], as has been done in Figure 9.9. The point representing this vowel has been distinguished from the others. It has been marked by an asterisk to show that this vowel does not have the lip rounding associated with the primary cardinal vowel in this area. It is not, however, really unrounded. The lips are fairly close together. In a more detailed phonetic analysis one could say that there are two types of lip movements. In one the corners of the lips are brought forward, so that they are somewhat protruded, and in the other they are simply narrowed vertically so that they may be said to be compressed. Note also that [e] in Japanese is slightly lower than it is in Spanish. This is the kind of small difference between vowels that is easily and conveniently expressible in terms of vowel charts.

Asterisks have also been used to represent the quality of some of the Danish vowels shown in the third chart in Figure 9.9. But in this case it is to indicate that those vowels differ from the primary cardinal vowels in the area by having more rather than less lip rounding. Danish has three front rounded vowels, only two of which are in phonemic contrast. The high front rounded vowel [y] contrasts with [ø] in some contexts and with [œ] in other contexts. All the Danish vowels shown in Figure 9.9 can occur in long or short form. The qualities of most of

FIGURE 9.9   The vowels of Spanish, Japanese, and Danish. Front rounded
vowels and back unrounded vowels are indicated by asterisks.

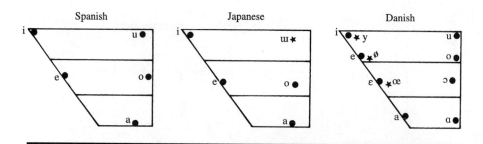

the short vowels are very similar to those of the long vowels, but in the case of
[a, ɔ, o], the short versions are slightly lower and more centralized. The accent
of Danish represented is rather conservative, and perhaps not typical of younger
speakers.

The three charts shown in Figure 9.9 are good examples of the way in which
vowels may be described. They are in part descriptions of the relative auditory
quality, in part articulatory descriptions. For the vowels in which the lip rounding
is the same as that of the primary cardinal vowels, they reflect the acoustic data
exactly. In these cases they are equivalent to plots of the first formant frequency
against the difference between the frequencies of the second and first formants.

Front rounded and back unrounded vowels cannot be represented in terms of
a vowel chart that assumes that the degree of lip rounding is like that of the primary cardinal vowels. In describing these other vowels, the degree of lip rounding must also be specified. One way of doing this is to use asterisks rather than
ordinary points. The asterisks indicate that the lip rounding is more like that of
the secondary cardinal vowels than that of the primary ones. The locations of the
asterisks indicate the vowel qualities in much the same way as the points indicate the qualities of the other vowels. It is as if they show what the formant
frequencies would have been had the lip rounding been like that of the primary
cardinal vowels.

When we consider the actual formant frequencies of front rounded vowels
and back unrounded vowels, we can see why these vowels are not quite so common in most languages. Adding lip rounding to front vowels lowers the higher
formants. As a result, a high front rounded [y] sounds as if it were between [i]
and [u], as we noted at the end of the preceding section when discussing Figure
9.4. Similarly, [œ], which is the front rounded vowel corresponding to [ɛ], has
a lower formant two than [ɛ]. When its formants are plotted on a formant chart,
it appears nearer the center. Conversely, removing lip rounding from the back
vowel [u] to produce [ɯ] raises formant two, so that it would also be nearer

the center of a formant chart. If the vowels of a language are to be maximally distinct from one another, then the front vowels will have to be unrounded, the back vowels rounded.

One of the forces acting on languages may be called the principle of *sufficient perceptual separation,* whereby the sounds of a language are kept acoustically distinct so as to make it easier for the listener to distinguish one from another. As a result of this principle, the degree of lip rounding can be predicted from the degree of backness and, to a lesser extent, the degree of height in by far the majority of languages. Front vowels are usually unrounded, and back vowels are usually rounded, with the degree of rounding increasing with the degree of height. In this way the vowels of a language are kept maximally distinct.

ADVANCED TONGUE ROOT (ATR)

Differences in vowel quality can usually be described in terms of variations in the degrees of height, backness, and lip rounding. But in some languages, there are differences in vowel quality that cannot be described in these terms. For example, in Akan (a West African language spoken mainly in Ghana) there are two sets of vowels that differ mainly in the size of the pharynx. In the one set, there are vowels in which the root of the tongue is drawn forward and the larynx is lowered, so that the part of the vocal tract in the pharynx is considerably enlarged. These vowels are called **Advanced Tongue Root** (or, more simply, **+ATR**) vowels. In the other set, there are vowels in which there is no advancement of the tongue root or lowering of the larynx (– ATR vowels). Figure 9.10 shows the shape of the vocal tract in two Akan vowels that differ in this way. In the +ATR vowel [e], the whole tongue is bunched up lengthwise in comparison with the –ATR vowel, here symbolized as [i̧]. We should also note that not all speakers of Akan make the difference between these two vowels in this way. Some seem to rely more on movements of the root of the tongue, and others more on differences in larynx height. What matters for the distinction between the two sets of vowels is that one should have a comparatively large pharyngeal cavity, and the other a comparatively small one.

In English, no pairs of vowels are distinguished simply by this tongue gesture although it does operate to some extent in conjunction with variations in vowel height. The tense high vowels [iː] and [uː], as in "heed" and "who'd," have a more advanced tongue root than the lax mid-high vowels [ɪ] and [ʊ], as in "hid" and "hood." However, the distinction between +ATR vowels and –ATR vowels is not the same as the distinction between tense and lax vowels in English, which was discussed in Chapter 4. The two sets of English vowel are divided by phonological considerations, such as the fact that lax vowels can occur before [ŋ] and tense vowels cannot, rather than by a particular tongue gesture or shape of the vocal tract.

| FIGURE 9.10 | Narrow (−ATR, broken line) and wide (+ATR, solid line) vowels in Akan, a language spoken in Ghana. |

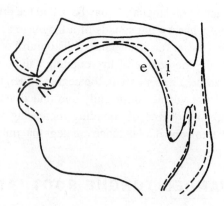

RHOTACIZED VOWELS

As we saw in Chapter 4, many forms of American English have rhotacized vowels in words such as "sir, cur, bird." We also noted that r-coloring can be produced in more than one way. Figure 9.11 shows the tongue positions of three different forms of American English [ɚ]. Some speakers use one of these, other speakers use another position. As shown by the heavy black line, the tongue can be bunched up in the center of the mouth, with the tip down and pulled back from the lower teeth. An important feature of this kind of rhotic articulation is that there is also a slight narrowing in the pharyngeal cavity. A second possibility, shown by the thin black line, is that the tip of the tongue can be raised to near the back of the alveolar ridge, forming a post-alveolar approximant. This is accompanied by a narrowing of the pharyngeal cavity at a slightly higher level. The third possibility, the gray line, is shown in the figure to indicate that there may be in-between positions. If you are a speaker of this form of American English, see if you can determine which of these articulations you use. One way of getting helpful information is to insert a toothpick between the teeth while you hold the position for the vowel [ɚ]. Does the toothpick touch the upper surface of your tongue, or is your tongue tip raised so that it touches the tip or the under surface of the blade of the tongue? It seems likely (see sources) that about 60% of speakers have the tip up, 35% have a bunched tongue position with the tip down, and the remainder, a small number, have an intermediate position.

Rhotacization is an auditory quality, which, like height and backness, is most appropriately defined in acoustic terms. In a rhotacized vowel (or portion of

| FIGURE 9.11 | Possible tongue positions for the vowel [ɝ] in American English. The tongue tip up post-alveolar approximant (thin black line) is the most common, followed by the bunched tongue (solid black line). The gray line indicates possible intermediate positions. |

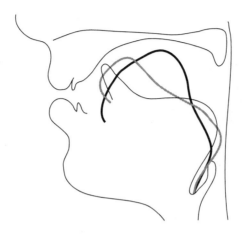

a vowel) there is a marked lowering of the frequency of the third formant. The frequencies of the first two formants determine the vowel height and backness. The frequency of the third formant conveys comparatively little information about either of these aspects of vowel quality. If you look back at Figure 8.7, you will see that the third formant falls only slightly throughout the whole series of nonrhotacized vowels. But, as you can see in Figure 9.12, there is a large fall in the frequency of the third formant in words such as "deer" and "bear," in which the ends of the vowels are considerably rhotacized in many forms of American English. Furthermore, throughout most of the word "heard," the third formant may be low, indicating that even at the beginning of the vowel there is a rhotacized quality.

NASALIZATION

In all the vowels we have been considering in this chapter so far, the soft palate has been raised so that there is a velic closure and air does not flow out through the nose. Vowels will be **nasalized** if the soft palate is lowered to allow part of the airstream to escape through the nose. The diacritic [˜] may be placed over any vowel to indicate that it is nasalized. Vowels of this kind are commonly called **nasal vowels.**

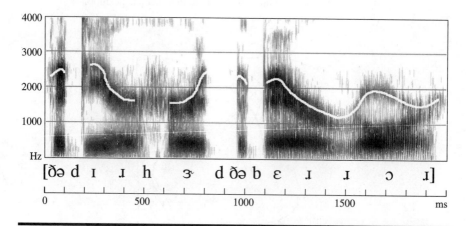

FIGURE 9.12 A spectrogram showing the lowering of the frequency of the third formant (and the second formant) during rhotacized sounds in a sentence in American English.

Learn to produce a variety of nasalized vowels. Start by saying the low vowel [æ̃] as in "man" [mæ̃n]. Alternate a series of nasalized and non-nasalized vowels, saying [æ æ̃ æ æ̃ æ æ̃]. You should be able to feel your soft palate moving up and down when you say these vowels. Try to say a whole series of nasalized vowels [ĩ ẽ ɛ̃ ã ɑ̃ ɔ̃ õ ũ]. Alternate each of these vowels with its non-nasalized counterpart.

Many languages have contrasts between nasal and oral vowels. Thus French contrasts "main" [mɛ̃] (hand) with "mets" [mɛ] (dish), and "ment" [mã] (lies, *vb.*) with "mât" [ma] (mast).

Consonants such as [m, n, ŋ] are, of course, nasals, but they are not *nasalized,* since this term implies that part of the air goes out through the nose and part through the mouth. Contrasts between nasalized and non-nasalized consonants do not occur in any language, but some consonants such as [w, j, ɹ, l] may be nasalized if they occur next to nasalized vowels. In Yoruba, the word for "they" is [w̃ɔ́], with the whole syllable being nasalized.

SUMMARY OF VOWEL QUALITY

Table 9.1 summarizes the discussion on vowels. There are two features of vowel quality—height and backness—that are used to contrast one vowel with another in nearly every language, and there are four other features that are used less frequently. Of the six features, three reflect relatively articulatory properties, and three reflect auditory properties, each of which may be produced in more than one way from an articulatory point of view.

TABLE 9.1	The features of vowel quality.
Quality	**Correlates**
height	frequency of formant one
backness	difference between frequencies of formant two and formant one
rounding	lip position
ATR	width of the pharynx
rhotacization	frequency of formant three
nasalization	position of the soft palate

SEMIVOWELS

Without being too precise about the meaning of the terms syllable and syllabic (a matter we will discuss in the next chapter), we can say that all sounds function either as the peaks of syllables, or at the syllable margins. Vowels are clearly at the peaks of syllables and are syllabic, consonants are generally not—although some consonants such as [l] and [n] can be syllabic in words like "shuttle" [ˈʃʌtl̩] and "button" [ˈbʌʔn̩]. We can also divide sounds into those that that have no obstruction in the center of the mouth, which may be called **vocoids,** and those that have such an obstruction, which will include most consonants. This gives us a pair of divisions that we can arrange as shown in Figure 9.13.

Given this division we can define vowels as syllabic vocoids and **semivowels** as nonsyllabic vocoids. The term semiconsonant is sometimes used for syllabic nonvocoids, but we will refer to them simply as syllabic consonants. Similarly nonvocoids are sometimes called true consonants, a term that could be applicable whether they are syllabic or not.

FIGURE 9.13	The two dimensions that are needed to divide sounds into vowels and consonants.

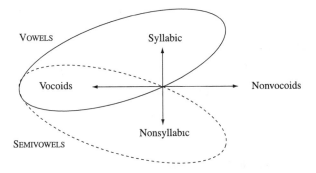

Here we are concerned with semivowels, which are vocoids that function as the beginning or end of a syllable. When at the beginning of a syllable, a semi-vowel usually consists of a rapid glide from a high vowel position to that of the following vowel. The semivowels in English are [j] and [w], which are like nonsyllabic versions of the English high vowels [i] and [u], respectively. In some languages (for example, French), there are the three high vowels [i, u, y]. In some of these languages, there is also a semivowel corresponding to the high front rounded vowel [y]. The symbol for this sound is [ɥ], an inverted letter *h*. Examples of words contrasting the three semivowels in French are given in Table 9.2.

Earlier in this chapter we noted that Japanese has a high unrounded vowel [ɯ]. It does not have spread lips like [i], but it has lips that are fairly close to-gether, compressed vertically, with the corners neither drawn back as in a spread vowel nor pulled together as in a rounded vowel. There is a Japanese semivowel bearing the same relation to this vowel as [w] does to [u] in English. The sym-bol for this semivowel is [ɰ].

Because a semivowel is a kind of approximant, it can be considered to have a particular place of articulation, just like any consonant. We have already noted that [j] is a palatal approximant and [w] is a labial-velar approximant. The semivowel [ɥ] is a labial-palatal approximant. We have not discussed this place of articulation before because approximants are almost the only sounds that are made using these two places of articulation simultaneously. The semivowel [ɰ] is a velar approximant.

When learning to produce the distinction between the French sounds / w / and / ɥ /, note that the English / w / is in between the two French sounds. It is not the same as French / w /. It is, of course, also true that / u / in English is in between the two French sounds [u] and [y]. As is often the case, when a lan-guage does not have to distinguish between two possibilities, it produces a sound that is in between the two. Recall, for example, the quality of English vowels before [ŋ] and before [r], where there are no oppositions between tense and lax vowels.

TABLE 9.2	Contrasts involving palatal, labial-palatal, and labial-velar approximants in French.				
Palatal		**Labial-Palatal**		**Labial-Velar**	
mjɛt	(crumb)	mɥɛt	(mute)	mwɛt	(sea gull)
lje	(tied)	lɥi	(him)	lwi	(Louis)
		ɥit	(eight)	wi	(yes)

In order to produce the French sound / w / as in "oui" [wi] (yes), start from a high rounded vowel that is fully back, like a cardinal [u]. Glide from this vowel very rapidly to the following vowel. The result will be similar but not identical to the English word "we" [wi]. Now try to say the French sound [ɥ] as in "huit" [ɥit] (eight). This time start from the secondary cardinal vowel [y], and glide rapidly to the following vowel.

It is also possible to consider the common form of English [ɹ], as in "red," as a semivowel. In the same way as [w] may be said to be a nonsyllabic counterpart of [u], so [ɹ] as in "red" may be said to be a nonsyllabic version of the vowel in "fur." From a phonetic point of view, regarding [ɹ] in "red" as a semivowel may be a valid description. But from a phonological point of view, it may not be appropriate in describing the sound patterns that occur in English.

SECONDARY ARTICULATION

It is appropriate to consider secondary articulations in conjunction with vowels because they can usually be described as added vowel-like articulations. The formal definition of a **secondary articulation** is that it is an articulation with a lesser degree of closure occurring at the same time as another (primary) articulation. We will consider four types of secondary articulation.

Palatalization is the addition of a high front tongue position, like that in [i], to another articulation. Russian and other Slavic languages have a series of palatalized consonants that contrast with their nonpalatalized counterparts. Palatalization can be symbolized by [ʲ] after a symbol. Russian words illustrating palatalized sounds are given in Table 9.3.

TABLE 9.3	Contrasts involving palatalization in Russian.

formə	(form)	fʲɛrmə	(farm)
vitʲ	(to howl)	vʲitʲ	(to weave)
sok	(juice)	sʲok	(he lashed)
zof	(call)	zʲof	(yawn)
pakt	(pact)	pʲatʲ	(five)
bɨl	(he was)	bʲil	(he stroked)
tot	(that)	tʲotʲə	(aunt)
domə	(at home)	dʲomə	(Dyoma [nickname])
kuʃatʲ	(to eat)	kʲuvʲɛtkə	(dish)

The terms palatalization and palatalized may also be used in a slightly different way from the way in which I have been using them so far. Instead of describing a secondary articulation, these terms may be applied in describing a process in which the primary articulation is changed so that it becomes more palatal. Thus sounds are said to be palatalized if the point of articulation moves toward the palatal region in some particular circumstance. For example, the English / k / in "key" may be said to be palatalized because, instead of the velar contact of the kind that occurs in "car" [kɑɹ], the place of articulation in "key" is changed so that it is nearer the palatal area. Similarly, palatalization is said to occur when the alveolar fricative [z] in "is" becomes a palato-alveolar fricative in "is she . . ." [ɪʒʃi]. A further extension of the term palatalization occurs in discussions of historical sound change. In Old English the word for "chin" was pronounced with a velar stop [k] at the beginning. The change of this sound into Modern English [tʃ] is said to be one of palatalization, due to the influence of the high front vowel. All these uses of the terms palatalization and palatalized involve descriptions of a process—something becoming something else—rather than a state, such as a secondary articulation.

Velarization, the next secondary articulation to be considered, involves raising the back of the tongue. It can be considered as the addition of an [u]-like tongue position, but without the addition of the lip rounding that also occurs in [u]. We have already noted that in many forms of English, syllable final / l / sounds are velarized and may be written [ɫ].

As an exercise, so that you can appreciate how it is possible to add vowel-like articulations to consonants, try saying [l] with the tip of your tongue on the alveolar ridge, but with the body of your tongue in the position for each of the vowels [i, e, ɛ, a, ɑ, ɔ, o, u]. The first of these sounds is, of course, a palatalized sound very similar to [lʲ]. The last of the series is one form of velarized [ɫ]. Make sure that you can say each of these sounds before and after different vowels. Now compare palatalized and velarized versions of other sounds in syllables such as [nʲa] and [ŋa]. Remember that [ŋ] is simply [n] with a superimposed unrounded nonsyllabic [u] glide (that is, an added [ɯ] glide).

Pharyngealization is the superimposition of a narrowing of the pharynx. Since cardinal vowel (5)—[ɑ]—has been defined as the lowest, most back possible vowel without producing pharyngeal friction, pharyngealization may be considered as the superimposition of this vowel quality. The IPA diacritic for symbolizing pharyngealization is [˷], exactly as for velarization. If it is necessary to distinguish between these two secondary articulations, then the IPA suggests using small raised symbols corresponding to velar and pharyngeal fricatives, representing a velarized alveolar nasal as [nˠ] and a pharyngealized alveolar nasal as [nˤ].

There is very little difference between velarized and pharyngealized sounds, and no language distinguishes between the two possibilities. In Arabic there is a series of consonants that Arabic scholars call emphatic consonants. Some of these sounds are velarized, and some are pharyngealized. All of them can be symbolized with the IPA diacritic [~]. (Arabic scholars often use a subscript [.].) There is some similarity in quality between retroflex stops and velarized or pharyngealized stops. This is due to the fact that in all these sounds the front of the tongue is somewhat hollowed.

Labialization, the addition of lip rounding, differs from the other secondary articulations in that it can be combined with any of them. Obviously palatalization, velarization, and pharyngealization involve different tongue shapes that cannot occur simultaneously. But nearly all kinds of consonants can have added lip rounding. In a sense, even sounds in which the primary articulators are the lips—for example, [p, b, m]—can be said to be labialized if they are made with added rounding and protrusion of the lips. Because labialization is often accompanied by raising of the back of the tongue, it is symbolized by a raised [ʷ]. In a more precise system, this might be taken to indicate a secondary articulation that we could call labiovelarization, but this is seldom distinguished from labialization.

In some languages (for instance, Twi and other Akan languages spoken in Ghana), labialization co-occurs with palatalization. As palatalization is equivalent to the superimposition of an articulation similar to that in [i], labialization plus palatalization is equivalent to the superimposition of a rounded [i]—that is, [y]. As we have seen, the corresponding semivowel is [ɥ]. Accordingly, these secondary articulations may be symbolized by a raised [ᶣ]. Recall the pronunciation of [ɥ] in French words such as "huit" [ɥit] (eight). Then try to pronounce the name of one of the dialects of Akan, Twi [tᶣi].

Table 9.4 summarizes the secondary articulations we have been discussing. As in some of the previous summary tables, the terms in Table 9.4 are not all mutually exclusive. A sound may or may not have a secondary articulation such as palatalization, velarization, or pharyngealization; additionally, it may or may not be labialized; and also it may or may not be nasalized. To demonstrate this for yourself, try to make a voiced alveolar lateral [l] that is also velarized, labialized, and nasalized.

TABLE 9.4	Secondary articulations.	
Phonetic Term	**Brief Description**	**Symbols**
palatalization	raising of the front of the tongue	sʲ lʲ dʲ
velarization	raising of the back of the tongue	sˠ ɫ dˠ
pharyngealization	retracting of the root of the tongue	sˤ ɫ dˤ
labialization	rounding of the lips	sʷ lʷ dʷ

EXERCISES

A Look at the positions of the tongue in the English vowels shown in Figure 1.8. It has been suggested (see Sources) that vowels can be described in terms of three measurements: (1) the area of the vocal tract at the point of maximum constriction; (2) the distance of this point from the glottis; and (3) a measure of the degree of lip opening. Which of the first two corresponds to what is traditionally called vowel height for the vowels in "heed, hid, head, had?"

_____

Which corresponds to vowel height for the vowels in "father, good, food?"

_____

Can these two measurements be used to distinguish front vowels from back vowels?

_____

B Another way of describing the tongue position in vowels that has been suggested (see Sources) is to say that the tongue is in a neutral position in the vowel in "head" and that (1) the body of the tongue is higher than in its neutral position in vowels such as those in "heed, hid, good, food"; (2) the body of the tongue is more back than in its neutral position in "good, food, father"; (3) the root of the tongue is advanced in "heed, food"; and (4) the root of the tongue is pulled back so that the pharynx is more constricted than in the neutral position in "had, father." How far do the data in Figure 1.8 support these suggestions?

C In the seventeenth, eighteenth, and early nineteenth centuries (see Sources), there were said to be three sets of vowels: (1) a set exemplified by the vowels in "see, play, father" (and intermediate possibilities), which were said to be distinguished simply by degree of jaw opening; (2) a set exemplified by the vowels in "fool, home, father" (and intermediate possibilities), which were said to be distinguished simply by degree of lip rounding; and (3) a set exemplified by the vowels now symbolized by [y, ø] as in the French words "tu, peu" (you, small), which were said to be distinguished both by the degree of jaw opening and the degree of lip rounding. These notions were shown in diagrams similar to that in Figure 9.14. How do they compare with contemporary descriptions of vowels? What general type of vowel cannot be described in these terms?

D Try to find a speaker of some language other than English. Elicit a set of minimal pairs exemplifying the vowels of this language. You will probably find it helpful to consult the pronunciation section in a dictionary or grammar of the language. Listen to the vowels and plot them on a vowel chart. (Do not attempt this exercise until you have worked through the Performance Exercises for this chapter.)

| FIGURE 9.14 | The vowel classification used by Helmholtz (1863), with keywords suggested by Ellis (1885). |

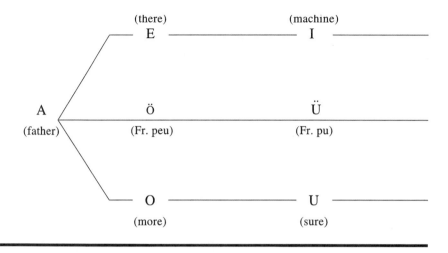

PERFORMANCE EXERCISES

The object of many of the following exercises is to get you to produce a wide variety of vowels that are not in your own language. When you can produce small differences in vowel quality, you will find it easier to hear them.

A Say the monophthongs [i, e] corresponding to at least the first part of your vowels in "see, say." Try to make a vowel with a quality in between [i] and [e]. Then make as many vowels as you can in a series between [i] and [e]. Finally, make a similar series going in the opposite direction—from [e] to [i].

B Repeat this exercise with monophthongs corresponding to the following pairs of vowels in your own speech. Remember to produce each series in both directions.

[ɪ–ɛ]

[ɛ–æ]

[æ–ɑ]

[ɑ–ɔ], if occurring in your speech

[ɔ–o] or [ɑ–o]

[o–u]

C Try moving continuously from one member of each pair to the other, slurring through all the possibilities you produced in the previous exercises. Do this in each direction.

D For each pair of vowels, produce a vowel that is, as nearly as you can determine, halfway between the two members.

E Repeat Exercises A, C, and D with the following pairs of vowels, which will involve producing larger adjustments in lip rounding. Remember to produce each series in both directions, and be sure that you try all the different tasks suggested in Exercises A, C, and D.

[i–u]

[e–o]

F Now repeat all the same exercises, but with no adjustments in lip rounding, using the following pairs of vowels. Go in both directions, of course.

[i–ɯ]

[e–ɤ]

[y–u]

[ø–o]

G Practice distinguishing different central vowels. When you have learned to produce a high-central unrounded vowel [ɨ], try to produce mid- and low-central vowels, which may be symbolized [ə] and [ʌ]. Try Exercises A, C, and D with the following pairs of vowels:

[ɨ–ə]

[ə–ʌ]

H Produce the following nasal and oral vowels. When making the nasalized vowels, be careful to keep the same tongue position, moving only the soft palate.

[i–ĩ–i]

[e–ẽ–e]

[æ–æ̃–æ]

[ɑ–ɑ̃–ɑ]

[o–õ–o]

[u–ũ–u]

I Now compare nasalized vowels with oral vowels that have slightly different tongue positions. Say:

[i–ĩ–ɪ–ĩ]

[e–ẽ–ɛ–ẽ]

[ɛ–ɛ̃–æ–ɛ̃]

[u–ũ–o–ũ]

[o–õ–ɔ–õ]

J Make sure that you can produce a variety of different vowels by saying nonsense words such as those that follow, preferably to a partner who can check your pronunciation.

ˈpetuz	syˈtøt	ˈmēnod
ˈtynob	diˈgɯd	pæˈnyt
ˈbɯgɛd	moˈpɑt	ˈdegũn
ˈnisøp	guˈdob	syˈtõn
ˈbædid	kɯˈtyp	ˈkøbẽs

K Learn to produce diphthongs going to and from a variety of vowels. Using the vowel symbols with their values as in English, read the following, first column by column, then row by row.

iː	ɪi	ei	ɛi	æi	ɑi	ɔi	oi	ʊi	ui	ʌi
ie	ɪe	eɪ	ɛɪ	æɪ	ɑɪ	ɔɪ	oɪ	ʊɪ	uɪ	ʌɪ
iɛ	ɪɛ	eɛ	ɛe	æe	ɑe	ɔe	oe	ʊe	ue	ʌe
iæ	ɪæ	eæ	ɛæ	æɛ	ɑɛ	ɔɛ	oɛ	ʊɛ	uɛ	ʌɛ
iɑ	ɪɑ	eɑ	ɛɑ	æɑ	ɑæ	ɔæ	oæ	ʊæ	uæ	ʌæ
iɔ	ɪɔ	eɔ	ɛɔ	æɔ	ɑɔ	ɔɑ	oɑ	ʊɑ	uɑ	ʌɑ
io	ɪo	eo	ɛo	æo	ɑo	ɔo	oɔ	ʊɔ	uɔ	ʌɔ
iʊ	ɪʊ	eʊ	ɛʊ	æʊ	ɑʊ	ɔʊ	oʊ	ʊo	uo	ʌo
iu	ɪu	eu	ɛu	æu	ɑu	ɔu	ou	ʊu	uʊ	ʌʊ
iʌ	ɪʌ	eʌ	ɛʌ	æʌ	ɑʌ	ɔʌ	oʌ	ʌʌ	uʌ	ʌu

L Try saying some of these diphthongs in one-, two-, and three-syllable nonsense words such as those that follow. These are good items to use in ear training practice with a partner.

tɪop	ˈdoebˈmɔid	sæoˈtɑoneu
tʌep	ˈdeubˈmɑud	sɔɑˈtɛonɪʊ
tɑɔp	ˈdɪʊbˈmʌɔd	soɛˈtæunue
tɛɑp	ˈdoebˈmoid	sɑʌˈtʊinui
toʌp	ˈdʊɛbˈmuɛd	sɔɪˈtɪunæɑ

M Now extend your range by including front rounded and back unrounded vowels as exemplified in the following:

iy	ey	ɑy	uy	yi	øi	ɯi	yø	øy	ɯy
iø	eø	ɑø	uø	ye	øe	ɯe	yɯ	øɯ	ɯø
iɯ	eɯ	ɑɯ	uɯ	ya	øɑ	ɯɑ	yu	øu	ɯu

N These vowels can also be included in nonsense words such as those shown here for both performance and ear training practice.

dɯeb	'tyæb'meyd	tɯy'neɑsʌø
diøb	'tuʊb'muød	tue'nøusʊɪ
deub	'tɔøb'mɑud	tɛɯ'noysæu
doub	'tøʊb'mɯɛd	tyɪ'nøysɔɔ
dæob	'tɯab'miod	taø'nɑesɪy

O Practice all the vowels and consonants discussed in the previous chapters in more complicated nonsense words such as the following:

ɣɑ'roʈiɸ	ŋɔvø'd̪eŋ̩	jæʒɯ'ɓeʃ
be'ɟɛʒuð	ɢaçy'bɨg	sy't'oʍɛk|
ɲi'ɖyxɛŋ̩	ʂeʕɔ'pæz	ʎɛ'nøk'æx
θæ'ɴɑkɯʃ	fiʀo'ceɬ	k!iɹu'god
ʐø'χoqɔl	heβɯ'ɟæt	wup'ɔ'k||em

SYLLABLES AND SUPRASEGMENTAL FEATURES

Throughout this book there have been references to the notion *syllable,* but this term has never been defined. The reason for this is simple: there is no agreed phonetic definition of a syllable. This chapter will discuss some of the theories that have been advanced and show why they are not entirely adequate. We will also consider **suprasegmental features**—those aspects of speech that involve more than single consonants or vowels. The principal suprasegmental features are stress, length, tone, and intonation. These features are independent of the categories required for describing segmental features (vowels and consonants), which involve airstream mechanisms, states of the glottis, primary and secondary articulations, and formant frequencies.

SYLLABLES

The fact that syllables are important units is illustrated by the history of writing. There are many writing systems in which there is one symbol for each syllable. A well-known present-day example is Japanese. But only once in the history of humankind has anybody devised an alphabetic writing system in which syllables were systematically split into their components. About 4,000 years ago, the Greeks modified the Semitic syllabary so as to represent consonants and vowels by separate symbols. The later Aramaic, Hebrew, Arabic, Indic, and other alphabetic writing systems can all be traced back to the principles first and last established in Greek writing. It seems that everybody finds syllables to be comparatively easy units to identify. But people who have not been educated in an alphabetic writing system find it much more difficult to consider syllables as being made up of segments (consonants and vowels).

Most syllables contain both vowels and consonants, but some, such as "eye" and "owe" have only vowels. Many consonants can also function as syllables. Alveolar laterals and nasals (as at the ends of "button" and "bottle") are common in English, but other nasals may occur, as in "blossom" and "bacon," particularly in phrases such as "the blossom may perish" and "bacon goes well with eggs," in which the following sounds aid the assimilatory process. Fricatives and stops may become syllabic in unstressed syllables as in "suppose" and "today," which may be [ṣ'poʊz] and [tʰdeɪ] in a narrow transcription. It is possible to consider all the cases in this paragraph as consisting of a consonant and an associated [ə].

Although nearly everybody can identify syllables, almost nobody can define them. If I ask you how many syllables there are in "minimization" or "suprasegmental," you can easily count them and tell me. In each of these words, there are five syllables. Nevertheless, it is curiously difficult to state an objective phonetic procedure for locating the number of syllables in a word or a phrase in any language; and it is interesting that most people cannot say how many syllables there are in a phrase that they have just heard without first saying that phrase themselves.

There are a few cases where people disagree on how many syllables there are in a word in English. Some of these are due to dialectal differences in the way that particular words are spoken. I would say that the word "predatory" has three syllables because I say ['prɛdətɹɪ]. Other people who pronounce it as ['prɛdətɔɹɪ] say that it has four syllables. Similarly, there are many words such as "bottling" and "brightening" that some people pronounce with syllabic consonants in the middle, so that they have three syllables, whereas others do not.

There are also several groups of words in which people do not differ in their pronunciation, but nevertheless differ in their estimates of the number of syllables. One group of words contains nasals that may or may not be counted as separate syllables. Thus words such as "communism, mysticism" may be said to have three or four syllables, depending on whether the final [m] is considered to be syllabic. A second group contains high front vowels followed by / l /. Many people will say that "meal, seal, reel" contain two syllables, but others will consider them to have one. A third group contains words in which / r / may or may not be syllabic. Some people consider "hire, fire, hour" to be two syllables, whereas others (who pronounce them in exactly the same way) do not. Similar disagreements also arise over words such as "mirror" and "error" for some speakers. Finally, there is disagreement over the number of syllables in a group of words that contain unstressed high vowels followed by another vowel without an intervening consonant. Examples are words such as "mediate, heavier, neolithic." Differences of opinion as to the number of syllables in these words may be due to differences in the way that they are actually pronounced, just as in the case of "predatory" cited earlier. But, unlike "predatory," it is often not clear if a syllable has been omitted on a particular occasion.

It is also possible that different people do different things when asked to say how many syllables there are in a word. Some people may pay more attention to the phonological structure of words than others. Thus many people will say that "realistic" has three syllables. But others will consider it to have four syllables because it is like the word "reality," which everybody agrees has four syllables. Similarly, "meteor" will be two syllables for some people, but three syllables for those who consider it is the same as the stem in "meteoric."

Judgments of the number of syllables in words such as "hire" and "hour" may also be affected by phonological considerations. Some people distinguish between "hire" and "higher" and pronounce "hour" so that it does not end in the same way as "tower." These people are likely to consider "hire" and "hour" to be monosyllables and "higher" and "tower" to have two syllables. But others who do not differentiate between "hire" and "higher" and who pronounce "hour" in the same way as "tower" may say that each of these words has two syllables. Thus two speakers may pronounce "hire" in exactly the same way, but one will consider it to have one syllable, and the other two, because of the way in which they pronounce other words.

Having cited a number of words in which there are problems in determining the number of syllables that they contain, it is important to remember that there is no doubt about the number of syllables in the majority of words. Consider a random list of words (the first word on each three-hundredth page of *Webster's New World Dictionary*), "compline, gauger, maroon, radiometer, temperate." There is complete agreement on the number of syllables in each of these words except for the last ("temperate"). In the case of this word, the disagreement is not over what constitutes a syllable but whether the pronunciation is [ˈtɛmpɹɪt] or [ˈtɛmpəɹɪt].

In looking for an adequate definition of a syllable, we need to do two things. We must account for the words in which there is agreement on the number of syllables, and we must also explain why there is disagreement on some other words. One way of trying to do this is by defining the syllable in terms of the inherent sonority of each sound. The **sonority** of a sound is its loudness relative to that of other sounds with the same length, stress, and pitch. Try saying just the vowels [i, e, ɑ, o, u]. You can probably hear that the vowel [ɑ] has greater sonority (due, largely, to its being pronounced with a greater mouth opening). You can verify this fact by asking a friend to stand some distance away from you and say these vowels in a random order. You will find that it is much easier to hear the low vowel [ɑ] than the high vowels, [i, u].

We saw in Chapter 8 that the loudness of a sound mainly depends on its acoustic intensity (the amount of acoustic energy that is present). The sonority of a sound can be estimated from measurements of the acoustic intensity of a group of sounds that have been said on comparable pitches and with comparable degrees of length and stress. Estimates of this kind were used for drawing the bar graph in Figure 10.1. As you can see, the low vowels [ɑ] and [æ] have greater sonority than the high vowels [u] and [i]. The approximant [l] has about the same sonority as the high vowel [i]. The nasals [m, n] have slightly less sonority than [i] but greater sonority than a voiced fricative such as [z]. The voiced stops and all the voiceless sounds have very little sonority.

The relative sonority of a number of the sounds of English.

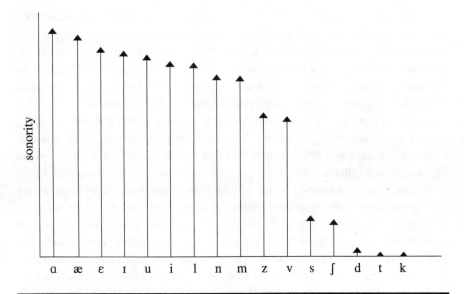

The degrees of sonority shown in Figure 10.1 should not be regarded as exact measurements. The acoustic intensity of different sounds may vary quite considerably for different speakers. Thus, in a particular circumstance one speaker may pronounce [i] with a greater sonority than [l], whereas another may not.

We can now see that one possible theory of the syllable is that peaks of syllabicity coincide with peaks of sonority. This theory would explain why people agree on the number of syllables in the majority of words. In words such as "visit, divided, condensation," there are clear peaks of sonority. In these words, each of the syllable peaks has much more sonority than the surrounding sounds. The theory also explains why there are disagreements over words such as "prism, seal, meteor." Different individuals may vary in the number of peaks of sonority that they have in some of these words. The final [m] in "prism" might have greater sonority than the preceding [z] for some people, but not for others. Similarly, the [l] in "seal" and the second [i] in "meteor" might or might not constitute distinguishable peaks of sonority.

A sonority theory of the syllable will not, however, account for all the observed facts. It obviously fails in a word such as "spa." This word is one syllable, but it must be said to contain two peaks of sonority. It consists of three segments, the first and last of which have greater sonority than the second. A sonority theory also fails to account for the difference in the number of syllables in the phrases "hidden aims" and "hid names." Each of these phrases contains the same sequence of segments, namely, [hɪdneɪmz]. Therefore, there are the same number of peaks of sonority. But the first phrase has three syllables, and the second has two.

There are also a number of words that many people can pronounce with or without one of the syllables. Typical of these words are "paddling, frightening, reddening." Each of these words can be said as two syllables, with the division between them as shown by the inserted period: [ˈpæd.lɪŋ, ˈfɹaɪt.nɪŋ, ˈɹɛd.nɪŋ]. Alternatively (still using an inserted period to show the syllable breaks), they can be said as three syllables, with a syllabic nasal or lateral in the middle: [ˈpæd.l̩.ɪŋ, ˈfɹaɪt.n̩.ɪŋ, ˈɹɛd.n̩.ɪŋ]. Some people claim that they make a distinction between "lightning" (in the sky) [ˈlaɪt.nɪŋ] and "lightening" (making light) [ˈlaɪt.n̩.ɪŋ] and between "codling" (a little codfish) [ˈkɑd.lɪŋ] and "coddling" (a way of cooking an egg) [ˈkɑd.l̩.ɪŋ]. In all these cases a sonority theory of the syllable is inadequate. The variations in the number of syllables cannot be said to be due to variations in the number of peaks of sonority.

One way of avoiding this difficulty is to say that syllables are not marked by peaks in sonority but by peaks in **prominence.** The relative prominence of two sounds depends in part on what their relative sonority would have been if they had had the same length, stress, and pitch; but it also depends in part on their actual stress, length, and pitch. Then we can say that, for example, the [n] in "hidden aims" constitutes a peak of prominence because it has more stress or more length (or both) than the [n] in "hid names."

The problem with this kind of definition is that one cannot state a procedure for combining sonority, length, stress, and pitch so as to form prominence. There is no way in which one can measure the prominence of a sound. As a result, the notion of a peak of prominence becomes a completely subjective affair, so that it does not really throw any light on how one defines a syllable. A sound is prominent because it forms the peak of a syllable; it is syllabic because it is prominent.

A completely different approach is to consider syllabicity not as a property of the sounds one hears but as something produced by the speaker. A theory of this kind was put forward by the psychologist R. H. Stetson. He suggested that every syllable is initiated by a chest pulse—a contraction of the muscles of the rib cage that pushes more air out of the lungs. Stetson made numerous observations of the actions of the respiratory system. But his claims about the actions of the muscles were nearly all deductions based on his observations of the movements of the rib cage and his measurements of the pressure of the air in the lungs. Unfortunately, subsequent direct investigations of the activity of the muscles themselves have failed to confirm his theory. It is clearly untrue to say that every syllable is initiated by a chest pulse.

Yet another way of considering syllables is to regard them as abstract units that exist at some higher level in the mental activity of a speaker. They may be necessary units in the organization and production of utterances. The support for this view comes from various sources. Consider, for example, the errors—the slips of the tongue—that people make when talking. Perhaps one of the commonest is the interchanging of consonants, so that "our dear queen" becomes "our queer dean." In virtually all cases of errors involving the interchange of consonants, it is not a matter of one consonant interchanging with any other consonant. Instead, it is always the case that there is an interchange between consonants in the same place in the syllable. Observations such as these are hard to explain unless we consider the syllable to be a significant unit in the production of speech. Further evidence of a similar kind is provided by descriptions of the sound patterns that occur in languages. We have seen in the earlier chapters that it is difficult to describe English (or, indeed, most languages) without considering syllables as units.

In summary, we can say that there are two types of theories attempting to define syllables. First, there are those in which the definitions are in terms of properties of sounds, such as sonority (acoustic energy) or prominence (some combination of sonority, length, stress, and pitch). Second, there are theories based on the notion that a syllable is a unit in the organization of the sounds of an utterance.

In one sense, a syllable is the smallest possible unit of speech. Every utterance must contain at least one syllable. It is convenient to talk of speech as being composed of segments such as vowels and consonants, but these segments can be observed only as aspects of syllables. A syllable can also be divided for descriptive purposes into its **onset** and **rhyme.** The rhyming part of a syllable consists of the vowel and any consonants that come after it—a fairly familiar notion. Any consonants before the rhyme form the onset of the syllable. The rhyme of a syllable can be further divided into the **nucleus,** which is the vocalic part, and the **coda,** which consists of any final consonants. Words such as "I, owe" consist of single syllables that have only a rhyme, which is also the nucleus. They have neither an onset nor a coda. Words such as "splint" and "stripes" are single syllables containing onsets with three consonants and codas with two consonants.

Sometimes it is difficult to say whether a consonant is the coda of one syllable or the onset of another. How do you divide a word such as "happy" into syllables? Some people will say it is ['hæ.pi], others regard it as ['hæp.i]. Another solution is to consider the [p] as belonging in both syllables, and to call it **ambi-syllabic.** The result of doing this would be to transcribe "happy" as ['hæpi] with no syllable division. There is disagreement among phoneticians as to the correct solution to this problem, and we will not discuss it further here.

Languages differ considerably in the syllable structures that they permit. As we have noted, English has complex onsets and codas. Hawaiian allows no more than one consonant in an onset, and none in the coda, so that every word (such as "Honolulu" and "Waikiki") ends in a vowel. Standard Chinese allows only nasal consonants in the coda, producing words such as "Beijing" and "Shanghai."

STRESS

Stress is a suprasegmental feature of utterances. It applies not to individual vowels and consonants but to whole syllables—whatever they might be. A stressed syllable is pronounced with a greater amount of energy than an unstressed syllable, and it is more prominent in the flow of speech.

English and other Germanic languages make far more use of differences in stress than do most of the languages of the world. In many languages, the position of the stress is fixed in relation to the word. Czech words nearly always have the stress on the first syllable, irrespective of the number of syllables in the word. In Polish and Swahili, the stress is usually on the penultimate syllable.

Variations in the use of stress cause different languages to have different rhythms. But we do not have a good way of describing these rhythmic differences. It used to be said that some languages (such as French) could be called syllable-timed languages in which syllables tend to recur at regular intervals of time. In contrast, English and other Germanic languages were called stress-timed in that stresses were said to be the dominating feature of the rhythmic timing. We now know that this is not true. In contemporary French there are often strong stresses breaking the rhythm of a sentence. In English the rhythm of a sentence depends on several interacting factors.

Perhaps a better typology of rhythmic differences among languages would be to divide languages into those that have variable word stress (such as English and German), those that have fixed word stress (such as Czech, Polish, and Swahili), and those that have fixed phrase stress (such as French). This is, however, another area in which phoneticians must do more research before there is an agreed typology that can be set forth in a textbook such as this one. There are many languages that do not seem to fit into any of these divisions.

In contrast to the nature of syllables, the nature of stress is fairly well understood. Stressed sounds are those on which the speaker expends more muscular energy. This usually involves pushing out more air from the lungs by contracting the muscles of the rib cage and perhaps increasing the pitch by the use of the laryngeal muscles. The extra activity may result in the sound having greater length. There may also be increases in the muscular activity involved in the articulatory movements.

When there is an increase in the amount of air being pushed out of the lungs, there is an increase in the loudness of the sound produced. Some books define stress simply in terms of loudness, but this is not a very useful definition if loudness is considered to be simply a matter of the amount of acoustic energy involved. We have already noted that some sounds have more acoustic energy than others because of factors such as the degree of mouth opening.

A much more important indication of stress is the rise in pitch, which may or may not be due to laryngeal action. You can check for yourself that an increase in the flow of air out of the lungs causes a rise in pitch even without an increase in the activity of the laryngeal muscles. Ask a friend to press against the lower part of your chest while you stand against a wall with your eyes shut. Now say a long vowel on a steady pitch and have your friend push against your chest at an unexpected moment. You will find that at the same time as there is an increase in the flow of air out of your lungs (as a result of your friend's push), there will also be an increase in the pitch of the vowel.

There is a final factor to note when discussing stress in English. We saw in Chapter 5 that a syllable in English is either stressed or not stressed. If it is stressed it can be at the center of an intonational pitch change so that it receives a tonic accent, which might be said to raise it to a more primary level of stress. If it is unstressed it can have a full vowel or a reduced vowel. In some views, a reduced vowel implies that there is a lower level of stress, but in the view expressed here this is not a matter of stress but of vowel quality. We also saw that there are pairs of words, such as "(an) insult" and "(to) insult," that differ only in stress. What happens when these words appear to lose their stress because of a heavy stress elsewhere in the sentence? Consider a pair of sentences such as "He *needed* an increase in price" and, with an equally strong stress on *"needed,"* "He *needed* to increase the price." The answer is that the stress difference between the two words is not completely lost. There may be no changes in pitch associated with the difference in stress, but there are still differences in the relative lengths of the syllables. A stressed syllable is pronounced with a greater amount of energy than an unstressed syllable, and this difference may be manifested simply in the length of the syllable.

LENGTH

The individual segments in a syllable may also vary in length. Many varieties of Scottish English make a length contrast between "week" [wik] and "weak" [wiːk], both having the same monophthongal vowel quality. In most varieties of English, variations in lengths are completely allophonic. We saw, for example, that the vowel in "bad" is predictably longer than the vowel in "bat," because, other things being equal, vowels are always longer before voiced consonants than before voiceless consonants.

Many other languages make considerable use of length contrasts. Long vowels contrast with short vowels in several languages—for example, Estonian, Finnish, Arabic, and Japanese. Danish examples are given in Table 10.1. Length may be shown by placing [ː] after a symbol or by doubling the symbol.

Contrasts between long and short consonants are not so common, but they do occur. Luganda has contrasts such as [ˋkkúlà], meaning "treasure," and [kúlà], meaning "grow up." Italian has contrasts such as "nonno" [ˈnɔnno] (grandfather) versus "nono" [ˈnɔno] (ninth) and "Papa" [ˈpapa] (Pope) versus "pappa"

| TABLE 10.1 | | Contrasts in vowel length in Danish. |

viːdə	"hvide"	(white)	vilə	"vilde"	(wild)	viːlə	"hvile"	(rest)
veːdə	"hvede"	(wheat)	menə	"minde"	(remind)	meːnə	"mene"	(mean)
veːdə	"væde"	(wet)	lɛsə	"læsse"	(load)	leːsə	"læse"	(read)
væːdə	"vade"	(wade)	mæsə	"masse"	(mass)	mæːsə	"mase"	(mash)

['pappa] (porridge, baby food). Long consonants (or vowels) that can be analyzed as double consonants (or vowels) are called **geminates.**

The Italian geminate consonants can be compared with the contrasts between
English consonants in "white tie" [waɪt.taɪ], "why tie" [waɪ.taɪ], and "white
eye" [waɪt.aɪ]. The difference is that in Italian a long consonant can occur
within a single morpheme (a grammatical term for the smallest meaningful unit).
But in English, geminate consonants can occur only across word boundaries, as
in the previous examples, or in a word containing two morphemes, such as "unknown" [ʌnˈnoʊn] or "guileless" [ˈgaɪlləs].

Probably one of the most interesting languages in the way that it uses length
is Japanese. Japanese may be analyzed in terms of the classical Greek and Latin
unit called a mora. A mora is a unit of timing. Each mora takes about the same
length of time to say. The most common type of Japanese mora is formed by a
consonant followed by a vowel. Japanese words such as [kakemono] (scroll)
and [sukijaki] (beef stew) each consist of four moras of this type. Note that in
the latter word the high vowel / u / is voiceless because it occurs between two
voiceless consonants; but it still takes about the same length of time to say as
do the vowels in the other syllables. Another type of mora is a vowel by itself,
as in the word [iki] (breath). This word has two moras, each of which takes
about the same length of time to say. A consonant cannot occur after a vowel
within a mora, but it too can form a mora by itself. The word [nippoŋ] (Japan)
must be divided into four moras [ni p po ŋ]. Although it has only two vowels,
it takes approximately the same length of time to say [nippoŋ] as it does to say
[kakemono] or [sukijaki].

PITCH

The pitch of the voice is determined by several factors. The most important is the
tension of the vocal folds. If the vocal folds are stretched, the pitch of the sound
will go up. Altering the tension of the vocal folds is the normal way of producing
most of the pitch variations that occur in speech. In addition, as we saw in the

section on stress, an increase in the flow of air out of the lungs will also cause an increase in pitch, so that stressed sounds will usually have a higher pitch. Finally, variations in pitch occur in association with the variations in the position of the vocal folds in different phonation types. Thus creaky voice usually has a low pitch as well as a particular voice quality.

Many different kinds of information can be conveyed by variation in pitch. As is the case with other aspects of speech sounds, some of this information simply indicates the personal characteristics of the speaker. The pitch of the voice usually indicates whether the speaker is male or female and, to some extent, his or her age. In addition, it conveys a great deal of nonlinguistic information about the speaker's emotional state—whether the person is calm or angry, or happy or sad. As yet, nobody knows if the pitch changes conveying this sort of information are universal. But it is apparent that speakers of many different languages have similar inflections when conveying similar emotional information.

There also seem to be some universal aspects to the ways in which languages use pitch differences to convey linguistic information. All languages use pitch to mark the boundaries of syntactic units. In nearly all languages, the completion of a grammatical unit such as a normal sentence is signaled by a falling pitch. The last syllable (or the last stressed syllable) is on a lower pitch than it would have been if it had been nonfinal. Conversely, incomplete utterances, such as mid-sentence clause breaks where the speaker intends to show that there is something still to come, often have a basically rising intonation. There are, of course, exceptions to these two generalizations. In some styles of English, for example, it is possible to have a rising intonation on many sentences. But the use of a falling pitch to mark noninterrogative sentences occurs in by far the majority of utterances.

Syntactic information is the only linguistic information conveyed by pitch in English and most other Indo-European languages. But in many languages, pitch variations have another function. Differences in pitch can be used to change the meaning of a word. For example, in Chinese, the consonant–vowel sequence [ma] pronounced with a high and level pitch means "mother," but the same sequence pronounced with a high falling pitch means "scold."

Pitch variations that affect the meaning of a word are called **tones.** The meaning of a word depends on its tone in the majority of the languages in the world. All languages also use intonation, which is the use of pitch variations to convey syntactic information. The intonation patterns are superimposed on the tones in a way that we will discuss later.

The simplest kind of tone language is that in which there are only two possible tones, high and low. In many Bantu languages, such as Shona (spoken in Zimbabwe), Zulu, or Luganda, every vowel may be classified as being on a high or on a low pitch. Thus, in Shona the sequence [kùtʃérá], meaning "to draw water," has a low tone on the first syllable and a high tone on the second and third syllables. But when this sequence is [kùtʃèrà] with low tones on each syllable, it means "to dig."

Tones may be transcribed in many different ways. One of the simplest systems is to mark a high pitch by an acute accent over the vowel [á] and a low pitch by a grave accent [à]. Middle pitches can be left unmarked. This is the kind of transcription I have been using in the examples cited in some of the tables illustrating sounds not found in English (see, for example, Tables 6.3, 7.5). In a language with three tones, such as Yoruba (spoken in Nigeria), the mid tone would be left unmarked. In this way we could transcribe a three-way opposition such as occurs in Yoruba: [ó wá] (he comes), [ó wa . . .] (he looked for . . .), [ó wà] (he existed).

Speakers of English often find it hard to consider the tone as an important, meaningful part of a word. But for speakers of a tone language, a difference in tone is just as significant as a difference in consonant or vowel quality. If you are trying to say "he looked for (something)" in Yoruba, and you say [ó wà] instead of [ó wa], it will sound just as odd as if you had said "he licked" instead of "he looked" in English.

Contrastive tones are usually marked over the vowel in a tone language. But they are often properties of the syllable as a whole. They can also occur on voiced consonants that can be regarded as syllabic. The Igbo (spoken in Nigeria) for "I'm beautiful" is [ḿ mà ḿ má]. Occasionally, tones occur on consonants that are not normally syllabic. In the section on length in this chapter, I transcribed the Luganda word for "treasure" as [`kkúlà], with a low tone mark before the first [k]. Obviously, the silence preceding a voiceless consonant cannot be said on a low pitch. Only voiced sounds can have a high or a low pitch. This tone had to be transcribed simply because (for reasons to be explained later) it is a necessary unit when considering the sound pattern of Luganda as a whole.

Tone languages make two slightly different uses of pitch within a word. In the examples given so far, differences in pitch have affected the lexical (dictionary) meaning of a word. But many, if not most, tone languages also use pitch differences to make changes in grammatical (morphological) meaning. Thus in Igbo the idea of possession—roughly the equivalent of "of" in English—may be expressed by a high tone. This high tone appears, for example, in the phrase meaning "the jaw of a monkey." The word for "jaw" is [àgbà] with two low tones. The word for "monkey" is [èŋwè], also with two low tones. But the phrase "the jaw of a monkey" is [àgbá èŋwè], with a high tone on the second syllable of the word for "jaw." Thus the English word "of" can sometimes be represented simply as a high tone on a particular syllable in Igbo.

Another example of the grammatical use of tone occurs in the tense system of Edo, spoken in Nigeria, as shown in Table 10.2. In what may be called the timeless tense (indicating a habitual action), there is a low tone on both the pronoun and the verb. In what may be called the continuous tense (indicating an action in progress), there is a high tone on the pronoun, a low tone on monosyllabic verbs, and a tone going from low to high on disyllables. In the past tense, there is a low tone on the pronoun, a high tone on monosyllabic verbs, and high to low on disyllables.

TABLE 10.2	The use of tone in part of the tense system of Edo.			
Tense	**Monosyllabic Verbs**		**Disyllabic Verbs**	
Timeless	ì mà	(I show)	ì hrùlè	(I run)
Continuous	í mà	(I am showing)	í hrùlé	(I am running)
Past	ì má	(I showed)	ì hrúlè	(I ran)

Before considering more complicated tonal systems, you should check that you can pronounce correctly all the tones that have to be pronounced in the examples cited in the previous paragraphs. You should, of course, say the high tones on a pitch in the upper part of your own pitch range, and the low tones on a pitch in the lower part. If you are working with a friend or with recordings of a speaker of a tone language, be careful *not* to imitate their exact pitches, unless they have just the same pitch range as you normally do. Contrastive tones must always be considered relative to the presumed mean pitch of the speaker. (One of my problems in doing fieldwork with speakers of tone languages is that they often say I am mispronouncing a word when I imitate them fairly exactly. I have a rather deep voice, and my repetitions are apt to be misunderstood unless I make a distinct effort to say them not in the same way as the speaker, but on a somewhat lower pitch.)

The tones in many languages can be described in terms of given points within the speaker's pitch range. If the speaker is aiming at a single target pitch for a syllable, the tone can be regarded as a level tone. Luganda, Zulu, and Hausa are examples of tone languages in each of which there are basically just two tones, high and low. Yoruba is an example of a tone language with three tones, high, mid, and low. Additional gliding tones do occur in Yoruba, but they can be shown to be the result of combining two of the tones within a single syllable. Tone languages with four pitch levels are somewhat more uncommon. Egede and Kutep (both spoken in Nigeria) have tones that can be distinguished as being top, high, mid, and low.

The tones of some languages cannot be conveniently described in terms of single points within a pitch range. In Mandarin Chinese, there are four tones, three of which involve gliding movements. Tones of this kind are called **contour tones.** When making tones of this type, the speaker's aim is to produce a characteristic pitch movement, rather than a single point in the pitch range. In addition to Chinese, many of the languages of Southeast Asia (for example, Thai and Vietnamese) have contour tones.

The transcription system that we have been using is sufficient for languages that have only level tones. It can be expanded to incorporate languages with four level tones, perhaps by marking the lower of the two mid tones with a horizontal bar, [ā], and leaving the upper one unmarked. But it cannot be used to specify accurately the tones of a contour tone language.

One way of representing contour tones is to consider five equally spaced points within the normal pitch range of a speaker's voice: (1) low, (2) half-low, (3) middle, (4) half-high, and (5) high. We can then describe a contour tone as a movement from one of these points to another. We can represent this information graphically. If we draw a vertical line to indicate the normal range of a speaker's voice, we can plot a simplified graph of the pitch to the left of this line. In this way we can form a letter-like symbol that represents the tone.

The four "tone letters" that are required for describing Mandarin Chinese are shown in the fourth column of Table 10.3. Each consists of a reference line to the right, preceded by a line indicating the pitch of the tone. Thus tone 1 is a high-level tone remaining at pitch level 5. Tone 2 is a rising tone, going from pitch level 3 to pitch level 5. Tone 3 begins by falling from pitch level 2 to the lowest possible level and then rises to pitch level 4. Tone 4 falls from pitch level 5 all the way to pitch level 1. It is usually impractical to use tone letters in a transcription of a language. A convenient system is to describe each tone in a particular language by means of tone letters and then numbers specifying the pitch levels, as in the third column, or tone letters, as in the fourth column, and then use superscript numbers, as in the fifth column in Table 10.3.

Other tone letters designed in the same way can be used for the description of tones in other languages. The tones of Thai are illustrated in Table 10.4. Note how the numbers that are conventionally used in specifying Thai tones do not have the same values as those conventionally used for Mandarin Chinese in Table 10.3. Tone 1 in Thai is a falling tone, whereas in Mandarin Chinese it is a high-level tone. In Thai there is also a fifth tone, designated the common tone, which is left unmarked in transcriptions.

Even in a tone language, the pitch of the voice changes continuously throughout sequences of voiced sounds. There are seldom sudden jumps from one pitch level to another. As a result, assimilations occur between tones in much the same way as they do between segments. When a high tone precedes a low tone, then the low tone will usually begin with a downward pitch change. Conversely, a

TABLE 10.3	Tonal contrasts in Mandarin Chinese.				
Tone Number	Description	Pitch	Tone Letter	Example	Gloss
1	high level	55	˥	ma^1	mother
2	high rising	35	˧˥	ma^2	hemp
3	low falling rising	214	˨˩˦	ma^3	horse
4	high falling	51	˥˩	ma^4	scold

TABLE 10.4	Tonal contrasts in Thai.				
Tone Number	**Description**	**Pitch**	**Tone Letter**	**Example**	**Gloss**
1	low falling	21	˩	naa^1	(a nickname)
2	high falling	51	˥	naa^2	face
3	high rising	45	˦	naa^3	aunt
4	low falling rising	214	˩	naa^4	thick
"common"	mid falling	32	˧	naa	field

high tone following a low tone may begin with an upward pitch movement. Considering two adjacent tones, it is usually the first that affects the second rather than the other way around. There seems to be a tendency in the languages of the world for tone assimilations to be perseverative—the tone of one syllable hanging over into that of later syllables—rather than anticipatory—the tone of one syllable changing because it anticipates that of the syllable yet to come.

Changes of tone due to the influence of one tone on another are called **tone sandhi.** Sometimes these changes are fairly complex. For example, in Mandarin Chinese the word meaning "very" is [hao^3], with a falling-rising tone. But in the phrase meaning "very cold!" it is pronounced with a high rising tone [hao^2 leeŋ^3]. In this way, Mandarin Chinese avoids having two falling-rising tones one after another. Whenever a tone-3 word is followed by another tone-3 word, the low falling–rising tone is changed into tone 2—the high rising tone. As another example of tone sandhi, we can consider what happens to compound words in Shanghai Chinese. The word for "sky" is [tʰi], with a pitch fall going from high (5) to low (1). The word for "earth" is [di], with a pitch rise going from low (1) to high (5). Put together, these form the word for "universe" [tʰidi], which has a pitch fall going from high on the first syllable to low on the second. Thus the pitch pattern associated with the first syllable has extended over the whole compound word. This is the general rule in Shanghai Chinese for compound words beginning with a syllable that is high falling when it occurs in isolation. The word for "symphony" is composed of the words meaning "exchange," "sound," and "song." When said in isolation, the first of these, [tʃiɔ], has a high falling tone (51); the second, [ʃiã], has a mid rising tone (35); and the last, [tʃʰiɔʔ], has a short high tone (5). But when put together to form [tʃiɔʃiãtʃʰiɔʔ] "symphony," the first syllable is high (5), the second mid (3), and the third low (1).

As I mentioned earlier, tone languages also use intonational pitch changes. In many tone languages, ordinary statements will have a generally falling intonation, and at least some questions will have a rising intonation over part of the utterance. Doubt, anger, excitement, and many other emotional signals will be conveyed by intonations not all that dissimilar from those in English, the distinctive tones of individual words being superimposed on the overall patterns.

As in English, the regular intonation of a sentence often marks syntactic boundaries. In most languages there is a downward trend of the pitch over a syntactic unit such as a sentence. This general pitch lowering is known as **declination.** In some languages, such as Hausa, declination involves the falling of the mean pitch level throughout the sentence. Both high tones and low tones at the beginning of a sentence are higher than they are at the end. A high tone at the end of a Hausa sentence may even have about the same absolute pitch as a low tone had at the beginning of the same sentence.

In other languages the declination may take a slightly different form. The low tones may remain at about the same level throughout the sentence, so that the declination affects only the high tones. In Luganda, there is a rule whereby high tones are lowered slightly whenever they are preceded by a low tone within the same sentence. This was the reason why I had to mark the low tone at the beginning of [`kkúlà] "treasure," even though it could not be pronounced. The high tone in this word is slightly lower than it would have been if this (silent) low tone had not been there.

To summarize, variations in pitch are used in a number of different ways. In the first place, they convey nonlinguistic information about the speaker's emotional state and, to some extent, personal physiological characteristics. Second, in all languages, differences in pitch convey one or more kinds of linguistic information. The linguistic uses of pitch are intonation (the distinctive pitches in a phrase), which in all languages conveys information about the syntactic components of the utterance, and tone (the distinctive pitches within a word), which may convey both lexical information about the meaning of the word and the grammatical function of the word. Within tone languages, the tones can be divided into contour tones, which require the specification of a change in pitch within the syllable, and so-called level tones, in which only a single contrastive height needs to be specified for each syllable, the pitch changes within a syllable being regarded as simply the result of putting syllables together to form a sentence.

STRESS, TONE, AND PITCH ACCENT LANGUAGES

It is clear that Chinese is a tone language, in which the meaning of a word is affected by the pitch, and that English is not, despite the fact that we can describe certain syllables in an English sentence as having high or low tones, as we saw in Chapter 5. The "tones" in an English sentence do not affect the meaning of the individual words, although they may affect the meaning of the phrase or sentence. English has stress contrasts, such as "below" versus "billow," but not tone contrasts.

So far we have been considering languages to be either stress or tone languages, but this is an oversimplification. There are some languages that have both. Pirahã, for example, a language spoken in the Amazonian rain forest, has two contrastive tones. The word / bagíai /, with a high tone on the second vowel (and low tones unmarked), means "friend," but / bagiái /, with the high tone on the next vowel, means "thief." Pirahã also has stress differences, in that / ga'ba /, a species of fruit, has stress on the second syllable, whereas / 'kaba /, "no," has stress on the first syllable. Both these words have two low tones. Thus Pirahã has both stress and tone from a phonetic point of view. However it should be noted that the stress differences in Pirahã are predictable from the phonetic structure of the words. It is the voiceless consonant at the beginning of / 'kaba / that causes it to have stress on the first syllable.

There are some European languages in which pitch plays a role in apparently distinguishing words. Swedish has stress differences that can be described in much the same way as stress differences in English. But it also has a pitch contrast between, for example, "anden" (the duck) and "anden" (the ghost). In the Stockholm dialect, the word for "the duck" has a high pitch early in the word, whereas "the ghost" may have two pitch peaks. Swedish phoneticians describe the difference as accent 1 versus accent 2. We should note, however, that this is not really a difference in tone. The base form of the word for "duck" is / and /, with the suffix / -en / making it "the duck." The word for "ghost" is / ande / with the suffix being simply / -n /. The difference in the composition of the words accounts for the difference in pitch. Pitch may be said to play a role in showing the forms of words in Swedish, but it does not otherwise distinguish meanings.

Scottish Gaelic spoken in the Outer Hebrides has words that differ in pitch, but again they are not really differences in tone. For example, "duan" / tuan / (song) contrasts with "dubhan" / tuan / (hook), the first word having a rising pitch, and the second word falling steeply at the end. Although these two words have identical sequences of segments and often have the same length, the second word is felt by speakers to have two syllables (as it did historically), and this affects the pitch. It is possible to argue that Scottish Gaelic is now becoming a tone language.

Japanese is a more striking case of a language that is in some ways between a tone language and a stress language. Words in Japanese have an accent on a particular syllable much in the same way as English words have one or more stresses. In Japanese the accent is invariably realized as a high pitch, so that Japanese is often called a pitch-accent language. Japanese words differ in the placement of the accent, giving rise to contrasts such as / kákiga / "oyster," / kakíga / "fence," and / kakigá / "persimmon."

EXERCISES

A People differ in their judgments of the number of syllables that there are in the following words. Ask several people (if possible, include some children) to say these words and then tell you how many syllables there are in each of them. Try to explain, for each word, why people may differ in their judgments, even if the people you ask are all in agreement.

laboratory _____

spasm _____

oven _____

prisoner_____

million _____

merrier _____

feral_____

B List four words for which the sonority theory of syllabicity is inadequate in accounting for the number of syllables that are present.

_____

_____

C Make a list of ten words chosen at random from a dictionary. In how many cases is there no doubt as to the number of syllables that they contain? Explain the reasons for the doubt in the case of the others.

_____

_____

_____

_____

_____

D Look at dictionaries or introductory textbooks on four or five foreign languages not mentioned in this chapter. Try to state whether they have variable word stress or fixed word stress, or whether stress does not seem to be a property of the word.

_____

_____

_____

E Again by looking at dictionaries or introductory textbooks, find examples of tone languages not mentioned in this chapter. For each language, try to state how many contrasting tones it has, exemplifying the distinctions between each of them with minimal pairs if possible.

_____

_____

_____

F In Luganda, many words fall into one or the other of two classes, each with a different pattern of permissible tones, as exemplified in the following lists:

I		**II**	
èkítábó	(a book)	àkàsózì	(a hill)
òmúꞌ ntú	(a man)	òmùkázì	(a woman)
òlúgúꞌ dó	(a road)	èm̀bwáꞌ	(a dog)
òkúwákáná	(to dispute)	òkùsálà	(to cut)

Describe the permitted sequences of tones in each class. (In fact, Class II is more complicated than is indicated by the data given here.)

_____

_____

G Roughly speaking, when making a declarative statement in Luganda, the initial vowel is dropped and the tones in Class I words become as shown here:

kìtábó	(it is a book)
mùꞌntú	(he is a man)
lùgúꞌddú	(it is a road)

State the rule affecting the tones in this grammatical construction.

_____

_____

PERFORMANCE EXERCISES

A Practice saying nonsense words with long and short vowels. Say partially English phrases such as those shown here. Try to make the length of each vowel independent of the quality—so that [bɪb] is as long as [bib]—and of the following consonant—so that [bip] is as long as [bib]. The syllables are included within a phrase so that you can make sure that you keep the overall rate of speech constant.

'seɪ	'biːb	əˈgɛn
'seɪ	'bib	əˈgɛn
'seɪ	'bɪb	əˈgɛn
'seɪ	'bɪːb	əˈgɛn
'seɪ	'biːp	əˈgɛn
'seɪ	'bip	əˈgɛn
'seɪ	'bɪp	əˈgɛn
'seɪ	'bɪːp	əˈgɛn

B Repeat this exercise with other syllables such as those shown in the following list. Continue using a frame such as "say _____ again."

buːd

bud

bʊd

bʊːd

buːt

but

bʊt

bʊːt

C Learn to differentiate between single and double, or geminate, consonants. Say the following:

e'pɛm	o'num	ø'zys
ep'pɛm	on'num	øz'zys
'epɛm	'onun	'øzys
'eppɛm	'onnun	'øzzys

D Take a sentence that can be said with strong stresses recurring at roughly regular intervals, such as the following:

What is the 'difference in 'rhythm between 'English and 'French? Say this sentence with as regular a rhythm as you can, while tapping on the stressed syllables. You should be able to say it slowly, then at a normal speed, and finally fast, in each case tapping out a regular rhythm. Now try saying it as a French-speaking person just learning to speak English might say it, with each syllable taking about the same length of time. Make regular taps, one corresponding to each syllable throughout the sentence. Say it slowly, at a normal speed, and fast in this way.

E One of the best ways of learning about suprasegmental features is to learn to say a short sentence backward. To do this properly, you have to reverse the intonation pattern of the sentence, make the aspiration come before rather than after voiceless stops, and take into account all the variations in vowel and consonant length due to the phonetic context. If you can make a recording of yourself on a computer, you may be able to judge how successfully you can do this by playing the recording backward, so that the reversed sentence should sound as if it had been said normally. Begin with a fairly easy phrase such as the following:

Mary had a little lamb.

Then go on with a more difficult one such as the following:

Whose fleece was white as snow.

In each case it is best to begin by making a narrow transcription of the phrase, including the intonation pattern, and then to write this in the reverse order.

F Practice tonal contrasts by learning to say the following set of words in Ibibio, a language spoken in Nigeria. Ibibio has three tones: high [´], low [`], and falling [ˆ]. The six contrasting patterns in disyllabic words are illustrated here. (Saying these words also gives you practice in saying the labial velar [k͡p], which is discussed in Chapter 7 at the end of the section "Places of Articulation.")

Tone Sequence	Example	Gloss
high followed by high	ák͡pá	expanse of ocean
high followed by low	ákù	priest
high followed by falling	ák͡pân	square woven basket
low followed by high	àk͡pá	first
low followed by low	àk͡pà	species of ant
low followed by falling	àk͡pɔ̂	rubber tree

G Cantonese Chinese has a different tone system from Mandarin Chinese (shown in Table 10.3). In Cantonese there are six tones that occur on open syllables and three that occur only on syllables containing a final consonant. Say each of the following Cantonese words:

Description	Pitch	Tone Letter	Example	Gloss
high	55	˥	si	poem
mid	33	˧	si	to try
low	22	˨	si	matter
extra low	11	˩	si	time
mid rising	35	˧˥	si	to cause
low rising	13	˩˧	si	city
high	5	˥	sik	to know
mid	3	˧	sit	to release
low	2	˨	sik	to eat

LINGUISTIC PHONETICS

This chapter will consider the way articulatory movements are organized and will look at some phonetic processes that affect the way languages get to be the way they are. We will then summarize ways of making linguistic phonetic descriptions, first by reviewing the system of phonetic transcription proposed by the International Phonetic Association and then by considering a set of features of speech sounds.

CONTROLLING ARTICULATORY MOVEMENTS

Throughout this book we have been considering speech mainly in terms of the articulations required for segments. But we have not really considered in detail how these segments are put together, simply acknowledging that all utterances involve coarticulations—the overlapping of adjacent articulatory gestures. Consonants vary their place of articulation so that they become more like the next sound. As we have seen, English / t, d / are usually alveolar stops, but when they occur before dental fricatives they are pronounced with tongue contact on the teeth, so that they become [t̪, d̪] as in "eighth" [eɪt̪θ] and "width" [wɪd̪ð]. (Some people pronounce the latter word with voiceless consonants at the end, making it [wɪt̪θ].)

Another noticeable change in the place of articulation occurs in the pronunciation of / k, g / before a front vowel as in "key, geese" [kiː, giːs] as compared with a back vowel as in "caw, gauze" [kɔː, gɔːz]. The different forms of / k /—the allophones—occur because of the influence of the following vowel. The whole body of the tongue has to be pulled up and forward for [i]. This action begins during the formation of the closure for / k /, which is consequently farther forward than the closure in the allophone of / k / before / ɔ /. In the latter case, the / k / anticipates the low back position of the body of the tongue in / ɔ /.

You should be able to feel that the place of articulation of / k / is much farther forward before a front vowel. Check that in your own pronunciation of "key" the articulatory contact is between the tongue and a point on the roof of your mouth near the hard palate. Now compare this with your pronunciation of "caw," in which the articulation is at the back of the mouth fairly low down on the soft palate.

Now try to find out whether there is as much variation in the place of articulation when the / k / occurs *after* vowels in words such as "peak" [piːk] and "hawk" [hɔːk]. You will probably discover that there is very little difference between these allophones of / k /. In general, English may be said to be an anticipatory language—that is, one in which the articulations of the sounds yet to come are anticipated to some extent. Some other languages, such as French or Italian, are more perseverative in that the articulation of one sound tends to persevere, or continue, into the following sound.

There are many other examples of the tendency of English to anticipate future articulations. We noted that when a stop occurs before another consonant—as in "apt" and "act"—it is unexploded, so that these words are pronounced [æpˈt] and [ækˈt], the diacritic [ˈ] indicating that the stop is unexploded. This may be regarded as a case of the articulation of the last consonant being anticipated during the closure of the previous consonant. The [p] in "apt" is unexploded because the closure for the [t] occurs before the lips come apart. French and Italian are more likely to have exploded stops, but in English, an articulator that is not necessarily involved in a given sound will nearly always start moving toward its position in the next sound in which it is the primary articulator. This phenomenon is known as **anticipatory coarticulation.** There are also cases in which the actions involved in making one sound continue into the next. For example, when "it is" [ɪt ɪz] is elided into "it's" [ɪts], the voicelessness associated with the [t] persists into the next sound. This is known as **perseverative coarticulation.**

We must also note that we often use different muscular actions to produce essentially the same sounds. Thus, as we have seen, pitch changes can be produced either by extra respiratory effort pushing the air out of the lungs more rapidly, or by increasing the tension of the vocal folds in one of a variety of ways, or by a combination of these techniques. I have recorded some speakers who produce the rising intonation at the end of tag questions (sentences such as "That's your book, isn't it?") mainly by extra respiratory effort, and others (the majority of speakers) who produce it mainly by increasing the tension of the vocal folds. Until I made these instrumental recordings, I could not tell the difference between these two groups of speakers. They all sounded very much alike. An appropriate phonetic description of these utterances would show no differences.

When the same sound can be produced by different actions, we can say that there is phonetic **motor equivalence** between these actions. It does not matter to the listener which of the equivalent motor actions is used when producing a given sound. Accordingly, it is also irrelevant to the description of speech from a linguistic point of view. When we are concerned with just the meaningful aspects of utterances, we want to characterize simply those things that speakers control, and to which listeners attend. Consequently, we describe tone and intonation in terms of variations in pitch, *not* in terms of actions of the larynx and the respiratory mechanisms.

The notion of phonetic motor equivalence can be further exemplified by reference to other material previously discussed. I deliberately gave a vague definition of what constitutes a stressed syllable (one "pronounced with a greater amount of energy than an unstressed syllable"). There are several different ways of producing greater respiratory energy, most of them producing precisely the same acoustic effect. To take two examples, we can contract the muscles of the rib cage (the internal intercostals), or we can push against the diaphragm harder with the abdominal muscles (rectus abdominis and others). Either of these actions will produce an increase in the pressure of the air in the lungs, and either will produce a stressed syllable. The precise action used is irrelevant to the phonetic specification. The particular muscular movements involved may be important to the speech pathologist or teacher of speech who is trying to alter the speaker's behavior. But phonetic descriptions specify the goals that speakers have, rather than the underlying muscular mechanisms.

Putting this another way, we can explain the phenomenon of motor equivalence in terms of what are called **coordinative structures**—physiological systems that act together to produce the required effects. Thus we can think of the variations in subglottal pressure that occur during an utterance as the product of a coordinative structure consisting of the lungs, the sensory systems that supply the brain with information about the state of the lungs (for example, whether they are expanded or whether they have very little air in them), the muscles involved in adjusting the positions of the rib cage and the diaphragm, and the central processes relating all these. The subglottal pressure that can be produced at any given moment is constrained by this coordinative structure. Similarly, the control of the tension of the vocal folds depends on a complex coordinative structure involving the laryngeal muscles, sensory information on the positions of the cricoid, thyroid, and arytenoid cartilages, and other factors. The control of the position of the lower lip depends on a coordinative structure involving the lip muscles and the muscles fixing the position of the lower jaw, and on information on the state of these and other factors, including the movements of the upper lip. When talking a speaker simply sets the goals for the actions of the vocal organs, and the coordinative structures make the required movements.

For further simple examples of coordinative structures, we will consider the production of vowels. As you can see quite easily for yourself, it is possible to produce the same vowel with many different jaw positions. Try to say [i] with your teeth almost together, and then say it again with the teeth fairly far apart. There need be very little, if any, difference in the sounds you produce. The same is true of many other vowels. In fact, it is possible to produce a complete set of English vowels with your teeth almost together or with them held apart by a wedge such as a small coin. Obviously, the motor activity must be very different in these two circumstances. When the teeth are held far apart, you can feel the muscles of the tongue raising it up in the jaw when you say [i]. When the teeth are close together, the raising of the jaw itself contributes greatly to the lifting of the tongue for [i]. You can also observe the results of the motor equivalence of different gestures that people use when making vowels by watching them say the words "heed, hid, head, had." You will probably be able to see that some people lower the tongue by lowering the jaw as they say this series of words. But others keep the jaw comparatively steady and simply lower the tongue within the jaw.

Motor equivalence nearly always involves parts of the speech mechanism being considered in more detail than is necessary for the description of differences in meaning. In each of the cases we have been considering, it has been possible to characterize the sounds in a unique way in physiological or articulatory terms. Thus if two sounds have the same pitch, they have the same rate of vibration of the vocal folds, irrespective of the mechanism used to produce the vocal fold vibrations. Similarly, the different ways of producing stressed syllables that we were discussing will all result in the same increases in subglottal pressure. Lastly, the different jaw positions in vowels will not affect the position of the highest point of the tongue or its shape relative to the upper surface of the vocal tract.

There are only a few cases in which it has been shown that a person can produce the same sound with different vocal tract shapes. When this occurs, the coordinative structures permit what we may call compensatory articulations. The first case is in producing r-colored vowels, which, as we saw in Chapter 9, can be made with the tip of the tongue up or with a more bunched tongue position farther back in the mouth. Another case involves rounded vowels that can be made either with a small amount of rounding and lowering the larynx or with a large amount of lip rounding and the larynx in a more raised position. Try saying the vowel [u] with a more lowered larynx than usual. Now say it with a normal larynx position and note the difference in sound. If you could make a spectrogram of these two sounds, you would find the frequencies of all the formants are lower when the larynx is lower. Now try saying [u] with a normal larynx position and then increasing the lip rounding. This will also lower the formant frequencies, so that it is possible to make a sound identical with the first [u] (the one with a lowered larynx). For high back vowels, lip rounding and lowering the larynx are compensatory articulations, each having the same acoustic effect.

In general, speakers are goal oriented. They produce utterances sometimes using one set of muscles and sometimes another, but always with reference to what they hear and what utterances sound like. They vary their vocal gestures and do whatever they have to do to get the sounds produced.

THE BALANCE BETWEEN PHONETIC FORCES

When we consider how sounds pattern within a language, we must take into account both the speaker's point of view and the listener's point of view. Speakers often like to convey their meaning with the least possible articulatory effort.

Except when they are striving for clarity of articulation, they tend to produce utterances with a large number of assimilations, with some segments left out, and with the differences between other segments reduced to a minimum. Producing utterances in this way requires a speaker to follow a principle of *ease of articulation*. The main way of reducing articulatory effort is by making use of coarticulations between sounds. As a result of coarticulations, languages change. For example, in an earlier form of English, words such as "nation, station" contained [s], so that they were pronounced ['nasion] and ['stasion]. As a result of coarticulation, the blade of the tongue became raised during the fricative, in anticipation of the position needed for the following high front vowel. Thus the [s] became [ʃ], [i] was lost, and the unstressed [o] became [ə]. (The "t" was never pronounced in English. It was introduced into the spelling by scholars who were influenced by Latin.)

Further examples are not hard to find. Coarticulations involving a change in the place of the nasal and the following stop occur in words such as "improper" and "impossible." In words such as these, the [n] that occurs in the prefix "in-" (as in "intolerable" and "indecent") has changed to [m]. These changes, which occurred before these words were borrowed into English, are even reflected in the spelling. There are also coarticulations involving the state of the glottis. Words such as "resist" and "result" are pronounced as [rə'zɪst] and [rə'zʌlt], with a voiced consonant between the two vowels. The stems in these words originally began with the voiceless consonant [s], as they still do in words such as "consist" and "consult," in which the [s] is not intervocalic. In all these and in many similar historical changes, one or more segments are affected by adjacent segments so that there is an economy of articulation. These are historical cases of the phenomenon of assimilation, which we discussed at the beginning of Chapter 5.

Ease of articulation cannot be carried too far. Listeners need to be able to understand the meaning with the least possible effort on their part. They would therefore prefer utterances that have sounds that remain constant and distinct on all occasions. Perceptually, what matters is that sounds that affect the meaning of a word should be sufficiently distinct from one another. A language must always maintain *sufficient perceptual separation*. Therefore languages constrain speakers so that they keep words sufficiently far apart. The language makes sure that there is sufficient perceptual distance between the sounds that occur in a contrasting set, such as the vowels in stressed monosyllables (as in "beat, bit, bet, bat," etc.).

The principle of perceptual separation does not usually result in one sound affecting an adjacent sound, as occurs with the principle of maximum ease of articulation. Instead, perceptual separation affects the set of sounds that potentially can occur at a given position in a word, such as in the position that must be occupied by a vowel in a stressed monosyllable. Articulatory processes are syntagmatic, affecting adjacent items in a sequence, whereas perceptual processes are paradigmatic, affecting the set of items that can occur in a given place in a sequence.

We have already noted some of the ways in which languages tend to maximize the perceptual separation between sounds. As we saw in Chapter 9, this tendency explains why some vowel systems are more likely to occur than others. If the vowels of a language are to be maximally distinct, the formant frequencies will be such that the vowels are as far apart as possible when plotted on a vowel chart. Consequently, there is a natural tendency in languages for vowels to be spaced at approximately equal distances apart and for them to be on the outside of the possible vowel area. This tendency is most evident in languages with a comparatively small number of vowels. There are hundreds of languages that have only five contrasting vowels (e.g., Spanish, Hausa, Japanese, and Swahili, to name four completely unrelated languages). In all these languages, the vowels are roughly evenly distributed so that there are at least two front vowels and two back vowels. There is no language in which there are only five vowels unevenly distributed so that all of them are front vowels. But there are, of course, many languages like English that have five front vowels and an approximately similar number of back vowels.

If there is a possibility for a pair of contrasting sounds to occur in the same place within a word, then there will be a tendency for the perceptual distance between them to be increased. Conversely, whenever a language does not distinguish between two similar sounds, the actual sound produced will tend to be in between the two possibilities. Thus, as we have seen, English distinguishes between voiced and voiceless stops as in "pie, buy." But this distinction cannot occur after / s /. Consequently, the stop in "spy" is in between these two possibilities (but closer to the stop in "buy").

Other examples of this phenomenon have also been mentioned. We saw that before [ŋ], English does not distinguish between tense and lax vowels. Consequently, the vowel that occurs in, for example, "sing," has a quality in between that of [iː] and [ɪ]. Similarly, there is no distinction between tense and lax vowels before [r]. The vowel in "here" in most forms of American English is also intermediate between [i] and [ɪ].

The principle of maximum perceptual separation also accounts for some of the differences between languages. French has two high rounded vowels, [u] as in "tout" [t̪u] (all) and [y] as in "tu" [t̪y] (you). These two possibilities are kept distinct by one being definitely a front vowel and the other definitely a back vowel. But English does not have this opposition. Consequently, the high rounded vowel that occurs in, for example, "who, two" varies considerably. In some dialects (for example, most forms of American English), it is a central or back vowel, and in others (for example, some forms of Scottish English), it is a front vowel not very different from French [y]. As far as this vowel is concerned, what matters most in English is that it should be high and rounded. Whether it is front or back is less important.

All these examples illustrate the way languages maintain a balance between the requirements of the speaker and those of the listener. On the one hand, there is the pressure to make changes that would result in easier articulations from a speaker's point of view. On the other hand, there is the pressure from the listener's point of view that requires that there should be sufficient perceptual contrast between sounds that are able to affect the meaning of an utterance.

THE INTERNATIONAL PHONETIC ALPHABET

One way of reviewing the notions of phonetic description is to consider the International Phonetic Alphabet (IPA). This is the set of the symbols and diacritics that have been officially approved by the International Phonetic Association. The association publishes a chart, which is reproduced (with permission) inside the front and back covers of this book. This chart is really a number of separate charts, which have been rearranged for this book. At the top inside the front cover is the main consonant chart. Below it to the left is a table showing the symbols for nonpulmonic consonants. To the right is the vowel chart. Inside the back cover there is a list of "Other symbols," and, below it, a table showing the diacritics. To the right there is a set of symbols for suprasegmental events, such as tone, intonation, stress, and length.

In the usual arrangement of the IPA chart, the material on the back page is placed below that on the front. It is an attempt to summarize a complete theory of linguistic phonetics in a single page, rather like a table of chemical elements summarizes a theorem of chemistry. The IPA chart does not try to cover all possible types of phonetic descriptions, including, for example, all the types of voice quality that distinguish one person from another or that characterize pathological forms of speech. Instead, it is limited to those sounds that can have linguistic significance in that they can change the meaning of a word in some language.

You should be able to understand all the terms in the consonant chart. If you have any problems, refer to the glossary at the end of the book. The symbols in this chart are arranged in such a way that if there are two items within a single cell, the one on the right is voiced. This enables the consonant chart to be taken as a three-dimensional representation of the principal features of consonants: where they are made (across the chart), their manner of articulation (down the chart), and the state of the glottis (within each cell).

The consonant chart thus summarizes the major features required for describing consonants. It even shows, by the use of shaded areas, which combinations of features are judged to be impossible. Thus it is considered that no language could have a velar trill or tap—a sound in which the back of the tongue vibrated or moved in a ballistic tap gesture against the soft palate. The blank cells on the chart—those that are neither shaded nor contain a symbol—indicate combinations of categories that are possible but have not been observed in any language.

For example, it is perfectly possible for a language to have a voiceless retroflex lateral fricative. No symbol was provided because there was no documentation in the phonetic literature of a language containing such a sound. But it in fact occurs in Toda, a Dravidian language spoken by about 1,000 people in the Nilgiri Hills in Southern India. This language has a contrast between a voiced retroflex lateral approximant [ɭ] and a voiceless retroflex lateral fricative. We will consider later how this sound should be symbolized.

Some of the other blanks and shaded areas should also be considered as simply reflecting the judgments of the phoneticians who drew up the chart. Go through each of these cells and see whether you agree with its assignment as a blank or a shaded area. For example, can you make a labiodental plosive? Some people have good teeth and can make a complete stop of this kind. But would it really be a possible speech sound in a language, which has to be capable of being produced by speakers with varying teeth placement? As another example, could you make a pharyngeal plosive? I think I can make a complete stop in the upper part of the pharynx, but there is no symbol for a sound of this kind because it is not used contrastively in any known language. On the whole, the makers of the chart have been fairly conservative in their addition of shading, only putting it in when it was reasonably clear that the sound could not be produced. It is quite certain that nobody could produce a voiced glottal stop (that is, a sound in which the vocal folds were simultaneously vibrating with normal voicing, and were also held tightly together), or a pharyngeal nasal in which the air was completely stopped by a closure in the pharynx, but nevertheless simultaneously escaped through the nose.

When considering the status of the rows and columns on the chart, it is worth considering the placement of [h] and [ɦ]. Are these sounds really glottal fricatives? As we noted earlier, [h] usually denotes a voiceless transition into (or, in some languages, out of) a syllable. Its place of articulation depends on the adjacent sounds. There is usually virtually no glottal friction (turbulent airflow) produced at the glottis. [ɦ] is also best regarded as a state of the glottis without a specific place; like [h], it is not a fricative. Both [h] and [ɦ] might have been better placed under "other symbols."

Below the consonant chart on the left there is a set of symbols for consonants made with different airstream mechanisms. The IPA recognizes three possibilities: clicks, voiced implosives, and ejectives. This does not mean that the IPA denies the existence of voiceless implosives. It is simply that the IPA considers them sufficiently rare not to necessitate separate symbols and would suggest using a diacritic. For example, a voiceless bilabial implosive, which occurs in only a handful of languages, can be symbolized by combining the voiceless diacritic with the voiced symbol, forming [ɓ̥]. The ejective symbol, ['], is like a diacritic in that it can be added to many different consonants, including fricatives, as exemplified by [s'].

The vowel chart on the right implies that there are three dimensions applicable to vowels: Front–back across the top of the chart, close–open on the vertical dimension, and rounding specified by the relative locations of members of pairs of vowels. Again, these are only the principal types of vowels. Other types, such as those that are nasalized or have an advanced tongue root, can be symbolized by adding diacritics.

The "other symbols" at the top left on the inside back cover represent sounds that could not be conveniently described in terms of the main sets of categories we have been considering. They include symbols for sounds with multiple places of articulation (labial velar and labial palatal) and the epiglottal sounds, which occur in Arabic, Hebrew, and some of the languages of the Caucasus. These sounds would have been hard to place on the chart without the addition of further columns that would have had a considerable number of empty cells.

The diacritic section of the chart allows a number of additional aspects of sounds to be represented by adding a mark above or below the symbol for the principal features of the sound. Some of the diacritics correspond to the provision of additional features or dimensions applicable to many different sounds. Thus additional states of the glottis are recognized by the provision of aspirated, breathy-voiced, and creaky-voiced diacritics. More specific features, such as particular tongue shapes, are recognized by providing diacritics for linguolabials, dentals, apicals, and laminals. Further vowel qualities can be symbolized with many of the other diacritics.

In addition, the IPA provides for the representation of stress, length, tone, and intonation. In the characterization of stress, only three possibilities are recognized: primary stress, secondary stress, and unstressed. There are four possible lengths: long, half-long, unmarked, and extra-short. The possibilities for tone and intonation allow for five contrasting levels and numerous combinations.

The IPA does not provide a symbol for every contingency, so when phoneticians come across some previously unrecorded event, they have to improvise. Let us now return to the question of how to symbolize the voiceless retroflex lateral fricative that occurs in Toda. One possibility that is always open to us is to use an asterisk, and add the following, after giving a consonant chart or transcription of Toda: "[*] represents a voiceless retroflex lateral fricative." Another possibility is to use the symbol for the voiced retroflex lateral approximant [ɭ] and add the diacritic [̥], which indicates that the symbol to which this diacritic has been added should be taken as representing a voiceless sound. It is sometimes difficult to add a diacritic below a symbol that itself descends below the level of the writing line. A possible way in this case is to put the [̥] slightly in front of the [ɭ], making [̥ɭ]. This symbol would really designate a voiceless retroflex lateral approximant, and an explanatory note would still be needed, saying "[̥ɭ] is a fricative rather than an approximant." However, this might almost be taken for granted, as no language contrasts any kind of voiceless lateral fricative with a voiceless lateral approximant made at the same place of articulation. Try saying a voiceless version of an ordinary English [l]. You will probably find that you are making a lateral [ɬ] with audible friction rather than a voiceless approximant.

The avowed aim of the IPA is to be able to symbolize all the distinctive sounds in languages. The intent is to represent by separate symbols the sounds that serve to distinguish one word from another in a language. The IPA would like to do this by using, as far as possible, ordinary letters of the roman alphabet or simple modifications of these letters. Occasionally, when this would mean the creation of a large number of symbols for a set of related sounds, the IPA favors the use of diacritics. This happens, for example, in the case of nasalized vowels, or ejective stops.

IPA symbols can be used in a variety of ways. There is no sense in which one can speak of *the* IPA transcription of a given utterance. Many styles of transcription are possible, as we saw in Chapter 3 in the discussion of English vowels. The relation between some different styles is summarized in Figure 11.1.

The first distinction is between a transcription which in some way reflects the systematic, linguistic, facts of the utterance being described, as opposed to one in which the symbols are used just to provide an impressionistic record of the sounds as heard—the kind of record that might be made by a linguist, totally without any preconceptions, hearing the first few words in a language that had never been transcribed before. In theory, an impressionistic transcription is one in which the symbols represent intersections of general phonetic categories.

Phoneticians very seldom make a totally impressionistic transcription. Generally, within a few minutes of starting to transcribe a language we have not worked on before, we begin to use symbols that rely on our linguistic hunches and preconceptions. We very soon stop noting small differences between repetitions of the same utterance, particularly if they are of the kind of which the speaker seems to be unaware. Virtually the only occasion when a completely impressionistic transcription is necessary is in the investigation of an infant's prelinguistic babbling.

Within the class of systematic (phonetic) transcriptions, there are two independent divisions. First, a transcription may be phonemic or allophonic. A phonemic

---

FIGURE 11.1   A schematic representation of some terms used for describing different types of transcription.

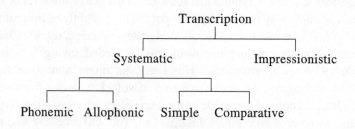

transcription is one in which all the different words in a language are represented by the smallest possible number of different symbols. An allophonic transcription is one that uses a larger number of distinct symbols, so that it can differentiate among systematic, allophonic differences in the sounds of an utterance.

As we noted when discussing the sounds of English, phonemic and allophonic transcriptions are related to each other by a set of statements that, by their application, convert the one form of transcription into the other. A phonemic transcription plus the statements convey exactly the same information as an allophonic transcription. The difference between these two types of transcription is simply whether the detailed phonetic information is made explicit within the transcription itself or within the set of statements that accompanies the transcription.

The other kind of distinction among systematic phonetic transcriptions is that between a simple and a comparative use of particular symbols. The simplest IPA symbols are those that use ordinary letters of the roman alphabet such as [a] and [r]. More exotic letters such as [ɑ, ɒ, ɐ] and [ʀ, ɹ, ɾ] convey greater phonetic detail. A transcription using more unusual symbols is called a comparative transcription, on the grounds that the use of more specific symbols implicitly reflects a comparison between the general phonetic values of the simple symbols and the more precise values of the exotic symbols. In general, as we noted earlier, a broad transcription is one that is both phonemic (as opposed to allophonic) and simple (as opposed to comparative). A narrow transcription may show allophonic distinctions, or it may show more phonetic detail by using more specific symbols, or it may do both these things.

When we think about transcriptions, we can see that phonology and phonetics are inextricably intertwined. It is generally recognized that phonology must rest on accurate phonetic observations. But it is equally true that most phonetic observations are made in terms of a phonological framework. The only pure phonetic description is the instrumental data derivable from a high-quality recording. As soon as the data is segmented or described in any way, then phonological considerations are bound to be present.

FEATURE HIERARCHY

The second way in which we will review phonetic descriptions is by considering a set of linguistic phonetic **features.** A feature, in this sense, is a component of a sound that may itself be composed of other features or may be a terminal feature. Each terminal feature specifies a set of phonetic possibilities. Thus there is a feature Place of articulation, which dominates terminal features like Labial and Dorsal, and these terminal features have particular values like [bilabial] and [labiodental]. Features form a hierarchy, some dominating other features, and some, the terminal features, consisting of a list of possible phonetic values. When discussing features, it is good to be careful to distinguish between the

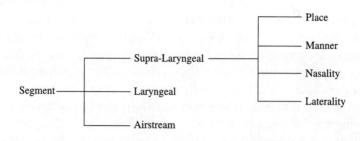

FIGURE 11.2   The supraordinate features in a feature hierarchy.

name of a feature and the possible values that it can take, a distinction that is not always made in books on phonetics and phonology. I will follow the practice of using a capital letter when naming a feature and putting square brackets around possible values that the feature may have.

The major linguistic features are shown in Figure 11.2. All sounds have some Supra-Laryngeal characteristics, some Laryngeal characteristics, and some Airstream mechanism. The Supra-Laryngeal characteristics can be divided into those for Place of articulation, Manner of articulation, the possibility of Nasality, and the possibility of being Lateral.

A detailed specification of the Place feature is given in Figure 11.3. The first division is into the major regions of the vocal tract, giving us the five features,

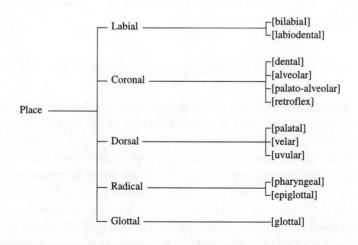

FIGURE 11.3   Features dominated by the feature Place.

Labial, Coronal, Dorsal, Radical, and Glottal. We used the first three of these terms in Chapter 1. Now we are adding **Radical** to apply as a cover term for [pharyngeal] and [epiglottal] articulations made with the root of the tongue. We also have a feature Glottal, with only one value, [glottal], to cover various articulations, such as [h, ʔ]. If we are to have a convenient grouping of the features for consonants, we have to recognize that Supra-Laryngeal features must allow for the dual nature of the actions of the larynx and include Glottal as a Place of articulation.

A sound may be articulated at more than one of the regions Labial, Coronal, Dorsal, Radical, and Glottal. We have described sounds such as [ɥ] that simultaneously have articulations that have feature values [labial] and [palatal], and [w], which is simultaneously [labial] and [velar]. Within the five general regions, Coronal articulations can be split into three mutually exclusive possibilities: Laminal (blade of the tongue), Apical (tip of the tongue), and Sub-apical (the under part of the blade of the tongue). The mutually exclusive possibilities for each of these and for the other places of articulation are shown on the right of Figure 11.3. Some of these possibilities have not been discussed in this introductory textbook, but they are all needed for describing the sounds of the languages of the world.

In a simple framework it is sufficient to consider Coronal to be a terminal feature like Labial and Dorsal, as shown in Figure 11.3. A more elaborate feature hierarchy would include the apical/laminal distinction we discussed in Chapter 7. In this way we could deal with a wider range of languages, using the distinctions shown in Figure 11.4.

The features for possible manners of articulation are shown in Figure 11.5. Four of the features we have been using—Stop, Fricative, Approximant, and

---

FIGURE 11.4   An elaboration of the feature Coronal.

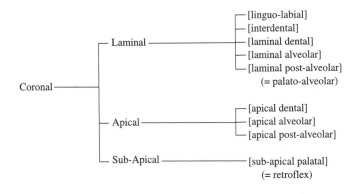

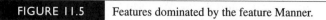

FIGURE 11.5 Features dominated by the feature Manner.

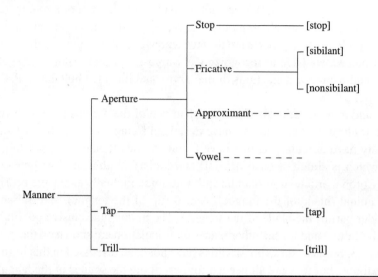

Vowel (without explicitly calling them features)—can be grouped together as aspects of another feature, Aperture. This grouping reflects the fact that the four features, Stop, Fricative, Approximant, and Vowel, are all dependent on the degree of closure of the articulators. In some older feature systems, these possibilities are split into two groups, but it is now thought better to recognize that they form a continuum. The changes in the pronunciation of my own name, for example, fall on this continuum. The name is of Danish origin. I pronounce it [ˈlædɪfoʊɡɪd] in English, with consonants as they once were in Danish. These stops first became fricatives, which later became approximants in Danish [ˈlæðəfoɣəd] > [ˈlæ̞ðə̞foʊɣ̞əd], making it apparent that there is a continuum going from [stop] through [fricative] to [approximant]. (Note the use of the diacritic [˳], meaning more open, turning the fricative symbols into symbols for approximants.) My name is simply two Danish words put together: "lade," a barn, and "foged," something like a steward or bailiff. Spanish also has a process whereby stops first become fricatives and then approximants.

The feature Stop has only one possible value, [stop], but Fricative has two, [sibilant] and [nonsibilant]. The possible values for Approximant and Vowel will be discussed in the next paragraph, but first we should note that there are two other Manner features, Trill and Tap, each of which have only a single possible value, [trill] and [tap]. The further relations among all the Manner features are beyond the scope of this book.

As shown in Figure 11.6, Approximant and Vowel dominate other features. There are five principal features, the first of which, Height, has five possible

FIGURE 11.6   Features dominated by the features Vowel and Approximant.

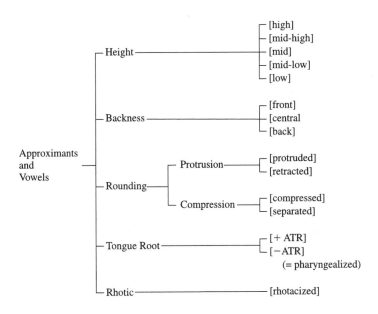

values: [high], [mid-high], [mid], [mid-low], and [low]. As far as we know, no language distinguishes more than five vowel heights. Backness has only three values, [front], [center], and [back]. As we saw in Chapter 9 when discussing Japanese [ɯ], there are two kinds of Rounding: Protrusion, with possible values [protruded] and [retracted], and Compression, with possible values [compressed] and [separated]. The feature Tongue Root has two possible values: [+ATR] and [−ATR]. Pharyngealized sounds may be classified as having the opposite of an advanced tongue root and are therefore [−ATR]. The feature Rhotic has only one possible value, [rhotacized].

Separate figures have not been drawn for the other two Supra-Laryngeal features, Nasality and Laterality, as each of them are themselves terminal features. Nasality has the possible values [nasal] and [oral]; Laterality has the possible values [lateral] and [central].

The Laryngeal possibilities, shown in Figure 11.7, involve three features. Glottal Stricture specifies how far apart the vocal folds are. Languages make use of five possibilities: [voiceless]; [breathy voice], as we saw in languages such as Hindi; [modal voice], which is the regular voicing used in every language; [creaky voice] in languages such as Hausa; and [closed] forming a glottal stop. Many in-between possibilities occur, but if we are simply providing categories for the degrees of glottal opening that are used distinctively, these five are

FIGURE 11.7   Features dominated by the feature Laryngeal.

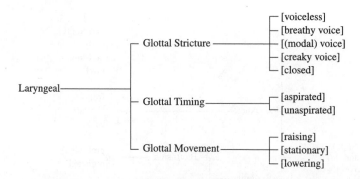

sufficient. A separate feature, Glottal Timing, is used to specify voiceless aspi-rated stops and breathy-voiced aspirated stops. A third feature, Glottal Movement, is also included among the Laryngeal features, to allow for the specification of implosives and ejectives. Some books, including previous editions of this book, prefer to consider these sounds as simply involving a different airstream mecha-nism. This is the way I began describing them at the beginning of Chapter 6. At the end of that chapter I included them in the summary of actions of the glottis. As pointed out there, they interact with other Laryngeal features and are accord-ingly put at this point in the hierarchy.

The arrangement in Figure 11.7 leaves the Airstream feature, shown in Figure 11.8, dominating only two features, Pulmonic and Velaric. Each of these has only one value. In a more elaborate arrangement it would be appropriate to con-sider whether the pulmonic airstream mechanism varied in force, but this possi-bility will not be considered here.

The figures discussed earlier provide a hierarchical arrangement of the fea-tures required to describe nearly all the sounds of the world's languages. Try working through this hierarchy from the top down, so that you get a complete specification of a variety of sounds. Table 11.1 gives a partial specification of a number of English segments.

FIGURE 11.8   Features dominated by the feature Airstream.

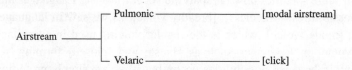

TABLE 11.1		A partial feature specification of some English segments (vowels that may not occur in all accents are omitted).	

Place	Labial		[bilabial]	p, b, m
			[labiodental]	f, v
	Coronal		[dental]	θ, ð
			[alveolar]	t, d, n, l, s, z
			[post-alveolar]	r
			[palato-alveolar]	ʃ, ʒ
	Dorsal		[velar]	k, g, ŋ
Aperture	Fricative		[stop]	p, t, k, b, d, g, m, n, ŋ
			[sibilant]	s, ʃ, z, ʒ
			[nonsibilant]	f, θ, v, ð
	Approximant Vowel	Height	[high]	i, u
			[mid-high]	ɪ, ʊ, eɪ, oʊ
			[mid]	ə, ɜ
			[mid-low]	ɛ, ɔ
			[low]	æ, ɑ
		Backness	[front]	i, ɪ, eɪ, ɛ, æ
			[back]	ɑ, ɔ, oʊ, ʊ, u
		Rounding	[rounded]	ɔ, oʊ, ʊ, u
			[unrounded]	i, ɪ, eɪ, ɛ, æ, ɑ
Nasality			[nasal]	m, n, ŋ
			[oral]	(all others)
Laterality			[lateral]	l
			[central]	(all others)
Laryngeal	Glottal Stricture		[voiceless]	p, t, k, f, θ, s, ʃ
			[(modal) voice]	(all others)

PERFORMANCE EXERCISES

The material at the end of this chapter is intended to help you review many of the sounds that have been described in previous chapters. It consists of real words in some different languages. If possible, you should compare your pronunciation of these words with that of a native speaker. Most of these sounds can be found on the Web site mentioned in the Preface. If the sounds are not available, you should try to pronounce the words just on the basis of the transcription provided. You might begin your review by trying to pronounce the data given in the following tables, which provide material on specific languages:

6.1	Lakhota	(ejectives)
6.2	Sindhi	(implosives)
6.3	Xhosa	(clicks)
6.5	Gujarati	(murmured vowels)
6.6	Thai	(stops)
6.7	Hindi	(stops)
7.1	Malayalam	(places of articulation)
7.2	Quechua	(palatal, velar, and uvular plosives and ejectives)
7.5	Margi	(prenasalized stops)

Now try to say the following words.

A Navajo

Navajo has a three-way stop contrast that will require your making voiceless unaspirated and ejective stops that do not occur in English. There are also several different affricates.

Voiceless Unaspirated	Voiceless Aspirated	Ejective
tota	tˣáːʔ	t'áh
"not"	"three"	"just"
hátítsɪ	tsʰah	ts'ah
"you will speak"	"awl"	"sagebrush"
	tɬʰah	niʃtɬ'aː
	"ointment"	"left"
tʃí	tʃʰaːʔ	tʃ'ah
"day"	"beaver"	"hat"
	bɪkʰáː	k'aːʔ
	"its surface"	"arrow"

B Zulu

Zulu has a series of clicks, which are similar to those in Xhosa.

Dental	Alveolo Palatal	Alveolar Lateral
kǀáːgà	kǃàːkǃá	kǁáːgà
"to whitewash"	"to undo"	"put into a fix"
kǀʰàːgá	kǃʰàːkǃʰà	kǁʰáːgà
"to identify"	"to rip open"	"to link horses"

Dental	Alveolo Palatal	Alveolar Lateral
g|ò:ɓá	g!ò:ɓá	g‖ò:ɓá
"to grease"	"to milk"	"to beat"
ìsì:ŋ|é	ìsì:ŋ!é	ìsì:ŋ‖é:lè
(kind of spear)	"rump"	"left hand"

C Burmese

Burmese contrasts voiced and voiceless nasals at four places of articulation.

Voiced Nasals	Voiceless Nasals
m̯ậ "lift up"	m̥ậ "from"
nă "pain"	n̥ă "nose"
ɲă "right"	ɲ̥ă "considerate"
ŋâ "fish"	ŋ̥â "borrow"

D Greek

Greek is one of the comparatively few languages that contrasts both voiced and voiceless palatal and velar fricatives. It also has interdental fricatives.

Dental		Palatal		Velar	
θiki	"box"	çɛɾi	"hand"	xɔma	"soil"
ðiki	"trial"	jɛɾi	"old men"	ɣɔma	"eraser"

E Ewe

Ewe contrasts voiced and voiceless bilabial and labiodental fricatives both intervocalically and in clusters with [1].

Voiceless Bilabial	éɸá	éɸle
	"he polished"	"he bought"
Voiceless Labiodental	éfá	éflé
	"he was cold"	"he split off"
Voiced Bilabial	èβè	èβló
	"Ewe" (the language)	"mushroom"
Voiced Labiodental	èvè	évló
	"two"	"he is evil"

F Zulu

In addition to a complex set of clicks, Zulu has several different contrasts involving laterals.

	Voiced Lateral Approximant	Voiced Lateral Fricative	Voiceless Lateral Fricative/Affricate
Alveolar	lálà "sleep"	ɮálà "play" [imper.]	ɬânzà "vomit"
Nasal + Alveolar		ínɮàlà "hunger"	íntɬ'àntɬ'à "good luck"
Velar			k͡ʟ'îná "be naughty"

The following exercises review vowels and semivowels. As noted in Chapter 9, the main features of vowel quality cannot be adequately described by means of written descriptions. Listen to recordings, or, if you can, find native speakers of some of the languages listed here, and try to imitate their pronunciation.

Note that the symbols do not have the same values as they do in the transcription of English.

G French

French has 12 contrasting oral vowels. (Some speakers of French do not make all these distinctions.)

li	"lit"	(bed)
le	"les"	(the, *plural*)
lɛ	"laid"	(ugly)
la	"là"	(there)
lɑ	"las"	(tired)
lɔk	"loque"	(rag)
lo	"lot"	(prize)
lu	"loup"	(wolf)
ly	"lu"	(read, *past part.*)
lø	"le"	(the, *m. sing.*)
lœʁ	"leur"	(their)
lɛ̃	"lin"	(flax)
lã	"lent"	(slow)
lõ	"long"	(long)
lœ̃di	"lundi"	(Monday)

French also has three contrasting semivowels.

mjɛt	"miette"	(crumb)
myɛt	"muette"	(mute)
mwɛt	"mouette"	(seagull)
lje	"lié"	(tied)
lɥi	"lui"	(him)
lwi	"Louis"	(Louis)
ɥit	"huit"	(eight)
wi	"oui"	(yes)

H German

German has so-called tense and lax vowels, which differ in both length and quality. The symbol [y] denotes a slightly lowered high front vowel—a rounded version of [ɪ].

tiːf	"tief"	(deep)
teː	"Tee"	(tea)
taːt	"Tat"	(deed)
toːt	"tot"	(dead)
'tuːtən	"tuten"	(toot)
'tyːtə	"Tüte"	(paper bag)
'tøːtən	"töten"	(kill)
tɪʃ	"Tisch"	(table)
tɛst	"Test"	(test)
'tatsə	"Tatze"	(paw)
tɔp	"Topp"	(top)
tʊʃ	"Tusch"	(flourish)
'tʏtəl	"Tüttel"	(dot)
'hœlə	"Hölle"	(hell)
'laɪtən	"leiten"	(lead)
'lautə	"Laute"	(lute)
'lɔʏtə	"Leute"	(people)

I Swedish

Swedish has long and short vowels; the short vowels are followed by long consonants. The symbol [ʏ] denotes a slightly lowered high front vowel—a

rounded version of [ɪ]. The symbol [ɵ] denotes a more centralized high
rounded vowel—a slightly lowered [ʉ].

ɹiːta	"rita"	(draw)
ɹeːta	"reta"	(tease)
ɹɛːta	"räta"	(straighten)
hæːɹ	"här"	(here)
ɹɑːta	"rata"	(refuse)
ɹoːta	"Rota"	(name of a valley)
ɹuːta	"rota"	(root)
ɹyːta	"ryta"	(roar)
ɹøːta	"röta"	(rot)
hœːɹ	"hör"	(hear!)
ɹʉːta	"ruta"	(window pane)
ɹɪtː	"ritt"	(ride, *n.*)
ɹɛtː	"rätt"	(correct, *n.*)
hæɹː	"herr"	(Mr.)
ɹatː	"ratt"	(steering wheel)
ɹɔtː	"rått"	(raw)
ɹʊtː	"rott"	(rowed)
nʏtːa	"nytta"	(use, *n.*)
ɹœtː	"rött"	(red)
ɹɵtː	"rutt"	(route)

J Vietnamese

Vietnamese has eleven vowels, including contrasting back rounded and unrounded pairs. Tones in this exercise are marked as follows: mid-level tone is
unmarked; high-rising tone has an acute accent [´].

Front	Back Unrounded	Rounded
ti	tɯ	tu
"bureau"	"fourth"	"to drink"
te	tɤ	to
"numb"	"silk"	"soup bowl"
té	ʌŋ	tɔ
"to fall down"	"favor"	"large"
æŋ	tɑ	
"to eat"	"we/our"	

FURTHER READING

Phonetics has been studied for many centuries. In this alphabetized list of books, I have limited myself to some of the more important books that have been published in the past forty or fifty years. Of course, many important findings have appeared in journals rather than in books. If you want to keep up to date in the subject, you should look at the following journals: *Journal of the International Phonetic Association, Journal of Phonetics, Journal of Speech and Hearing Research, Language and Speech,* and *Phonetica,* as well as more specialized journals in other fields, such as acoustics (notably the *Journal of the Acoustical Society of America*), linguistics, speech pathology, and particular language areas.

Phonetic Dictionaries

Jones, Daniel. *English Pronouncing Dictionary*, 15th ed. (edited by Peter Roach and James Hartman) Cambridge: Cambridge University Press. 1997.

Wells, John. *Longman Pronunciation Dictionary*. Harlow, U.K.: Longman, 1990. 2nd ed. Harlow: Pearson Education, 2000.

Both these dictionaries are great reference books that all students of phonetics should consult.

General Books on Phonetics

Abercrombie, David. *Elements of General Phonetics*. New York: Aldine, 1967. A classic book on a number of the most important concepts in phonetics. It is very easy to read and a good introduction to the topics selected, but it is somewhat limited in scope.

Catford, John C. *Fundamental Problems in Phonetics*. Bloomington: University of Indiana Press, 1977. Not a beginner's book, but a good account of the phonation types and aerodynamic processes involved in speech production.

Celce-Murcia, Marianne, Donna Brinton, and Janet Goodwin. *Teaching Pronunciation: A Reference for Teachers of English to Speakers of Other Languages*. Cambridge: Cambridge University Press, 1996. A good book for teachers.

Clark, John, and Colin Yallop. *An Introduction to Phonetics and Phonology*. Oxford: Blackwells, 1995. Covers much the same ground as here, but more specifically aimed at linguists.

International Phonetic Association. *The Handbook of the International Phonetic Association.* Cambridge: Cambridge University Press, 1999. A reference book that every student of phonetics should possess.

Johnson, Keith. *Acoustic and Auditory Phonetics* Oxford: Blackwells, 1997. An up-to-date account of acoustic phonetics, paying special attention to how we hear sounds.

Ladefoged, Peter. *Elements of Acoustic Phonetics.* 2nd. ed. Chicago: University of Chicago Press, 1996. A basic account of just those aspects of acoustics that are relevant for students of phonetics. The second edition is considerably enlarged and contains an introduction to computer speech processing.

Ladefoged, Peter. *Vowels and Consonants.* Oxford: Blackwells, 2000. A shorter, simpler, more casual introduction to phonetics than this book. It comes with a CD illustrating all the sounds of the International Phonetic Alphabet and sounds from many different languages.

Ladefoged, Peter, and Ian Maddieson. *Sounds of the World's Languages.* Oxford: Blackwells, 1996. An attempt to give a comprehensive account of all the different sounds that have been reported in the world's languages.

Laver, John. *Principles of Phonetics.* Cambridge: Cambridge University Press, 1994. An extensive overview of the field.

Lieberman, Philip, and Sheila Blumstein. *Speech Physiology and Acoustic Phonetics.* Cambridge: Cambridge University Press, 1988. An introductory textbook concerned with experimental phonetics.

Maddieson, Ian. *Patterns of Sounds.* Cambridge: Cambridge University Press, 1984. A survey of the sound systems of more than 300 languages, providing a basis for a description of a number of universal phonetic tendencies.

Pickett, J. M. *The Acoustics of Speech Communication: Fundamentals, Speech Perception Theory and Technology.* Allyn and Bacon, 1999. This book goes considerably further than other introductory books on acoustic phonetics, discussing several aspects of speech perception.

Pike, K. *Phonetics.* Ann Arbor: University of Michigan Press, 1943. Subtitled "A Critical Account of Phonetic Theory, and a Technique for the Practical Description of Sounds," this is a classic book for advanced students.

Pullum, Geoffrey, and William Ladusaw. *Phonetic Symbol Guide.* 2nd. ed. Chicago: University of Chicago Press, 1996. An invaluable reference book describing a wide variety of phonetic symbols, including all the symbols of the IPA.

Stevens, Kenneth, *Acoustic Phonetics.* Cambridge, Mass.: MIT Press, 1999. Clearly the leading technical book, describing everything that is known about the acoustics of speech

Zemlin, W. R. *Speech and Hearing Science.* Englewood Cliffs, N.J.: Prentice-Hall, 2nd. ed. 1981. A good account of the anatomy and physiology of the vocal organs.

GLOSSARY

Note: The explanations given in this glossary should be regarded not as formal definitions, but as general guides for use in review.

Advanced Tongue Root (ATR) Having the root of the tongue pulled forward so as to widen the pharynx (and, often, to raise the body of the tongue nearer to the roof of the mouth). Pharyngeal sounds are [–ATR], as the pharynx is narrowed.

Affricate A stop followed by a homorganic fricative.

Allophone A variant of a phoneme. The allophones of a phoneme form a set of sounds that (1) do not change the meaning of a word, (2) are all very similar to one another, and (3) occur in phonetic contexts different from one another—for example, syllable initial as opposed to syllable final. The differences among allophones can be stated in terms of phonological rules.

Alternations Variations in words that can be described in terms of phonological rules(for example, the difference between [aɪ] and [ɪ] in "divine–divin(ity)."

Alveolar An articulation involving the tip or blade of the tongue and the alveolar ridge, as in English [d] in "die."

Alveolar ridge The part of the upper surface of the mouth immediately behind the front teeth.

Alveolo-palatal A post-alveolar consonant made with considerable raising of the front of the tongue, making it equivalent to a palatalized palato-alveolar. Polish and Chinese have alveolo-palatal fricatives, [ɕ, ʑ].

Ambisyllabic Belonging to two syllables. A consonant such as [p] in "happy" is sometimes said to be ambisyllabic.

Anticipatory coarticulation An action in which one of the speech organs that is not involved in making a particular sound moves toward its position for a subsequent sound. For example, the rounding of the lips during [s] in "swim" is due to the anticipation of the lip action required for [w].

Apical An articulation involving the tip of the tongue.

Approximant An articulation in which one articulator is close to another but without the tract being narrowed to such an extent that a turbulent airstream is produced. In many forms of English, / j, l, r, w / are approximants.

Articulation The approach or contact of two speech organs, such as the tip of the tongue and the upper teeth.

Arytenoid cartilages A pair of structures at the posterior ends of the vocal folds. Their movements control different phonation types.

Aspiration A period of voicelessness after the release of an articulation, as in English "pie" [pʰaɪ].

Assimilation The change of one sound into another sound because of the influence of neighboring sounds, as in the change of underlying [n] to [m] in "input"

['ɪmpʊt] or of underlying [z] to [ʒ] in "does she" ['dʌʒʃi].

Back vowels Vowels in which the body of the tongue is in the back part of the oral cavity (mouth). The vowels [u, o, ɔ, ɑ] form a set of back reference vowels.

Bark scale A scale in which equal intervals of pitch as perceived by listeners are represented by equal distances on the scale.

Bilabial An articulation involving both lips, as in English [m] in "my."

Binary feature A feature (for example, Lateral) that can be used to classify sounds in terms of two possibilities.

Breathy voice Another name for murmur, a type of phonation in which the vocal folds are only slightly apart so that they vibrate while allowing a high rate of airflow through the glottis, as in Hindi [bʱ].

Broad transcription A transcription that does not show a great deal of phonetic detail, often a simple phonemic transcription.

Cardinal vowels A set of reference vowels first defined by Daniel Jones. The vowels of any language can be described by stating their relations to the cardinal vowels.

Citation form The form a word has when it is cited or pronounced in isolation.

Click A stop made with an ingressive velaric airstream, such as Zulu [ǁ].

Closed syllable A syllable with a consonant at the end, as the first syllables in English "magpie, pantry, completion."

Coarticulation The overlapping of adjacent articulations.

Coda The consonants occurring after the vowel in a syllable.

Contour tone A tone in a language such as Chinese that has to be specified as a gliding movement within the pitch range.

Coordinative structures The functional organization of a group of muscles into a single unit.

Coronal Sounds articulated with the tip or blade of the tongue raised toward the teeth or the alveolar ridge (or, sometimes, the hard palate), such as [θ, s, t].

Creaky voice See *Laryngealization.*

dB (decibels) A measure of the relative intensity of two sounds, corresponding to ten times the common logarithm of the power ratio of the two sounds. The power ratio is the square of the amplitude ratio so this is equivalent to twenty times the common logarithm of the amplitude ratio of the two sounds.

Declination The general downward trend in pitch in a syntactic unit such as a sentence in many languages.

Diacritics Small added marks that can be used to distinguish different values of a symbol. For example, the addition of [˜] distinguishes a velarized from a nonvelarized sound, as in [ɫ] as opposed to [l].

Diphthong A vowel in which there is a change in quality during a single syllable, as in English [aɪ] in "high."

Dorsal Sounds articulated with the back of the tongue.

Dorsum The back of the tongue.

Downdrift The tendency for the pitch to fall throughout an intonational phrase.

Downstep Lowering of a high pitch accent or high tone after a similar high pitch accent or high tone.

Ejective A stop made with an egressive glottalic airstream, such as Hausa [k'].

Epenthesis The insertion of one or more sounds in the middle of a word, such as the pronunciation of "sense" as [sents].

Feature A component of a sound that may itself be composed of other features or may be a terminal feature. Each terminal feature specifies a limited set of discrete phonetic possibilities with specific phonetic properties.

Flap An articulation in which one articulator, usually the tongue tip, is drawn back and then allowed to strike against another articulator in returning to its rest position.

Formant A group of overtones corresponding to a resonating frequency of the air in the vocal tract. Vowels are characterized by three formants.

Frequency The rate of variation in air pressure in a sound.

Fricative Narrowing of the distance between two articulators so that the airstream is partially obstructed and a turbulent airflow is produced, as in English [z] in "zoo."

Front vowels Vowels in which the body of the tongue is in the front part of the oral cavity (mouth). The vowels [i, e, ɛ, a] form a set of front reference vowels.

Geminate Adjacent segments that are the same, such as the two consonants in the middle of Italian "folla" ['folla] (crowd).

Glottal An articulation involving the glottis, as [ʔ] in many forms of English "button" ['bʌʔn̩].

Glottalic airstream mechanism Movement of pharynx air by the action of the glottis. Ejectives and implosives are produced with a glottalic airstream mechanism.

Glottis The space between the vocal folds.

Hard palate The bony structure that forms the roof of the front part of the mouth.

Homorganic Made with the same place of articulation. The sounds [d] and [n], as in English "hand," are homorganic.

Implosive A stop made with an ingressive glottalic airstream, such as Sindhi [ɓ].

Impressionistic transcription A transcription in which the symbols indicate only the general phonetic value of the sounds.

Initiator A prime mover of an airstream. The closed glottis is the initiator in glottalic egressive stops.

Intensity The amount of acoustic energy in a sound.

Interdental Articulated with the tongue between the upper and lower teeth. Many speakers of American English use an interdental articulation in words such as "thick, thin."

Intonation The pattern of pitch changes that occur during a phrase, which may be a complete sentence.

Intonational phrase The part of an utterance over which a particular intonation pattern extends.

Labial An articulation involving one or both lips, such as [f, v, m].

Labialization A secondary articulation in which lip rounding is added to a sound, as in English [ʃ].

Labial velar (labiovelar) An articulation involving simultaneous action of the back of the tongue forming a velar closure and the lips forming a bilabial closure.

Labiodental An articulation involving the lower lip and the upper front teeth.

Laminal An articulation made with the blade of the tongue.

Laryngeal The region of the vocal tract at the glottis in which consonantal articulations such as [h, ʔ] are made.

Laryngealization Another name for creaky voice, a type of phonation in which the arytenoid cartilages hold the posterior end of the vocal folds together so that they can vibrate only at the other end, as in Hausa [ɓ̰].

Lateral An articulation in which the airstream flows over the sides of the tongue, as in English [l] in "leaf."

Lateral plosion The release of a plosive by lowering the sides of the tongue, as at the end of the word "saddle."

Lax A term with no specific phonetic correlates, used when dividing vowels into classes on phonological grounds. In English, the lax vowels are those that can occur in monosyllables closed by [ŋ] such as "sing, length, hang, long, hung."

Linguo-labial Articulated with the tongue near or contacting the upper lip.

Lip rounding The action of bringing the corners of the lips toward one another so that the mouth opening is reduced.

Liquid A cover term for laterals and various forms of r-sounds.

Locus The apparent point of origin of the formants for each place of articulation.

Loudness The auditory property of a sound that enables a listener to place it on a scale going from soft to loud without considering the acoustic properties, such as the intensity of the sound.

Monophthong A vowel in which there is no appreciable change in quality during a syllable, as in English [ɑ] in "father." Compare *diphthong*.

Motor equivalence Two different gestures of the vocal organs that will produce the same sound.

Motor theory of speech perception The notion that listeners perceive some aspects of an utterance by reference to their own activities, considering what they would have to do in order to make similar sounds.

Multivalued feature A feature such as Height that can be used to classify sounds in terms of more than two possibilities.

Murmur Another name for breathy voice, a type of phonation in which the vocal

folds are only slightly apart so that they vibrate while allowing a high rate of airflow through the glottis, as in Hindi [bʱ].

Narrow transcription A transcription that shows phonetic details (such as, in English, aspiration, length, etc.) by using a wide variety of symbols and, in many cases, diacritics.

Nasal A sound in which the soft palate is lowered so that there is no velic closure and air may go out through the nose, as in English [m] in "my."

Nasalization Lowering of the soft palate during a sound in which air is going out through the mouth, as in the vowel [æ] between nasals in English "man."

Nasal plosion The release of a plosive by lowering the soft palate so that air escapes through the nose, as at the end of the word "hidden."

Nasal stop A complete stoppage of the oral cavity so that the airstream passes only through the nose. Usually nasal stops are simply called nasals.

Nasal vowel A vowel in which part of the airstream passes out through the nose.

Nucleus The center of a syllable, usually just the vowel.

Obstruent A fricative, stop, or affricate.

Onset The consonants occurring before the vowel in a syllable.

Open syllable A syllable without a consonant at the end, as the first syllables in English "beehive, bylaw, sawing."

Oral stop Complete stoppage of both the oral and nasal cavities, as in [b, d, g].

Palatal An articulation involving the front of the tongue and the hard palate, as in English [j] in "you."

Palatalization A secondary articulation in which the front of the tongue is raised toward the hard palate, as in the so-called soft sounds in Russian.

Palato-alveolar An articulation between the tongue blade and the back of the alveolar ridge.

Perseverative coarticulation The persistence of an aspect of the articulation of one sound into the following sound. For example, the nasalization of a vowel after a nasal consonant.

Pharyngeal An articulation involving the root of the tongue and the back wall of the pharynx, as in the Arabic [ʕ].

Pharyngealization A secondary articulation in which the root of the tongue is drawn back so that the pharynx is narrowed, as in some so-called emphatic consonants in Arabic.

Phoneme One of a set of abstract units that can be used for writing a language down in a systematic and unambiguous way. See also *allophone.*

Phonology The description of the systems and patterns of sounds that occur in a language.

Pitch The auditory property of a sound that enables a listener to place it on a scale going from low to high, without considering the acoustic properties, such as the frequency of the sound.

Plosive A stop made with a pulmonic airstream mechanism, such as in English [p] or [b].

Post-alveolar An articulation involving the part of the alveolar ridge posterior to the point of maximum curvature, for example [ʃ] in English or [ɳ] in Malayalam.

Prominence The extent to which a sound stands out from others because of its sonority, length, stress, and pitch.

Pulmonic airstream mechanism The movement of lung air by the respiratory muscles. Most sounds are produced with a pulmonic airstream mechanism.

Radical An articulation made with the root of the tongue.

Reduced vowel A vowel that is pronounced with a noncontrasting centralized quality, although in the underlying form of a word it is part of a full set of contrasts. The second vowel in "emphasis" is a reduced form of the vowel / æ /, as in "emphatic."

Retroflex An articulation involving the tip of the tongue and the back part of the alveolar ridge. Some speakers of English have retroflex approximants in "rye" and "err." Retroflex stops occur in Hindi and other languages spoken in India.

Rhotacization The auditory property known as *r-coloring* that results from the lowering of the third formant.

Rhotic A form of English in which / r / can occur after a vowel and within a syllable in words such as "car, bird, early." Most forms of Midwestern American English are rhotic, whereas most forms of English spoken in the southern part of England are nonrhotic.

Rhyme The vowel (nucleus) and any consonants occurring after the vowel in a syllable.

Rounded A sound with added lip rounding.

Secondary articulation An articulation made by two of the organs of speech that are not involved in the primary articulation. The English alveolar lateral at the end of a syllable, as in "eel," is often made with the back of the tongue raised, and thus has the secondary articulation of velarization.

Semivowel A sound articulated in the same way as a vowel, but not forming a syllable on its own, as in [w] in "we."

Sibilant A speech sound in which there is high-pitched, turbulent noise, as in English [s] and [ʃ] in "sip" and "ship."

Soft palate The soft, moveable part of the palate at the back of the mouth.

Sonority The loudness of a sound relative to that of other sounds with the same length, stress, and pitch.

Spectrogram A graphic representation of sounds in terms of their component frequencies, in which time is shown on the horizontal axis, frequency on the vertical axis, and the intensity of each frequency at each moment in time by the darkness of the mark.

Stop Complete closure of two articulators. This term usually implies an oral stop—that is, complete closure of two articulators and a velic closure, as in English [b] in "buy." But nasals, as in English [m] in "my," can also be considered stops.

Stress The use of extra respiratory energy during a syllable.

Strong form The form in which a word is pronounced when it is stressed. This term is usually applied only to words that normally occur unstressed and with a weak form, such as "to" and "a."

Suprasegmental features Phonetic features such as stress, length, tone, and intonation, which are not properties of single consonants or vowels.

Syllable A unit of speech for which there is no satisfactory definition. Syllables seem to be necessary units in the mental organization and production of utterances.

Systematic phonetic transcription A transcription that shows all the phonetic details that are part of the language and can be stated in terms of phonological rules.

Tap A rapid movement of the tip of the tongue upward to contact the roof of the mouth, then returning to the floor of the mouth along the same path.

Target position An idealized articulatory position that can be used as a reference point in describing how a speaker produces utterances.

Tense A term with no specific phonetic correlates, used when dividing vowels into classes on phonological grounds. In English, the tense vowels are those that can occur in stressed open syllables such as "bee, bay, bah, saw, low, boo, buy, bough, boy, cue."

ToBI A system for transcribing the intonation of utterances in terms of a sequence of pitch accents—H(igh) and L(ow) and combinations—on stressed syllables, intonational phrases, and boundaries, together with a set of Break Indices indicating the degree of connection between adjacent words ranging from 1 (close connection) to 4 (maximum break).

Tone A pitch that conveys part of the meaning of a word. In Chinese, for example, [ma] pronounced with a high-level tone means "mother" and with a high falling tone means "scold."

Tone sandhi A change of tone due to the influence of neighboring tones.

Tonic syllable The syllable within a tone group that stands out because it carries the major pitch change.

Trill An articulation in which one articulator is held loosely near another so that the flow of air between them sets them in motion, alternately sucking them together and blowing them apart. In some forms of Scottish English, [r] in "rip" is trilled.

Unrounded An articulation in which the lips are in a spread or neutral position.

Uvular An articulation involving the back of the tongue and the uvula, as in French [ʁ] in "rouge" [ʁuʒ].

Velar An articulation involving the back of the tongue and the velum, or the soft palate, as in English [g] in "guy."

Velaric airstream mechanism Movement of mouth air by action of the tongue. Clicks are produced with a velaric airstream mechanism.

Velarization A secondary articulation in which the back of the tongue is raised toward the soft palate. In many forms of English, syllable final [ɫ] as in "hill" is strongly velarized.

Velic Involving the upper surface of the velum, or soft palate, and the pharynx. A *velic closure* prevents air from escaping through the nose.

Velum The soft, movable part of the palate at the back of the mouth.

Vocal tract The air passages above the vocal folds. The vocal tract consists of the oral tract and the nasal tract.

Vocoid A sound with no obstruction in the center of the mouth. Vowels and semivowels are vocoids.

Voice bar A dark area near the baseline in a spectrogram, indicating voicing during a consonant.

Voiced Having vibrations of the vocal folds during an articulation, as in English [m] in "me." In a partially voiced sound, vocal fold vibrations occur during only part of the articulation, as often in English [d] in "die."

Voiceless Pronounced without vibrations of the vocal folds, as in English [s] in "see."

Voice Onset Time (VOT) The moment at which the voicing starts relative to the release of a closure.

Weak form The unstressed form of any word, such as "but" or "as," that does not maintain its full form when it occurs in conversational speech.

SOURCES

Some of the data presented in this book are from published sources or from personal communications from colleagues.

The IPA charts inside the front and back covers have been reproduced with permission from the International Phonetic Association. Inquiries concerning membership of the Association should be addressed to the Secretary, International Phonetic Association, Department of Linguistics, University of Victoria, Victoria, B. C. V8W3P4 Canada. E-mail: esling@uvic.ca

Many of the statements on English allophones in Chapter 4 are based on observations by my colleagues of the TIMIT database and other databases that reflect the pronunciation of a large number of American speakers of various dialects.

The recordings for the pitch curves in Chapter 5 and the spectrograms of American English were provided by my colleague Bruce Hayes.

The photographs of the glottis in Chapter 6 were taken by John Ohala and Ralph Vanderslice.

The relation between frequency in Hz and pitch in Bark is given in: Schroeder, M. R., B. S. Atal, and J. L. Hall (1979). "Objective Measure of Certain Speech Signal Degradations Based on Masking Properties of Human Auditory Perception." In B. Lindblom and S. Öhman (Eds.), Frontiers of Speech Communication Research (pp. 217–229). New York: Academic Press.

The x-rays of cardinal vowels used in Figure 9.3 were published in: Jones, S. "Radiography and Pronunciation." British Journal of Radiology, New Series, Vol. 3 (1929), 149–50.

The acoustic data on the formant frequencies of vowels (Figure 8.7 and 9.1) are from: Petersen, G. E., and H. L. Barney. "Control Methods Used in a Study of the Vowels." Journal of the Acoustical Society of America, 24 (1956), 175–84. Holbrook, A., and G. Fairbanks. "Diphthong Formants and Their Movements." Journal of Speech and Hearing Research, Vol. 5 (March 1962), 38–58.

The data for the plots of different accents of English are from: Hagiwara, R. (1995) "Acoustic Realizations of American / r / as Produced by Women and Men," unpublished Ph.D. dissertation, University of California, Los Angeles (Californian English); Hillenbrand, J., L. A. Getty, M. J. Clark, and K. Wheeler

(1995). "Acoustic Characteristics of American English Vowels." Journal of the Acoustical Society of America, 97(5), 3099–3111 (Northern cities); and Deterding, D. (1990). "Speaker Normalisation for Automatic Speech Recognition," unpublished Ph.D. dissertation, University of Cambridge (BBC English). The data on American English / r / are also from Robert Hagiwara's Ph.D. dissertation.

The data on Spanish vowels in Chapter 9 are from: Delattre, Pierre. "Comparing the Vocalic Features of English, German, Spanish and French." International Review of Applied Linguistics, Vol. 2 (1964), 71–97. The data on Japanese vowels are from: Mieko Han. Japanese Phonology. Tokyo: Kenkyuusha, 1962. The data on Danish vowels are from: Fischer-Jørgensen, Eli. "Formant Frequencies of Long and Short Danish Vowels," in Studies for Einar Haugen, ed. E. S. Firchow et al. The Hague: Mouton, 1972.

The x-rays of the Akan vowels (Figure 9.6) were provided by Mona Lindau.

The description of vowels mentioned in the first exercise at the end of Chapter 9 is published in: Stevens, Kenneth N., and Arthur House. "Development of a Quantitative Description of Vowel Articulation." Journal of the Acoustical Society of America, Vol. 27 (1955), 484–93.

The description mentioned in the second exercise at the end of Chapter 9 was suggested by Morris Halle and Kenneth N. Stevens. Historical descriptions of vowels mentioned in the third exercise may be found in: Helmholtz, Hermann. *Sensations of Tone.* First published in German in 1863, the fourth edition was translated by A. J. Ellis and published in English in 1885. Reprint. New York: Dover Publications, 1954.

Much of the data on particular languages is from my own fieldwork, usually conducted with the invaluable assistance of other linguists who were more familiar with the languages being investigated. Many of these data have been published with appropriate acknowledgments to the linguists who were the original sources, in *Sounds of the World's Languages,* Peter Ladefoged and Ian Maddieson, Oxford: Blackwells. 1996.

As noted in the Preface, much of the data in the tables and exercises is included in the UCLA database on *Sounds of the World's Languages,* which is available on a set of disks for Macintosh computers and partially available on the Web at a site also noted in the Preface.

INDEX

Terms in **bold** are also in the glossary.